MEJI

10TH ANNIVERSARY
SPECIAL EDITION

MILTON J DAVIS

MVmedia, LLC
Fayetteville, GA

MVmedia, LLC
PO Box 1465
Fayetteville, GA 30214

Publisher's Note: This is a work of fiction. Names, characters, places, and incidents are a product of the author's imagination. Locales and public names are sometimes used for atmospheric purposes. Any resemblance to actual people, living or dead, or to businesses, companies, events, institutions, or locales is completely coincidental.

Book Layout ©2017 BookDesignTemplates.com
Cover Art by Mshindo Kuumba
Cover Design by Kecia Stovall

Ordering Information:
Quantity sales. Special discounts are available on quantity purchases by corporations, associations, and others. For details, contact the "Special Sales Department" at the address above.

Meji Special Edition/Milton J Davis. – 2nd ed.
ISBN 978-0-9992789-5-6

Contents

To the Ancestors

Two must become one

INTRODUCTION BY CHARLES R. SAUNDERS

Ndoro and Obaseki. Warrior and mystic. Twin brothers rescued from ritual infanticide, only to be separated not long after their birth. Two paths to follow. One destiny to fulfill.

In *Meji,* Milton J. Davis has created an African-oriented fantasy epic that is wide-ranging and deeply engrossing. The novel is set in Uhuru, an Africa that is not the same as the one we know. Uhuru is a continent in which the cultures of our world's Africa developed in different directions, leading to a setting that is at once familiar and exotic.

Meji is a huge tapestry of a tale that encompasses a multitude of characters and a vast variety of cultures, tribes and kingdoms. Yet for all its twists and complexities, the story is tightly knit – told the way an African *griot* would tell it, strumming his *kora* as his audience listens raptly in the flickering glow of firelight ...

As you join Obaseki and Ndoro on their separate and ultimately converging journeys through the heart of Uhuru, you will see how deeply the author has immersed himself in the ocean of African history, folklore and mythology, and how he has rearranged those elements in an entirely new way.

I know how Milton felt as he was writing *Meji* – for I've swum in that ocean myself. Many years ago, I studied sources similar to the ones Milton has perused, and invented an alternate Africa of my own: Nyumbani, the continent though which the heroic warrior Imaro wanders. My woman-warrior character, Dossouye, lives in yet another parallel version of the Bright Continent.

At that time, I knew the potential existed for the conception of many other variations on classic African themes. A limitless number of stories were waiting to be written by other authors. Consider the dozens, if not hundreds, of ways the legend of King Arthur has been retold. That's just one story, from one culture. Africa, with its hundreds of cultures stretching back to the beginning of humanity, offers infinite opportunities for stories of fantasy and sword-and-sorcery – or, as I prefer to call it, sword-and-soul.

In *Meji*, Milton has made full use of those opportunities. From the *umuzis* of the Sesu to the desert stronghold of the Ihaggaren; from the cosmopolitan city of Mawena to the river kingdom of Tacuma, the author's vivid prose sweeps the reader along on a wave of pulse-pounding action, vivid description and agonizing moral dilemmas.

You will meet a wide array of characters as you accompany the twin protagonists on their quest to transform the Two into One – from the haughty to the humble, from the virtuous to the vicious, from the divine to the demonic. And the women of Uhuru are equal to – and sometimes more than a match for – the men.

When I first read *Meji*, I was profoundly impressed by the sheer scope of the endeavor and the narrative skill of the author. *Meji* is a story that needed to be told – and for Milton J. Davis, it is only the first of many.

Read on, and become One with the Two ...

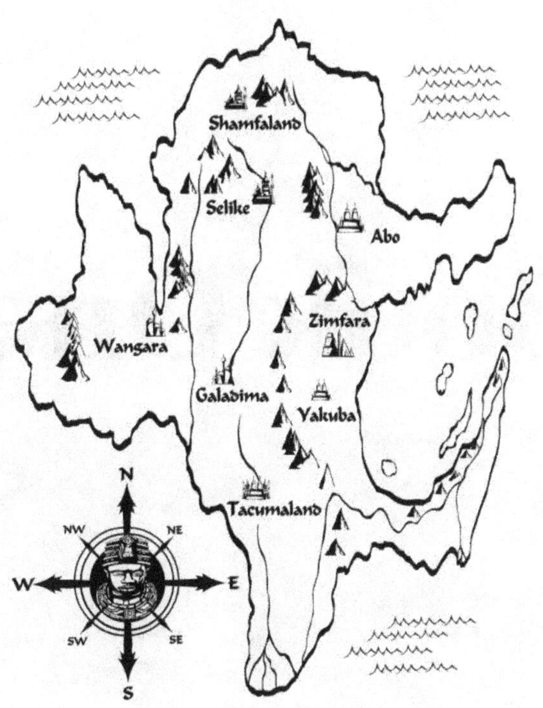
Shamfaland
Selike
Abo
Wangara
Zimfara
Galadima
Yakuba
Tacumaland
N
NW
NE
W
E
SW
SE
S

Uhuru

Book One

1

A yellow moon shimmered above Sesuland, casting its hue across the rolling grasslands. Atop a low rise overlooking the Kojo River, the inhabitants of Inkosi Dingane's umuzi attempted to sleep despite the unusually bright night. Restless cattle crooned at the sky, their wild brethren answering with agitated tones. Dry season had come early and pushed away the shroud of moisture obscuring the stars in the expansive sky. Soon it would be time for the Sesu to pick up their shields and assegais and march against their enemies. Dry season was war season, and the Sesu had a way with war.

The sound of cowbells and drums exploded from the royal compound beyond the cattle pen. Royal messengers dashed among the huts with wavering torches, their voices filled with excitement. The day the Sesu waited for was finally at hand; inkosi Dingane's great wife Shani was in labor. Dingane squatted outside the birthing hut, his mind in turmoil. Every scream sent a wave of fear racing through him. Though his other wives had borne him many children, this would be Shani's first and his most glorious. This child, this boy, would be his successor. Dingane took great pains to make sure he did nothing to offend the spirits during the pregnancy, lest they curse Shani's unborn child. He spent many nights awake imagining how he would raise his heir, teaching him the ways of a Sesu warrior and the secrets of the inkosi. By the time he was of age, the elders of the tribe would dare not select anyone else to succeed him. He would be by far the one most capable of leading the Sesu to future greatness.

A strange cry escaped the hut. Dingane jumped to his feet and ran to the entrance. A hand reached out and stopped him; no man, not even the inkosi, was allowed into the birthing hut. Thembile, Shani's maid, emerged.

"Send for Mulugo," she said urgently. "Something is wrong."

Dingane turned to his bodyguards and pointed to a young warrior leaning on his spear.

"Zenzele, go find Mulugo and bring him here quickly!" he ordered.

He turned back to Thembile. "Is the baby in trouble?"

"I do not know," Thembile replied. "Only Mulugo can answer that question."

Zenzele returned with Mulugo. The medicine-priest wore one of his many masks, his mayembe clutched in his bony right hand. His brown eyes locked on Dingane, and the inkosi took a step away. He did well to hide his fear of the old priest before his warriors, though he knew his façade did not fool Mulugo. The priest gestured toward the hut. Dingane pulled aside the cloth covering the entrance, careful not to look. Mulugo entered and Dingane quickly let go of the cloth.

Dingane crouched beside the entrance, rocking back and forth on his heels as he offered his prayers to Unkulunkulu. His son was being born and the turmoil inside sent his stomach churning in pain. Every scream sent him reeling more. Any more and he would have to send his warriors away. He must not show weakness, no matter how much he felt it.

Shani screamed again, pulling Dingane to his feet. He rushed into the hut, his heart pounding like a celebration drum. Three faces met his; the cowering gaze of the midwife, the scowl of Mulugo and the exhausted smile of Shani. Dingane smiled until he saw what his wife held. Shani had given birth to twins.

"You are cursed," Mulugo said. "You prayed for sons and Unkulunkulu has given them to you.

The joy faded from Shani's eyes. "What does he mean, Dingane? What is he saying?"

Thembile placed a cool rag on Shani's forehead. "Calm yourself, my queen. Do not worry."

"Twins are an abomination, a bad omen to the tribe," Mulugo announced. "They must die."

"No!" Shani screamed. She clutched her crying babies close to her breast.

"They are my sons!"

Her desperate eyes sought Dingane. "You cannot let him do this."

Dingane looked away from his Great Wife and glared at Mulugo. What the priest said was true, but he would not be denied a son. The thought of not having an heir overwhelmed his fear.

"My sons will not die," he declared.

Mulugo held his mayembe out to Dingane, the ornate spirit-filled animal horn inches from the inkosi's face.

"You are a fool!" Mulugo replied. "You stand here naked to Unkulunkulu and deny his will for your own vanity. The Sesu chose you to lead us for your strength and wisdom, and you return our favor by damning our souls!"

"Be quiet, old man!" Dingane spat. "Do you read the mind of the Eye now?" Despite his anger he felt Mulugo's words. The Sesu followed him as long as he protected them and their beliefs.

"No, Dingane, I do not know the mysteries of the Eye. But I know the heart of the Sesu." Mulugo shook his mayembe, and then let it drop to his side.

Dingane felt trapped. He looked into Shani's terrified eyes, at his sons searching their mother's breasts, at the ancient wisdom carved in Mulugo's face. He could not deny the Sesu, yet he could not deny Shani and himself.

"Will the spirits be satisfied with one?" he asked.

"Dingane, no!" Shani exclaimed.

"Ukulunkulu's favor is not open for barter," Mulugo warned.

"This is no bargain. Take one of the boys. The other shall live as I please."

Mulugo glared at Dingane then stormed from the birthing hut. Shani did not give up so easily.

"You can't do this, Dingane!" she pleaded. "These are our children!"

Dingane gazed into Shani's damp eyes, his face set hard. Over the years he had given in to his sweet flower many times. Now there was no room to give.

"Shani, you must try to understand. This is a terrible but necessary thing. I have already asked too much when it comes to your wishes. I cannot ask anymore."

"It is so easy for you," Shani said. "You did not carry them. You did not feel your body grow plump with life, two lives. You did not feel the love grow as well."

"You are not the only one grieving," Dingane said. "But Sesu ways are strict and necessary, just as those of your people."

"The Mawena do not kill their twins," Shani snapped.

"But the Sesu do," Dingane replied.

Shani looked away from Dingane. For a long moment they both were silent, then finally Shani spoke.

"I will do as you wish, but I will choose which child will live."

Dingane nodded his head, relieved to be released from such a burden. He stood to leave the hut, but Shani raised her hand.

"I want one week to make my decision."

"It must be tonight." Dingane's voice was stern.

Shani's eyes narrowed. Her small mouth formed a rigid line as she spoke. "My son will not die a stranger to me. If he does, I will, too."

Dingane's hard look softened with fear. "Whatever you wish."

"I will see no one except Husani and Thembile."

"No one," Dingane replied. "But if you choose which one to keep, I will choose his name."

Shani lowered her head. "As you wish, my husband."

Dingane turned and left the hut. Mulugo waited as he emerged.

"Where is the child?" Mulugo asked.

"You will have him soon enough," Dingane replied. Mulugo scowled, spun and stomped away muttering. Dingane refrained from imagining what curses the medicine priest weaved against him. His first priority was to fulfill Shani's demands. He summoned Zenzele once again.

"Bring Husani to me," he ordered.

Zenzele ran into the darkness and returned quickly with Husani. Shani's personal bodyguard was a tall, broad man, characteristic of the Mawena. He carried a shield and short spear, his hair cropped short in the Mawena style. His clothes were Mawena as well; green pants that ended at his thick calves and a loose-fitting shirt with long sleeves of the same hue. There was no doubt where his loyalties lay.

"The Great Wife has asked that you stand guard of her hut during her recovery," Dingane said to Husani. "No one is to enter or leave except you or Thembile."

Husani nodded in acknowledgement. With that Dingane turned away and went to his umuzi.

"Husani," Shani called out. "Are you there?"

"Yes, inkosa."

"Enter, please."

The warrior stooped low and entered the birthing hut. Shani sat in the background, cradling her babies. She looked up, and then struggled to her knees.

"My queen!' Thembile exclaimed, 'you mustn't!"

"Help me," Shani demanded. Thembile went to Shani and helped her to her feet. Shani swayed, the pain burning through her loins as she stood.

Thembile grabbed her. "Please, inkosa, you must rest!"

Shani looked past Thembile to Husani. "You have always been faithful to me."

Husani's eyes narrowed. "What do you wish, my inkosa?"

Shani looked at them both, the fear radiating from Thembile's timid eyes, the strength of Husani's stare. They would do anything she asked, each for their own reason. But they would do it. She handed the twins to Thembile.

"Take them," she said. "This is Ata, and this is Atsu. Tonight, you will take them to Mawenaland."

Fear took hold of Thembile's face. "We cannot do this!"

"It is what our queen wishes," Husani said, reminding Thembile of her first loyalties.

Thembile paced. "We will be caught. Dingane will kill us all."

"You must leave tonight," Shani said, ignoring Thembile's comments. "Dingane will not visit this hut for one week, nor will anyone else."

"Not even Mulugo?" Husani asked.

"Especially not Mulugo."

Shani saw the concern in Husani's eyes. "I will be fine. I have enough food. All I need is rest."

"And after a week?"

"That is in Olodumare's hands," she replied. "Now go. Take my sons to our people."

Husani bowed and went for the hut entrance. Thembile did not move. Her eyes pleaded with Shani, but the inkosa was unmoved.

"Come, sister," Husani urged. "We waste precious time."

Thembile gave Shani one more glance then hurried out of the hut, Husani close behind.

Shani stared for a moment where Thembile stood holding her babies in her trembling arms. She could not cry or mourn, for the fatigue finally overcame her and she collapsed where she stood.

Mulugo sat naked in his hut surrounded by the swirling grey smoke of a smoldering dung fire. His eyes closed, he concentrated with every speck of his being to control the anger and fear threatening to break the mental dam holding back the dangerous emotions. This was not the time for random action, he thought to himself; he must marshal the weaknesses invading his mind and transform the useless energy into decisive action.

He saw his death in the eyes of the twins, just as the babalawo foretold. As a young medicine priest visiting the city of Abo, he humored himself by seeking his fortune from a decrepit babalawo whose name did remembered. The toothless man sat at the edge of the marketplace that long ago was shared by Sesu and Mawena, offering fortunes and remedies for a handful of kola nuts.

"Two kola nuts, young Sesu," the man coughed. "I see Fate's web in the bones."

Mulugo remembered how he laughed at the man, an arrogant sound expressing his contempt for everything Mawena.

"A fortune from a Mawena is worthless," he told the old man.

The babalawo's face went from smiling to stern. "For you, young warrior, I will read the bones for free." He tossed the bones at Mulugo's feet, his eyes rolling back to white.

"A great medicine priest you will become, but your path will be cleared by treachery and deceit. Power without respect shall be your reward until that day when the one who is two brings an end to your dark days."

Mulugo felt fire in his veins as if the words were uttered moments ago instead of the countless seasons passed. He chanted, the rhythmic words soothing the anger that lapped at the rim of his control.

"I ask for a fortune and you give me a curse," he spat at the old man. Mulugo shoved the man into the dirt and threw the kola nuts in his face. The old man looked at Mulugo, managing to grin.

"Your life is a curse, young Sesu," he replied. "It will be a long life, a very long life."

The heat rose in the hut and Mulugo sweated. His life had been long. His climb to the high priest of Sesuland had been a journey of deception and cruelty, but he had done no different than any ambitious man seeking power. He never experienced the touch of a woman; the chance of eternity through children was never to occur. Still he thought the words of the beggar fortune teller mere coincidence until saw Dingane's twins and realized the power of the old Mawena.

"The One Who is Two," Mulugo whispered.

He had to kill them soon. Every moment they lived they grew stronger. The blood of a chief flowed through their veins, two souls blessed by a lineage superior to his own. Though twins, he saw the difference. One cried with the soul of the world, his only concern the fear of this strange world and the hunger in his belly. The other sat quietly, his eyes drinking in the new world about him, seeing everything within and beyond a normal Sesu's sight. He was the one who had to die first, the one Mulugo would have chosen if given the chance. Dingane's weakness ruled once again and the Mawena cow had her way.

The swirling smoke came less random, moving with a pulse that claimed life from nothing. Faces appeared before Mulugo, faces of the spirits to which he offered his dark libations nightly in hopes they would strengthen him in his time of need.

"The Weak One calls," they whispered. "He has seen his death and is afraid."

"Silence!" Mulugo shouted. His ancestors mocked him, but the truth was that he was more powerful than they had ever been when they were alive. It was this new borne power that summoned his oldest uncles from the Zamani to serve him in the life they would never know again.

"The abomination is here, born with the blood of chiefs and the power to see beyond seeing. How do I stand against this?"

"Only one of twins can bring your demise," they sang. "Make the herbs that bring the sleeping sickness and serve it to Shani. The child eats what the mother eats. An adult will sleep, but a child will die."

Mulugo smiled. It was a simple task, something well within his skills to perform. He jumped up and ran to his shelves, selecting the perfect plants to carry out this task. The abomination would die as many other new born, and no one will be the wiser. Mulugo sprinkled the leaves into his worn stone mortar and began his task, humming a chant as he prepared his freedom.

* * *

The sun rose impatiently over the Sesu pastures, eager to get about its celestial business. Warm rays of light pierced the hut in which Dingane slept. One sliver touched the chief's face and he sprang from his cot as if burned. He leapt from the cot and bolted from the hut, spurred by the message sent to him from his ancestors while he slept.

In his dream Mulugo had defied him. The old wizard had taken matters into his own hands, invading the birth hut and killing both babies with his jagged metal knife. Shani's screams rang in his head as he neared the hut, his breathing heavy and desperate. He looked about for Husani but the warrior could not be found. Dingane yanked the hut door aside and charged in. Shani's head rose slowly from her cot, her eyes wet and red. The babies were gone. He ran, headed to Mulugo's abode, his eyes wide with anger. Striding into the wizard's hut, he found the old man sitting before a small stone table, his ancient hands slowly grinding a collection of herbs.

"Damn you, Mulugo!" he shouted. He attacked the medicine priest, wrapping his hands around the Mulugo's neck. Mulugo struggled to speak, pounding Dingane's arms feebly. He stopped suddenly, throwing his hands out behind him and finding his cane. His breath escaping him, Mulugo touched Dingane lightly on his leg. Searing pain rushed through the inkosi's body; he released the priest and fell away, clutching his calf. Mulugo leaned against the stone table in the center of his hut, gathering his breath.

"The night has driven you mad!" Mulugo gasped.

"You killed my sons!" Dingane shouted.

Mulugo looked at Dingane. "I have not touched the abominations. I have been doing what I can to deflect whatever evils your decision has brought to us."

Dingane stood. "But they were not in the hut! Shani was crying, and I dreamed..."

Dingane fled the hut, Mulugo following as closely as he could. By this time the commotion had passed throughout the village and everyone crowded about the birthing hut, curious to know what was afoot. Dingane's warriors cleared a path as the chief returned and charged inside.

Shani waited for him. She sat erect, covered in fresh clothing Thembile brought her the night before, her composed face hiding her pain.

"Where are my sons, woman?" Dingane shouted. "Where are Husani and Thembile?"

"Gone," Shani replied, her voice strong and firm. "The Mawena do not kill their twins."

"Do you know what you have done?" Dingane shouted. He grabbed her by the wrists and yanked her to her feet, ignoring her grimace.

"I bent the rules for you, Shani. Yesterday I defied Mulugo and the elders for you. And this is how you repay me?"

"You did nothing for me," Shani replied. "If that was so you would have spared both my sons."

Dingane let her go, his face a mirror of disgust. "I expected you to be a Great Mother worthy of this tribe. My dowry to your father was more than he asked because of what I thought you were worth. I was wrong."

"I am Mawena," Shani said. "I will not let my children die."

Dingane spat on the floor of the hut and left Shani sobbing. When he emerged Mulugo was waiting.

"What has happened?" he demanded.

"Shani sent the twins to her people."

A gasp rose from the crowd. Mulugo threw his medicine stick to the ground and pointed a crooked finger at Mulugo.

"See what has happened so soon, inkosi of the Sesu! The evil befalls us!"

Dingane ignored Mulugo's gesticulations, turning his attention to Gamba, the leader of his personal guard.

"Gather an impi of my finest warriors and send for my weapons."

"Where are you going?" Mulugo asked.

"After them," Dingane replied. "The boys are with Husani and Thembile. They had a head start, but Thembile will slow Husani down."

"I will go with you," Mulugo decided. "We must wait no longer. When we find them, we must kill one immediately."

"I will not slow down for you, old man"

"You will not need to," Mulugo replied.

Gamba returned with the warriors. He helped Dingane don his headdress and strapped his shield and assegais across his back. Dingane looked over his men and was satisfied with Gamba's choices.

"Impi kimbia!" he shouted, and they set off at a warrior's pace. Mulugo followed close behind, resting in his litter as his porters kept pace with the warriors. They ran through the streets of Selike, urged on by the chants of the Sesu. Men, women, girls and boys all shouted for their success. The throng followed them to the edge of Sesuland, and then watched as their inkosi and his warriors disappeared into the grassy horizon.

* * *

Husani gazed on the grasslands from his perch, searching for signs of pursuit. He and Thembile reached the hills just before dawn, finding a place to rest before continuing their journey to Mawenaland.

He turned back, watching Thembile suckle the twins, absorbed in the nurturing of Shani's children. Though she did her best, they would never reach Mawenaland. An impi was surely pursuing them by now, an impi with no woman or babies to slow them down. He had to do something if the twins were to make it to Mawenaland. What, he did not know.

"How are they?" he asked Thembile.

"As well as can be expected," she replied.

Husani crouched closer to Thembile. "We must go now."

Thembile glared. "The babies need more rest. I am not even finish feeding them!"

"They will have all the time they need to feed in Mawenaland," Husani replied in a harsh ton.

Thembile pulled the babes from her breasts. Their feeble cries tore at her heart; she pleaded with Husani once more

"Just a few more minutes," she begged.
Husani said nothing for a moment, his mind elsewhere. When he finally turned his attention back to Thembile, his expression echoed his resolve.

"Take your time, Thembile. We can wait."

Thembile fed the babies until they were full then placed them in the woven basket. She looked about for Husani but could not find him. He had apparently slipped away while she nursed. Thembile sang, more to soothe herself than the sleeping twins. Death was following her; she felt its press upon her back, its putrid breath cold against her flesh. She should have fled Shani's hut as soon as the inkosa stated her intentions. But now she was part of this foolish scheme, too afraid to say no when asked.

Husani reappeared suddenly from the bush. "Are you ready?" he asked. Thembile checked the babies one last time. "Yes, I am," she answered.

"Good," Husani said. He took his wrist knife and handed it to Thembile.

"Mawenaland is not far from the base of the hills. If you follow this path, you should reach it by sunset."

"What are you talking about?" Thembile replied. "We cannot separate!

Husani placed his hand on Thembile's shoulders. "Listen to me. Dingane has surely discovered the babies are gone by now and an impi has been sent after us. Together we are too slow."

"Then we will die!" Thembile exclaimed.

"No, woman, listen to me," Husani insisted. "Just inside the woods of Mawenaland is Koso. When you come across the Kosobu, show them my knife. They will make sure you and the babies get to Abo."

Thembile realized what Husani was going to do. She never doubted his bravery, but to see him, his handsome face resolved, she then knew what a true warrior he was. She took the knife, placing it in the basket with the twins. She touched Husani's cheek.

"I will pray for you," she whispered.

"And I for you," Husani replied. "Now go."

Thembile picked up the basket, trotting down the path Husani described to her. Husani watched until she disappeared, then covered her tracks. He returned to his perch and waited.

The sun dangled low on the western horizon when Husani spotted the impi. They were moving fast; at their current pace they would reach the hills in minutes. Their chant reached his ears and made him smile.

"Come for me, Sesu," he said. "You will surely get me."

He rose and set off, climbing up a path in the hills that ran opposite of the trail leading to Mawenaland. He ran long enough to make sure the Sesu warriors would not overtake him before he reached his destination. Once he was sure of his distance he walked, saving his energy for what lay ahead.

The impi picked up the trail not far from the village. There was no rest, no easing of the pace; the Sesu had been defied and revenge was demanded. But Dingane would make sure that revenge only went so far. He would have his son.

By midday the hills that separated Sesuland from Mawenaland were in view. Dingane increased the pace, knowing the longer they traveled without seeing their prey the better their chances at reaching Abo. The warriors responded with a war chant, beating their assegais against their shields. We are coming, they chanted. We are coming for you.

Dingane led his warriors into the hills, their stride still strong despite the miles they'd traversed. It did not take them long to find the Mawena camp.

"The ashes are still warm," Dingane remarked. It took a moment to find the trail leading away from the Mawena camp. The impi set off again, their energy renewed.

The trail snaked upward through the hills, meandering like the gemsbok which created it. The natural growth of grasses faded with each step, usurped by low shrubs and weak trees as they drew closer to Mawenaland. The Sesu paused at the top of the hill then plunged into a dense tangle of bush and trees. The path narrowed, and the Sesu were forced to travel single file.

The slim path slowed them down considerably, the thistles from the encroaching bushes slashing their bare arms and legs. A wicked thorn bit into Dingane's calf and he dropped to his knees in pain, his hand grasping his wounded limb. No sooner had he descended that he heard a wet thump behind him. He turned to see the warrior behind him fall, an assegai buried in his chest. The others raised their shields and formed the tortoise around their inkosi, protecting him from the deadly missiles raining down on them. As suddenly as the barrage began it stopped. Dingane broke free of the formation, running at full speed through the narrow path. Fury consumed him as he looked for Husani, promising himself the Mawena would die a painful death when he was finally captured.

Husani leaped in his path. He slammed into Dingane, knocking the inkosi off his feet and into the brambles. Dingane scrambled to keep his balance, but Husani pushed him further into bush, the thorns tearing into his face and torso. The biting of the bush was punctuated by a searing stab into his right thigh. Dingane held back a scream as Husani leapt back, a look of grim satisfaction on his face.

"You will die, fool!" Dingane shouted.

"I know," Husani replied. The Mawena jumped over Dingane and charged the approaching Sesu warriors. Dingane watched Husani plunge into his men, using the narrow path to his advantage. Five Sesu fell before Husani was finally overwhelmed, his large frame disappearing under an avalanche of Sesu blades.

The warriors freed Dingane from the shrubs. As soon as he was clear he shoved them away.

"Come! We must go."

"Inkosi, your leg," Gamba said.

"Are you a healer now, Gamba? Follow me!"

Dingane place his full weight on his wounded leg and shouted. Determined to go on, he took another step. The pain overwhelmed him and he collapsed into the arms of his men.

When he awoke, he was stretched out on a hide cot, Mulugo squatting beside his leg, pressing the wound with a poultice. The medicine priest raised his eyes slowly to meet Dingane's.

"It is happening as I foretold," Mulugo said.

"Be quiet," Dingane ordered. "I will not stop until I have my son back."

Mulugo looked exasperated and turned his attention back to the wound. "We must go back to the umuzi. Your wound is bad, and I do not have the proper herbs to heal it. I did not expect to be saving a life, only taking one."

Dingane gritted his teeth. "We are not going back without my son. Do the best you can." He rose up on his elbows and called for Gamba.

"Make me a litter quickly," he commanded. Gamba trotted off to do his job.

"Even you cannot deny what is happening," Mulugo said. "Can't you feel the unbalance? Both boys must die!"

Dingane glared at the medicine priest. "Listen to me, old man. One son will die; the other will live. If you mention this to me again, I will cut your throat."

Mulugo looked stunned. He backed away from Dingane. "I am returning to the village. I will no longer be a part of this evil."

"You will do no such thing," Dingane said. "You came this far, you will go all the way. Do you understand?"

For once Dingane was privileged to see fear in Mulugo's eyes. Maybe the medicine priest thought him mad; it didn't matter to Dingane. The only thing that mattered was his son.

Dingane tried walking but the pain was too great. Gamba returned quickly with the litter. Dingane struggled in and nodded to Gamba. "I am ready."

Gamba bowed to Dingane. "Impi kimbia!" he shouted. With the command the impi fell into ranks and began the run to Mawenaland.

* * *

Thembile scrambled down the goat path leading to the forest. The fear that had been held in check by Husani's presence was upon her in full fury, riding her harder than the babies she bore against her breasts. The sun was setting, the long shadows of the nearby forest creasing the hills. Thembile would give anything to be among them, hidden in familiar darkness. But as soon as she reached them she realized she'd been too long among the Sesu. The forest engulfed her, the sky above becoming an ominous canopy of leaves.

"Oya protect me!" she prayed as she ran on.

The trail widened as it progressed into the trees, the signs of human habitation growing more numerous. Thembile knew she was close to a village, but her legs would carry her no longer. She would never make it before dark; she would have to sleep in the forest. She stopped and then gingerly stepped from the trail into the bush. She found a good spot, a large tree surrounded by a stand of saplings. She put the babies down and cleared a spot to sit. The twins slept, exhausted from the journey and lack of milk.

"Poor little ones," she whispered. "Your lives begin so hard."
She woke them and offered them her breasts and they suckled eagerly. She sang to them, knowing that any sound might attract danger but too tired to care. When the babies were finished she laid them on the blanket then lay beside them, clutching Husani's knife in her small hands.

It seemed only moments had passed when Thembile jumped up, startled by harsh clanging. Sunlight broke through the canopy, stinging her eyes and frightening her even more. She found the babies and calmed somewhat, then leaned against a tree to orient herself. The clanging came from a herd of goats passing along the path, shepherded by a group of young boys. One of the boys approached her, his eyes searching the bush for the source of the scream.

"Habare!" she called out. The boy looked suddenly in her direction.

"Umzuri," the boy replied. "Who are you, mother?"

"I am Thembile. I need your help."

"Wait here. I will go back to the village and bring help."

"What is your village?" Thembile asked.

"Koso."

The boy ran through the brush and back to the path, calling his cohorts. Two younger boys appeared, and the eldest pointed to Thembile. The boys nodded then went to her.

The younger boy took off his shoulder pouch and handed it to Thembile.

"Here, eat. Paki said you looked hungry." Thembile had not thought about food until that moment. She accepted the pouch eagerly.

"Are these your babies?" the other boy asked.

"No," Thembile replied, her mouth stuffed with food. "They are the sons of inkosa Shani, Great Wife of inkosi Dingane and daughter of Oba Noncemba.

The boy stepped away from the sleeping children, showing his respect.

"We will protect you until Paki returns."

Thembile smiled. "I am honored to have such fine warriors to watch over us."

The boys made good company, sharing their food and conversation. It seemed only a moment passed before the eldest boy returned, bringing with him a group of warriors from the village. The younger boys moved aside quickly, leaving Thembile to confront the warriors alone. The eldest of the men stepped forward, a graying beard bordering his cherubic face, his stomach protruding past his waist belt. His left hand carried a worn shield, his right an assegai with an extremely long blade. In other circumstances Thembile might have found him amusing, but the threatening look on the man's face emphasized the seriousness of her situation.

"Paki says you are Shani's handmaiden."

"I am."

"And these are her children?"

Thembile nodded.

The man smirked. "Then where is the Great Wife?"

"These babies are twins," Shani replied. "The Sesu consider them abominations, and the medicine priest said they must die. Shani did not want this, so she sent Husani and me..."

One of the younger warriors came forward. "Did you say Husani?" he asked.

"Yes, yes. He gave me this to show anyone who found us."

She revealed Husani's knife. The old warrior looked at the young man.

"It is his knife," the young man said. He looked at Thembile. "Where is he?"

Her eyes watering as she replied. "He stayed behind to slow down the Sesu pursuing us."

The young man's face became somber, his fingers absently rubbing the cowry shells about his neck. The older warrior motioned to Thembile.

"Come with us."

Koso bordered the Bose, a wide, lethargic river shadowed by trees bent over its muddy waters. Cone shaped houses of wood and mud lined the narrow streets leading from the river's edge into the forest. The entire village smelled of fish. For Thembile it was a welcomed change from cow dung. The warriors took her to the meeting tree, a huge ancient plant surrounded by the village elders. The chief sat in the center, his head covered by a crown woven in the kente of his family. He seemed young for a chief, but his bearing reflected his position. Each elder wore his family kente, signifying a group of great power. She knelt, placing the basket with the babies before the elders and touched her head on the ground.

"I am Olatunde, chief of the Koso. You carry the children of Dingane?" the chief asked.

Thembile felt fear in her throat. "Yes, baba."

The chief rubbed his chin. "We are not friends of the Sesu. They raid our farms and steal grain for their cattle. I have no reason to save the sons of an enemy."

The thought of harm coming to the infants forced Thembile's fear aside. "These boys are not Sesu. They belong to Shani, daughter of Oba Noncemba, your oba. I have promised to take them to him and I will, with or without your help."

Olatunde held up his hand. "I didn't say we wouldn't help you. I wanted everyone at this council to understand why we will help. We are, after all, Mawena. We are proud of the blessing Shani sends us."

He raised his hand and the younger warrior came forward.

"Jelani will take you and the babies to Abo by boat. Dingane chases you, but the boats will take you faster. You must leave now."

Thembile bowed to the chief. "I thank you for your kindness. Olodumare keep you."

Jelani led Thembile to the awaiting boats. There, she was greeted by a tall, beautiful woman; her head wrap and dress signifying the chief's clan.

"I am Zuwena, wet nurse for the chief's family. I will care for the children."

Thembile clutched the babies, reluctant to give them up.

Zuwena gave the handmaiden a sympathetic smile. "It is all right. You are tired, and your milk is weak."

"Will we take the same boat?" Thembile asked.

"Yes," Zuwena replied. Thembile handed the babies to Zuwena slowly, still wary to give up the boys despite being surrounded by people willing to help her.

"They are fine boys," Zuwena remarked. "They will grow into great men."

"If they live," Thembile replied.

Jelani helped Thembile and Zuwena into the boat. There were three boats in all, the front and rear boat containing oarsmen and archers. Jelani prepared a place for Thembile, a cot with a lambskin blanket.

"You can rest here," he said. "If I know Husani, your journey was hard."

"He was a brave man," Thembile replied.

"I know. He was my brother."

Thembile smiled at Jelani, the resemblance now apparent. She lay down on the cot as the boats got under way. Knowing of Husani's brother calmed her; everything would be all right; of this she was certain. Once in Abo, Oba Noncemba would handle the situation and the babies would be safe. She closed her eyes and let the rhythm of the boat lull her to sleep.

* * *

Oba Noncemba slept fitfully in the bedchamber of his palace, unaware of the crisis approaching his city. Though very much the grandfather, he had a youthful look about him despite the gray speckled hair on his head and the white beard. The privileges of higher status had not contributed to his waistline; he was as fit as his days as a warrior oba leading his armies in conquest of the kingdom now known as Mawenaland. The last decade he spent not as a warrior but a diplomat, securing the borders of his realm through trade, negotiation and marriage. The ancestors blessed him with few sons but many daughters and these had married the princes of many surrounding realms, making them family. All had married well except Shani. Noncemba stirred in his sleep as he recalled his youngest daughter which he had not seen since she married Dingane, chief of the Sesu. He did not like the young Sesu, but it was a marriage he could not avoid. The Sesu were growing numerous and powerful under Dingane's rule, rising from a small tribe of cattle raiders to a unified force. Though still not a kingdom, the young chief was powerful enough to request a bride.

Noncemba sat up in his bed just before the messenger entered.

"My oba, forgive my intrusion. You are needed urgently at the meeting tree!"

Noncemba did not question the messenger's summons. He dressed and followed the man through the palace and into the courtyard. The wide area brimmed with people; spectators sat upon the bleached white walls, a curious murmur drifting into the enclosure. The elders sat below the branches of the enormous baobab, a tree older that the ancestors, its canopy shielding the entire courtyard. They were flanked by his generals dressed in red kapok and chain mail, each wearing their headdress rank except Kumba, their leader and Noncemba's closest friend. Before them a small group knelt, their heads touching the ground. Noncemba's anxiety increased as he recognized them as Kosobu. This was definitely a Sesu matter; the Kosobu lived along the river separating Mawenaland from the Sesu grasslands. As he approached them a woman lifted her head and struck the oba still. It was Thembile, Shani's handmaiden, and she held twins in her arms.

"What have the ancestors blessed us with?" he whispered.

"A blessing and a curse," Kumba commented.

Noncemba walked up to Thembile and knelt before her. The spectators gasped while the elders frowned at such a break in protocol.

"Are they my grandsons?" he asked.

"Yes, my oba. This is Ata, and this is Atsu. The inkosa sent them to you for your protection."

Noncemba was well aware of the Sesu attitude towards twins. Many of the Kosobu were orphaned Sesu hidden among the reeds of the river by their desperate mothers. The Kosobu found them and took them in without question.

"The Sesu will be angry," Elder Kosoko said. The elder stood, a tall, thin man twice the age of Noncemba. His family was among the First of Mawenaland and had produced its share obas in the past.

"They will demand that we kill them."

"Killing twins is not our way," Kumba snarled.

"Everyone here knows this," Noncemba replied. "This is a serious matter, one that could lead to war if not handled carefully."

"Then let war come," Kumba said. "For the past ten years we have danced with the Sesu. It is time we crushed them and their ambitions like dung flies."

A whisper of approval meandered among the spectators. Noncemba's royal stool was brought to him by his attendants. He sat before his people, returning to tribal protocol.

"One hunts the lion with skill, not anger," he said. "The Sesu are a concern, but so are the Kossi, the Burundi and the

Fah. Mawenaland is strong enough to defeat any of these lands alone, but defeating one makes us vulnerable to another. We must consider our response carefully."

"How can we appease the Sesu without killing the twins?" Elder Kosoko asked. "They know Thembile brought them here. They will come to you and ask for justice."

"Inkosi Dingane does not want to kill them both," Thembile said.

Noncemba eyes widened in time as a gasp rose from the throng.

Thembile dared to lift her eyes again. "Dingane wished to keep one to be his heir for they are his first children from Shani. The medicine priest insisted they kill them both but the inkosi refused. Inkosa Shani told Dingane she would choose which one would live, but she sent them both to you."

"You didn't make this journey alone," Kumba said. "Who helped you?"

Thembile's head sagged. "Husani."

"Where is he?" Noncemba asked.

"He stayed behind in the hills to slow the Sesu impi pursuing us. He told me to go to Koso. He said they would bring me to you."

Noncemba nodded. "You have served my family well. You and the others may go to my palace and rest."

Noncemba's servants led Thembile and the Kosobu into the palace. Noncemba turned to the elders.

"Dingane's desire for a son is our advantage," he said. "Come, let us prepare for our visitors."

The Sesu impi had been on the trail since morning. Despite the burden of carrying Dingane they made good time, arriving at the outskirts of Mawenaland by midday. They rested briefly, long enough to eat and quench their thirst. Then they marched again, their chants muffled by the encroaching forest.

The trail ended its meandering and widened into a well-used road. Wooden huts peered through the trees, but no people were visible. Word of the impi had preceded it, and the Mawena were staying clear. Dingane rose from his litter as they climbed a heavily forested hill, anticipating the scene about to unfold before him.

They reached the crest of the hill and Dingane raised his hand, halting the impi. Below them was the city of Abo, the heart of Mawenaland. Cylindrical wooden houses topped with conical thatch roofs peppered small plots of farmland. The plots grew smaller as the homes pushed closer to the city. In the city the dwellings consisted of stone and were grouped according to clan. Each clan enclosed its homes with white clay walls painted with the family kente. The center of this magnificent sprawl was filled by the royal compound of Oba Noncemba. A massive stone fence encircled a large pasture filled with cattle, the wealth of many tribes before Dingane's eyes. Noncemba's hilltop palace marked the nucleus of the royal compound. The extravagant homes of his clan members peppered the hillsides. Beside the palace the meeting tree thrived, a massive plant older than the ancestors. Below its branches the elders of Mawenaland waited.

"Put me down!" Dingane demanded.

"But Inkosi, your leg!" Gamba replied

"Down!" Dingane ordered. He was eased down and stood immediately. The pain throbbed in his leg, but he ignored it. Noncemba would not see him as a cripple.

The Sesu proceeded, their wary eyes noting every movement and shadow. The streets were completely deserted; the Mawena had obviously been warned of the impi's arrival and were prepared. As they entered the inner city, a commotion drew their attention. Mawena warriors appeared and quickly closed ranks behind them, careful to stay out of spear range. Though they outnumbered the Sesu intruders, their advantage didn't lull them into foolishness. A lion fights more ferociously when cornered; no less would be expected from the Sesu.

The gates to the royal compound were open. Mawena elders sat patiently below the branches of the meeting tree, each man draped in his family cloth pattern. In the center sat Noncemba on a gilded stool with a leopard skin cushion. He was draped with a kente robe adorned in elegant patterns of red, purple and green. A black cap studded with thick gold buttons covered his head. He wore a thick serpentine gold bracelet on his right wrist; a cluster of gold cubes tied together by a leather cord circled his left wrist. More gold cubes dangled from leather bands surrounding his ankles, spilling over his sandals. Golden rings shaped in the patterns of animals and proverbs decorated every finger. There was a time when Dingane was in awe of the Mawena. Even now it was hard for him to suppress his admiration. But time taught him the meaning of true power, which did not lie in elaborate clothing and trinkets. He was Noncemba's equal in every way. The Sesu had become strong under his rule, strong enough for Noncemba to offer Shani to him as his great wife.

Dingane halted his warriors outside assegai distance of the meeting tree, a sign that he meant no violence.

"Mulugo, come with me," he said to the medicine-priest.

Mulugo's litter was lowered and the old man took his place beside Dingane. As they neared the tree, Dingane recognized Thembile kneeling beside Noncemba. She had shed her Sesu garments for Mawena clothing. In her arms was the bundle that Dingane sought.

It was Dingane who spoke first. "Habare, baba."

"Umzuri, Dingane," Noncemba replied. "It's been a long time, my son."

"I am not here to chat," Dingane replied. "I want my sons."

"You mean your son," Noncemba replied. On the oba's signal Thembile rose and walked to Dingane, extending the bundle. Dingane took it and turned back the cloth. There was only one child.

"What have you done?" Mulugo demanded. "Where is the other child?"

"What difference does it make?" Noncemba replied. "The child was to be killed, so we saved you the trouble."

"Where is the body?" Mulugo asked.

Noncemba scowled. "What are you implying, magic man?"

Mulugo's face twisted with skepticism. "You are the boy's grandfather. Would you really kill the son of your daughter?"

Noncemba glared at the medicine priest, his hand tightening on his staff. "The blood of the Mawena is strong in my grandsons. To waste it sickens us all. But our tribes are bonded; my grandsons are Sesu and subject to your ways. Shani was wrong to send them here. We carried out your deed because of this disgrace."

Noncemba stood, raising his staff. The Mawena warriors stormed forward, surrounding the Sesu. Noncemba smiled.

"Do not push this issue, my son. We have suffered enough with your ways this day."

Dingane trembled with rage. He stared at Noncemba, his strength occupied by keeping his assegai in his hand.

"I need someone to nurse the child during the journey back to Selike," he finally said, his voice trembling.

Noncemba nodded and turned to Thembile. She walked to Dingane, staring directly into his eyes, her loathing for him apparent to everyone. But she was not alone. A warrior stepped forward with her, a young man Dingane quickly recognized as being related to Husani.

"Thembile and Jelani will return with you," Noncemba said. "I trust you will make sure no harm comes to them?"

"I will," Dingane replied.

"Then I wish you a safe journey home," Noncemba said.

Dingane turned away without a reply. He stormed through his warriors, the pain in his leg insignificant against the rage in his head. The Sesu warriors followed with Thembile and Jelani the last of the group.

"He insulted you!" Mulugo exclaimed. "He dishonored the Sesu!"

"The Mawena are strong," Dingane replied. "Do you see?" He waved his hand to acknowledge the numerous warriors shadowing their retreat.

"Our time will come, Mulugo," he continued. "Mawena bone will one day shatter beneath Sesu feet. That I promise you."

* * *

Kumba approached Noncemba and fell to his knees.

"What is your command, my Oba?"

Noncemba rested his chin on his fist. "Follow them until they leave our land. I don't want anyone doubling back. If any of Dingane's warriors break rank, kill them."

A wicked smile came to Kumba's face. "It will be our pleasure to serve the Oba."

Kumba stood and marched to his warriors. He shouted the order to march; the warriors formed ranks and trotted from Abo to catch the Sesu.

Noncemba watched until the army left the gates of the city. He turned to his closest servant.

"Bring me my grandson."

The servant returned with the infant wrapped in a blanket of royal kente. Shani's son stared directly into his grandfather's eyes with intensity beyond his few days of life.

"You must name him," Elder Kosoko advised.

"You have your grandfather's face and your mother's eyes," Noncemba said. He raised the infant over his head for all around him to see.

"Behold my grandson," he announced. "He will be known as Obaseki Noncemba."

The elders bowed their heads, whispering the name to the ground that held the bodies of their ancestors. Noncemba lowered the baby then looked upon him again.

"I hope you live up to your name, little one." Noncemba handed his grandson back to the servant then with a waving of his staff, lead the procession of elders and warriors back into the walls of the Inner City.

2

Ndoro crouched beside the thorn fence surrounding Shani's umuzi, swinging a gnarled branch back and forth. On the other side of the fence Sitefu attacked Amanzi relentlessly as the others boys looked on, his zinduku smacking Amanzi's head repeatedly. Amanzi backed away, clearly giving up the fight.

"Say it!" Sitefu shouted. "Say it!"

Amanzi looked desperate. He tried to fight back, but Sitefu was just too fast. He finally dropped his sticks.

"You are my master," he said.

With that Lungile stepped between them. He was the inqwele, the leader of the herd boys, the best stick fighter among them. He was in charge of sparring.

"It is over," he said. "Sitefu, tend to Amanzi's wounds."

Ndoro knew Sitefu would win. Amanzi was afraid of him like the other boys his age. Ndoro wasn't afraid. He wanted to join them and spar with them, but his world ended at the thorn fence. Momma would take a switch to him if he tried to venture outside the Royal Umuzi, so he would sit and watch the other boys filled with longing and anger.

A strong calloused hand lifted him and he laughed.

"Put me down!"

Jelani's other hand went under his other arm and he laughed again.

"Look, another monkey in the umuzi. I guess I'll throw this one out, too!"

Jelani swung him over the brambles and spun him around.

"Let me go! Let me go!" Ndoro squealed.

"I do, and your momma would skin me," Jelani replied. "Come, little monkey; it's time to eat."

Jelani let him go and Ndoro landed on his feet. He looked up at the burly bodyguard, grinning and lifting his eyebrows. Jelani grinned back.

Ndoro sprang like a gazelle, bounding to the hut. Jelani ran after him, surprised at how hard he had to run to catch up with the boy. He caught him only a few paces from the hut, grabbing him under the arms again and lifting him up.

"Your faster than you ought to be, little monkey."

"I'll beat you soon, big monkey."

Jelani put him down. "You probably will."

Shani emerged from her hut with a smile for her son.

"Ndoro, were you at the fence again?"

"Yes, momma. Sitefu and Anzani sparred today and Sitefu won. He's fast like the cheetah, but I'm faster. I could beat him."

Shani looked at Jelani and he looked away.

"Don't spend so much time watching those boys. You have chores to do. I need your help."

"The other boys don't help their mommas. They watch the herd and stick fight. The girls stay at home."

He folded his arms across his chest. "I am not a girl."

Shani turned her back on him. "Come inside. The food is ready."

Ndoro trudged into the hut, his head low. He sat cross-legged before the fire and Shani handed him a bowl of uPhutu porridge. He stared into the bowl.

"Momma, inkosi Dingane is my father?" he said.

Shani stopped eating, her face pensive. "Yes, Ndoro, he is your father."

"Then why aren't I in an intanga?"

"You are too young."

Ndoro scooped a spoonful of porridge and chewed slowly. Shani watched him nervously.

"Amanzi is my age, I think. He is in an intanga," he said. "His father is not inkosi, but he is in an intanga."

Jelani frowned at Shani and left the hut with his bowl.

"We won't talk about this tonight," Shani said. "Eat you uPhutu and go to sleep."

Shani left the hut looking for Jelani. He sat by his hut eating his porridge. She marched up to him and gripped her amble hips.

"Is there something you wish to say?" she asked.

"You are his mother and I am your servant," Jelani replied. "It's not my place to comment on the raising of Ndoro."

"But you disapprove."

Jelani sat down his bowl and stood, towering over her. He had grown into a man since leaving his people eight years ago to serve Shani as his brother had years ago. Unlike his brother, he was not one to hold his opinion.

"You can't continue to hide him from the facts," Jelani said. "It's time he understood his place."

"He's just a boy," Shani protested. "I want him to enjoy his life as long as he can. He will have plenty of time to suffer."

"Ndoro will be a Sesu warrior one day. It is a hard life of struggle for respect and status. The sooner he begins to make his place among his own, the better his chances will be to remove the curse that looms over him."

"He's just a boy!"

"You will do what you want, inkosa," he said. "If you want Ndoro to have any kind of chance among his own you must let him go. It will be hard and painful, but it will make him the warrior he must be to endure this life."

"What if they don't accept him, Jelani? What if they deny him his place?"

"Then he will have to force acceptance on them," he replied. "The world of men is merciless, inkosa. No man is given status. He must earn the respect of his peers. If Ndoro can accomplish this he has a better chance of being acknowledged by Dingane."

Shani sat in the dust and dropped her head in her hands. "Will you help him, Jelani?"

"It is not my place," Jelani replied unhappily.

"You are the only man he knows. You must help him."

"The Sesu won't approve."

Shani lifted her head, her lips bunched in anger. "This is a Mawena decision. The Sesu will not recognize my son so they have no say in his upbringing. Train my son, Jelani. Make him a warrior, a Mawena warrior."

Jelani looked at the inkosa, a smiled forming on his handsome face. "Is this your command?"

Shani sat up, straightening her back and raising her head. "It is my command."

"I will start tomorrow." Jelani finished his bowl. "Good night, inkosa."

Shani smiled. "Good night, Mawena."

"Ndoro, wake up."

Ndoro struck at the hands shaking him, kicking out his legs against his cot.

"Come on, little monkey. It's time to rise."

The voice calling him wasn't the soothing tone of his momma. His eyes snapped open to Jelani's face.

"Jelani?"

The warrior stepped away, folding his hands across his chest. "Stick fighters rise early in the morning to practice their skills."

Ndoro jumped off the cot. "I'm a stick fighter!"

"Come then. Let's see what you know."

Ndoro chased Jelani outside. He ran to the thorn fence, fishing out the sticks he'd hidden the day before. When he turned around Jelani held two sticks of his own.

Ndoro let out a yell, charging and flailing. Jelani laughed, stepped aside and tripped the boy. Ndoro fell on his face, jumped to his feet, found Jelani and charged again. After the third fall and a bloody nose, Ndoro stopped charging. He glared at Jelani, his face caked with dirt, blood running out his nose and over his lips. His narrow shoulders rose and fell with his heavy breath.

"You're . . .not . . . supposed . . . to . . . move!"

"That's the Sesu way," Jelani replied. "Two fools smashing at each other until someone gets tired and the other one cracks his head. The style favors the strongest man."

Ndoro dropped his arms, confused by Jelani's words.

"It's the way the boys fight and the way the men fight. It's the right way."

Jelani crossed his arms. "If it's so right, why didn't you hit me?"

"Because you're a big monkey!"

Jelani laughed. "You're almost right. I am bigger than you. Sitefu is bigger than you, too."

Ndoro dropped his sticks and sat hard. "Then I'm not big enough to beat Sitefu."

Jelani came to him and pulled him back on his feet. “Yes, you are little monkey. Come, let’s clean you up and start over. This time I’ll show you the right way to fight.”

Jelani led Ndoro to the river. The warm water soothed his wounds and lifted his mood. Jelani had beaten him bloody and never raised his sticks. He dodged like the springbok evading the shumba.

He dunked his head underwater and shook it.

“I am ready,” he announced.

They walked back to the umuzi and practiced the rest of the day, stopping only for a bit of food and water. Ndoro was relentless, listening to Jelani every word, repeating every motion as best he could. As the sun disappeared behind the undulating horizon their practice ended. Man and boy slumped to the ground, arms sore and but spirits high.

“Shango, boy!” Jelani exclaimed. “Do you ever get tired?”

Ndoro lay on his back, gazing at the emerging stars above. “I am a stick fighter. I never get tired.”

He didn’t remember falling asleep. He didn’t feel Jelani lifting his limp form and carrying him to the hut, humming to him like a baby. He woke for a moment when he felt the familiar contours of his cot and heard the voice of his momma.

And so it was for a month, early rising, day long practices, then tired dreamless sleep. Shani suffered for her little man as she watched Jelani’s stern but careful training. He pushed the boy without sparking his anger. Ndoro seemed to enjoy the punishment, his well of energy challenging Jelani’s endurance.

Jelani’s touch woke Ndoro. He sprang up in his cot ready for another day of practice.

“No practice today, little monkey,” he said. “Today you take our goats to the pasture across the river.”

Ndoro mouth gaped.

“You do know how to do this don’t you?”

Ndoro nodded.

“Then get to it, little monkey. The goats are hungry.”

Shani was waiting with a bowl of uPhutu. She smiled, but her eyes expressed her worry.

“Be careful, Ndoro.”

“I will mamma.”

Ndoro finished his porridge and ran to the umuzi, sparring sticks in his right hand, his herding stick in his left. Shani held the gate open for him and he drove the goats down the hill and across the river to the grasses below. He felt the boys' eyes on him, their faces unreadable. Most of all he noticed Sitefu. He watched Ndoro, his mouth curved to slight frown. Ndoro's stomach rumbled in nervous excitement. Sitefu would have to approach him to establish his place among the other herd boys. The older boys, the ones watching cattle, seemed not to notice him at all. They talked among themselves, teasing and laughing, a few of them threatening each other to sparring.

He found a good spot of grass and halted his goats. Ndoro sauntered to a nearby acacia and sat beneath its thorny branches. He placed his sticks at his side, leaned against the smooth tree trunk and waited.

It wasn't long before a procession of boys came in his direction, each one herding his own goats. Sitefu led them all, his eyes focused on Ndoro in a way that made the younger boy nervous. His nervousness dissipated as Sitefu drew closer; he wasn't as big as Ndoro thought. Ndoro was actually taller than the boy, although at only eight seasons old his physique was just a thin layer of skin and muscle. Sitefu's body was lean and muscular like a leopard and like a leopard he could be powerful. Ndoro witnessed that in Sitefu's fight against Amanzi. But Ndoro was no Amanzi. He was a stick fighter, a Mawena stick fight, and he was anxious to find out where that would take him among his peers.

Sitefu wasted no time. He strode up to Ndoro, fighting sticks in his hand and touched the boy on his head.

"I am you master," he announced.

Ndoro picked up his sticks and stood. "No one is my master."

Ndoro did not see Lungile until he stepped between the boys.

"You can't fight him," Lungile said.

"Why? He is in my intanga. I must prove to him that I am his master."

"Mulugo said we should not talk to him. He is cursed."

Ndoro's eyes widened. "Cursed? I am not cursed! I am the son of Inkosi Dingane!"

"The inkosi is not above the ancestors," Lungile replied. "You shouldn't be alive."

Ndoro's hands tightened around his sticks. No matter what Jelani taught him, he would not strike at Lungile. He wasn't afraid of him; he knew he couldn't beat him, at least not yet.

"If I was supposed to be dead I would be," Ndoro retorted.

"You need to learn respect, dead boy," Lungile said. "Sitefu, if you want to fight him, go ahead."

Lungile smirked and walked away. Ndoro's mouth opened in shock. The inqwele was not watching the match, which meant if he won it would mean nothing.

Sitefu didn't care. His stick flew at Ndoro's head, barely missing as Ndoro stumbled away. He staggered away, Sitefu flailing at his head and knees. Ndoro avoided most of the blows but the ones that landed stung his pride more than his skin. He sidestepped, dodging Sitefu's charge and giving himself time to settle down. Sitefu's stick smacked against his blocking stick and Ndoro swung at his attacker's head. Sitefu was quick; he pulled his head back and the stick missed. Ndoro brought the stick down, feinting at Sitefu's knees then swung at his head again when the boy dropped his blocking stick. Stick met skull and Sitefu winced. Ndoro frowned; there was no blood so the fight was not over. He dodged a wild swing and smacked his stick against Sitefu's ribs, followed by another blow to his head. There was blood this time; Ndoro grinned in triumph and stepped away, his hands raised in victory.

Sitefu did not stop. The stick smashed against Ndoro's ribs, knocking the wind out of him. He fell to his knees gasping. Sitefu beat him on his back and head while the other boys cheered. Ndoro scrambled about on hands and knees, blackness blotting out the pain. Lungile would not stop his beating; Jelani was too far away to help him. The rules of sparring did not apply anymore. Jelani warned him but he did not believe him.

Ndoro flipped around and kicked Sitefu's ankles, knocking him down. He came to his feet and kicked Sitefu in the face. The boy rolled onto his back, blood pouring from his nose. Ndoro raised his stick and struck him again across the forehead, raising a welt.

"I am your master!" he shouted.

A hard stick struck him across the back. Ndoro spun around, swinging his stick. Pain exploded in his stomach; he doubled over and the pain appeared across his back. Ndoro gritted his teeth, fighting back the tears struggling to escape his eyes and the darkness seeping into his head. The blows came so quick the pain felt continuous, cascading over him. The blows ceased amid yelps and the thump of feet against the grass. He felt himself rising.

"I'm here, little monkey," Jelani whispered

Ndoro smiled as he let the darkness take over, happy to be away from the pain.

* * *

He didn't open his eyes when sound finally came back to his ears again. He couldn't understand the words floating over him but the anger in them was clear. He remained still, listening as the words began to make sense.

"This is your fault!"

"How can you blame me for this? You are the one who has disowned him. Did you keep him alive for this? His own intanga did this to him!"

"They will be punished."

"I don't care what happens to them. I care about our son."

Ndoro opened his eyes to the dim interior of his momma's hut. Her back was to him, the faint light from the dying fire illuminating her familiar outline. Jelani stood beside her, his arms folded across his chest. Inkosi Dingane, his baba, stood in front of momma, his features hidden by her body. Ndoro tried to move to see his baba's face but he didn't want them to know he was awake.

"What do you want me to do?" Dingane raised his hands. "I told you to keep him in the umuzi. Mulugo spreads his lies every day. Everyone either hates him or fears him."

"I tried, but he insisted," Shani said. "Jelani said it was best."

Dingane rushed to confront Jelani. "So this is your doing, Mawena."

Jelani did not move.

"Jelani is trying to make him a man," Shani said.

Dingane glared at Jelani a moment longer then looked at Shani.

"Shani, you must understand. I am bound by tradition. There is only so much I can do. He must do the rest himself."

"Then let him," Jelani said. "You can't make them accept him, but you can make them follow tradition. Ndoro is Sesu and should be treated so. He should be with his intanga. He should earn his place among them with his stick fighting skills. Anyone who violates Sesu law should be punished. If you refuse to treat him as your son, at least treat him like a Sesu."

Dingane glared at Jelani for a moment, then his expression softened.

"I will see to it," he said.

His baba walked away from Jelani. He moved Shani aside and approached Ndoro. Ndoro opened his eyes fully, staring into his father's eyes.

"Baba," he said.

Dingane leaned towards Ndoro until their foreheads touched.

"My son," he whispered.

Dingane pulled away, turned and left the hut.

Shani rushed to Ndoro and held him close.

"Momma, where is baba going?"

"Don't worry, little monkey," she said, using Jelani's pet name for him. "How do you feel?"

"Good, momma," he lied.

"You must rest now," she said. "In time you will feel better."

"Baba said I can be with my intanga."

Shani's face turned solemn. "Yes, he did. But you must understand, Ndoro. Many Sesu don't think you should be here. They will do whatever they can to disgrace you. Some will try . . . they will try to . . ."

"Kill me?"

Shani's eyes glistened. "You must be strong and wary. Your father cannot help you."

"Jelani will," Ndoro said.

"Yes, I will," Jelani replied. "Now sleep. Tomorrow will be an early day."

Ndoro smiled at them both. Dingane was his father, but momma and Jelani were his family. He could deal with any challenge as long as they were with him. He hugged momma, her smell soothing his mind. He lay on his cot, closed his eyes and once again fell into a peaceful slumber. The next time he awoke, he would wake as a Sesu.

3

Adesina cried, his legs tangled beneath his narrow bottom, his arms hanging at his side. His small brown head hung back so far only his chin and nose could be seen above his neck. He wailed from deep inside in his throat, a sound that should have echoed between the family compound walls of Abo. But only one person heard his cry, and that person had had enough.

"Shut up, Adesina!" Obaseki shouted. The young prince lay on his bed, his eyes clinched, hands over his ears. His feet dangled over the edge of his bed, kicking at Adesina.

"Don't do that!" Lewa scolded. She looked at both boys with sympathetic eyes too beautiful to belong to a twelve-year-old girl.

"He misses his momma," she explained.

"Why doesn't he miss her somewhere else?" Obaseki fussed. "I'm sleepy!"

"Salako performed a cleansing spell and drove him away."

Obaseki slammed his fist like hammers against the bed.

"I hate Salako!"

"Seki?"

Thembile opened his door and stepped into his room, concern and fear in her eyes.

"Who are you talking to?"

Obaseki opened his eyes to his aunt and sat up on his bed. Adesina continued to wail, but Thembile didn't hear him. She didn't see him either, nor did she see Lewa frowning at her.

Obaseki learned long ago that some of his friends were special. Only he could see them, but Salako could feel them. He hated Salako.

"No one," he answered.

Thembile saw the lie in his face and shrugged.

"I don't believe you, but I don't want to know. Do whatever you need to do and get some sleep. Kumba is leading weapons training tomorrow and he will hear no excuses."

"I will, aunt."

Thembile looked around the room one more time, rubbing the charm bag around her neck and whispering before she left.

Obaseki put his hand over his ears again. Adesina continued to cry despite Lewa's cooing.

"Okay, Adesina, I'll do it," Obaseki said.

Adesina looked at him, his shoulders trembling. "You will?"

Obaseki let out a defeated sigh. "Yes. Now stop crying!"

Lewa folded her slim arms across her budding chest. "Don't play with him, Seki. If you're not going to do it, don't say it."

"I said I would."

"How are you going to get out of the palace? You're an heir."

"I'll figure something out after I get some sleep!"

He fell back on his bed with a thud. When he looked up Adesina was gone. Lewa remained.

"You didn't leave."

"I never do."

Obaseki shrugged. "You can stay as long as you're quiet."

He lay back down on the bed and closed his eyes.

"Seki?"

Obaseki sprang back up. "What?"

"Goodnight."

The morning sun rose into a clear blue sky, its brilliant light reflecting off the stark white walls of the royal palace. Servants swept the royal courtyard clear of debris, preparing for the Oba's daily conference with the elders. Outside the palace walls other servants prepared meals, white smoke rising from the short chimneys protruding from the tops of the rotund ovens. The smell of fresh bread seeped into Obaseki's room, stirring his senses and waking him. He rose, looked about for Adesina and was pleased in his absence. Lewa was still there, staring at him from her corner.

"You slept well," she said.

Obaseki nodded as he put on his kente robe. He reached over his bed to the shelf and took down his sparring stick and shield, his face curled up in a frown. He hated weapons training; he would rather go to the ovens and help the cooks prepare the meal. He was fascinated by the preparation, the way the flour rose into tasty hard bread loaves, the aroma of the goat stew and the constant singing of the servants as they worked. Sometimes he wished he was just another boy, following his father to work in the fields or into the forest to hunt, or better yet pushing a canoe into the Kenji to cast the net for fish. But instead he was the grandson of Oba Noncemba, son a mother he never met and a father no one spoke of.

He trudged out of his room into the morning brightness. His cousins emerged from their rooms, bright and eager for the day's lesson. They separated, seeking their favorites among the crowd, every one of them avoiding Obaseki. He glared back at the ones brave enough to look at him and they glared back, shaking their sticks in his direction. He didn't bother to return the threat; they knew they couldn't beat him despite his apathetic attitude. It was his luck to have ability in something he despised.

He was the last to line up. Kumba stood under the ironwood tree shielding the practice courtyard, his dark hard face wrenched in disgust. His wide bare chest bore the scars of battles fought and won, his thick arms showing stretch marks made by muscles larger than the skin was meant to sheath. A leather kilt wrapped his narrow waist; thick thighs emerging from the hem, narrowed briefly at the knees then spread into muscled calves almost as thick as his thighs. Some said Kumba could crush the skull of a buffalo with one blow of his right fist while ripping the horn from a charging rhino with his left hand. Obaseki believed them.

"Oba Noncemba is cursed by the ancestors!" he growled. "His daughters have given him weaklings instead of warriors!"

His stared through the others, focusing on Obaseki. "So, you finally decided to join us?"

"Yes, uncle." Obaseki's words were more respectful than his tone.

"Save your defiance for sparring," Kumba snapped. "Your cousins are eager to show you what they learned since last we met."

Kumba turned his broad back to his pupils and commenced the drill. The boys followed him the best they could, their movement weak shadows of the warrior's precise execution. Still, they were improving. The drills continued until noon before Kumba raised his hand. The boys stopped and fell into the dirt, everyone except Obaseki. He was too angry to be tired, because Adesina had returned and brought his wailing with him.

"You said we would see mamma today!" he screamed.

"Will you leave me alone?" Obaseki shouted back before he realized what he had done.

"So, young prince, I'm bothering you?" Kumba loomed over him, blocking the sun with his massive frame.

"No uncle, I..."

The stick hit him despite his quick block. He rolled in the dirt, his head hurting more than his body. He kept rolling until his bumped into the ironwood.

"You are fast, I grant you that," Kumba commented. Kumba grabbed him by the arm and dragged him away from the others. He shoved him down, and then folded his arms across his chest.

"I know about the ghosts," he said. "Personally, I don't believe it. You are not a medicine priest. You are a prince, and you have the potential to be a damn good warrior, but you must concentrate, Seki."

Obaseki glanced away towards Adesina who continued to cry. He brought his eyes back to Kumba.

"I will try, uncle."

Kumba sighed. "Go home, Seki. You've done enough today. Think about what I've said."

Obaseki stood and trudged to the palace, Adesina trailing and wailing. He was almost home when Lewa appeared at his side.

"You promised, Seki."

"He promised he would stop."

"He won't stop until you take him home."

Obaseki stopped walking, looking around to make sure no one was watching before he answered.

"It's not that easy. I'm not supposed to leave the palace compound. It's forbidden until I become a man."

"You can sneak out."

"How?"

"I can show you."

He looked at Lewa, her face confident. Adesina cried.

"Okay," he said. "Let's go."

Lewa turned and led them to the cooking pots. The servants were busy with the midday meal, swirling about the open fires and smoking ovens as they sang one of their many work songs. The aroma of simmering goat reminded him of his hunger and he rubbed his stomach. The cooks noticed his gesture and laughed.

"The little prince is hungry!" they sang. Omope, a huge gregarious man with a greasy smile grabbed his hand and led him to a stool beside one of the largest ovens. He opened the iron door, extracted a bread loaf and handed it to Obaseki. "Thank you, Omope" He bounced the treat from hand to hand while it cooled, then took a big bite. The bread melted in his mouth and he moaned.

Lewa's expression was not a happy one. "Seki, let's go."

"Not until I finish my bread," he mumbled.

"Now!" Lewa swung and smashed her hand against a calabash on the table beside Obaseki. The water splashed his face and soaked his bread. Everyone turned, their eyes fearful. Omope scrambled to him with a towel.

"I am sorry, my prince. Please forgive us!"

"It's not your fault." Obaseki glared at Lewa who stood with a smirk on her face.

"The bread was good. I must go."

Obaseki wiped himself and followed Lewa. He pretended not to see the servants clutching their talismans and whispering prayers.

Lewa led him to the commissary area behind the kitchens. All the food for the palace was received, inspected and sent to the kitchens from the area.

"We'll hide in the storage hut until the next wagon of grain comes," she said. "We can sneak inside while the others are unloading. We'll have to make sure we jump off in the city. If not, we'll end up in the countryside outside the main gate."

Obaseki nodded. His defeat complete, he opened the door to the hut and walked inside. The smell of rotting grain attacked his nose and he stumbled back.

"It stinks!"

Adesina's abrasive wailing overpowered his repugnance and he went inside. The trio sat patiently, Adesina's crying subsiding to whimpering. The clatter of ox hooves and wooden wheels finally reached their ears and they sat up straight. The door swung wide and grain poured into the hut like water. The torrent hit Obaseki, pushing him back into the hut. Grain dust filled his nose and lungs, choking him. Before he could cry out the grain flood halted. He tried to move but couldn't.

"I'm stuck," he whispered.

Lewa wasn't paying attention to him. "The wagon is leaving!"

Obaseki dug himself free as fast as he could. He peeked outside to make sure no one else was present before charging out of the hut after the wagon. Lewa and Adesina were on the wagon, holding up the canvas that once covered the grain. He grabbed the back of the wagon and jumped on, crawling under the canvas before the farmers noticed.

This was too much for a crying spirit, he thought. He'd almost died in the grain hut, and now he was violating a sacred rule older than any elder alive. He didn't dare imagine what kind of punishment awaited him if his grandfather discovered him gone. He lifted the canvas slightly, peering out onto the scene fading behind him. He could see the palace spires rising over the commissary and the kitchens, their gold caps glistening in the blue sky. Someone might be looking for him right now. Soon the Atuegbu, his grandfather's elite guard, would be scouring the palace grounds, Thembile following them with worried eyes and wringing hands. She would be blamed and punished. Thembile didn't deserve punishment, though. She was afraid of him, but she did her best to ignore his friends and had covered up for him when others thought his behavior strange. She even defended him before his grandfather, something that most didn't have the courage to do.

He was going back, he decided. He would find another way to get Adesina quiet, one that didn't involve Thembile being disciplined. He lifted the canvas to see the palace gates behind him, the high wood and iron doors that concealed the Royal

Palace from Abo in mysterious splendor. He was outside for the first time in his life.

Lewa's voice killed his astonishment.

"Get ready, Seki. We're almost there."

"Where?"

"The main market," Lewa replied. "Adesina's mother goes there every day with bushels of yams. Her stall is in the center of the market."

"I should go back," Obaseki said. "This isn't right."

"It's too late now," Lewa said. "We're here."

A confusing bouquet of smells and sounds penetrated the coarse fabric hiding him, enticing him to look. A crush of people surrounded the wagon, some buying, others selling, all engaged in a daily ritual that existed long before Abo claimed to be a city. He jumped from the back of the wagon, his body filled with wonderful energy as he watched the Mawena selling their goods. He was lost in the crowd immediately, pushed and jostled by the constant torrent of sweating bodies. A familiar whine penetrated the noise, accompanied by the same annoying face.

"Momma is not here!" Adesina screamed.

"Yes, she is," Lewa assured him. "Come, follow me."

Obaseki followed Lewa, pushing through the crowd as they inched their way to the central market. He was so focused on keeping up with Adesina and Lewa that he didn't notice the curious stares transforming into shocked faces as the Mawena recognized the royal pattern of his kente robe. No one could remember seeing a member of the royal household outside the palace at such a young age; no one had ever seen a member of the royal family outside the royal palace alone. When they reached the central stalls everyone knelt, their heads touching the ground.

Obaseki had just realized the commotion he instigated when Adesina shrieked.

"Mamma! Mamma!"

The woman bowed before them, a basket of yams resting beside her. A colorful scarf covered her head, helping to obscure her face. Obaseki walked to her and squatted before her.

"Please, aunt, rise and face me. I have something to tell you."

Adesina's momma lifted her head just enough to look into Obaseki's eyes. He smiled, and she smiled back. She was a handsome woman with a comforting smile.

"What do you wish of me, young prince?"

"I have come to speak to you of your son."

Adesina's momma sat up straight. "My son? My son is dead."

"I know, but he is not happy. Salako drove him from his home. He misses you."

Anger seeped into the woman's face. "You have no right to torment me even if you are a prince. Whoever told you these things did not mean for you to use them this way."

"Adesina told me," Obaseki replied nervously. Others had sat up, listening to the conversation.

"Tell her I miss my tum-tum," Adesina whispered.

"He missed his tum-tum," Obaseki said.

The woman's hand clamped over her mouth as tears welled in her eyes. "Where is he? Where is my Adesina?"

"He is here. He wishes to come home."

The woman was about to answer when broad man with the face of Adesina appeared, grabbing her by the arm and pulling her away as he glowered at Obaseki.

"Who are you?" the man demanded. "You are no medicine priest. Adesina's spirit tormented us day and night with his wailing. He is gone. It is time for him to move on."

"But he wants to go home," Obaseki pleaded. "He will be quiet if you lift the spell and let him come home."

The man rushed Obaseki and pushed him to the ground. The crowded gasped, many falling back to their knees and hiding their faces in the dirt.

"No, Olujimi" the woman exclaimed. "He is a prince! You mustn't touch him!"

"I don't care what he is. He has no right to tell us our business. Salako told us what to do and it worked."

Olujimi pulled his orinka from is waist belt, brandishing the war club over his head. "Go back to the palace, young prince. Leave us common folk alone."

The assegai struck Olujimi with a force that spun him around, knocking the orinka from his hand. Adesina's father grabbed the shaft protruding from his arm in reflex; his teeth clinched in anger and pain. The man who threw the spear walked up to his victim. He was clad in a leather shirt covered by chain mail, a conical helmet on his head. A curved sword hung from his waist belt that held his leather kilt around his narrow waist. He placed a sandaled foot on Olujimi's wounded arm and jerked the spear free. Olujimi passed out.

The man approached Obaseki and knelt before him. It was Aditola, his grandfather's senior bodyguard.

" prince, I was sent to bring you back to the palace."

Obaseki nodded. He was relieved that the Atuegbu had found him, but he knew what it meant. His grandfather was angry.

The warrior glanced back at Olujimi. "Did he harm you?"

"No!" Obaseki blurted. "It was I who harmed him."

He went to Adesina's mother. She hovered over her husband, her voice soft and as she prayed.

"I am sorry, aunt," he whispered. "I was only trying to help Adesina."

"He was a selfish boy," she replied. "It is why the ancestors took him so young. Tell him to go. This is his fault. He has caused this by not respecting us. He is no longer wanted."

Obaseki looked about him. Lewa stood beside him, looking sad enough to make him want to cry, but Adesina was gone. Obaseki knew he was gone for good.

"He is gone, aunt. I am sorry."

Obaseki returned to the warrior. More Atuegbu arrived, forming a wall between Obaseki and the others.

"I am ready," he said.

Aditola nodded and they marched away from the market, Obaseki in the middle of the ranks, his head down in sorrow and shame. He did not understand this strangeness about him, this ability to see spirits as if they live, to talk to those long since dead as if they still existed. But he would try; one day he would discover the purpose of it all. He would do it for himself. He would do it for Adesina.

4

Inaamdura sauntered through the central courtyard of the Yellow Palace, her delicate hands folded behind her back. Her dark brown face was a sculpture of composure, her strong cheekbones and narrow nose like her mother. A collection of colorful beaded necklaces rose from her slim shoulders to just below her chin, each one a token of admiration from a hopeful suitor. Her shapely body was covered by a thick yellow robe that fell to her sandaled feet, protecting her from the cool winds that blew down from the towering mountains watching over Kampera. She was her mother's eldest and most beautiful daughter, and she was well aware of her status.

She halted before the ornate wooden door leading to her mother's personal garden. She was about to enter when a familiar giggle drew her attention. Inaamdura grinned.

"Bikita, how many times have I told you not to spy on me?"

Little Bikita hugged Inaamdura from behind, pressing her cheek into her sister's back.

"Where are you going?"

"You know where I'm going, and you know you can't follow."

Bikita worked her way around Inaamdura and gazed into her eyes. She was as much as her father's daughter as Inaamdura was her mother's, a handsome child with a round face and dancing eyes. Her beaded braids played about her high forehead as she nuzzled her sister.

"You could take me if you wanted."

Inaamdura knelt, looking her precious sister in the face. Her mother taught her to conserve her emotions in all relationships, but she could not deny Bikita. Her effervescence wore away the hardest barrier she could ever erect, so she gave in and loved Bikita like she loved no other.

"Look, Kita, do you want to see me in trouble with mamma?"

Bikita frowned. "No."

"That's what will happen if I take you in the garden. Momma will take a switch to me and beat me until I bleed."

Bikita gasped. "No! Momma wouldn't do that to you. You're her favorite."

"Favorite or not, I can't take you into the garden. Now go and play. Your time in the garden will come soon enough."

Bikita clasped Inaamdura's face between her hands and kissed her on the nose.

"Bye, Rah-rah!" Bikita said.

She skipped away across the courtyard and into the palace. Inaamdura watched her with a bit of joy and sadness. Her time in the garden would come and her childhood would end. It was the price she would have to pay for the privilege of being the daughter of Azana.

Inaamdura opened the door of the garden and was rushed by the heavy scent of flowers. The garden bloomed constantly, populated with flora that displayed their enticements in an unending sequence of colors and aromas. She followed the granite path to the acacia tree dominating the center of the garden, its seductive white blooms a contrast to its sharp thorns. Below its broad canopy Azana sat on her cushioned ironwood stool, staring at her daughter with her intense black eyes. Their likeness was disturbing, a resemblance so close that those looking at a glance might mistake one for another. But where Inaamdura's face and body expressed the softness of youth, Azana's suffered with the hardness of age.

Azana gestured for Inaamdura to sit and she did so, folding her legs beneath her as he sat at her mother's feet.

"You are late," Azana said.

"I am sorry, momma."

"You must handle Bikita sternly or she will ruin you."

"I know momma. I will try harder."

"You will not try; you will do. You have no more time, Inaamdura. Events are moving faster than I expected."

Inaamdura stiffened. It was not her mother's way to rush into action.

"What has happened?" she asked.

"My eyes have seen the Sesu moving towards the border with intent. My ears have heard inkosi Dingane talk of empire, of building a city to rival Abo of the Mawena and of making the grasslands the home of the Sesu."

"What of our overtures?"

"Dingane has agreed to take Amadika as his Great Wife, but only because of the disfavor Great Wife Shani suffered from the birth of her twins and her defiance of Sesu tradition."

"It is not right to ask a woman to choose between her children," Inaamdura said, letting her anger slip.

"That was an unnecessary comment," Azana scolded. "It is not our concern of what is right or wrong among the Sesu."

"If Dingane has agreed to marry Amadika, why are you concerned?"

Azana reached out her hands and Inaamdura stood then helped her mother to her feet. They walked along the path, their feet crushing the colorful collage of petals scattered before them.

"Dingane may be too strong for Amadika. She may not be able to fulfill her duty as a Bonga wife."

"So, what do we do?"

"I don't know. Dingane has invited us to attend the Mkosi ceremony. Your father thinks it is a waste of time, but I insisted that we attend. My ears tell me the Mkosi ceremony is the most important of all Sesu festivals, one in which all the Sesu attend to confirm the soul of their nation. We will have a chance to see what the Sesu have to offer the Shamfa. Besides, if would be an insult if we did not attend."

They walked together silently, enjoying the coolness of the day. Inaamdura found her mother's company best when they didn't speak. She felt close to her in those silent moments, sharing the love that she knew her mother would never express verbally for it was not her way. She was the perfect Bonga wife, bred to lead her husband to greatness. While her father performed the ceremonies, and made the speeches all men desired of their kings, it was Azana who bore the burden of running the nation as she ran her home. She made the decisions of the kingdom; Muchese made sure they were carried out. The nation wore a Shamfa face, but it was ruled by a Bonga hand.

Her mother broke the silence as always.

"You will accompany your father and me to Sesuland. Amadika will remain here."

"Shouldn't she go as well?" Inaamdura asked. "It is she he is to marry."

"The Sesu are not like us, daughter. Their way of life is simple and hard. It is not the life for a Bonga wife, but we all must make sacrifices for the pride of our family. If Amadika sees what her future holds too soon, she will cause difficulty."

Inaamdura stopped to watch a thorn bird land in the acacia, working its way through the dangerous thorns with ease.

"We will leave in two weeks," Azana said. "Make sure you handle your affairs."

Inaamdura knew of what affairs her mother spoke of.

"I will, momma."

"Good. Now leave me to my garden. I wish to feed the birds."

Inaamdura left her mother to her joy. Leaving the garden was a great relief until she stepped into the courtyard. Twaambo was waiting for her, standing with his legs spread in a powerful stance, his right fist pressed hard into his armored hip. He was in full Shamfa warrior regalia, which he always wore in public. Twaambo was as serious as her mother, but held none of her solemn ways. In fact, Twaambo was very un-Shamfa like. His dark brown eyes were intense; his brows always close together as if in constant contemplation. She could not deny that he was handsome, but there was no difficulty in reserving her emotions towards him. She did not like Twaambo. She would marry him, but she did not like him and she suspected she never would.

"Hello, Twaambo," she said.

"Inaamdura, it is good to see you."

Inaamdura walked by Twaambo and he followed.

"What are you doing here?" she asked.

"There is something I wish to show you."

Inaamdura turned to look at her fiancé, flashing a wicked smile.

"I cannot see that until we marry."

Twaambo looked shocked. "I did not mean..."

Inaamdura laughed. "I know, Twaambo. Now what is it you wish to show me?"

"It is not here. I must take you there. It will require a week's travel. I spoke to Muchese and he gave his permission. The proper escorts will accompany us, of course, and a company of my finest warriors will join us as well."

"I cannot go," Inaamdura said.

"You haven't even asked what I planned to show you."

Inaamdura stopped in the courtyard, grasping Twaambo's hands in hers.

"Our family had been invited to attend the Mkosi ceremony in Sesuland. My mother asked that I accompany her. I'm surprised baba did not mention this to you."

"It is not your place to go," Twaambo said angrily.

"It is not you place to question the decision of the Queen Mother," Inaamdura snapped.

Twaambo backed down, but only slightly.

"I agree, but isn't it odd that the daughter destined to marry the inkosi does not attend his people's most sacred celebration?"

"Amadika will attend many Mkosi celebrations in the future."

"The Sesu are not worthy of the Shamfa's attention," Twaambo spat. "Give me two regiments and one dry season and the Sesu would no longer exist."

"You are the perfect diplomat," Inaamdura said with a smile.

"I would be angry with you if you weren't so beautiful,"

Twaambo replied. He squeezed her hand and Inaamdura feigned a blush.

"You should leave, Twaambo. I have much to do before I leave, and you are a distraction; a pleasant distraction, but one just the same."

Twaambo bowed. "You will go with me when you return?"

"Yes, Twaambo, I will. Now go."

Twaambo left the courtyard. Inaamdura watched him, trying her best to summon some kind of emotion towards her husband to be with no success. She understood the words of her mother and she saw the wisdom in them, but she knew her mother did not always heed her own advice. She loved her father. She would not admit it, but she saw it in her mother's eyes when she looked at him.

She stepped into the dim light of the Queen's House, the living quarters of the Yellow Palace, following the carpeted floors to the ironwood staircase leading to her room. She had chosen the smallest room of the palace as her own, preferring the limited space to a large expanse begging to be filled. Her tastes were modest; her room held only a small bed, two chests of drawers for her small wardrobe and an elaborately carved mahogany chest. The one window of the room looked out to the mountains where she would gaze at the cloudy peaks for hours. She sat before the portal, looking out onto them again. She always wondered how long they had stood, watching indifferently over the comings and goings of men and animals, observing the world change below them while they remained the same; silent, powerful and unmoving. One day she would rule an empire as strong as the mountains, a dynasty that would outlive its founders. Twaambo was a strong and ambition man, although she worried about his aggressive streak. It would take time, but he would eventually carve out his own land to the east of Shamfa among grasslands and forest of the highlands. They would rule together, in time challenging the Shamfa and the Bonga for dominance of the valley. This was her secret ambition, to sit in the garden with her mother not as an obedient daughter, but as an equal.

"Inaamdura?"

Amadika poked her head into the room, her worried frown ruining an otherwise pretty face. She stepped inside, shuffling to her sister's bed to sit. Amadika was the sister that looked like the child of Muchese and Azana, possessing the sweet, child-like face of her father and the feminine voluptuousness of her mother. Her ways were a mix as well, sometimes playful and energetic, sometimes solemn and serious. She also possessed a sense of dread which was uniquely hers, a trait that annoyed Inaamdura to no end.

Inaamdura turned and smiled. "Hello, little sister."

"Don't use your charms on me," Amadika snapped. "I'm not one of your dogs sniffing about. Twaambo told me you're going to Sesuland with momma and baba."

Inaamdura sat silent while she fought to control her anger. Twaambo would pay for this, but first she would deal with Amadika.

"Inkosi Dingane has invited momma and father to the Mkosi ceremony. Mother asked that I accompany them."

Amadika slammed her fist on the bed. "Why was I not told? I'm the one promised to marry Dingane. I should go, not you!"

"Listen to you," Inaamdura admonished. "You sound like Bikita. That's the reason momma did not ask you to go. The last thing she needs is for you to get in front of the inkosi have one of your fits."

"And what if I do? At least he'll know I don't want to marry him."

Inaamdura felt pain rising in the back of her head. "You would jeopardize the alliance between Shamfa and Sesuland?"

"Twaambo says we don't need the Sesu," Amadika answered. "He says we could break them like sticks if they attacked Shamfa."

"Twaambo is no expert on war," Inaamdura replied. "How many battles has he won? How many lands has he conquered? If momma believes the Sesu are necessary allies, they will be. Don't let Twaambo's ego infect your reason. Remember your duty."

Amadika face became composed. "Twaambo deserves a woman that believes in him."

So, there it was. She always knew of Amadika's infatuation with Twaambo as a child, but apparently that infatuation had lingered. She was not about to be dragged into a fight with her sister about a man, let alone Twaambo.

"If I tell you something, you must keep it a secret," Inaamdura said.

Amadika looked skeptical. "What?"

"Promise me you won't tell anyone, not even Twaambo."

Her sister hesitated. "I won't tell him."

"The purpose of our journey is to determine whether the Sesu are worthy allies. Most of all, momma wishes to meet Dingane face to face to determine whether he is a suitable match for you."

Amadika's eyes brightened. "Really?"

"Yes. It is important for any alliance to be as strong as possible. If you and Dingane are not a good match, the alliance will fail."

"I hear the Sesu are savages," Amadika whispered. "They still live in grass huts and the men have as many wives as they can afford. It's disgusting."

Inaamdura place a light touch on Amadika's shoulder. "I will look out for you, little sister. If Dingane is just one speck less the man Twaambo is, I will speak strongly against him."

"Thank you Rah-Rah," Amadika said as she hugged her.

"Now go," Inaamdura ordered. "I need a nap."

Amadika hugged her again and pranced from her room. Inaamdura waited until she knew her sister was far away before snatching up a brush from her vanity and hurling it across the room. Amadika tried her patience to no end. She refused to accept the fact that her future had been decided. She would marry Dingane no matter what mother thought of him. The deal had been struck; there was no going back. Twaambo was not an option. It was time for her to grow up and face facts; maybe her marriage to Dingane would be the slap to bring her to her senses. Inaamdura rose from her chair and fell onto her bed face first and arms spread, embracing the mattress like a long lost love. She tried to sleep but her stomach fluttered as she thought of seeing the Sesu for the first time. Were they the savages everyone thought they were, or were they equal to the Shamfa in culture and power? She hoped for Amadika's sake the latter was true.

The days leading to their journey passed quickly for Inaamdura. Azana decided to place her in charge of selecting the entourage accompanying them to Sesuland. It was a test to determine if she was astute in Shamfa politics and Inaamdura approached the task carefully. She kept the group small, 10 families total. The Shamfa families outnumbered the Bonga as a reminded of their lower status. She selected three members from each family; an elder, a warrior and an attendant. Her only difficulty was Twaambo's family. His father, Sipole Sishokwe, was an obvious selection. He was her father's closest friend and ally. By right the warrior should have been Twaambo, but he would not go. He would be as volatile as Amadika and sure to cause trouble. She left the task of Twaambo's refusal to her mother who handled the situation calmly yet stern, leaving neither father nor son able to argue the decision. In the end her mother showed her approval by sending her a flower from her garden, a beautiful protea which she placed in a jade vase on the chest by her window.

The caravan assembled at the stone road surrounding the Yellow Palace outside the Mansa's Wall. Each family supplied its own ox drawn wagon, each transport covered by a canvas depicting the family patterns. Muchese's wagon was yellow, the only wagon constructed entirely of wood strengthened by protective metal strips. The huge vehicle was harnessed to six oxen bred to pull the tremendous weight. During war the wagon served as Muchese's command hut, but on this day its stark interior gave way to a woman's touch. The supply wagons were loaded with enough provisions to feed them for the entire journey even though they expected Sesu hospitality once they reached the ceremony. If that occurred, they would share what they brought with the less fortunate on their return trip through Sesuland. The gesture would not be forgotten and would leave a good impression on the common folk from which many of Dingane's warriors originated.

One company of warriors was selected to provide protection for them. They were the Twon, her father's personal company consisting of warrior from the main Shamfa clans. Each man brought three mounts; a stallion, a mare and a donkey to carry their provisions. They were impressive in their leather caps and breastplates, the chain mail sleeves extending beyond their short-sleeved cotton shirts. Metal studded strips of leather hung down over most of their riding pants, with leather boots protecting their legs up to the knees. Curved sabers hung from their waists, their hands holding long lances crowned with broadleaf blades. Half the company was positioned at the head of the train, the other half at the rear. They sat stoically, waiting with the others for Muchese and Azana to emerge from the palace.

A formal announcement had not been made concerning the journey but the throng appeared just the same, lining the eastern avenue originating at the Mansa's wall. The road passed through the main market, the merchant district and Bonga district before emerging through the Eastern gates out into the grasslands. People jostled for position on the road's edge to see the train, fist fights erupting as tempers grew short and the temperature rose.

Muchese stood in the window, looking down on the agitated crowd. Inaamdura watched her father for the indication that they should leave but he seemed in no particular hurry. He looked down at the restless crowd and smiled.

"Can you hear them?" he asked her. He turned to show the brilliant smile that was the trait of his clan, a countenance that Bikita had inherited and Amadika tried to imitate.

"They call for you, baba," she said.

Her mother sat on the lounge, her face showing her displeasure.

"Are you done toying with your people?"

Muchese smiled at his wife despite her remark.

"You are a brilliant woman but you know nothing of ceremony. The people need spectacle. They need to wait impatiently to see their mansa, for they know their mansa blesses them with his presence."

"Then bless them, my husband. The day grows short and we have much ground to cover before nightfall."

Muchese pouted then left the window. He was dressed in parade garments, a golden headring with a bull head symbol in the center. He was bare-chested with braided golden armbands encircling each bicep. Gilded rings adorned every finger, each shaped in the symbol of the Shamfa clans. His black toga fell to his sandaled feet. He departed the room; Inaamdura and her mother close behind. Twon escorts met them as they entered the courtyard, leading them through the palace gates and to the awaiting wagon. The guards opened the doors but Muchese refused to enter.

"You two get inside," he commanded. Inaamdura was puzzled, which showed on her face.

"Ceremony, my daughter," he said. "Now, get inside!"

Azana rolled her eyes and entered the wagon. Inaamdura followed, sitting on the calfskin bench closest to a viewing port. She watched as her father walked up to the ox driver and took his whip. He snapped the whip and the wagon lurched, Inaamdura falling onto the bench. She looked at her mother and she shrugged.

The families saw them approach and their warriors banged their shields in approval. A roar rose from the crowd and the people surged forward to view Muchese. The line of warriors held firm, keeping the East Road clear for the train. Drummers played furiously, accompanied by a host of bembira players and the voices of thousands of Shamfa and Bonga. They followed the train through the Mansa's market where the merchants had closed their shops in anticipation of the day. The train crept deliberately through the city, eventually passing through the massive iron doors of the fortified wall. Muchese continued to lead his wagon until they were out of sight of the city. The caravan halted and he returned the ox driver's whip. His warriors helped him into the wagon.

"We can make good time now," Azana said.

"My lovely wife is always so serious," Muchese said as he approached her. He sat hard beside her and kissed her full on the mouth. Azana shoved him away playfully, slapping him lightly on the shoulder.

"Muchese! This is no time for play!"

Muchese kissed her again then fled to Inaamdura's side.

"Look, Dura. You are looking at a sight as rare as a hyena with a beard. It is a Bonga woman that truly loves her husband!"

"Sometimes I wish I didn't," Azana replied. "I would leave you and watch this village you call a mansadom crumble."

"That it would do without your stern hand," Muchese admitted.

"Inaamdura, ride with our warriors. Your mother and I have things to discuss."

"Yes, father." She signaled the ox driver from the portal and the wagon halted. A horse waited for her when she exited the wagon, held in place by Sipole himself.

"Come," he said. "I was looking forward to riding with you."

"Thank you, uncle." Inaamdura climbed onto the mount and rode off at a trot with her future father in law.

"You know I am angry with you," he said. "Twaambo should be here protecting you and serving me."

"It was my mother's decision," Inaamdura replied.

"Nonsense. I know Azana well, and she could care less if Twaambo came with us or not. You told her he could not go."

Inaamdura decided not to play coy. "Yes, I did."

Sipole sniffed. "Twaambo told me of his conversation with you and Amadika. I admit my son talks too much, but it was not your place to punish him. You should have come to me."

There was a hint of anger in Sipole's voice which told her she had made the right decision. Sipole only demanded Twaambo's council in matters of war.

"I apologize for my rashness," she said. "I miss Twaambo's company as much as you, uncle. I will make it up to you both when we return to Kampera."

Sipole nodded then turned his attention to the journey. "This journey will not be so pleasant once the road ends. The grasslands are not as smooth, and Sesuland is filled with hills, rocks and rivers. You'll be glad you took a horse by the time we get to Selike."

"Is that the capital city?"

Sipole laughed. "City is a relative term. To the Sesu it is a metropolis, but to you it will appear a maze of villages. The Sesu have no need for cities. They have no goods to trade and their craftsmanship is limited to their clothes, weapons and trinkets. They value nothing but their cattle and their honor. I still don't understand why an alliance with them is so important."

"Weren't the Shamfa once the same as the Sesu?" she asked.

Sipole glanced at her with a respectful eye. "Yes we were, but that is why Disingwayo broke away and led us to where we are today. He saw the potential in us and knew it would not be fulfilled adhering to the old way."

Inaamdura had listen to her father tell the story of Disingwayo, "The Banished One," and how he forged the Shamfa in the shadow of the mountains and on the backs of the Bonga. It must have been an exciting time, full of danger and uncertainty. She often imagined herself living in those times as Disingwayo's Great Wife, fighting side by side with her husband and helping him build an empire between the mountains and the river. She hoped the same future waited for her with Twaambo.

"Twaambo has found his destiny on the other side of the mountains," Sipole continued.

"What?" Inaamdura eyes went wide.

Sipole looked at her then laughed. "Oh, I'm sorry. He wanted to show you himself. I guess I spoiled the surprise."

"He said he had something to show me," she said.

"I will speak no further," Sipole finished. "I have said enough."

By nightfall they were near the frontier, the land claimed by both Sesuland and Shamfa. The road had faded away hours ago but so far the ground was smooth enough to continue at a steady pace. The wagons were circled and camp set up for the night. Inaamdura returned to her father's wagon exhausted but happy. Sipole's slip had her mind racing as she thought of the possibility of a new land, an unexplored country open to the rule of Twaambo and herself. She wished she had stayed in Kampera and followed her fiancé to this new world and her new future. Sesuland suddenly felt vile in her mouth, like a sour fruit that once held the promise of sweetness. She would be sure to visit Twaambo as soon as she returned. There seemed to be much they needed to discuss.

She found her mother and father sitting outside the wagon on their stools, both holding long sticks in their hands. They seemed to be doodling in the dirt, drawing lines and circles with exuberant gestures and excited voices.

"Who in their right mind would want to take this road?" her mother said.

"The smart warrior," Muchese replied. "The key to victory is to do the unexpected. History is replete with leaders who thought their people were safe because of a false belief. The raging river is always passable, the impenetrable forest is penetrable, and the highest mountain will someday be climbed."

Inaamdura saw a crude map of Uhuru traced into the dirt, the major cities marked with dots. Muchese was attempting to draw a line through Sesuland to Mawenaland, but Azana kept erasing the line with her right foot.

"Why must you always disagree with me?" her mother asked. "Haven't I given you great council since the day we joined?"

"Yes, you have, Azana. But you must understand that war is as much about chance as it is about logic. Sometimes one must take a chance to be victorious."

Inaamdura cleared her throat to announce her presence.

"Come to me, child," her mother said. "Your father is teaching me the science of insanity."

Muchese laughed and the three spent the rest of the night feasting, discussing, arguing and laughing. Inaamdura tired before them both and went to sleep early. When she awoke sunlight was still weak in the clear sky. A sudden jolt of the wagon had awakened her; she sat up to see her mother and father were not in the wagon. She dressed quickly and went outside. The ox driver was hastily hitching the oxen to the wagon.

"Where are my mother and father?" she asked.

"They are ahead with the others. They went out to meet with the Sesu."

"The Sesu are here?"

The ox driver smiled. He was naked except for his loincloth, a narrow short man with hard muscles and wrinkled skin.

"The Sesu always come in the dawn," he said. "They believe their magic is stronger then. It is also the time they choose to attack."

Inaamdura ran to the center of the wagon circle. Her father sat on his royal stool flanked by her mother and Sipole. The other nobles stood behind them, their attendants holding their family icons. The Twon formed two lines on either side of the nobles, fully armed and emotionless.

Inaamdura came to her mother's side and finally saw them. She counted ten warriors, each man covered in elaborate outfits of cow tails that hung from their necks, arms, waists and legs. Each man wore a plume of feathers on their heads, some large enough to obscure their faces, other with a simple arrangement in the back and a single feather in the front. The man in front was a towering figure, his broad chin shadowed with a grey-black beard. His balding head barely held his head ring, the remaining hairs woven around it to hold it in place. His garments were understated compared to his companions; a single stork feather rose from the front of his leopard headband, a cluster of lourie feathers adorning the back. A leopard claw necklace encircled his neck. He regarded Inaamdura for a moment then turned his attention back to Muchese.

"As I said, your wagons will slow us down. Dingane sent us as an escort, but we do not wish to be late for the ceremony."

"I understand your concern, Madikane," Muchese said. "We are honored that Inkosi Dingane chose to send an induna of such a high rank to escort us to Selike. We would feel terrible if our cumbersome caravan should delay your arrival. But our wagons contain tribute to your inkosi that we would be embarrassed to enter your royal umuzi without."

Madikane stood silent, rubbing his grizzled chin. "You can bring the wagons, but we must leave now. We're two days from Selike, but with the wagons it will take us five. Send a messenger when you are ready to depart. We will await you at the Mpanda."

Madikane brought his right hand across and hit his chest with his fist. Muchese and the other men returned the gesture. The Sesu sprang to their feet and Madikane led them away, but not before taking another glance at Inaamdura.

"Well, that was interesting," Muchese said as he rose from his stool. "I didn't expect them so soon."

"They have probably been following us for days," Sipole replied. "They were waiting for the right moment to approach."

"The Twon have that effect on people," Muchese said. "They are a fearsome group."

Sipole laughed. "We are at the border of Sesuland. We saw what Madikane wanted us to see."

"Enough of this," Muchese said, clearly irritated by Sipole's words. "We must break camp. Our hosts are waiting."

Inaamdura was so involved in her father and Sipole's squabbling she did not notice her mother until she spoke.

"What did you think of the Sesu?" she asked.

"Oh, mother! I didn't see you."

"What did you think?"

Inaamdura could not hide her feelings. "They were impressive."

"Madikane seemed to think the same of you."

"He noticed that I was late, nothing more."

"I don't have to tell you the effect you have on men," her mother said. "Stay close to your father and the Twon. I don't trust these Sesu."

Sipole's words were proven true as they approached the Mpanda River. The massive Sesu encampment sprawled on both banks. Naked children shouted as the train was spotted and the Sesu warriors among them responded with alacrity. Inaamdura was fascinated with how fast they ran, charging up the hill with incredible speed and surrounding the wagons before the Twon could take position around Muchese's wagon. Madikane was the first to reach them.

"You must stay among yourselves," he advised. "The Mkosi is a proud time for the Sesu, and nothing would be prouder than a warrior killing an enemy on his way to pay respect to the inkosi."

"What of your men surrounding us?" her father asked.

"They will obey my orders as long as you do. Stay with your people until we reach Selike."

Madikane was about to leave when he saw Inaamdura. This time his stare was deliberate.

"This is my daughter, Inaamdura," Muchese said, his voice tight.

"Is this the one promised to Dingane?"

"No."

Madikane smiled. "Good."

He turned and marched away. His men formed a perimeter around the wagons.

Muchese turned to her, his face serious. "Get inside the wagon, Inaamdura. I want you to stay there until we reach Selike."

"But baba, the wagon is hot and I cannot see well."

"Get inside the wagon!" he shouted.

Inaamdura was stunned. She couldn't remember the last time her father yelled at her. She backed away from him then turned and ran to the wagon. She clamored inside and was greeted by her mother.

"Your father is doing what is best for you."

"I am not afraid of the Sesu or Madikane."

"This has nothing to do with being afraid. Madikane is taken with you. I have given one of my daughters to the Sesu and I will not give another."

Inaamdura felt a chill like the mountain winds. She sat, resigned to watch the journey to Selike from inside the royal wagon.

And what a journey it was. The wagons did slow down the procession, but in truth the Sesu didn't seem to mind. They set out in early morning, a chorus of drums and voices calling for the departure. The warriors led the way, followed by their attendants. The women followed, the married women covered in cotton cloth dressed with multi-colored beads adorning their necks and ears. The single girls wore only a small beaded skirt around their waists, their breasts exposed. They all walked together and they sang the entire day. The warriors sang first, then the boys, the married women, the single women and the old. As soon as one group was done the other began. Inaamdura did not understand the words, but the feeling was intoxicating. She spied what she could through the wagon vents, but had a better view at night when she was allowed from the wagon. She ate quickly then ran to the wagon perimeter to watch the Sesu celebrate throughout the night, the warriors' martial steps athletic and threatening, the single women moving their bodies to attract the attention of the single warriors. She watched them until her mother forced her back into the wagon.

As they drew closer to Selike they met other bands of Sesu heading to the ceremony. The volume of the singing increase as the bands joined together, the clans greeting each other as family. The warriors were the exception. The rivalry between the regiments was immediate. The warrior danced before each other, their movement more threatening and aggressive. The Shamfa were introduced to a more ominous tradition among the Sesu; the stick fight. Warriors from different regiments would face each other in a circle of bodies, brandishing long sticks with small shields. After a round of boasting and dancing they would attack each other in a blur, striking at their opponent's body and occasionally taking a swing at the head. Some warriors dropped their stick and conceded to their opponent, who would help the man to his feet in good spirits. Others would fight until a blow to the head knocked them unconscious. The victor would immediately drop his stick and tend to the defeated one, a gesture that was approved by the losing regiment. Inaamdura watched as much as she could, fascinated by the endless energy of the Sesu. At night when she was allowed outside the wagon she would hurry to the edge of the encampment and sit, watching the Sesu under the protection of a squad of Twon.

By the fourth day their journey to Selike had become a procession of thousands. For as far as she could see in every direction were Sesu men, women and children, walking and singing. The stick fighting had ceased; the warriors, women, girls and boys all sang the same song. They swayed like grass with the wind, each person in perfect time with the person beside him or her. Inaamdura found herself moving with them despite the jolting ride inside the wagon. That night as she sat at the wagon boundary with the Twon, Madikane approached. He was alone and without his weapons, a dagga pipe in his hand. He offered it to the Twon and they refused with their silence. Inaamdura rose immediately to return to the wagon.

"What do you think of the Sesu?" Madikane called out.

Inaamdura halted. She knew she shouldn't speak to Madikane; it was obvious he was interested in her as a potential wife and neither her mother nor father wished to give him any reason to hope.

"I am destined to marry another," she said. "He is man of great standing in our land, and refusing him would cause a rift that would be difficult to repair."

Madikane took a long drag on his pipe and let the smoke seep from his lips.

"You are not one to waste words, are you?"

Inaamdura shared a smile with Madikane that was more generous than he deserved.

"To answer your first question, I find myself growing more impressed with your people every day. You seem to possess a joy the Shamfa lost long ago."

"The Shamfa are our cousins," Madikane replied. "The marriage of Dingane and Amadika only legitimizes what is well known."

He took another drag from the pipe and closed his eyes. "The Shamfa have strayed too far from the Untuni traditions. You have gained much, but you have lost much as well. Maybe the Sesu will teach you how to live again."

One of the Twon guards grasped her arm. "Princess, we must go now."

Inaamdura freed herself from his grasp. "You are here to protect me, not give me orders. You forget your place."

Anger flashed across the Twon's face but was quickly replaced by a subservient smile. He bowed and stepped away.

"What is that song everyone is singing?"

Madikane grinned. "We are calling for the inkosi," he replied. "We are asking him to show himself so we know he is still alive and the Sesu are still favored by Unkulunkulu."

"You know Dingane well?"

"I do. I am his senior induna, chosen because my clan is the strongest in Sesuland. I command six thousand warriors and my umuzi is second in size only to the inkosi. Not only do I know Dingane well, he knows me very well also."

Inaamdura picked up a challenging tone in Madikane's voice. He was apparently a powerful man in his own right, which was why he showed an interest in her. He was seeking his own alliance with the Shamfa.

"What does he look like?"

Madikane frowned. "You will have to see for yourself tomorrow." He took another drag on his pipe then sauntered away, disappearing in the darkness.

Inaamdura began to call him back but realized the futility of the effort. She felt tired; it was late and she needed to rest for tomorrow. She turned to her bodyguards, eyeing the one that tried to rush her earlier.

"Now it is time for us to go."

The Twon took up beside her and they walked back to the royal wagon, Inaamdura anxious for the coming of the next day.

The morning came with a chorus of shrill voices just after dawn. The Sesu women sang a song that resonated throughout the grasslands, waking everyone for the final march to Dingane's royal umuzi. Inaamdura sprang awake to their call and was met by the angry stare of her mother.

"You spoke to Madikane last night," she hissed.

"I did," Inaamdura replied. "I told him I was promised to another."

"I told you to stay away from him."

Inaamdura sat up. "I thought you trusted me, mother. I have done nothing to make him think there is an opportunity for an alliance between him and the Shamfa. It is obvious he wishes to raise his status among the other indunas, and a Bonga wife would give him that edge."

Azana smiled. "You are truly my daughter. I knew he was interested, but I underestimated his intentions."

"Don't worry about me, mother. I have your instincts. I am concerned about Amadika. Are you sure she is strong enough to handle Dingane?"

Azana sat beside Inaamdura and placed her hand on her arm. "As much as I would like to hope, Amadika's marriage to Dingane will not help our cause. The union will make us allies by blood and allow us to focus on other more important matters."

"So, she is a gift?" Inaamdura tried to hide the disapproval in her voice. Her failure was reflected in her mother's stern gaze.

"Amadika's fate is as it should be. She is too weak to be an asset to any noble man. She will be a good Sesu wife and bear Dingane many sons. She should be grateful that I find any use for her at all."

Inaamdura had enough of the conversation. "I would like to go outside for a moment before our journey begins, mother. The wagon gets stuffy as they day wears on, so I am grateful for any fresh air I can get."

"Your father has lifted his restriction." Azana rose to her feet. "Since we are so close to the Royal Umuzi, he feels Madikane will behave himself for the remainder of the journey. You can ride with us."

Inaamdura smiled; the news of her freedom was enough to cool her down. She followed her mother out of the wagon and ran to her mare tethered to provision wagon. She mounted and rode back to the royal wagon to join her mother and father. They rode to the front of the train and took their place at the center of the Shamfa royal procession.

They were a tiny part of a massive human herd, an endless march of thousands of Sesu headed to a sacred destination. As they crossed the Nzolo River the singing resumed, a song that begged for the inkosi to show himself to his people. They walked up the hill before them, the gentle slope an easy climb for the multitude. Inaamdura felt the excitement rise in her with every step. She was no longer an observer; she was a follower, a part of a ceremony she knew nothing of but anticipated more than anything in her short life. By the time they reached the crest of the hill she thought she might scream to release the tension inside her. When she looked out over the hill at the scene below her, all she could manage was a startled whisper.

Thousands of grass huts covered the land, domiciles so recent they were green with new grass. Columns of smoke spiraled into the sky forming a grey haze over the encampments. Through the smoke she saw the Royal Ikhanda, the umuzi of Inkosi Dingane. It covered the entire face of the hill, the outer thorn fence circle three miles at its widest point and ending at the entrance to the ceremonial grounds. An inner fence encircled the ceremony courtyard. At the north end of the courtyard was the cattle pen holding the famous white cattle of the Sesu inkosi. Above the cattle pen was a smaller cluster of huts, the largest occupying a space close to the entrance to the pen. Thousands of huts rested between the outer umuzi and the cattle pen wall.

The Shamfa followed their Sesu companions to a clearing on the left of the royal umuzi. The regiments separated, each claiming an area based on its rank. Madikane's warriors signaled the Shamfa to follow them. They made their way through the multitudes on a ragged road leading to the Royal Umuzi. Madikane's clan halted outside the thorn fence and set up camp, the women and children immediately gathering grass to build their huts. The Shamfa circled their wagons and set up their camp.

Inaamdura followed her mother and father to Madikane. The induna sat below an acacia with his senior warriors while his wives labored on the huts. Muchese dismounted and approached the men with great ceremony.

"Inkosi Madikane, I thank you for your protection during our long journey. I will be sure to share my complements with Dingane when we meet later today."

"You will not see the inkosi today," Madikane replied. The Mkosi ceremony begins at first light tomorrow and will continue for three days. Dingane will receive you after the ceremony is complete. He has asked that I assist you until then."

Muchese was not happy. "I understand the importance of your ceremony, but I too have a kingdom to rule, and any time I spend away from my duties is a disservice to my people. If Dingane would give us just a moment of his time it will insure that we had the opportunity to discuss important matters if for some reason we must leave before the ceremony's end."

Madikane stood to face Muchese. The Twon moved to flank their leader and Madikane's warriors came to their feet.

"No one can see the inkosi before the ceremony. If your duties are more important than your alliance with the Sesu, leave now and bother us no further. I for one will not try and stop you. I warn you though; Dingane will see your early departure as an insult."

Inaamdura was puzzled by her father's impatience. It was not his way to hurry a diplomatic opportunity, especially one involving someone as important as Dingane.

"I ask your pardon," her father said. "It is not my place to disrupt the traditions of anyone, let alone the Sesu. We will retire to our wagons and look forward to our meeting with the inkosi."

They mounted and rode back to their camp. Inaamdura pulled her mare close to her father, hoping he would share explain his hastiness. He said nothing, his mouth set in a rare frown as he leaned forward on his stallion. Once they reached the wagons he dismounted quickly and scurried to the royal wagon, closing the door hard behind him.

Inaamdura turned to her mother, her expression asking the question she could not speak.

"He is afraid of them," Azana said. "He has seen enough to realize the Sesu are a larger threat than he anticipated."

"What do you think?" Inaamdura asked.

"I am concerned," she admitted. "It is apparent my eyes and ears see and hear both ways. I had no knowledge that the

Sesu were this numerous. I fear we may have played the wrong hand with these people. We may have to fight them despite the marriage alliance."

The thought of the Shamfa at war with the Sesu made her stomach churn. Her sister would be a hostage among the Sesu if that occurred, and she was not sure the Shamfa could defeat such a large and virile people.

"It might be best we wait until we meet Dingane before we make any assumptions," she replied. "His intentions may not extend to Shamfaland."

"We have determined as much," her mother replied. "Believe me daughter, if this Dingane reveals himself as a person we cannot trust, there will be no marriage. The inkosi of the Sesu may find himself a head short of his ambitions."

Azana placed a reassuring hand on Inaamdura's shoulder. "Come, Dura. Let us rest. I hear the Mkosi is a long monotonous thing. We must not be caught snoozing by our hosts."

The day crept by like a bush snail. Despite her mother's advice Inaamdura scampered around the wagon camp too excited to sleep. Instead she watched the Sesu go about their daily routines. Many of the people stared at the wagons, a mode of transportation uncommon among the Sesu. Children ran up to her to play despite their parents' protests, but they were chased away by the warriors guarding the wagons. The singing was more random, bursting out unexpectedly among the young girls and the warriors. No songs filled the day like those on the march. Inaamdura suspected the Sesu were saving their energies for the next three days so she finally decided to go to sleep. The royal wagon was too hot, so she ordered a servant to make her a bed beneath the wagon to protect her from the sun and the curious. Inaamdura crawled onto her bead and tried to imagine what she would experience over the next three days as the Sesu celebrated these sacred days.

The sound of footsteps woke her. Inaamdura peered from under the wagon and saw movement in the distance. She crawled out to see most of the camp asleep except for a few Twon on guard duty. The shuffling came from outside their camp; she stood and walked to the perimeter to find the source of the commotion.

She startled the guards as she approached.

"How can I help you, princess?" he asked.

"What is going on?"

The Twon shrugged. "Who knows with these monkeys? Some of the warriors are gathering before the entrance of Dingane's umuzi."

Inaamdura straightened her back and assumed a regal pose. "Show me."

The Twon led her to a place where the warriors were in full view. They were covered in cow tails and feathers grander than those she saw on the march. A bonfire burned in the center of Dingane's umuzi surrounded by figures moving in time to a rhythm that carried on the wind down to her ears. The warriors did not move; they stood like trees, as if their feet held onto the ground like roots. The drumming was joined by a low chant from the figures around the bonfire and the warriors marched into the umuzi, swaying from side to side in a trance-like motion. Inaamdura watched them make their way up the avenue into the ceremonial area, holding her breath like a child watching something sacred for the first time.

She never saw the warriors. Her concentration was broken by grunts and she turned away from the spectacle to see her Twon bodyguards lying on the ground grimacing. A band of Sesu warriors stood over them; Madikane stared at her with his hungry eyes.

"This is not for you to see," he stated. "Go back under your wagon."

For a brief moment Inaamdura reeled from true terror. Her protection lay at her feet and Madikane stood before her with his men. He could take her if he wanted; there was no one to stop him. She would have to control the situation.

"You had no right to attack my men," she said. "They did not know this was a sacred ceremony."

"They could have asked," Madikane said, smiling.

"You said Dingane asked you to watch over us. Is this the way you treat guests?"

Sounds rose from the camp. Inaamdura glanced backwards and saw more Twon coming her way, led by her father.

"Warn the others," Madikane said. He reached out and grabbed her by the wrist, squeezing until it hurt. "This ceremony is not for you."

Inaamdura managed to snatch her arm away which seemed to amuse Madikane. He raised his assegai and his men followed him into the darkness.

This time her father was more relieved than angry.

"What did that man do?" he demanded.

"We saw a procession of warriors march into Dingane's umuzi," Inaamdura replied. "Madikane said it was not for us to see. Our Twon paid for their curiosity."

"Are you okay?"

"Yes, father." Inaamdura strode back to the wagon and crawled back under with as much dignity she as she could display. Once on her cot, she broke out in a sweat, her body trembling. Madikane was beginning to scare her despite her resolve against fear. She decided it would be better for her and the Shamfa party that they get close to Dingane as soon as possible, before Madikane made his own decision on their fate.

The intense morning sun rose with the voices of Sesu. The melody wrapped around Inaamdura and woke her, its beauty a salve to the night's confrontation. Everyone in the camp was awake, preparing themselves absently while the voices of the Sesu women held their attention. Inaamdura's attendants swarmed around her, moving her to a secluded area surrounded by heavy cloth. Inside was her bathing tub, the perfumed wood adding its aroma to the singing. Inaamdura's attendants undressed her and she stepped into the soothing warm water. The attendants scrubbed her quickly, their complements on her beauty barely noticed. She sensed this day; there was an energy that seemed to hang in the air. She was trying to understand what she felt when one of her attendant's voices finally broke through her musing.

My princess, will you wear this?"

Inaamdura looked at the squat woman. She held a small beaded skirt in her hands, the type worn by the single Sesu women.

"Who gave you this?" she asked.

"Induna Madikane," she replied. "He said all must follow Sesu tradition during the Mkosi ceremony."

Inaamdura harbored no modesty, but she was not about to give Madikane a glimpse of what he could never have.

"Take it away," she commanded. The attendants dressed her in traditional Shamfa ceremonial clothing. The beads encircling her neck were uncomfortable, but she was pleased to finally be able to wear a full set like her mother. Massive gold leaf earrings dangled from her ears, presents from Sipole. When she stepped from behind the curtain, her mother and father were waiting.

"My beautiful daughter," Muchese exclaimed. "Come, the warriors are waiting to escort us to Dingane's umuzi."

Her mother nodded her approval and they proceeded to the wagon circle edge. Madikane and his warriors waited, donned in their finest cow tails and feathers, their shields groomed and assegai blades gleaming in the morning light. Madikane looked at her and she saw the disappointment in his eyes.

"Induna, we are ready," her father announced. Madikane nodded and signaled his men. They led the way to the umuzi entrance, the Shamfa walking in single file behind Muchese flanked by Madikane and his warriors. They were among the first groups to enter the umuzi, following a procession of warriors and elders of higher rank. The thorn fence walls were higher than she realized, towering easily over the tallest of Madikane's men. Sunlight disappeared as they entered the corridor and Inaamdura felt an unwelcome hand on her shoulder.

"You did not wear my gift," Madikane said.

"I have explained to you my feelings. You would do well to understand."

Madikane laughed. "You are stubborn like a warthog. The man who marries you will bear many scars from your tusks."

When they emerged into the light of the ceremonial grounds Inaamdura was trembling again. The small Shamfa band was surrounded by the might of Sesuland. She realized they were as much captives as they were guests, that any demand the Sesu might impose on them would have to be agreed to or they could be killed. If Madikane asked for her before Dingane, her father could not refuse.

Madikane led them to the front of the gathering. Another thorn fence stood before them separating the courtyard from the royal umuzi and Dingane's compound. The inkosi's wives sat on either side of the cattle pen, each draped in leather skirts and shirts covered by exquisite beadwork necklaces, bracelets, and belts. She counted ten wives total, five on either side of the entrance. She noticed an empty leopard skin covered stool. This was the position reserved for the Great Wife, the honor her mother and father hoped Amadika would fill. She searched the faces of the other wives wondering if she could spot the fallen wife whose fateful decision had given Dingane the son he craved and condemned him at the same time.

They were led to a clearing to the right of Dingane's stool.

"This is your place of honor," Madikane said. "You should have no trouble seeing the ceremony."

"Many thanks, induna," Muchese replied. The entourage took their seats, a nervousness running through them. No sooner had they seated themselves did the Sesu warriors leap to their feet in unison and began to sing. The song boomed throughout the umuzi, ringing in Inaamdura's head. Others on the outside began to sing as well.

"They are calling him," Madikane said, managing to sit beside her. "They are begging him to show himself."

Inaamdura barely heard him. She watched the entrance to the umuzi, anticipating Dingane's entrance. She was trembling again, but this time she shook with excitement, not fear. The moment she had waited for was at hand.

Dingane emerged from the royal compound, his entire body wrapped in a suit of woven grass. Only his face was visible, and it was a handsome, regal face. His dark brown eyes stared forward as if in a trance, the wrinkles in his forehead giving him the look of wisdom. He held a gilded assegai over his head, the shaft grasped in his left hand, the right hand just below the blade. A single file of elders followed behind him, each covered in white robes decorated by white and red beds. Each walked with a staff topped with a golden figure representing their clan.

Dingane walked past his wives and stopped in front of them. The elders took their places behind him and sat cross-legged on the ground, laying their staffs before them. The inkosi of Sesuland turned slowly to either side, displaying the golden assegai to everyone on the ceremonial ground.

He spoke with a resonant voice that reached down into Inaamdura and grasped her heart.

"Where are my people? Who stands behind me before the ancestors?"

The people responded with the Song of the Inkosi, The Strong Bull. As the Sesu sang the praise of Dingane, Inaamdura knew her life was to change this day. No matter who her parents had chosen, she would marry Dingane. This was the man who would give her an empire to rule. Let Amadika have Twaambo; let the Bonga cry and protest on the broken promise. Her future was not wandering mountain pastures seeking glory. It was in front of her, it surrounded her. Her future was among the Sesu.

Dingane danced, moving his muscular body with the grace of a leopard. He thrust his assegai in mock battle, performing the ritual dance known only by the inkosi. Inaamdura watched him move, drinking in every motion. She wanted to dance with him, matching his martial steps with a dance of joy. When he finally finished she was disappointed. The medicine priests approached him and tore off the grass clothing while chanting. When they were done he stood naked, his chest rising and falling with his exertion. His wives came to him then, dressing him as they sang, wrapping his leather loincloth around his waist followed by a kilt of bright white brushed cow tails hanging from a belt of red beads. They fastened a breastplate of leopard skin around his chest and clamped golden armbands about his massive biceps. A necklace of leopard claws was secured around his neck. The last of his wives marched to his side, placing his headdress over his head ring, a thick head band of leopard and otter skin, a single stork feather rising from the front. Dingane nodded to her then sat among the elders. He nodded his head and the ceremony continued.

The remainder of the ceremony meant nothing to Inaamdura. The procession of the regiments performing their sacred dances, the homage paid to the ancestors by the elders, even the sacrifice of the black bull by the bare hands of the youngest regiment did not stir her. She could not take her eyes off Dingane. She watched him as he watched the others, fascinated by his every gesture. Somewhere during the ceremony, he looked at her for a brief moment, a slight smile on his face. She smiled back and looked away, but she could not deny what she felt. She was so enthralled with him that she did not notice when the ceremony ended. The warriors trailed out of the royal umuzi, their voices lifted in song with the other Sesu. The soul of the Sesu had been replenished; Dingane was still favored by the ancestors. The harvest would be bountiful and the raids successful. The Sesu would still be masters of the grasslands.

"Come. It's time to see the inkosi," Madikane ordered.

Muchese was flustered. "Induna, we haven't had time to prepare!"

"It takes no time to say what is on one's heart if those words are true," Madikane replied.

Muchese looked at Azana and his shoulders slumped. "What of our tribute?"

"The inkosi will receive your gifts later," Madikane answered. "Come, we are wasting time."

The Shamfa delegation hastily gathered their possessions and followed Madikane to where Dingane sat with his wives, the elders and his highest-ranking indunas. Madikane stood before his inkosi. He dropped to his knees, touched head to the ground then came back to his feet.

"Inkosi, once again the ancestors smile on you and your greatness. I present to you the Shamfa. They have come to pay their respects"

Dingane nodded to Madikane. The warrior took his place behind the inkosi with the rest of the indunas. Muchese took this as a sign.

"I am Muchese, inkosi of the Shamfa and friend of the Sesu. We are honored to have been invited to such a powerful ceremony. Surely the ancestors will grant you a bountiful harvest."

Dingane seemed almost annoyed with Muchese's patronizing chatter. His attention went immediately to Inaamdura. Their eyes met, and she turned away. Her heart fluttered again, and she hid her face behind her veil.

"I am glad you came," Dingane replied. "Most nobles declined our invitation in fear of our land and our people, though you have come despite the warnings. I too am honored by your presence."

Madikane leaned forward, whispering in Dingane's ear. Inaamdura went cold inside. He was making his move and there was nothing anyone could do to stop him. Once Dingane made his intentions clear her parents would be in no position to refuse the offer without destroying any chances of alliance with the Sesu.

"Is this the daughter I have heard so much about?" Dingane asked.

"No, inkosi," Muchese replied. "This is my daughter, Inaamdura. She accompanied us as a companion to my wife, Azana."

"Step forward, Inaamdura, so that I might see you better." Inaamdura glanced at her father for his permission. He nodded, his face tight with worry. Inaamdura rose, walking with a grace that only she could display under such circumstances.

"How may I serve you, inkosi?" she asked.

"Madikane tells me you are a smart woman, a true Bonga like your mother."

"I have been raised well," she replied. "Though I cannot say if my strengths are worthy of a noble husband."

"Why is that?"

"My skills have not been tested. I will not have the opportunity until I am married."

Dingane rubbed his chin. "Tell me about your sister."

"I think my father and mother would do better justice than I, inkosi. A sister's opinion may be tainted by different memories."

"I wish your opinion."

Inaamdura hesitated, looking back at her mother and father's anxious faces. She could describe her sister generously, but then she would lose this captivating man sitting before her. She risked causing a rift between the Shamfa and the Bonga if she made her play. She looked at her mother and father one last time before she spoke.

"My sister is a sweet child. She is strong in her likes and dislikes, and she is easily influenced. I am sure she is in love with my betrothed, though she would deny it if you asked her."

"That's interesting, but it's not what I asked you," Dingane said. "Will your sister make a good wife?"

"It depends what type of wife the inkosi wishes. If you wish a woman that will heed Sesu traditions, conform to the ways of her adopted people and bear healthy children, then my sister will make a fine wife. But if you wish a companion, an advisor that will teach the Sesu how build a kingdom in the grass, a wife that can control the operations of the empire that her husband creates, my sister is not the wife for you."

Dingane leaned back on his stool. "Who is this woman that can be such a companion?"

Inaamdura gave Dingane a smile that removed any doubts of her intentions. "I think the inkosi knows the answer to his question."

"Inaamdura, what are you doing?" her father shouted.

Dingane leaned to the side and glared at her father. "I would appreciate your respect while I talk to your daughter."

Inaamdura could not see her father's face, but she was certain it was not pleasant.

"We have settled the marriage arrangement," Muchese protested. "You are to marry Amadika."

Dingane ignored him. "Would you accept me as your husband if I asked?"

"It depends on what the inkosi offered me," Inaamdura replied.

Dingane and his indunas laughed hard at her response. Sipole did not see the humor.

"You are disgracing my son!" he yelled. "Muchese, the Bonga will not tolerate such an insult!"

Dingane jumped to his feet, his face deathly serious. "You may be a man of influence in Shamfa, but you are nothing here. Speak again and my warriors will wash their spears in you."

Again, he looked at Inaamdura. "What do you wish?"

"To be your Great Wife," she replied.

"It is yours to have," Dingane said.

Inaamdura knelt before Dingane to cover the weakness in her knees. "Then ask for me to be your wife. I will accept."

"Inaamdura, no!" her father pleaded.

"I think your daughter has made her choice, Muchese, and it is my choice as well. I wish to marry your daughter Inaamdura and make her my Great Wife. She will remain among us until the day of the wedding ceremony to learn the ways of her new people."

Dingane stood, passing his gaze among the elders, the indunas and his wives.

"Do you accept the decision of your inkosi?"

A cheer rose among the Sesu, drowning out the protests of the Shamfa delegation. Inaamdura took a deep breath and finally turned to face her people. Her father stared at her, his mouth wide in shock. Sipole glared at her, his intentions clear in his malevolent eyes. She finally looked at her mother. Her face was emotionless for a moment, but then her mouth moved, and a smile formed on her face. Inaamdura smiled as she read her mother's words.

"Well done, my daughter. Well done."

5

Obaseki clinched his teeth and closed his eyes, trying his best to hold back the laughter threatening to break free. He sat cross-legged beside his younger cousins on a zebra skinned rug, his arms resting on his knees, his clean-shaven head encircled by a thin golden band marking him as a prince. His kente robe hung from one shoulder, the bold yellow, orange and black pattern matching that of his cousins and his grandfather. He attempted to look regal, but the unexpected grin on his face could not be contained. It wasn't his fault; Lewa was being silly again.

Oba Noncemba cleared his throat and Obaseki managed a few more moments of stillness. His grandfather sat before the royal household flanked by his senior officers. The dry season was coming to an end, the air thick with moisture, the gathering clouds a sign of the coming rains. His grandfather had finally returned from war, but not with the victory he coveted. For six months he fought relentlessly against the Dumani, driving them from the eastern borders of Mawenaland and into the peaks and valleys of their own soil. He trapped them, positioning his army to deliver the final blow when the plan fell apart. A mistake had been made; a decision that spared the Dumani army from a final crushing defeat and insured that the Dry War would continue into the next year. Worst of all, the blunder had been committed by his own son, Obeseki's uncle Azikiwe.

Lewa sat beside his uncle, making faces at him as he prostrated before Noncemba and Kumba. Obaseki snorted and his grandfather jerked his head towards him.

"I am sorry, Grandfather," he said.

Noncemba glared at him then turned his attention back to his son.

"There is no reason to discuss your offense, Azikiwe," he said. "What I and the elders wish to know is why."

Azikiwe raised his head. He was an odd-looking man who barely resembled his father. His eyes always seemed locked in a state of shock, giving him a comical appearance despite his best efforts at a serious countenance. His broad nose was definitely a trait of his father's, but his round face and weak chin was his own. There was no fear in his wide brown eyes as he spoke.

"I positioned my men at the pass as you suggested, but I was concerned about the cliffs over our position. If the Dumani managed to gain the higher ground, we would be destroyed. I sent my reserves to cover the paths leading to the cliff tops to prevent such a maneuver."

Kumba stepped forward, his large hands folded behind his back. He had removed his tattered kapok uniform and stood before Azikiwe in his leather and steel under armor, his sword still at his side. He was the only person allowed to carry a weapon in Noncemba's presence.

"Your orders were to hold the pass, Azikiwe," he said.

"As I said I was protecting my men from attack from above."

"That's not true," Kumba replied.

"How would you know?" Azikiwe snapped. "I did as I was told."

"You were told to guard the pass with all your men," Kumba retorted. "Why did you send your cavalry away?"

"The cavalry had the best chance to reach the cliffs before Dumani archers could take position."

Kumba paced. "So, you made the decision to protect your position?"

Azikiwe shoulders lifted. "Yes, I did."

"So, you think I am a fool."

"I said no such thing."

"You might as well have!" Kumba retorted. "Only a fool would have sent you to block the path without considering the bluffs above you. It was my orders you followed."

"I was not told the cliffs had been considered in the battle plan. If I had been present at the war council, I would have known."

Kumba stopped pacing, looking at Noncemba. He took his position beside the oba and sat.

"You let the Dumani break through to prove a point?" Noncemba asked.

"I did not say that. Had I been privy to the battle plan I would not have divided my forces."

"Your word games are tiresome," Noncemba said. "The ancestors have cursed me with an only son who cares more about his feelings than his family. You are no use to me."

If Noncemba's words stung, Azikiwe showed no signs of pain.

"If you gave me the chance to show you my talents, you would be proud," Azikiwe retorted.

"You cannot display what you don't possess." Noncemba's expression transformed from anger to disgust.

"You've resisted my teaching your entire life, now you jeopardize the existence of our people because of your foolishness."

Azikiwe rose and approached his father.

"Let me finish what you began. Give me command of the warriors and I will run the Dumani down and destroy them."

"That opportunity has passed," Noncemba replied. "You had your chance at the pass, but you chose to make a statement."

The courtyard was silent for too long a moment. Even Lewa was still. She sat beside Azikiwe, her arm resting on his shoulder. Obaseki shook his head angrily at her. She looked back and smiled but did not remove her arm.

"Let everyone hear my words," Noncemba announced. "I decree that my son, Azikiwe, disgraced his family and his people by his actions in battle. For this he will be punished."

Noncemba stood before his son. Azikiwe prostrated and Noncemba put his left foot on his head.

"Although you have failed me, you are still my son. You will take a regiment of your choosing to the eastern borders. Once there you will build a fort and enforce the boundaries between Mawenaland and the Kossi. You shall not return from this duty until the Kossi have been defeated or offer terms. If you cannot follow my orders, maybe you will do better by following your own."

Noncemba removed his foot from Azikiwe and the young man stood before his father.

"I will not fail you again, baba," Azikiwe promised.

"We will see," Noncemba replied. The oba trudged back to his golden stool and sat heavily on the silk cushions. Lewa stepped back as Azikiwe came to his feet, backing away until he was outside the courtyard. His face remained expressionless as he turned away and disappeared into the streets. Lewa came to Obaseki's side and sat.

"You almost got me in trouble!" he whispered.

"They cannot see me," she replied sweetly. "I am for your eyes only."

"You must behave," he said. "We must respect my grandfather."

"He's not my Oba," Lewa protested.

"Shhh!" His cousins were looking at him and whispering.

The royal family waited as the other noble families left the courtyard in an ordered procession by rank. The royal family dispersed soon afterward, everyone heading for their sector of the compound. Obaseki stood with his cousins to leave when he heard his name called.

"Obaseki, come," Noncemba said.

Obaseki clinched his teeth and approached his grandfather, prostrating before him.

"Get up, boy. There are no formalities between you and me."

Obaseki rose with a grin.

"It is because of your mother that I am so lenient with you," Noncemba explained, patting Obaseki on his head. "You are also my eldest heir."

"What about uncle?"

"Apparently you did not understand what happened here today. Your uncle will never be my heir. Even if I wanted to select him it would not be possible now. He has disgraced himself too many times. The elders and the noble families would protest his selection. That brings us to you."

Obaseki's mouth became so dry his response resembled a croak. "Me?"

"Yes, you. Your condition has disturbed me for some time now. When you were a boy your oddities could be explained and ignored. But you are a man now and this problem must be addressed."

Salako stepped forward and Obaseki stepped back. The old man steadied himself with a short walking stick crowned with gold carved in the shape of a sleeping crocodile. He wore a white robe barely visible under the talismans and gris-gris hanging from his waist and charms dangling from gold chains around his narrow neck. Salako shuffled up to Obaseki and circled him as he always did, shaking his head and waving his horsetail swatter.

"I cannot help him," Salako announced. "His gift is well beyond my understanding. You must seek Fuluke, the Man of the Woods. He will know what to do."

"You must go to this man, Seki," Noncemba said gently. Maybe he can give us understanding so we can see the benefit of this...talent."

"I don't want to go," Obaseki said. "I can make them go away on my own."

Noncemba rested his chin in his hand. "You have no choice. You will leave in the morning. I suggest you say your goodbyes. I don't know how long this will take, but you may be gone for a long time"

"Grandfather, please."

Noncemba waved him silent. "I don't want to send you to this Fuluke, but I must try to solve this puzzle. This "sight" of yours may be a gift or it may be a curse. I must trust Salako's suggestion. He has served our family for many years and has never led us wrong."

Obaseki dropped his head. His grandfather had been kind to him, kinder than with his own. He would not make a decision that would harm him.

"I will pack my things for the journey," Obaseki said.

"Your servants will do that for you," Noncemba replied.

Obaseki bowed to his grandfather and trudged away. Lewa followed behind him.

"He is sending you away!"

Obaseki shrugged. "There is nothing I can do about it."

"Who is this Fuluke?"

"I don't know. Grandfather thinks he will be able to help me."

Lewa stopped, placing her hands on her hips. "There is nothing wrong with you."

"Let's not talk about it." Obaseki felt queasy. He put his hand on his stomach and rubbed it.

"You are afraid," Lewa said.

He could not deny how he felt. She had been his friend for as long as he had memory, his constant companion for all his years. She had even walked with him during his initiation rites despite his protests.

Obaseki was quiet the rest of the day, wandering about the palace with Lewa tagging along, answering her questions with short angry answers. Sometimes he wished she would go away and let him have some time to think alone. But she never left unless she chose to, which was when he made her angry. He tried his best to upset her, but she persisted, staying at his side until he went to sleep later that night.

He awoke with the morning drums, his possessions resting at the foot of his bed in a neat pack. Lewa was awake as well, sitting at the foot of his bed as always.

"You were very noisy last night," she said.

"I was dreaming.""

"About what?"

"Will you leave me alone?" Obaseki shouted.

"No."

He flung his headrest at her and watched it pass through her, slamming against the wall and breaking.

"See what you made me do? Why don't you just go away?"

Lewa eyes glistened. "Why are you so mad at me?"

"If I didn't see you, I wouldn't have to go away!"

Lewa said nothing, her head sagging. Obaseki's anger trickled away.

"If you didn't see me, I would have to go away." She dropped to her knees, looking at Obaseki with pleading eyes.

"I don't want to go there. I want to stay here with you."

Obaseki looked into Lewa's pleading eyes and sighed. The Spirits talked about There often, most of them afraid to leave the familiarity of Mawenaland for the next world that waited for them. Salako told him that all spirits must eventually move closer to Oyo, returning from where they came. But it was

Mawena nature to be afraid of the unknown in death, even though they swore their belief in life. So they would linger, living their lives as they had when alive until even that existence no longer satisfied them. That's when they became trouble and had to be driven away.

A bodyguard stuck his head into Obaseki's room. He looked at him oddly, and then quickly formed his expression to one of respect.

"Omoba, we are ready to depart," he said. "Oba Noncemba wishes to speak to you before you leave.

Obaseki nodded and the bodyguard left.

"Come on, Lewa. My grandfather waits."

They walked down the bleached white corridor into the central courtyard. His grandfather sat alone under the acacia, fanning himself with his swatter, a kola nut lodged firmly in his jaw. He motioned for Obaseki to sit beside him.

"Your mother was my favorite," he said. "I know a father shouldn't cherish one child over another, but I could not help myself. She was a bright girl, with a smile that shamed the sun and eyes that glittered like stars in the dry season sky. She was strong, too. Not physically strong, but strong of mind and spirit."

Noncemba lowered his head then sighed.

"The worst day of my life was when she married Dingane. It was necessary, for the Sesu were becoming a nuisance and I did not have the strength or the resources to fight them. I invited Dingane to meet and form an alliance. He suggested a marriage to seal our agreement and he chose Shani to be his wife. I had no choice; they were married, and I have not seen her since."

"At least you know what she looks like," Obaseki said.

Noncemba smiled and patted Obaseki's head. "Yes, I do. You have her eyes and her smile, Obaseki. When I look at you I have my daughter back."

A shadow of sadness hung over his grandfather and Obaseki could sense its weight. He wanted to grasp his hand, but he was unsure of his reaction. He continued to sit motionless, watching his grandfather look into the distance with painful eyes.

"Your mother sent you to me to save you," Noncemba finally said. "I tried to raise you as she would, but this sight of yours seems to be getting in the way."

Obaseki felt brave enough to speak. "What I see is real, baba. The Spirits are like you and me.

"I know they are real," Noncemba replied. "But it is not your place to see them. You are of royal blood. Even the Sesu blood that runs in you speaks of a noble past. Leave the Spirits to the medicine-priests. That is why I'm sending you to Fuluke. It is my hope that he will be able to free you of this handicap and send you back in full strength to receive your birthright."

Obaseki could do nothing but nod his head. Lewa was close by, her touch colder than usual. His grandfather's words frightened her.

"Do whatever this Fuluke tells you, Obaseki. He will not harm you because he knows that if he does he'll have to deal with the fury of the Mawena. There is not enough herbs and spells in the world that could stop me taking my revenge. The more you obey, the faster he will be able to bring you back from the valley of ghosts."

Obaseki resisted the urge to look at Lewa. "I will do as you say, grandfather."

Noncemba signaled one of his servants to step forward. The woman knelt beside the oba, extending her hands that held a rectangle of gold, the bull leopard icon impressed on its surface. The servant hung the necklace around Obaseki's neck and stepped away.

"You wear my symbol," Noncemba said. "This will guarantee you safe passage throughout Mawenaland. Be safe, Obaseki."

"Thank you, grandfather." Obaseki bowed to his grandfather and stood. A rush of sadness overwhelmed him and he lunged, throwing his arms around Noncemba's neck and hugging him tight. Noncemba's eyes widened then closed as he smiled.

"I'll miss you, too," he said. "Come, now. You are a prince."

Obaseki was sure to wipe his eyes before letting his grandfather go. He turned and marched away, Lewa trailing behind him.

"I'm sorry," Lewa said.

"It's not your fault," Obaseki replied. "The ancestors have given me this ability for some reason. I hope Fuluke can show me why."

His escort waited for him outside the palace. Ten Atuegbu milled about, each covered in royal kapok, their swords dangling from their leather shoulder sheaths. Each man held double blade lances. They snapped to attention when they noticed Obaseki, clearing away to reveal a final surprise. A pure white stallion waited, draped in a royal red kapok outfit matching the pattern of the Atuegbu. The saddle straddling the stallion's back was a beautiful object obviously from the saddle smiths of Bosede, polished black leather studded with gold and a horn crowned with cowry shells. Obaseki ran to his mount and clambered onto the horse before his servants could assist him. Lewa approached the beast warily. The horses turned in her direction and snorted, pounding their feet into the dirt nervously. His escorts looked about for the source of their mounts agitation, but they could not see the girl. Lewa backed away, turned and ran, disappearing into crowded street. Obaseki almost called out to her, but stopped. Doing so would only bring more attention to him, which he wished to avoid.

Obaseki looked for Lewa as they rode down the broad avenue leading to the western gate, ignoring the praise calls and bows of the people surrounding him. The gate masters manning the ramparts beat their drums in a solemn rhythm that barely covered the shrieking joints of the massive metal gate as it swung open. Obaseki raised in his saddle, scanned the throng for Lewa, his heart beating faster the further they galloped away from the central city. His nervousness increased when he realized Lewa was not the only one missing. They were all gone, every one of them. The Spirits that had shown themselves to him entire life were nowhere to been seen.

"I must go back," Obaseki whispered. "I must go back to the palace."

Dapo, the leader of the escort, a serious man with deep eyes and a stern face, rode up to his side.

"Omoba, what is the matter?"

Obaseki reached out to him, almost falling off his horse.

"Dapo, I have to go back."

Dapo's expression softened. "I'm sorry, Omoba. Oba Noncemba gave me specific orders to deliver you to Fuluke. I cannot let you go back."

Obaseki pushed Dapo away and grabbed the reins of his mount. Dapo signaled his men and they crowded around Obaseki, hemming him in.

"Let me go! I order you to let me pass!"

"I am sorry, Omoba. I cannot."

Dapo nodded his head and Obaseki was swept off his horse by a strong arm. He tried to struggle but the man was too strong. He was in the grasp of Malomo, a hulking figure known throughout Mawenaland for his strength. He tied Obaseki's hands quickly then placed him back on his horse. Dapo grabbed the reins.

The fight left him as suddenly as it come. Obaseki slumped forward, his head resting on his mount's neck. He kept his eyes closed as they rode, not knowing when they left the city behind and entered the countryside. The despair he felt in the city subsided the further they traveled until he felt strong enough to lift his head. The sun descended behind the trees, leaving a familiar void that darkness rushed to fill. Abo had disappeared beyond the western horizon. Obaseki was lethargic, swaying with the rhythm of his stallion, his mouth dry. He tried to speak but only croaked.

Dapo heard him and slowed his mount to fall in step with Obaseki.

"It is good to see you awake, Omoba," he said. "We will camp soon. There is a village up ahead that will give us shelter for the night."

Dapo handed Obaseki a water calabash and he drank greedily, almost choking on the cool liquid. No sooner had his thirst been quenched did he regret the decision. As his energy returned the emptiness inside him reappeared, not as intense as it was leaving Abo, but painful just the same. If this was the way his life would be without the Spirits he wanted no part of it. He would rather die than live the rest of his life feeling so bad.

They found the village at dusk. It was small; a cluster of a dozen huts circling a wide clearing. Obaseki and his protectors entered through the dilapidated gate dangling from a ragged thorn fence. The ditch behind the fence was filled with debris. It was a poor attempt at security, more a bluff than anything else.

No one came to greet them. Dapo ordered one of his men to check the huts. The man went from hut to hut, exiting each one alone. Dapo frowned and climbed from his horse.

"We will camp here tonight," he said.

The Atuegbu had no problem finding firewood. They built a huge fire in the center of the village then searched the vacant domiciles until they located iron pots for boiling sorghum and a clay oven sturdy enough to bake bread. Malomo helped Obaseki from his horse and guided him to the fire. He spread a blanket and motioned for Obaseki to sit. Once he was seated Malomo freed his hands.

Obaseki rubbed his wrists as he watched the others cook and set up camp. The void inside was not as severe as earlier. Obaseki thought it was because he was far away from Abo, but the answer became obvious as he peered into the darkness persisting around the huts. Something moved beyond the flickering firelight, something strange yet familiar. The people might have left the village, but the Spirits had remained.

Dapo noticed his stare and an uncomfortable look came to his face.

He stood before Obaseki and handed him a bowl of porridge.

"Thank you," Obaseki said.

Dapo nodded. He squatted before Obaseki and bowed his head.

"My prince, I know it is not my place, but I wish you would not look in such a way into the darkness. Although my men are brave and would fight any foe on my command, they are wary of spirits, especially being so far away from the city. If they see you with that look in your eyes they will be unnerved."

"I will try my best to control my strangeness," Obaseki replied.

"I did not mean to insult you."

"Of course you didn't." Obaseki turned his back to Dapo and ate his porridge. He listened as Malomo walked away to join his comrades opposite the fire. The big man sat between them, keeping his eye on Obaseki while speaking and laughing with his brethren. Food made him sleepy; he lay down on his kapok blanket and quickly gave into the night.

The village came alive in his dreams, the huts transforming into brightly colored buildings with newly thatched roofs. Handsome people sauntered back and forth across the clearing, the men bare-chested with red kilts tied around their waists and heavy necklaces dangling from their necks. The women were dressed the same, their beaded kilts shorter to display their elegant legs. Children darted about, singing in a language that seemed familiar, yet he couldn't understand. They stopped suddenly, looking about as if something had intruded upon their peace. One man turned to face him, then another. Soon the entire village walked towards him, their curious stares changing to anger. Obaseki felt their fear and realized he was not dreaming.

"Seki! Seki!"

Obaseki turned to the voice that called his name. Lewa stood outside the thorn fence jumping up and down and waving her hands furiously.

"Get out of the village!" she yelled.

Obaseki jumped to his feet. The spirits milled about his escorts, their pleasant countenances replaced by hungry stares. He ran to Lewa, stopping only when he felt her cold arms wrap around him.

"Come on! Let's get away!" he cried.

"No," Lewa replied. "You're safe now. They cannot get out. The thorn fence is gris-gris to keep them in."

Obaseki understood. "And it kept you out."

Lewa nodded.

The spirits looked at him a moment longer then turned their full attention to the sleeping Atuegbu. Lewa pulled him away.

"Come, Seki. You don't want to see this."

Obaseki snatched away. "We have to help them."

"We can't. Once they entered the village, they cannot leave."

"What will they do to them?"

"They will feed the spirits."

The spirits hovered close to the sleeping men, their spectral mouths expelling a chant in an ancient tongue. Obaseki felt the words seep into him, summoning him toward the spirits. Lewa held onto him.

"Don't listen to them, Seki. Listen to me."

Lewa's voice grounded him. He backed away as white shadows formed about the Atuegbu. The chants grew louder as the auras lifted from the men and passed into the spirits. Each warrior took a final exaggerated breath then fell still.
Obaseki looked helplessly at his men then turned away, following Lewa into the forest. She led him through the darkness as if the sun shone; following a trail he could barely see.

"Where are we going?"

Lewa turned to look at him. "Back to Abo."

Obaseki snatched his hand away from her. "I can't. I promised my grandfather I would find Fuluke."

"You're so stupid!" Lewa snapped. "You almost died in the village and you don't know where Fuluke lives. You have no choice but to go back."

Obaseki sat down in a pile of wet leaves. He understood his grandfather now, which made him even more determined to find Fuluke.

"Take me to a dry spot," Obaseki said. "I need to sleep. In the morning we will find Fuluke."

"No!" Lewa shouted. She let go of him and disappeared into the trees.

"Lewa! Come back!" Obaseki waited for a reply that never came. He slumped against a tree, knocked down by waves of despair, fear and desperation. He was lost, his men dead and Lewa had abandoned him. He closed his eyes and with no other alternative, he slept.

The morning came with humming. Obaseki listened, his eyes closed. He stayed motionless as the humming increased. The sound was replaced a foul odor.

"You can open your eyes if you wish," the voice said.

Obaseki eyes flew open despite his fear. A man squatted before him clothed in a tattered, oversize animal hide pulled tight around his waist with a grass cord. Gris-gris covered the hide, some Obaseki recognized but many other unrecognizable. He had the face of a grandfather but moved with the dexterity of one much younger. Every hair on his face was grey, from his thick eyebrows to his beard.

"Who are you, uncle?" Obaseki asked.

"Fuluke," the man replied, "and you are Obaseki."

Obaseki was dismayed by the sight of the ancient medicine-priest. Though his face projected the image of a wise and learned man, his ragged clothing and his smell made the young prince wary.

"How do I know you're him?" Obaseki asked.

"You don't," Fuluke answered. "Come, I have food and medicine at my hut. By the look of things, you need both."

Obaseki sat still. This man could be Fuluke or some bandit attempting light banter until his cohorts arrived to rob him.

Fuluke peered over Obaseki's shoulder. "What is her name?"

Obaseki turned his head. Lewa stood behind him glaring at the old man, her small fists shaking.

"You can see her?"

Fuluke smiled. "I cannot see her but can feel her. That makes all the difference."

The faint sun streaming through the gaps in the leaves weakened as clouds moved in.

"Her name is Lewa. She wants to stay with me so she won't get killed. She is afraid that if I forget her, she will fade away and be nothing."

"I see," Fuluke said. He stood then extended his hand. "Come. We have much work to do in a short time."

Obaseki refused the stranger's hand. He stood on his own and gathered what little he was able to bring the night before. Lewa grabbed him by his arm.

"Don't go with him Seki. He is evil like the spirits in the village."

Fuluke turned, his face concerned. "You went into the village?"

Lewa's hand covered her mouth and she backed away. Obaseki gazed at the old man, a smile forming on his face.

"Yes, we went into the village," he replied.

"That is what happened to your men. I am sorry. The spirits of Okuthe are vengeful. They carry a grudge that time has not healed, and they despise the living."

"Why didn't they attack me?"

"That's a good question. That's why your grandfather sent you to me."

Fuluke leaned on his walking stick. "You are a strange one, Obaseki. You live among the living, yet you exist among the dead. This is not a natural state."

Lewa had regained her strength and moved beside him. "Do not listen to him, Seki."

"Mawena were not meant to exist in two worlds. We must choose one or the other. To move in body and spirit is to disrupt the world that Oyo created."

Fuluke stared at Lewa and she grasped Obaseki's arm again.

"I did not ask to be different," Obaseki argued.

"No, you did not," Fuluke agreed. "But we cannot ask for the life we want to lead. We must accept Oyo's gift with humility and live the life that has been woven by the threads of time. But you can make one choice, Obaseki. You can choose to live among the living and separate yourself from the spirits. If you can do this, you will have the life the ancestors have chosen for you."

Obaseki pulled his arm away from Lewa.

"No, Seki," she cried. "Don't go. Don't leave me."

Obaseki turned and looked at his lifelong friend, her glistening eyes almost making him turn back.

"I have to try, Lewa. I promised by grandfather."

"Then you will lose me," she whispered.

Obaseki gazed at Lewa, concentrating on every part of her. No matter what Fuluke taught him, he wanted to remember her always. He managed to smile, and then turned away.

"I love you," she whispered. "I will wait for you, Seki. I promise."

Obaseki turned back. Lewa was gone. He couldn't see her, but worst of all, he could not feel her.

Fuluke grasped his shoulder and squeezed it gently.

"Come, son," he said. "You have much to learn."

Obaseki tore his eyes away from where Lewa had stood. Fuluke patted his shoulder then headed into the forest. Obaseki followed and they disappeared into a wall of leaves and darkness.

6

Shange kaVilakaze strode the perimeter of the royal umuzi in search of Shani's hut. He was a walking legend, one of Sesuland's greatest warriors second only to Dingane. He moved with exaggerated arrogance, his muscled shoulders swinging back and forth in time with the stride of his thick legs. His golden headring gripped his head so tight wrinkles creased his brow. Facial and body scars made him appear older than his thirty-five years but to him they were symbols of bravery far beyond a mere simba mane or ostrich feather. It was rare to see him in the city, let alone stalking the huts of Dingane's wives. A lesser man would be dead, struck down by Dingane's guards without question. But he was Shange, with certain privileges associated with his rank.

Shange reached the last hut, the home of Shani. Shange felt sadness upon seeing the dingy hut, a sign of Shani's fall from Great Wife status. She had been spared physical death, but in some ways exile was just as final. Her disobedience concerning the twins could not go unpunished, though even in this Dingane displayed his usual leniency towards his former Great Wife. He stripped her of her status, moving her to the smallest wife hut. She was denied the use of the household servants and required to make her own way while raising Ndoro on her own. She was allowed the company of Jelani and Thembile, but she could never return to Mawenaland again. Any other wife would have faced shunning or death for such an act. While others criticized Dingane for his decision, Shange saw no wrong in it. He had always favored Shani. She was beautiful and strong, the type of woman normally frowned upon among the Sesu but admired by the Mawena. Shange wore the headring signifying his eligibility for marriage, but he had taken no bride. Shange lived for battle; he had no time for family and idleness. Glory was earned on the battlefield, not the yam field. If he ever was to take a wife, it would be a woman like Shani.

She emerged from her hut, radiant despite her worn clothes and faded beads. Shange surprised her and she jumped back into her hut with a squeal.

"Forgive me inkosa," he said, honoring her despite her lowered status. "I should have announced my approach."

Shani emerged from the hut with a welcoming smile. "No, Shange, don't apologize. It's rare that we get visitors."

Shange felt uncomfortable looking into Shani's desperate eyes. She should have been allowed to return to her people. She was unworthy of this torment.

"I am looking for Ndoro," he finally said.

Shani's expression moved from desperate to wary. "What do you want with him?"

Shange raised his head regally. "Has Ndoro completed his initiation rites?"

"Yes," Shani confirmed. "The elders did not perform them. Jelani did."

That was disappointing, Shange thought. Shange had much respect for the Mawena, but no matter what the stigma, Ndoro was Sesu and should have been initiated properly into manhood.

"Is he part of an induna?"

"Yes, but they do not accept him."

Shange began to doubt his decision. Ndoro was clearly the outcast he had heard he'd be. If he was not accustomed to the camaraderie of an induna he might be more of a hindrance than a help.

"Where is he?"

Shani pointed to the river. "He is with Jelani."

She stepped closer to Shange, her face hard like a lioness.

"You will not harm my son, Shange."

Shange smiled at her boldness.

"I bring no harm to the son of Dingane," he replied. "I offer him a chance for honor. I have planned a cattle raid and I have picked Ndoro to join my party."

Shani covered her mouth with her hands to hide her shock. "Dingane is allowing this?"

"This is not the inkosi's decision," Shange replied. "Every man must be blooded before he can wear the headring and claim a wife. You know this."

"Sesu rights have not applied to Ndoro."

Shange shrugged his shoulders, his first slip of respect before the inkosa.

"He shall have his chance. Maybe the ancestors will favor him and drive the demon from his body."

Shani dropped her hands, revealing her anger as she glared at him.

"Like I said, he's at the river. Goodbye, Shange."

Shange followed the twisting road down into a steep drift. At the bottom of the narrow valley the Mfululo flowed, lined by small trees and wavering shrubs. A familiar sound came to his ears, the ringing of metal meeting metal and the clash of cowhide shields. Jelani and Ndoro sparred near the river's edge, their only spectators a mixed herd of zebra and wildebeests more interested in the spring grass than fighting men. Shange found a comfortable clump of grass and sat. Ndoro's stature impressed him. At twelve he was as tall as Jelani, although still not filled out with the muscles his Sesu bloodline promised. His face was a perfect blend of Dingane and Shani, his eyes a strange light brown. They locked on Jelani like the stare of a lion on the hunt as they circled each other, probing in vain for the opening the experienced Mawena would never reveal.

Jelani's shield dropped slowly, a feint Shange spotted easily. Ndoro sprang at the trap, his assegai flashing forward with a speed as surprising as his strength. Despite the set-up Jelani barely dodged the strike. With a flick of his wrist he struck Ndoro's elbow with his shield. Ndoro winced, dropping his assegai as the burning pain ran up his arm to his shoulder. Before Jelani could strike Ndoro spun away, throwing his shield at Jelani in frustration. Shange shook his head; the boy was acting his age now.

Shange stood noisily and Ndoro reacted, snatching his assegai from the ground and throwing it directly at him. Shange was so impressed he almost lost his life, raising his shield at the last minute and knocking the spear aside. Ndoro recognized the warrior, his mouth wide with shock. He dropped to the ground, touching his head to the dirt. Jelani remained standing, his face filled with suspicion.

"Get up, boy," Shange said. "I am no inkosi."

"Forgive me," Ndoro said. "You startled me."

"I would hate to see your reaction if you knew I was coming." Shange stopped before Jelani and nodded. The Mawena nodded in return, still not speaking.

"I am leading a raid on the Jamburu tomorrow," Shange told Ndoro. "You will accompany me as my attendant."

"By whose authority?" Jelani challenged.

"I need no authority," Shange replied. "The boy is of age and I am his elder. My status allows me to choose who I wish, and I have chosen him."

"What does the inkosa say of this?"

"Don't make me speak of Shani in front of the boy," Shange warned. "He needn't be reminded."

"I will go," Ndoro said.

Jelani cut his eyes at Ndoro. "You are not ready."

"That is my decision, Mawena. From what I have just seen he's better prepared than most his age. You've done a good job, Jelani, but it's time Ndoro learned the ways of battle from a Sesu warrior."

Shange saw Jelani's forearm tense, the tip of his assegai rising. He smiled, hoping the Mawena would lose his composure and attack. It would be a good death for either of them. Unfortunately, Jelani relaxed, the spear tip dropping towards the ground.

"Meet me here tomorrow," Shange finished. "The Jamburu village is three days away. Make sure we have enough provisions for the journey."

Shange marched away to his umuzi in the hills beyond Selike.

"What are you thinking?" Jelani growled.

"It is time, Jelani," Ndoro replied. "I am of age and it is time I began to build my herd. I know Shange will get most of what we take, but if I do well I will get something. It won't be much, but it's a beginning."

"This has nothing to do with your skills or your wealth," Jelani shot back. "This is about your life. Did it occur to you that Shange might have been sent by Mulugo?"

Hatred flashed across Ndoro's young face. "Shange would not answer to that baboon. He is a honored warrior. His magic is strong. He does not need Mulugo's tricks."

"You never know what a man owes another man," Jelani replied. "If Shange is with Mulugo, he may attack you away from Selike. You can't stand against him alone and you know your induna won't help you."

"So be it. I am tired of living in disgrace. If Shange decides to kill me at least if can be said that Sesu's greatest warrior had to do the deed. Momma will be free of this prison and allowed to return to the Mawena."

"I can't stop you," Jelani admitted. "If you're intent on going, let's get back to our practice. There are some things I must show you that may keep you alive long enough to see a second raid."

Darkness had long cast its shadow on the umuzi when they returned to Shani's hut, firelight beckoning them through the door slats. Jelani retired to his hut outside the thorn fence. Ndoro moved the door aside and ducked into the hut.

"Hi, momma." His voice was soft, his way of apologizing for being late.

Shani kept her back turned to her son to hide her joy. She was afraid Shange might have taken him or worse still, decided to kill him without the excuse of a cattle raid. She stirred the iron pot full of goat stew slowly, aware of how famished Ndoro might be.

"Where have you been?" she snapped. "I had to take the cattle to the high grass myself."

"I'm sorry, momma," Ndoro said. "Jelani decided I should practice longer since..."

"Since what?" Shani turned to face her son.

"Momma, Shange came to me today. He chose me to go on the cattle raid with him."

"What does Jelani think about this?"

"He thinks Mulugo is behind this. He thinks Shange will try to kill me once I am away from Selike."

"What do you think?"

Ndoro sat on the floor. "I don't care."

Shani rushed Ndoro, grabbing his shoulders and shaking him with all her might.

"Do you want to die? You would leave me alone?"

Ndoro reached out and hugged his momma. "I don't want to leave you, mama. You know I don't. But I am tired of this way of life. If I return people will respect us and leave us alone. Maybe baba will come see us."

Shani stroked his hair. He was so big now, a man by years but still a boy.

"Don't risk your life for something that will never happen," she whispered. "You are a man and must make your own decisions. I will not make you weak with my worries. If you wish to go on the cattle raid, go. I will pray that Shango watches over you and brings you back to me."

Shani let her son go and went back to her pot, scooping out a bowl of stew and handing it to him.

"How long will you be gone?"

Ndoro slurped down the stew and wiped his chin. "Three days."

Shani's eyebrows rose. "Three days? I don't have enough time to gather food for three days. I can barely keep food in our bowls day to day."

Ndoro lowered his bowl, anger evident in his eyes. "I am the son of Dingane. I should not have to scrounge for food."

"You must learn to accept your place," Shani said, barely able to keep the anger from her voice. "I will gather the food with Jelani's help."

Ndoro slammed his bowl down. "I'm not hungry anymore." He crawled to his sleeping cot and lay down with his back to his mother.

Shani's mind swirled with a mixture of anger and sympathy. She picked up the bowl and went outside to scrap it clean. Jelani sat before the hut, his dagga pipe hanging from the corner of his mouth.

"He shouldn't go!" she blurted. "You know that."

Jelani nodded his head and removed the pipe from his mouth. "I can't stop him. He is a man now, inkosa."

Shani ran to Jelani then grasped his wrists. "He should not suffer for my discretion. If he was in Abo he would be a great warrior, a noble among men. Instead he is an outcast."

"He is also a meji," Jelani replied. "He will rise above his adversity. He has the fighting skills of men twice his age and the wisdom of his grandfather. The ancestors have blessed him despite his circumstances."

Shani kissed Jelani's wrists. "Thank you for your words."

"I wish I could offer more."

Shani smiled. "I am still Dingane's wife. Now is not the time for us." She pushed him away. "Take care of my son. He may need your words to soothe his disappointment."

When Ndoro awoke the next morning, Jelani waited for him. He held a hunting bow in his right hand and a throwing knife in his left. A bundle of throwing spears rested on his back

"Wake up, little monkey. The day is short, and we have much to do."

Ndoro ran into the hut, emerging with bow, arrows and spears. They crossed the river and traveled well beyond the city into the midst of the savannah. Below them thousands of herd animals wandered the grasses, barely noticing the two men staring down on them from the rise. Striped indube bachelor stallions jousted among themselves as the luckier ones kept a careful eye on their mares and colts. Springboks and gazelles grazed nervously, always on the lookout for the majestic shumbas and stealthy ingwes that lurked in the high grasses. The two hunted until nightfall, downing a fine springbok that that they smoked throughout the night.

Jelani and Ndoro sat before the fire outside Shani's hut, the succulent smell of the springbok spreading with the smoke. Shani came out to sit with them. It was a clear, warm night with a slight breeze that played about them. Ndoro gazed into the fire, watching the flames dance.

"There are some that can read fire," Jelani said. "They say that fire is the spirit of the ancestors. The story of every man lives in the flames. If a man could read the fire, he would already know his life."

"Don't tell him such things," Shani scolded. "He has enough to worry about."

Ndoro turned his head to Shani. "Jelani did not have to tell me, momma. I have watched the flames all my life."

"What do they say, Ndoro?" Jelani asked.

"They say I will be a great warrior one day. They say the Sesu will bow before me as they do my father, and I will have thousands of huts surrounding my umuzi. My thorn fence will bulge with white cattle, and my wives will be the most beautiful daughters of my allies and enemies."

"So much from such a little fire," Shani commented. "Come, you must sleep. If you are to travel with Shange, your journey will be fast and hard. He takes only the best warriors with him and raids the strongest villages."

Ndoro looked at Jelani and the warrior nodded his head. He kissed his mother and went inside to his cot by the clay chimney. Momma made fun of his words, but he had seen it in the flames. Maybe not exactly as he told it, but just the same he was destined to be inkosi. But first, he must be a warrior.

The morning came too soon for Ndoro. He was stirred from his dreams by Shani, shaking him by his shoulders.

"Wake up, warrior," she whispered. "Shange will punish you if you are late."

Ndoro jumped from his cot and almost knocked Shani down. He grabbed her before she hit the dirt, pulling her up with his left arm.

"I've got to go momma. Pray for me."

Ndoro ran out of the hut and into Jelani. This time he wasn't fast enough and they both tumbled into the grass.

"Slow down, boy!" Jelani admonished. "Shange won't leave without you."

Ndoro whistled in frustration. He found his hatchet and shoved it back into his belt then gathered his throwing spears. His iklwa was by his shield and he crawled over to them, snatched them up and sped away.

Shange and the others waited by the river. Ndoro recognized faces in the group and grimaced. There were twenty Sesu, ten warriors and their attendants. As soon as the warriors saw him they confronted Shange, yelling and gesturing towards him. He knew the warriors Shange had gathered and he knew their attendants. Dabule, Hamu, Thuka, Amanzi, Senzan and Sitefu; all were members of his intanga. This would not be a good journey.

He finally drew close enough to hear the warriors' argument.

"He cannot go!" the tall man with a massive plume sticking from his headring argued. "He is bad luck!"

"Are you afraid of Mulugo, Ziwedu?" Shange asked calmly. "If you are, then maybe you should take off your headring and wear your wife's skirt."

Tantashi laughed. Ndoro knew Tantashi; he was a lean, handsome man with bright eyes and a generous smile. He wore a simple leopard headdress and a necklace of leopard claws.

"The boy is harmless," he said. "If he is cursed then the ancestors will deal with him, not us."

Big Bekuza shook his head. "These are Jamburu cattle we're talking about. They will be watching their herd carefully, so it is likely we'll get in a fight. If we do, I want the spirits with me, not against me."

"You should stay home, Bekuza. You are too fat to run from the Jamburu."

Shange gave the rest of the warriors a mean look. "You are wasting my time. Ndoro is going. If you have a problem, leave now. I'll be sure to have the maidens share their beaded skirts with you when I return."

Ndoro stood beside Shange, his smile disappearing when he saw the snarl on the warrior's face

"You're not worth the trouble you're causing, but it's too late for me to change my mind. My umuzi is too far and my sons are too young. Pick up my things and let's go."

Shange jumped into the river and waded across. The other warriors looked at each other, waiting for someone to leave. Tantashi laughed and followed Shange, as did Bekuza. Ziwedu rubbed the gris-gris strung around his neck and walked into the river. The others, not wanting to be labeled cowards, finally followed.

The pace was brisk but tolerable. Ndoro ran awkwardly at first, struggling to handle Shange's gear with his own. By the time they reached the first rest spot he was comfortable. Shange halted under the shade of a large acacia tree, dropping his shield and assegai.

"Why are we stopping here?" Ziwedu asked. "This is a shumba tree. Look at the bones."

"If they return our cattle raid becomes a shumba hunt," Shange replied.

"Ndoro, set up my sleep roll and get me some water. There is a waterhole in that direction. Be careful of the crocodiles. I don't want to have to sleep on the ground."

Ndoro was off before Shange's last words were from his mouth. The other boys followed him, and the task soon became a race. Ndoro climbed the hill well before the others and froze at the crest. A pride of shumbas languished at the edge of the waterhole. Five females and two males slept by an indube carcass while the cubs gnawed on the remains.

"Let's go back," Sitefu said from behind him. "It is too dangerous."

"My father will beat me if I come back with no water," Dabule said. He was the smallest of their age group, smaller than his brother Pukane who was only eight.

Ndoro crouched, staring at the shumbas. If he worked his way to the right, he could reach the closest edge of the waterhole without disturbing the shumbas. Sitefu looked at him, his face bunched in anger.

"No, Ndoro!" he barked. "If you go we all must go!"

Sitefu grabbed his shoulder and Ndoro shrugged him off.

"Don't touch me again, goat." Ndoro crept down the hill until the dingy water shimmered before him. He dipped his water bag into the water, letting it settle as it filled, then made room for the other boys. They each took turns, watching the shumbas and the frolicking cubs.

Amanzi was filling his bag when the fly bit his cheek. He yelped, and the cubs froze, looking in their direction.

"Run!" Ndoro shouted. The boys streaked up the hill while the cubs ran to the females, their weak cries loud enough to stir their slumbering parents. Ndoro looked as he reached the hilltop and saw the shumbas on their paws, their narrow pupils looking into his. He ran for the warriors as the shumbas roared.

Shange was on his feet, assegai in hand. The other warriors scrambled for their weapons as boys ran by, all of them except Ndoro. He dropped his water bag and took up his assegai with the warriors as the shumbas approached.

"Everyone to me!" Shange shouted. The warriors came together forming a wall of cowhide shields, the points of the assegais sticking out from the gaps. The shumbas milled about, roaring at the formation but were experienced enough to know this would be no easy kill. They trotted away, the males the last to leave after a half-hearted charge at the warriors. Ndoro held his fear down as he stood with the warriors, fighting the tremor that threatened to shake his assegai from his hand.

Once the shumbas disappeared over the hill the formation broke and Shange ran to the edge, peering down the hill to make sure the beasts were no longer a threat. He spun about and charged Ndoro, slamming his shield into the boy and knocking him into the dirt.

"I ask you to bring me water and you bring a pride as well!"

Ndoro was more embarrassed than hurt. He could stand Shange's punishment alone, but he would not tolerate it before the eyes of his age-group.

"I did what you asked. If I had come back with no water, you would have beat me just the same."

Shange glared at him. "That is true, but in trying to avoid punishment you almost killed us all."

Shange backed away. "Set up my camp and prepare my meal. When you are done take your sleeping roll and set it at the hill over the waterhole. You will protect us from your friends tonight."

Ndoro felt the eyes on him as he did as he was told. He set up his cooking pots and prepared izikobe with strips of dried rabbit. After the izikobe was done, Ndoro prepared himself a bowl, grabbed his sleeping mat and headrest then went to the hilltop.

Shange had done him a favor. Ndoro wanted to come with Shange because of the honor, but he was not prepared for the loneliness he felt among the raiding party. All his life he'd dealt with the alienation, the stigma of being born a twin and the accusations of Mulugo. But Momma and Jelani were always there at the end of the day, giving him words of encouragement and strength. Now he was alone, staring at the others as they ate. There would be no reassurance words or soothing hugs. If he was lucky the punishment would not last beyond the night. Ndoro was not lucky. After a restless night watching the waterhole for signs of the shumba's return he was awakened by a sharp kick in the ribs by Shange.

"Today you will apologize to your brothers by carrying their load. They are waiting for you."

Ndoro rose slowly. He looked into Shange's eyes and for a moment he thought he saw a glint of uncertainty in the warrior's face. The emotion fled as quickly as it appeared and Shange strode away. His brothers came single file, Sitefu leading them. Sitefu lifted the shoulder strap of his bundle and dropped it over Ndoro's head and onto his shoulder, the narrow leather strip digging into his bare skin.

"Look my brothers," he shouted. "An ass wandered into our camp last night. Let's load it up quickly before it runs away!"

The boys' laughter was forced. Ndoro stared at each one as they put their bundles on his shoulders. Hamu, Thuka and Dabule were enjoying themselves, but Shapi and Zibe were clearly uncomfortable. Amanzi was afraid, his hands shaking as he eased his bundle over Ndoro's head.

"I'm sorry," he whispered. "My father said he would beat me if I did not join the others. I fear him more than I fear you."

"I will do my best to change that," Ndoro whispered back.

Amanzi's eyes widened and he stumbled back, turned and ran away. Senzan dodged his flight, walking up to Ndoro with neither fear nor pleasure in his eyes.

"Do you have any sheepskin or cloth with you?" he asked.

"Yes."

"Put it between your shoulders and the straps. It will ease the pain."

Senzan sat his bundle at Ndoro's feet. "I will help you."

"No," Ndoro replied. "Don't get in trouble because of me."

Senzan nodded and walked away. His older brother Dabaze ran up to him and shoved him. Senzan shoved him back. He would do anything to aggravate his older brother, even helping the outcast. Dabaze trailed behind Senzan, yelling at him the entire walk back to the group.

Ndoro listened to Senzan's advice. He took the sleeping rolls off his shoulder and tore a piece of cowhide from his loin-cloth. He laid the skin on his right shoulder and put the rolls back in place. By the time he was done the raiding party had moved on. He could barely see them on the horizon, their shimmering shadows obscured by rising heat and dust. There was no way he could catch up with them, so he walked, the sleeping rolls slapping against his ribs with every step. Ndoro finally lost sight of the group and followed them by tracking. Trotting alone through the grass and shrubs he felt relieved and afraid. He was happy to be away from the tension of the raiding party, but he knew being alone made him vulnerable to attack by a pride of shumbas or hyenas. As the sun descended behind a clump of low hills to the west, Ndoro picked up his pace. He was a good hunter, but darkness would hide their trail. He had no intention of spending the night in the wild alone.

He spotted the flicker of their fire as the sun carried the last shreds of daylight behind the hills. The stares of his companions ranged from surprised to indifferent, but the look in Shange's eyes was best put as impressed anger.

"That demon inside you must be a luck talisman," Shange said as he took his sleeping mat. "You made it in spite of yourself."

Ndoro handed everyone their mats then set about preparing a meal for Shange and himself. He was famished from the long walk and extra burden, but he knew Shange would not let him eat more than his allotted share. If he could get away from the group for only a moment, he could chew on the dried strips of springbok that lay hidden in his pouch. He was lucky, for after their meal Tantashi revealed his dagga pipe, which brought wide smiles to all the warriors. The attendant boys would not be able to share, but they moved close to the circle in hopes they would be able to feel the effect of the burning dagga. He waited until the voices were loud and distracted before he made his way into the darkness, stealing a thick burning stick from the fire to use as a torch. He settled under a low tree and propped his torch against a large granite rock resting far enough from the tree as to not cause a fire and to prevent drawing any night hunters to his sleeping area. The meat was tough but welcomed; Ndoro rested his back on the tree and closed his eyes, letting the sounds of the night take him away from the struggles of the day. Sleep captured him like an unseen trap and he dreamed of a life that could never be, a life as the favored son of Dingane, leader of his intanga and eventually inkosi of the Sesu. Warriors from the farthest ends of Sesuland would dance in his umuzi and sing his praises as he handed them their shields to march and subdue his enemies. His wives' huts would be as numerous as the grass and his cattle countless. By the time Shange jostled him awake the sun was high on the horizon. He had overslept, but so had Shange. The sour smell of dagga clung to the warrior's skin like sweat.

"Damn Tantashi!" Shange snapped. "I should have made him leave his pipe. Now we are late!"

He lifted Ndoro to his feet by his right arm. "You were smart not to smoke."

Ndoro rolled his sleeping mat. "I'm am sorry, Shange. I will make breakfast quickly."

"We don't have time. The Jamburu will arrive at the high pastures tonight. We must be in place before they arrive, or we will never be able to get the cattle."

He placed his hand on Ndoro's shoulder and smiled. It was the first sign of friendliness the boy had received since leaving his mother and Jelani.

"Everyone will carry their own weight today. We will run until we reach the Old Men."

Shange waited until Ndoro was packed and they ran to meet the others. They followed Shange, the warriors in single file from highest to lowest rank. The boys followed, arranged in the same pecking order. Ndoro was last, but he didn't mind. It was the closest he had felt to the group during the entire trip. For the moment, he was Sesu.

It was the hardest day of the trek. Shange set a fast pace that never slowed. They ran across the short grass, through the welcomed shade of scattered acacias and around the enormous herds of zebras, wildebeests, elephants and the host of other creatures that filled the lands of the Sesu. They stopped briefly for water along the river, only to see Sitefu almost lose his head to a hungry crocodile. Azani spotted the creature moving in and saved Sitefu by screaming and running away from the banks. The crocodile lunged just as Sitefu lifted his head and stood. The warriors drove the beast away as they did the shumbas, but Sitefu's nerve fled with the beast. He refused to approach a waterhole afterwards.

By dusk the crowns of the Old Men appeared on the horizon, their grey ice caps a jarring contrast to the heat swirling around the weary runners. Ndoro's heart banged against his chest like a war drum; his left side felt as if someone had driven an assegai into him and left it to rot away. He was sure he would never make it to the ambush; he was more tired than he could imagine anyone could be without dying. As the sun crept closer to the top of the Old Men the pace increased. Ndoro's eyes went wide. How could he keep this up?

"We're not far," Shange shouted. "Stop hobbling like monkeys and run like Sesu!"

They trailed Shange into the valley of the Old Men. Throughout their run the river had never been far away, meandering between the grasslands and hills like an indecisive lover, teasing each one relentlessly for over a thousand strides. The river led them into a narrow valley, only a few strides of rock between them and the grey stone peaks known as the Old Men. The slice of land became so narrow that Ndoro thought they would surely have to swim the rest of the way to the pastures. He was not a good swimmer and the river between the walls of the Old Men was swift and angry, careening off huge boulders and swirling around unseen barriers. The path finally broadened and steepened; soon the river ran below them. The land beneath his feet began to level when Shange finally stopped running.

Everyone fell where they stopped except Shange and Ndoro. Ndoro doubled over, his hands grasping his knees as he heaved. The others sprawled about on the rocky crest, moaning, cursing or a combination of both.

Shange looked at them all and spat. "I have brought women with me to do warriors' work."

He walked up to Ndoro and shoved him. "Where is my food?"

Ndoro looked at Shange bewildered. "Your food?"

"You are my servant, are you not?"

Ndoro straightened and went to his pack. He removed his cooking pot.

"Come," Shange said. "I will show you where to find wood and water."

Shange led Ndoro into the pastureland. The side of the mountain sloped gently into a vast grassland ringed by low shrubs and sparse trees. The grasses teemed with large herds more numerous and larger than anything he had seen in Sesuland. Directly opposite them a range of low hills rose from the plains. The river flowed to his right, resuming its broad and laconic nature.

"An alert scout would see us enter the pastureland no matter what we do," Shange said. "We will camp in the trees below and wait for the Jabaru to arrive."

"How will we see them through the trees?" Ndoro asked.

Shange smirked. "We won't have to see the Jamburu. Their cattle wear huge bells around their necks that wake the ancestors and their warriors sing as bad as they sing loud. We will wait until nightfall and then strike."

Ndoro looked at the Shange with grudging admiration. "Why are you telling me this?"

"Because you will lead the boys into the valley to gather the cattle once we drive off the Jamburu."

For a moment Ndoro felt pride, but his reality was always near. “The other boys won’t follow me.”

“They will if I tell them. Now go fetch water and cook my food. There is a stream in the bush about five strides away.”

The others came down into the brush and set up camp. The boys began cooking and serving food, each one glancing at Ndoro as they passed but saying nothing. Each one except Sitefu.

“The others are afraid of you,” he said. “Shange leads this party, but he is not inkosi. No matter what he says, in Selike I am the elder.”

“We are not in Selike,” Ndoro replied. “In Selike I cracked your head like a melon and helped you heal. Here I won’t be as generous.”

“You are a demon,” Sitefu spat. “I hope Mulugo kills you soon.”

Ndoro glared at Sitefu as he sauntered away. He was about to follow him when Shange’s voice broke his anger.

“Where is my food?” he shouted.

Ndoro took the uPhutu to Shange. Shange tasted the porridge then nodded in approval.

“Don’t worry about Sitefu,” he said. “You will be equals when we return to Selike. Then you can challenge him to a stick fight and give him the beating he deserves...in public.”

Shange shared a rare smile with Ndoro. He grinned as he returned to the others and ate his meal.

“What are you smiling about?” Sitefu asked.

Ndoro didn’t answer. He kept smiling and eating as he imagined his stick breaking on Sitefu’s head.

Ndoro sat awake that night while the others slept, peering through the trees onto the grasslands below. Despite Shange’s confidence, Sitefu’s words bothered him more than they should. He had not thought about Mulugo since their journey began and he was glad of it. The medicine-priest lurked about his life like a starving hyena, waiting for the chance to kill him. When he was young he was afraid of the old man, but now he just wanted to be rid of him. Maybe he could convince Shange in taking him in to live at his umuzi. He could attend him on his adventures and learn the Sesu ways from a true legend. He decided he would ask Shange when they returned. Ndoro finally lay on his mat and drifted to sleep.

Ndoro was awakened by jangling bells and singing voice.

"Jamburu," he whispered.

He scrambled over to wake Shange, but the warrior shoved him away.

"I hear them!" he growled.

Shange came to his feet and kicked everyone awake. He had especially hard words for the other warriors.

"The pride of the Sesu surrounds me and a boy had to tell us the Jamburu are coming."

Everyone grabbed their weapons and shields then worked to the edge of the thicket. The cattle descended the hill in single file, flanked by Jabaru herders. The Jamburu were tall, lithe men draped in red robes that hung from one shoulder. Their shaved heads glistened with sweat as they clambered down the trail using their tall spears like walking sticks. They were terrible singers, at least to Ndoro, but their songs scattered the other beasts and warned the predators of their coming. The Jamburu herded their cattle to the choicest grass then drove off a skittish herd of zebra. Ndoro counted fifteen Jamburu. There were no boys among them, just herders and warriors. While five of the men stood watch over the cattle, the others set about gathering sticks and straw. Some of them wandered to the tree line, close to where the Sesu were hiding. The warriors grabbed their assegais as the Jamburu moved closer to their position. The foragers were satisfied before they reached the Sesu and returned to their brothers. They build grass huts in a circle around their cattle and settled in for a few weeks of grazing, or at least they thought.

The Sesu warriors watched the Jamburu all day, never moving from their positions. Ndoro and the other boys scampered about silently, making food for the warriors and tending to their weapons. The immediacy of action pushed all differences aside as the party prepared for the raid. The day seemed to stretch on forever, the sun taking its time across the sky, descending into the horizon with aggravating patience.

Shange stood soon as the sun disappeared into the horizon. Without a word the other warriors grabbed their weapons and followed him through the thicket and down into the grassland. Ndoro and the boys ran to the higher ground to watch the men work their way to the Jamburu.

"Can you see them?"

"Barely," Ndoro answered. "They are crouching low and using their shields to hide."

"If we can see them the Jamburu can," Sitefu said.

"The Jamburu are busy watching their cattle."

"Everyone be quiet!" Ndoro snapped.

They watched the warriors work closer and closer to the Jamburu umuzi. As the sun slipped completely below the horizon the warriors disappeared, swallowed by the valley darkness. The only light came from the Jamburu campfires that flickered like stars on the valley floor. There was a commotion in the camp, shapes flashing by the fire.

"Something is wrong," Ndoro said.

"I can't see anything," Sitefu replied.

"The Jamburu are moving."

Ndoro eyes went wide and he ran from the others to his sleeping mat. He grabbed his assegai and shield.

"What are you doing?" Sitefu demanded. "Shange told us to stay here!"

"It's an ambush!" Ndoro replied. "They know the warriors are coming!"

Ndoro burst through the bush as the Jamburu camp came alive with torches. The Jamburu warriors ran into the grasses shouting and waving their assegais. Shange stood and waved his shield. The other warriors emerged and charged with him. Before they could clash the Jamburu archers let loose their poison arrows, taking down half the Sesu. The archers had no time for a second volley; Shange was among them, his assegai flashing like lightening.

Ndoro was close enough to see the battle was not going well for the Sesu. Shange held his ground but the other warriors were overwhelmed by the Jamburu. He ran faster, fueled by anger as he watched his comrades fall one by one. Soon Shange stood alone, his shield held high, blood running down his arm and onto his assegai. Three dead Jamburu lay at his feet; the others taunted him, jabbing their assegais at him but none daring to move close. Shange yelled back, daring the warriors to come closer. Behind them an archer crept closer, his bow loaded and drawn.

"Shange!" Ndoro shouted, but it was too late. The archer let loose the arrow and it pierced Shange's thigh, knocking him to one knee. One Jamburu warrior leapt at the wounded Sesu and discovered his mistake too late. Shange sprang back to both feet, slapped the man's shield aside and stabbed him, driving his assegai through the man's chest and out his back. He kicked the man off his spear. The others stepped back, waiting for the poison to take effect.

The Jamburu warrior never saw Ndoro. His back was turned to the boy as he ran hard and knocked the man on his face then stabbed him in the throat. Ndoro trampled the man's body, running to stand beside Shange.

"What are you doing here?" Shange hissed. "I told you to stay with the other boys!"

"You are the only warrior left alive," Ndoro answered.

Shange smiled. "Then it will be a good death."

He stumbled and Ndoro leaned against him to keep him from falling.

"This is a good poison," Shange said. "I will be dead soon, though there is no honor in killing a man like a spring-bok."

"You will die honorably, Sesu."

The speaker broke from the circle, tall and thin like the others with muscles more defined. He wore no headdress, but a necklace of leopard claws rested around his neck. He smiled as he stepped forward, his eyes on Shange.

"Your taste for Jamburu cattle has finally caught up with you, Shange," he said.

Shange managed to laugh despite his obvious pain. "Bamuthi, I should have killed you when I took your herd."

"It looks like I will sing the praise song tonight," Bam-uthi said. He jumped at Shange and Ndoro stepped between them, his leaf shield covering him from ankles to chin, his asse-gai hidden. He charged Bamuthi Sesu style, ramming his shield into the Jamburu's and pushing him back. Ndoro hooked his shield under Bamuthi's and with a yell, jerked his arm back and opened the Jamburu to his thrust. Bamuthi turned sideways and Ndoro missed, his blade grazing the Jamburu's ribs.

Bamuthi brought his shield back, striking Ndoro on the head. Ndoro hit the ground hard, but he felt no pain. The blow broke the calabash that held his rage and it spilled over him like a flooding river. He rolled back onto his feet and attacked Bam-uthi again, beating the man relentlessly with his shield, jabbing with his assegai when an opening appeared. Flashes of other faces jumped between him and Bamuthi but he swept them aside, determined to strike down the arrogant Jamburu. Every-one and everything that ever stood against him during his brief lifetime walked with the legs of Bamuthi and Ndoro was determined to crush it once and for all. Fear shaped the Jamburu's face and he fought without skill but with desperation. Ndoro saw a small opening, a glimpse of flesh open to his assegai. He stabbed, opening the vein of Jamburu's neck. The warrior yelled and dropped his shield, grabbing his neck, blood seeping through his fingers. He fell to his knees, his wide eyes staring at Ndoro then fell dead onto his face.

Ndoro stood over Bamuthi, his shoulders heaving with each breath. The rage subsided and fatigue dropped on him like stone. He crumpled onto his hands and knees, retching until there was nothing left. He fell back onto his backside and looked about. They were all dead; every Jamburu sprawled about him in a circle.

"You killed them all," he heard Shange said. "You killed them all."

Ndoro turned to see the warrior sitting on the ground with him, holding his wounded leg.

"You must have helped me," Ndoro replied. "I could not have done this."

"I did nothing." The confidence was gone from his voice, replaced by a tone of bewilderment. "I saw you do it. I saw it all."

Ndoro stood. The moon was high above, its weak light forming small shadows about the Jamburu herd. He grabbed Shange's arm.

"What are you doing?" the warrior asked.

"We must go before more Jamburu come," Ndoro said. There was no rage to protect him, only the fear of a boy too far from home.

"There are no more Jamburu. You killed them all."

Shange gathered his feet under himself and assisted Ndoro in lifting him. He winced as he put weight on his leg.

"I won't make it," Shange admitted. "The poison is slow but sure. Take the herd; you deserve it. Let me die here with honor."

Ndoro leaned against Shange. "I am you attendant. I will take you to your umuzi. Your medicine priest will know what to do."

He carried Shange across the grasslands, through the trees and up into the bush. He hoped the other boys would be waiting for them, but he was disappointed. They were gone. The boys had fled in haste, leaving sleeping mats, pots and headrests behind. Ndoro eased Shange down against a small tree and built a fire. He made uPhutu for the both of them, adding his last strips of springbok.

"Here." He gave Shange a bowl. "You must eat to stay strong."

Shange snatched the bowl and attacked the porridge, finishing it before Ndoro could sit. Ndoro filled his bowl again then made some porridge himself. He said nothing to Shange, afraid of what words might come from his mouth. Something was inside him; he was certain. There was no way he could have defeated so many men by himself, seasoned Jamburu warriors equal to the best Sesu. He had killed his first men as if it was nothing. He sat eating porridge with the same hands that had just slain men. A smile came to his face. He was a Sesu now, a blooded warrior. His father could deny him many things, but he could not deny him that.

Shange groaned. Ndoro dropped his bowl and went to him.

"Get away!" Shange scolded him. "I don't need a nursemaid. Let me die in peace."

"I can't," Ndoro replied. "I will take you back to your umuzi, so your medicine priest can heal you."

Shange chuckled. "By the morning I won't be able to walk. Are you going to carry me for three days? Even you don't have the strength. Bring me Tantashi's dagga pipe and let me smoke myself to oblivion. By the time the hyenas come I will be dead and blissful."

Ndoro set out Shange's sleeping mat and headrest. "We will leave in the morning."

Shange laughed. "Your demon is strong, but not smart."

Shange fell asleep so quickly Ndoro thought he'd died. Ndoro remained awake, watching the camp until daylight struggled over the shoulders of the Old Men. He grabbed his assegai and shield and proceeded down the hill to the neglected Jamburu herd. Using the skills taught to every Sesu boy from birth, he went to each bovine and removed the cumbersome bells dangling from their neck. He then herded the cattle, driving them up the hill, through the thicket to the camp. Shange was awake when he returned, propped up on his elbows.

"So, you have decided to claim your prize?"

Ndoro did not smile. "The cattle will help me take you home."

Shange looked puzzled but did not argue. The cattle grazed on the short grass under the trees, ignoring Ndoro as he gathered branches and the blankets abandoned by the others. By the afternoon he had fashioned a respectable litter which he attached to the most docile of the cattle. He led the young bull to Shange.

"Can you get in?" he asked.

Shange looked at the litter with disdain. "I will not return to Sesuland like a cripple!"

"You don't have the strength to walk and I am not going to leave you here for the hyenas," Ndoro said. "When we get to Sesuland you can use your strength to walk into your umuzi in pride. For now, you need to get on."

Shange dragged himself onto the litter. "Why am I listening to a boy? I am a grown man with wives and cattle, yet I listen to a boy with the soul of a demon."

Shange's words stun. "I am no demon!"

Shange nestled into the litter and closed his eyes. "That is the thing about demons. A Sesu does not know if he has one inside him. I think all men do. It is what makes us brave and gives us strength. But just like Unkulunkulu made shumbas different in size and strength, so it is with men. Until I met you, I did not know a single man with a demon inside him stronger than mine, and you are still a boy."

"You don't think I am a curse to the Sesu?"

Shange laughed. "I wish I possessed such a curse! Dingane is a fool to ignore you. He will never have another son with your strength."

Ndoro squatted near the warrior. Shange's encouraging words were the first he'd ever heard from someone other than Momma and Jelani.

"Mulugo says I am cursed because I was born meji."

"Mulugo is a fool as well. He is a medicine priest because he was afraid to answer Dabulamanzi's call to war. In the early days the Sesu marched every dry season. Many Sesu became healers and diviners to avoid the inkosi's call to the umuzi.

"Baba believes him."

"I said Mulugo was a fool, I did not say he was without power. I have seen him do amazing things, but I have also witnessed him condemn good Sesu for his own ends. Everything he has done has benefited Dingane until you. For him to go against the inkosi means you are a greater threat to him than Dingane's anger."

Ndoro did not understand Shange's words. What could he do to Mulugo? An assegai was no match against a medicine priest's charms and spells.

"Well, boy, what are you waiting for?" Shange complained. "If you're determined for me to die in shame then get on with it!"

Ndoro drove the herd up the Old Men and down into the river valley. He lost many along the narrow pass to the swift river currents and the occasional lurking crocodile in the slow eddies and pool. As they passed from the rocky riverbanks to the savanna, the dangers turned from water and reptiles to shumbas and hyenas. Although his priority was to get Shange home safe, he cursed with every cow or bull lost.

Shange's health diminished with every passing day. By the third day he no longer spoke, swaying back and forth in the litter, his eyes half-closed and his mouth locked in a delirious grin. He was dying; Ndoro had no doubt. Keeping the herd was slowing him down. By the sixth day he abandoned them to the wilds, keeping only the bull pulling Shange's litter. They rested only when the bull would go no further, the stubborn bovine halting to graze and loll about at one waterhole or another. Ndoro took no rest, keeping a constant eye out for any predator and trying to get Shange to eat.

Eight days later they reached Sesuland. Ndoro trudged behind Shange and the bull, too weary to celebrate his return home. Shange's umuzi was another day's walk away and his legs burned, but he would not stop. He was too close.

He picked up his pace until he walked beside Shange.

"Master Shange, we are home," he said. "Soon you will hear the songs of your village. They will welcome their warrior home with a great celebration."

Shange said nothing. His eyes were closed, and the smile had long left his face. Ndoro refused to think he was dead although he knew it was possible. He prodded the bull on, determined to reach the umuzi before the end of the day.

He spotted the impi a half a day away from his destination. There were ten men total, their head plumes bouncing against the undulating hills from where they came. Their broad chests were hidden by the brushed white cow tails hanging down from their necks to their waists. They ran hard, their chant drifting on the breeze to Ndoro's ears. He stopped, pulling back on the rope around the bull's neck and waited for the warriors to come to him.

The first to reach him was a broad man as tall as Shange with a large chest and larger stomach.

"You are the one called Ndoro," he said.

Ndoro nodded.

"The boys said you were dead, that you died with Shange and the others."

"You can see they lied. They were too busy running away to know what happened."

Another warrior stepped forward as the others ran to Shange's side. This man was much younger, a leopard cap ringing his bald head, a plume of ostrich feathers rising out of the back.

"The boys said the warriors were dead and Shange was struck by an arrow. How did you rescue him?"

Ndoro lowered his head. "I killed the Jamburu."

The warriors looked at each other then back at Ndoro.

"We thank you for bringing our inkosi back. Come with us. We have food and a good medicine priest to tend to you and Shange."

"I think Shange is dead."

The old warrior laughed. "Shange is not dead. He would not dare die away from his umuzi. Come, everyone is waiting for us."

Ndoro hesitated. He could go with these men and become part of Shange's umuzi. Shange wouldn't dare deny him after saving his life but he would give up any claim as Dingane's heir if he did.

"Thank you, but I must return to Selike."

The warriors raised their shield in respect and headed back to the umuzi with Shange and the bull. Ndoro watched them until they disappeared over the rise before heading to Selike. He set a warrior's pace, reaching the Mfululo by nightfall. Ndoro took his time crossing the shallow river, savoring the sight of home and his mother's hut. He was halfway up the hill when the door of the hut swung open and Jelani emerged. Ndoro cleared his throat and Jelani jumped with his sword ready.

"Ndoro? Ndoro!"

Jelani charged down the hill and ran into Ndoro so hard they fell. He heard a shriek and in moments his mama was with them, the three of them rolling in the dust. The pain and fatigue were gone, replaced by joy he thought he could never feel.

Jelani lifted him from the ground and Shani squeezed him as tight as she could.

"You are not dead!" she exclaimed. "You are not dead!"

"No, mama, not yet."

"I told you those boys were lying," Jelani said. "I could see it in their eyes, especially Sitefu."

Shani looked him over, running her hand over his body. "You are hurt. Here, coming inside."

Shani dragged him into the hut and pushed him down on his cot. She ran over to a small box by the chimney and returned with an armload of calabashes. She went to work on his wounds as he lay down and fell asleep, lulled by the sing-song rhythm of his mother's voice.

The next day was strange in its normalness. No one came to the umuzi even thought Ndoro was sure the word had spread of his return. Shani tried to persuade him to remain in the hut, but Ndoro refused. He took the cattle out into the grazing fields. Sitefu and the other boys tended their family herds, but they would not look at him. One boy broke away from the others, driving his herd towards Ndoro. Ndoro recognized Senzan and grinned. The bold boy left his herd, marching directly to Ndoro.

"So, you are alive," he said.

Ndoro nodded.

They walked side by side not saying a word, tending their cattle together. Ndoro could stand the silence no longer.

"Why did you run?"

Senzan continued walking, staring at the ground. "Sitefu told us to. He said we would be killed once the Jamburu finished with the warriors. They all ran, but I didn't, at least not at first."

"You stayed?"

Senzan stopped and looked at Ndoro. "I wanted to be sure my brother was dead. I wanted to tell my baba that he was dead, that I saw him killed. I saw you reach Shange and I saw you fight. Then I ran."

"I don't remember killing anyone, Senzan. I remember attacking Bamuthi, but I don't remember the others. I thought Shange was helping me."

"No, it was you. You were a storm and the Jamburu were sticks in your path."

Ndoro felt an odd sensation. He looked away from Senzan and saw the source. Mulugo stood at the edge of the grass, his eyes set back deep in his head, his mouth trembling. His lips strained to form silent words. Ndoro had stood watching the priest curse him before, but the anger coming from him seemed deeper this time. Then he saw it, and he understood. He knew why the Jamburu waited for them; he knew why they brought archers with poison arrows. Mulugo's eyes went wide and a surprised look overcame his face. The medicine priest turned and ran back to the village.

"I must go, Senzan," Ndoro said. "Do yourself a favor and stay away from me. You are lucky only your brother died."

Ndoro rounded up his cattle then herded them back to the umuzi. He could tell no one what he sensed, because no one would believe him. It was a feeling confirmed by an expression. Everyone believed Mulugo wished him dead; no one would believe he would kill one of the Sesu's greatest warriors to accomplish it, not even his mama and Jelani.

Ndoro drove the cattle into the enclosure, securing the thorn fence behind them. Shani met him on his way to the hut.

"You are back early," she said. "Are you feeling well?"

"I am a little tired."

"I told you to rest. You just came back yesterday. Go inside. Jelani and I will tend to things."

Ndoro laid on his cot and fell into a deep, dreamless sleep. When he finally awoke, Shani stood above him, a look of terror on her face.

"You must come outside now," she said.

Ndoro scrambled off his cot and ran outside. The hut was surrounded by Sesu warriors dressed in full ceremonial garb, hundreds of men covered in braided cow tail necklaces and leggings, with feather plumes rising from their leopards and otter skin caps. They carried the battle shields of Shange, black cowhide with three white spots in the center. They saw him and dropped to one knee in unison.

"Ushange!" they barked.

One warrior stepped forward bearing a white shield with a black circle on top and bottom. He stood a head taller than Ndoro without the spectacular eagle feather headdress towering above him. The face was familiar; the man was definitely related to Shange. He scrutinized Ndoro for a moment then smiled.

"Ndoro kaDingane, I am Mayinga kaShange, son of Shange kaVilikaze. I have come to inform you that inkosi Shange is dead."

The words hit Ndoro like a war club. He wanted to fall to his knees and curse Mulugo, but he had to show dignity before the son of the only Sesu that believed in him.

"The ancestors have chosen a strong bull," he said.

Mayinga nodded. "The elders of our umuzi have honored me with their choice as inkosi. I would have rather served beside my father than in his place, but I do not try to understand the wisdom of the ancestors."

Mayinga turned and raised his shield. "Shingwa! Dabaze!"

Two warriors sprinted forward to Mayinga's side.

"My father told us of what you did. We are thankful that you brought him back to us so he could die with honor among his own. He asked that we give you his shield and assegai as thanks. May his nyama add to your strength and protect you from your enemies. We also gathered what was left of the cattle you brought from Jamburuland."

The warriors placed the shield and assegai at Ndoro's feet. Mayinga grasped Ndoro's shoulders, looking him in the eye as an equal.

"Whatever is your fate, Ndoro kaDingane, the warriors of kaShange will always be with you."

Another commotion drew his attention. Dingane's warriors marched across the royal umuzi led by Dingane's senior induna, Qethuka. He was simply dressed, apparently not expecting the visit of Shange's warriors. The grey-haired man was plainly out of breath as he stood beside Ndoro. He glanced at Ndoro, clearly angry, and then smiled at Mayinga.

"Inkosi Dingane has heard of Shange's death and his sorrow is larger than the sun," he said. "We hope that his son will follow his father in respecting the rule of the Inkosi over the Land between the Mountains."

"My allegiances are those of my father's," Mayinga replied. "The kaShange remain the friends of Dingane...and his son."

Mayinga raised his assegai and his warriors stood. He spun and ran, his warriors making a path as he ran through them. As he crossed the river they turned and followed. The kaShange left the way they came, running and chanting until they disappeared over the rolling hills in the eastern horizon. Quethuka glared at Ndoro.

"Inkosi Dingane knows the story of the cattle raid. You may have deceived the kaShange, but the inkosi is no fool. Still, Mayinga is a valuable ally and he seems to favor you. You and your mother will have access to the royal umuzi and your food will be provided by the royal household."

"Will my father come see us?" Ndoro asked.

"Of course not," Qethuka snapped. "He is still Sesu, and you are still a meji."

Qethuka walked away, Dingane's guardsmen close behind. Ndoro wanted to be angry, but he could not muster the energy. The words of Mayinga stayed in his head, bringing with them hope. He would see his father again one day, he was sure now. Shange's honor would one day make it come to pass. He knelt, picking up the assegai and shield of Shange and walked back to his mother's hut amid the murmurs of the curious. He looked at them all, smiled and closed the door behind him.

7

War season was over. The monsoons had come, the sky a perpetual gray, the rain continuous. Roads that once made way for warhorses and wagons became rivers of mud and water, virtually impassable. It was a time to rest, heal and plan.

Azikiwe watched the torrential rain from the window of his main palace and cursed the ancestors. It was his luck to be so close to crushing the Kossi army only to have the rains arrive early. He had no choice but to pull back or be trapped deep in Kossiland with no clear road to receive provisions from Baba-Ile, his main fortress. Few bridges spanned the Kalu River and those were overwhelmed by the rising water. The monsoon rains transformed the lazy trickle into a muddy torrent. He would have to settle for a temporary victory and hope that the Kossi would not reoccupy the lands he cleared during his campaign.

Isala sat up, letting the white cotton sheets fall away from her naked form.

"Come back to bed, Azikiwe," she whispered.

Azikiwe turned and grinned, his large eyes growing even wider as he admired her. Her dark skin was flawless and smooth like onyx, her full lips parted slightly as her brown eyes stared back at him. Perfect, beautiful, passionate Isala made his exile bearable. Five years had passed since he was banished from Abo by his father, but the anger burned in him as if the punishment had occurred moments ago. The first four years were a jumble of battles won and lost, but gradually he and his Tijuku elite gained the upper hand against the tenacious Kossi. In the last year he had finally been able to accomplish what his father sent him north to do, and he had done it on his own.

Azikiwe sauntered back to the bed, dropping his robe along the way. War and leadership had hardened his body and mind since his days in Abo. Anyone who knew him then would hardly recognize him. He climbed back into the bed and wrapped Isala with his arms, kissing her fiercely. The made love furiously, their grunts and cries rising above the rumbling clouds and drumming rain. When they were done Azikiwe threw the sheets on the floor and jumped out of the bed, breathing heavily.

"You're a lioness," he said.

Isala sighed as she rolled onto her stomach. "Only for you, my lion."

Azikiwe picked up his robe and put it back on. "I have a meeting with Chimela in a few moments. Call for a servant to draw my bath."

Isala rose from the bed reluctantly and dressed. "Shall I accompany you?"

"No, you may not," he replied. "I need some strength left."

Isala grinned then left the room. Azikiwe found himself back at the window staring into the rain. It was time to bring this war to an end. Despite his success, the new prosperity in the North and the company of Isala, Azikiwe wanted to go home. No matter what he accomplished in the north, it would never equal the prestige of Abo and the comfort of being among his family. He could not return until he defeated the Kossi and he was determined that the next dry season would mark the beginning of his return to Abo.

A servant entered the room and immediately fell to the floor, flattening himself in complete submission.

"Oba, your bath is ready," he announced.

Azikiwe stepped over the man, walking to the end of the granite hallway and down the ironwood stairs to the baths. The granite tub was filled with warm water and fragrant oils which soothed his mind as he entered. He climbed inside then sat against the back of the tub, letting his head fall back on the cushioned headrest as closed his eyes and dreamed of Abo. His musing was interrupted by a deep growl.

"And how long was I supposed to wait while you took your beauty bath?"

Azikiwe opened his eyes to the great bulk that was Chimela. The commander of his army stood with his legs spread, his massive hands balled into fists pressed against his hips. Muddy leather riding boots covered his huge feet, climbing his calves to his knees, the tops draped by dark brown pantaloons. A thick belt circled his wide waist and supporting his sword and scabbard. His shirt was covered with fetishes and talismans.

This huge man standing in his bath room was his best and most loyal friend, choosing to leave in exile with him despite the protests of his family and his mentor, Kumba. Azikiwe was the first to admit he would not have survived in the north without Chimela's abilities and council.

"You know as well as I how important it is to keep the customs of civilization in the frontier," Azikiwe replied. "You smell like you need a bath."

Chimela began removing his shirt. "I guess now is as good a time as any."

Azikiwe jumped out of the bath laughing. "Wait your turn!" He dried himself and dressed as Chimela waited.

"I'm surprised to find you alone," Chimela said. "Where is your woman?"

"She is in the bedchambers."

Chimela frowned. "You spend too much time with her. She will not be accepted in Abo."

"Who says she will ever see Abo?"

"You must have faith. We will return to Abo as heroes, my brother."

Azikiwe reached up and patted his friend on the shoulder. "Come, let's get this over with."

Azikiwe followed Chimela down the hall to the conference room. Rich woven carpets draped the walls, each representing the various villages, cities and tribes of the Mawena borderlands. The corners of the room held abstract soapstone carvings of leopards, the royal symbol of Noncemba's clan. A large ebony wood table filled the center of the room, standing on a massive rug woven in the kente pattern of his family. A map of Mawenaland and Kossiland was carved into the surface of the table. Wooden pegs carved in the shape of Mawena and Kossi warriors lined the edge of the table.

"Don't you ever stop planning?" Azikiwe asked his friend.

"The Kossi outnumber us," Chimela replied matter-of-factly. "You know this as well as I. The only way we can keep them at bay is to stay ahead of them."

"I am tired of keeping them at bay. It is time we ended this game."

Chimela leaned against the table and stared. "And how do propose we do this? We have just enough warriors to patrol the border. Our advance into Kossiland was pure luck. The rainy season benefited us just as much as the Kossi."

"What if we concentrated our forces into a massive, decisive strike?"

Chimela frowned. "Where do we strike? If we attack any of the Kossi cities near the border we accomplish nothing. The only way an attack you suggest could work is if we..."

"...struck the heart of Kossiland," Azikiwe finished.

Chimela's expression was not complimentary. "You have finally lost your mind."

"Have I? Let's see. To strike the heart of Kossiland, we must break every rule of war as we know it."

Azikiwe walked to the war table and set up the warrior pieces. Each piece represented a Mawena or Kossi regiment, depending on the shape. Azikiwe placed the pieces on the board according to his latest briefing from Chimela. Chimela studied the placement and nodded in approval.

"This was the position of the Kossi army before the rainy season. We pulled back because our position in Kossiland was unsustainable," Azikiwe said. "The Kossi army pulled back as well. As a matter of fact, most of their army has gone home to their villages to plant their fields."

"As has ours," Chimela said.

Azikiwe smiled. "That leaves us with a standing army of four regiments, three warriors and one cavalry. If we include my Tijuku the total increases by one regiment."

A gleam came to Chimela's eyes. "The Kossi has no standing army, though their oba's guard totals three thousand, four thousand counting the city guard."

Chimela rubbed his chin. "This is an interesting exercise, but by the coming dry season Kossiland would be back to full strength."

"Who said anything about waiting until the dry season?"

Chimela stepped back from Azikiwe. "You can't serious! The roads are impassable, the men are tired and healing and the priests are still pouring libations to the Kossi dead."

Azikiwe was undaunted. "We can use the forests instead of the roads if we divide our army into small units and attack on foot. The men are tired and hurt, but gold, salt and loot has always brought out the best in a warrior. The priests are always busy pouring libations. But most of all, the Kossi won't be expecting it."

Chimela went to the table and began shuffling the figurines about, pausing to study each scenario before shuffling them again. Azikiwe sat on his stool and waited patiently while his friend searched for a flaw in his plan. After an hour the big man stepped away from the table, sweat beading on his forehead, his massive hands gripping his waist belt.

"This could work," he finally said.

Azikiwe smiled. "Do you really think so?"

Chimela's smile was all the answer he needed. "There are a few issues that need to be worked out, but they're minor."

"So, my friend, who will buy the beer when we return to Abo?"

"I will!" Chimela bellowed. "And I will buy it with Kossi gold!"

Chimela rushed Azikiwe and lifted him in the air in one of his familiar but painful hugs. "You are truly Oba Noncemba's son!"

Azikiwe regained his breath as Chimela put him down.

"There was a time I would have considered that a compliment," he said. "I'm going back to my bedchamber. I think you have a few details to take care of, my friend. I wish to be ready to proceed in two weeks. Can I trust you?"

"Of course!" Chimela charged out of the conference room. Azikiwe strolled down the hallway and returned to the bedchamber and found Isala waiting for him.

"What do you wish, my Lion?"

"I wish to take you to Abo and proclaim you my Great Wife," he said, pulling her feet and spinning her around.

"I wish to give you gold dust to sprinkle in your hair and amber to wear around you lovely neck. But instead, I will have to give you Povo."

Isala broke away from their dance and gave Azikiwe a serious look. "My oba, what are you talking about?"

"Don't worry about it, little bird," he answered. "These sorts of things need not concern you. Come, let us walk."

"But it is raining, my oba."

Azikiwe smiled. "Only on the outside, Isala; only on the outside."

* * *

The days passed, and the rains continued. Chimela worked relentlessly on Azikiwe's plan, concentrating his forces at Baba-Ile. The fort had been evacuated of everyone except the Tijuku and the royal court. Secrecy was the rule; anyone looking the slightest suspicious of the activities surrounding the main fort was killed. As for Azikiwe, he continued his daily routine, unconcerned about the details of the coming campaign. He had ultimate trust in Chimela; his friend would let him know the details at the right time.

That time came during a Monday morning meeting with the village elders of a Kossi vassal village. Azikiwe struggled to stay awake as the tattered old men complained about the occupying Mawena. Chimela appeared behind the men, an angry look on his face. Azikiwe sat up on his stool.

"I will deal with your concerns later," he said to the elders. The old men bowed and left the chambers, glancing at Chimela in obvious fear.

"Well my friend, are we ready?"

Chimela said nothing until he was face to face with Azikiwe.

"Why do you want to march on Povo?" he asked.

"I think I explained that to you," Azikiwe replied.

Chimela folded his arms across his chest. "You told me what I wanted to hear. Why do you want Povo?"

Azikiwe smiled. "You're losing your touch, my friend. It took you longer than I expected."

Chimela waited for an answer.

Azikiwe stood and began to pace. "The Kossi raid Mawenaland not for loot but for slaves. Their oba possesses vast plantations surrounding the city that supply his merchant fleet with goods to trade across the ocean. If I can defeat the Kossi, I can establish a power base independent of Abo. Instead of Mawena working the plantations it will be Kossi men and women bearing the yoke."

"And when was I to be told of this?"

"When it was necessary."

Chimela found a stool and dragged it before Azikiwe. He dropped his bulk down hard and the stool cracked.

"This doesn't feel right, Azikiwe. This is beginning to resemble a rebellion."

This was no time for his sarcasm, Azikiwe thought. He sensed the struggle in his friend and had to choose his words carefully. Chimela was many things, but he was no traitor. He sat on the ground before Chimela, noting his friend's surprise in the slight raise of his eyebrows.

"I thought you knew me better to think I would ever challenge my father's right to rule," Azikiwe began. "He was chosen by the Queen Mother and confirmed by the elders. It is his right to rule."

Chimela nodded his head in agreement.

"You also know what my father thinks of me," Azikiwe said as he dropped his head.

Chimela shifted on his stool. "Sometimes fathers are so busy correcting our faults they fail to see our attributes."

Azikiwe knew Chimela would understand this path of argument. His own father had admonished him for choosing the life of a soldier to that of a priest, the profession of his lineage. Chimela's family disowned him for his decision. Kumba's clan adopted him and raised Chimela as one of their own.

When Azikiwe raised his head, his eyes were glistening. "When he feels his time is near, he will not select me as a candidate for oba."

"You do not know this, Azikiwe. Defeating the Kossi may change his opinion of you."

"I wish it were so, but I know better, friend. I gave up on that dream long ago. He fancies my nephew Obaseki now."

Chimela chuckled. "The one who sees ghosts? I seriously doubt that."

"I may be wrong, but I'm sure I am not being considered. What I fear is what will happen afterwards. Whoever is selected may fear my claim. He may decide to simplify matters. If that happens I must have a refuge and a position of strength to protect myself and those who follow me."

"So, this is your plan for Kossiland?"

"Yes, it is."

Chimela moved from his stool to sit beside Azikiwe. "You plan to pledge your loyalty to your father?"

"Of course."

Chimela rubbed his chin. "This changes things. I envisioned a plan that would lay ruin to Povo and the surrounding villages. We would burn Diallo's plantations and destroy his docks. As we marched back to the river we would let the warriors plunder whatever stood between us and home as a reward for their victory."

"We need to keep as much intact as possible," Azikiwe said.

"I know." Chimela stood and extended his hand. Azikiwe let his friend pull him to his feet and they hugged.

"You are my best friend, Chimela. Thank you."

"Keep your thanks. We are outcasts together. You will have your foundations before the rains cease. Kossiland will be ours."

Chimela walked to the door. "We will be ready to move in a week."

"I will be ready as well."

Chimela scowled and Azikiwe read his thoughts.

"I have to go," he said. "It is my place. The men will expect it."

Chimela strode back to Azikiwe with such force the prince was not sure of his intentions.

"This will not be a dainty march down a wide avenue," Chimela said. "The forest will be wet and miserable. We will have nothing to eat but cold hardcake and what we can steal from the local farmers. I can't afford anyone on this march that is not a fighting man, which means you must leave your servants behind unless they can wield a sword and a shield."

"I know the trials of the march, my friend. I was a soldier once."

"Excuse me for saying, my Oba, but your status shielded you from much of what most warriors have to endure. I'm not sure you are prepared for this type of battle."

"I'm going, Chimela. I say this as your oba, not as your friend."

Chimela flinched and Azikiwe immediately regretted his words. It was seldom when he had to use the power of his lineage on his friend, but he knew Chimela would not allow him to come on the march otherwise.

"As you wish...oba. You will be part of my group and dress as a common warrior. You will do as I order until I am sure the battle is won. We will reveal you to our men as if you had arrived at the moment of glory."

His friend always managed to find a way to be defiant.

Azikiwe bowed slightly. "As you wish, my commander."

"This is not a game, Azikiwe," Chimela warned. "Please take this seriously."

"I do, Chimela. Believe me, I do."

They parted ways, Chimela to his warriors and Azikiwe to the courtyard. The rain has stopped for a moment, the clouds thinning to tease those below with the promise of sunshine. Isala would take advantage of the respite for a walk so he was not surprised to find her stepping gingerly across the muddy expanse. Her servants walked beside her, their arms flying out to catch her at the slightest hint of a fall.

"You walk through the mud like you were born to it," he shouted.

Isala turned and smiled. "Are you calling me a buffalo?"

Azikiwe stomped through the mud to her side. He dismissed her servants and wrapped his arms around her.

"I must tell you something of great importance. I trust you with this knowledge as a pledge of my desire for you to be my Great Wife."

Isala eyes were wide and gleaming. "What is it?"

"In one week we march against Povo."

Isala's hand flew to her mouth. "Attack...Provo? How can you do this? This is the rainy season. The warriors won't be ready."

"Their men won't, but the Tijuku will."

Azikiwe shared his plan with Isala who looked at him in disbelief. By time he was done the clouds bulged above them, robbing the sky of its hope. Drizzle fell, covering her tight curls with a sensual sheen. Her beauty could not hide her emotions. She was very upset.

"What is wrong, sweet one?" he asked.

"I am honored to be by your side, my Oba, and I sense you plan is a good one. Despite my feelings for you I am still Kossi, and the thought of my people subject to the whims of Oba Noncemba sickens me."

"You will never answer to Abo," he assured her. "Kossiland will be in my charge."

"You will defy your father for my people?"

"No, I will defy my father for you."

Isala threw her arms around his neck and kissed him hard. "You will be a kind oba for my people."

"Only if you promise to be by my side, Isala. I will have only one wife, and it will be you."

Isala placed her head on his chest and Azikiwe hugged her.

"I am already yours," she whispered.

They kissed again as the rain fell heavier. Isala grasped his hand and pulled him toward the palace.

"Come, we must get out of the rain," she urged.

"You go on," Azikiwe said. "I have a visit I need to make."

Azikiwe watched her run into the palace before continuing across the courtyard to the stables. The servants immediately fell to the ground, burying their faces into the mud. Three Tijuku appeared before him and bowed.

"Bring me my horse," he ordered.

The Tijuku rushed into the stable and returned with Azikiwe's stallion. The four of them mounted and galloped through the mud and the iron gate. Azikiwe led the men down the Oba's Highway towards Abo. They rode at a constant gallop until they reached a small road that intersected the highway. Azikiwe reined his horse and jumped on him into ankle deep mud. He ignored the filth on his boot, proceeding down the road without his bodyguards. He would need no protection in this place, for it was the Oba's woods, home of the Oba's priest.

The narrow path widened into a broad highway flanked by massive ironwood trees. They were in straight order, too perfect to have grown naturally. Azikiwe looked to either side, almost expecting to see the ancestors that dwelt among them watching one of their own perform the same ritual many of them had performed when a part of the living world. He was not a priest, nor was he Obaseki, so the spirits remained invisible to him, the occasional rustle of leaves the only sign of their presence

When he reached the ceremonial grounds, the priests were waiting. They sat in a semi-circle before an ancient baobab so wide a village could live inside its hollow trunk. The mammoth tree towered over its brethren, its dense roots and dense canopy sucking the life from them. The priests were as silent as the tree, unmoved by the constant rain.

Azikiwe dropped to his knees before them. He reached into his robes, extracting a bundle wrapped in an elaborate kente blanket. He bowed and extended the bundle.

"Uncles, I come to you for your favors," he said. "This is a symbol of my respect for you and the spirits of these woods."

Azikiwe kept his eyes closed as the bundle was taken from his hand. He knew its contents; there was more gold dust in the calabash than gold in the entire city of Abo. He didn't come to the sacred woods to ask the ancestors favor; he came to buy it.

"This is a generous gift," they said in unison. "But what is gold to those gone beyond? Your offering will afford us much, but what do you bring for those who have gone before you?"

"I have nothing, my uncles, that will sway my fathers before me," Azikiwe admitted. "But if they grant me this victory over Kossiland, their rewards will be unlimited."

The grove shook with hysterical laughter. "You wish to bargain with the ancestors? That is like holding smoke in your hand. Bring us something you value more than gold and victory will be yours."

Azikiwe thought on the request. There was little in this world that meant more to him than gold. The power he possessed was nothing to the ancestors. He could think of only one thing, and she was not negotiable.

"I will not give you Isala," he said

"Then you have nothing for us. Go and win your war alone."

Azikiwe jerked his head up angrily but the priests were gone. He ran to the hollow baobab tree and charged inside. Stools sat around a smoldering fire, sleeping cots braced against the inside trunk. He tore the hovel apart but found neither the priests nor his gold. He left the tree and the grove with a bitter taste in his mouth. Chimela warned him long ago never to go into battle without the blessing of the ancestors, but he was not about to give up the only person he truly loved. Nothing was worth that price.

The Tijuku were waiting as he exited the grove. He climbed on his horse, looking one more time at the grove, angry that he wasted his time.

"I want this place burned to the ground when the dry season comes," he said. "It is useless to me."

He reined his horse and galloped back to Baba-Ile.

Chimela adjusted Azikiwe's chain mail, pulling each buckle tight. He stood back to observe his work then handed the prince a black kapok tunic.

"The cloth is treated to repel the rain and the kapok will stop poison arrows," he said.

"Do you expect us to encounter archers?"

"Not during the attack," Chimela replied. "Our scouts tell us there are First Men in the Kossi forest, and they hate the Kossi the same as Mawena. The will not attack us in force, but if one of the bastards thinks he can kill one of us and escape he will try."

"We should have cleared the forest of them before the attack," Azikiwe said.

"It would be easier to eat every leaf on every tree," Chimela said. "It's a minor risk, but we must be prepared. Our group will be the largest and the most likely to draw attention."

Azikiwe knew why. The group had been doubled in size to protect him. The plan was to separate the army into ten-man units, each unit with a Kossi scout to lead them to rendezvous point on the banks of the Kossi River. There they would form into a complete unit and quick march to Povo. Mawena merchant spies had informed them there were no walls surrounding the outer city; only the royal grounds with its prosperous plantations were walled. The docks were unprotected as well. The Kossi were apparently very confident in their ability to protect their capital city.

Chimela began to wrap his turban when Isala entered the stables.

"I would like to wrap my Oba's turban," she said.

Chimela glared at the woman. "She should not be here," he hissed.

"I know how you feel about protocol, my friend, but it is alright."

He turned to his woman and motioned for her to come forward. Isala went to Chimela and took the black cloth from him. She turned to Azikiwe and pulled him to her with the cloth.

"Don't go," she whispered.

"We had this discussion and I won. Now wrap my turban."

Isala draped the cloth over his shoulders. She reached into her dress and revealed a piece of amber strung on a simple leather cord which she hung on Azikiwe's neck.

"Wear this for me," she said. "It will bring you back to me."

"Chimela will bring me back to you," Azikiwe said. "My turban, please."

Isala wrapped the cloth around his head into a perfect turban. She kissed his cheek then left the room, glancing back with a smile.

Chimela returned then handed him a standard issue sword, a plain steel blade with an iron hilt and wooden scabbard.

"We are ready now," Chimela said.

"May the ancestors protect us," Azikiwe replied.

The Mawena force slipped from the fort at dusk under the cover of shadows and rain, following their scouts until they were well beyond the Kossiland-Mawenaland border. Once they were deep in the forest they built huts for the night, Azikiwe sharing shelter with Chimela. They broke camp before dawn and continued their march, fighting the dense woods and brush for every step. Azikiwe struggled more than the others; too many years had passed since he took part in a hard march. His legs felt as if the bone had disappeared as they wavered with every step. His men offered their hands but he refused, determined make his own way. When the night came he helped build his hut then collapsed onto his cot exhausted.

Chimela estimated a twelve day march to the rendezvous point but the heavy rain and dense forest slowed them. Azikiwe worried that the others had arrived and were waiting anxiously for them. The longer they gathered, the more likely they would be discovered. Every group had been instructed to remain secluded until he and Chimela arrived, but it would be nearly impossible to hide such a large force for any extended period of time. Chimela tried to increase the pace but the forest fought back, tangling their arms and legs with vines, striking their faces with sharp branches and wounding them with thorns and stinging insects. When they finally stumbled out of the woods to the clearing they were totally drained.

Azikiwe fell to his knees gasping for breath. He lurched forward and found himself staring into the face of a dead Mawena warrior.

"Chimela!"

Azikiwe jumped to his feet and yanked his sword free. Kossi warriors rushed from the woods on the other side the clearing, their white robes and turbans in contrast to the Mawena dark disguises. The Mawena charged as well, Chimela well in front of the others, his massive sword gripped with both hands. He slammed into the Kossi vanguard, scattering them with one massive swing and decapitating a hapless warrior in front of him while slicing another man's arm off with the same stroke. Azikiwe and the others fell in beside him and the struggle began in the downpour. As he fought with all his strength he realized his dream was at an end. The Kossi had discovered his plan; how, he did not know. At least he would die fighting and be spared the humiliation of his father's admonishment.

The Kossi pulled back. Azikiwe and the others gave chase, led by the unstoppable Chimela. The massive warrior turned the tide of battle single-handedly, his speed and fury unmatched by the Kossi mass. Azikiwe found a reason for hope. Maybe they would not march on Povo, but they just might survive this attack and make their way back to Baba-Ile. Strength flooded his legs as he chased the remaining Kossi back into the woods. He was about to let out a victory cry when the Kossi archers emerged from the brush.

The Mawena halted. Chimela turned to Azikiwe, his eyes sorrowful.

"Go back, Azikiwe. The ancestors are not with us today."

He turned and charged the archers, his men following in silent determination. Azikiwe sprinted to the other side of the clearing surrounded by his Atuegbu. He stopped at the woods' edge and turned back.

"Oba, we must go now before they catch us!" one of his guards urged.

Azikiwe glared at the man. Chimela and his men were close when the archers let loose their first volley. Half of the men went down, Chimela taking an arrow in the shoulder. He broke the shaft with his free hand and continued charging, swinging his sword over his head. The second volley fell more men but the Mawena continued their assault. Chimela broke another arrow from his chest. He slowed but he continued forward, curses flying like spittle from his mouth. The Kossi archers fumbled with their arrows as huge bleeding Chimela ran down upon them. They broke and ran, throwing their bows into the mud and fleeing into the trees. Chimela was alone, charging forward, yelling and waving his sword. The Kossi warriors reappeared like hyena pouncing on a wounded prey. Like a cornered lion Chimela fought, slashing and hacking the growing number of Kossi warriors. The objective was no longer to defeat the Mawena; it was to kill this unrelenting warrior decimating their ranks.

The Kossi surged again and Chimela went down under a torrent of blades. Azikiwe had seen enough; he would tell the story of his friend's final stand, holding him up to the highest honor.

"We can go now," he said. He turned away just as a volley of Kossi arrows fell upon them. A sharp pain pierced his back and Azikiwe fell to his knees. The wound took whatever energy remaining in him. He slumped to his knees, easing himself down into the wet underbrush. There was no use fighting any longer. He hoped the ancestors would be kinder to him that he was to them. He placed his face against the wet grass, closed his eyes and let the darkness take him.

* * *

Azikiwe awoke in darkness, a damp stench heavy in the stale air. The pain in his back had diminished to a dull throb. He lay still, waiting for his eyes to adjust to the darkness but they refused. He realized he was no longer outside; he was inside some chamber that blocked the light.

He tried to rise but was too weak. How long had he been in this room? Where was he? The realization that he had been captured made him weaker. He had failed to conquer Povo and he had failed to escape. The best that could happen to him was that he would die in this darkness, saving himself and his father the disgrace.

That grim hope was taken away with the rattling of metal and squealing hinges. A door appeared; dim light creeping into the room. A Kossi warrior stepped into the chamber followed by two men dressed in grey tunics and black shorts. They held short metal studded clubs in their hands as they advanced toward him.

"Is this the one?" the warrior asked.

One of the grey men nodded his bald head. The men rushed forward, pinning Azikiwe to the rotted straw. The warrior bent over him and reached into his shirt, extracting the amber necklace."

"It's him. Bring him."

The grey men lifted him to his feet and carried him out of the chamber. The dim light hurt his eyes, so he kept them closed as they took him to another chamber and stripped of his clothes. Azikiwe yelled as they dropped him into a tub of hot water and scrubbed him with coarse brushes, shocking him out of his melancholy.

The grey men raised him from the tub and dried him with soft towels. The warrior stepped forward and bowed, extending a bundle of clothes to him.

"Oba Azikiwe, Askia Diallo wishes you to join him at the palace as soon as you are able. He sends these garments with his apologies."

The robes were Mawena constructed with the finest cotton cloth and trimmed in royal kente. Azikiwe dressed as the trio watched, his mind working furiously to figure out what was happening. Once he was dressed the Kossi warrior smiled and bowed again.

"Please follow me," he requested.

Azikiwe trailed the warrior through the plain building and out into the brilliant sunlight. He stopped, shielding his eyes from the intense brightness. The light dimmed quickly; he turned to his right to see another man standing beside him holding an elaborate royal umbrella over him. The large man was dressed only in a loincloth with an iron slave band encircling his right bicep. The man was Mawena, one of the many captured by Kossi slave raiders. He did not recognize Azikiwe, but he turned away in respect.

He was in Povo. The smell of the sea burned his nostrils, the sharp blue sky dotted with high white clouds and seagulls. White washed stone homes with blue roofs lined the broad paved avenues leading the royal wall protecting the Askia's palace. Kossi crowded the streets, moving with their characteristic saunter, no one in any hurry to reach their destination. Their sing song dialect was pleasant to the ears, making the city seem like a continuous celebration to his unfamiliar ears. No one seemed to notice him; Azikiwe assumed they saw him as just another noble visiting the Askia. Only the warrior and the prison guards seem to know his true identity outside the palace.

He followed the warrior to the wall gates. The gate entrance was a towering door of metal inlaid with golden threads that wove abstract images of the Askias past and their military triumphs. Mawena images were just as numerous as Kossi, although his people were almost always shown in chains or in poses of death. Two warriors holding tall assegais flanked the gate. They bowed and stepped away as the gate was raised.

Azikiwe hesitated. He was being set up, but for what he did not know. His escort stood beside him.

"Please continue, Oba. The Askia is waiting."

Azikiwe entered the palace compound of Askia Diallo. The wealth of the Kossi was immediately evident everywhere he looked. The common tabby stone of the highway was replaced by elaborate mosaic tile of blue and white which led to the gilded palace gate. Towering bleached white walls punctuated with narrow towers at each corner enclosed the palace. The palace gate stood as high as the wall, thick planks of wood bolted together by wide straps of iron and inlaid with gold and cowry shells. A golden octopus filled the center of the gate, the clan totem of Kossi's royal family. The broad building wore a dome blue as the sea. Although their kingdom extended deep into the interior, the Kossi were and would always be a people of the sea.

Askia Diallo sat on a gilded throne before the entrance of his palace, flanked by the Kossi elders and backed by his personal guard. He was dressed simply in the traditional Kossi white pants and robe, a simple golden ring with milky white pearls encircling his head. His dark brown complexion reminded Azikiwe of Isala. He seemed young, but there was hardness in his smile that betrayed his age.

Askia Diallo rose as Azikiwe approached and bowed. The others did the same, remaining in the submissive pose until the Mawena sat on the cushioned stool before Diallo's throne. Diallo sat and smiled.

"I am honored. I apologize for your terrible treatment. My men did not know you."

A dull pain appeared in Azikiwe's stomach. "How did you find out who I was? How did you discover our plans?"

Diallo's face became sad. "I must apologize again. We are a proud people, but not as numerous or brave as you Mawena. We must fight our wars in different ways which require our people to make personal sacrifices for the good of us all. Isala is one of those people. She is one of our best."

Nausea swept over him and he swayed, weak from the word of his betrayal. She had marked him with the amber necklace, so they would be sure to find him.

"She said she loved me," he stammered.

"I'm sure she does," Diallo replied. "You are a handsome man and you offer much to a woman of her status. But that is the beauty of Isala. She does her duty for her Askia despite her feelings. She is a true treasure."

Diallo leaned forward and placed his hand on Azikiwe's shoulder.

"I did not bring you here to embarrass you, my friend. Your plan was brilliant and would have succeeded if not for Isala. Your men fought valiantly, especially your friend Chimela. He will always be remembered by my warriors with great respect. Many sons in Kossiland will bear his name."

Diallo leaned back into his throne, his face distraught. "I am troubled, Azikiwe. I see before me a brave man, a hero of Mawena who deserves to be respected by his people and more importantly, honored by his father."

"Do not speak of him," Azikiwe spat.

"We must," Diallo replied. "Your father is the scourge of us both. It is said that a common enemy forges unlikely friendships."

Azikiwe resisted Diallo's logic. "My father is not my enemy."

"He is certainly not your friend. He banished you to the outskirts of his kingdom and forced you to take a terrible risk to regain his favor. Word of your defeat had surely reached Abo, yet no delegation has come to ransom your freedom. He has left you here to die, Azikiwe. Your fate is in my hands."

"Then be done with it," Azikiwe retorted. "My skull is ready to take its place in your collection."

"I have no intentions of executing you. I see us both as victims, Azikiwe, victims of the rivalries of our fathers. But my father is dead and yours has disowned you. This is our opportunity to end the fighting between our people and come together for the prosperity of us all."

Azikiwe's head began to throb. "What are you asking me?"

"I wish to see peace between the Kossi and the Mawena. With your father in power that is not possible."

Azikiwe fought to stay upright in his stool. "Forgive my inattention, Askia. It has been days since I've eaten, I think."

"I understand. We will talk again after you have had time to rest."

Diallo signaled his bodyguards and they came forward. Azikiwe's escort helped him to his feet and led him to a small house beside the palace. He stepped through the wooden door and was relieved. A small bed rested against the wall; beside it was a table covered with fruit and a simmering pot of stew. He stumbled to the table and attacked the stew, almost spilling it as he devoured it. With his stomach settled and his headache gone he collapsed onto the bed and fell into a dreamless sleep. He had no idea how long he slept when a woman's voice stirred him awake.

"My Oba?"

Azikiwe sat up to see Isala at the foot of his bed. She rushed him before he could speak, kissing him and pushing him back onto the bed. He wanted to hate her, but his body responded hungrily to her touch. He held her tight in his arms, kissing her everywhere. Her love for him was a lie, as was everything Diallo said to him, but he didn't care. The lie in Povo was better that the truth waiting for him in Abo. Diallo was true about one thing; for him to be his own man, he had to rid himself of his father.

When they were done Isala tried to lie beside him, but he pushed her away. She seemed shocked, her eyes wide and glistening.

"What is wrong?" she asked. "Have I offended you?"

Azikiwe rose from the bed and dressed.

"I need you to take a message to Diallo," he said. Pain and confusion had fled his mind, leaving him free to make a clear decision unfettered by the opinion of his father and his people.

"Tell the Askia I wished to meet with him," he continued. "Not as Kossi and Mawena, but as brothers."

8

Dingane and Inaamdura sat side by side under the solitary baobab dominating the Royal Courtyard. A messenger knelt before them, resplendent in his white robe and cap, the royal insignia of Shamfa dangling from his neck on a thick gold chain. He extended his arms, handing a message scroll to the inkosi. Dingane, covered in brushed cowtails from neck to ankles, sneered at the messenger and looked to his wife. Inaamdura took the scroll from the Shamfa messenger's trembling hands and nimbly untied the cords binding in together. She took her time, unraveling the leather strips with a delicacy they did not deserve. She was splendid as always, her head shaven and adorned with a simple golden cord. She'd shed her admiration beads the day she wed Dingane, replacing them with a single necklace of amber and gold. She still wore her Bongo robes, refusing to adopt the drab cloaks of married Sesu women. She did succumb to their intricate beadwork, wearing a belt of white and red beads; a clear symbol of her supreme status among Dingane's other wives.

She hesitated to unravel the scroll. She knew what it contained; it was a message as inevitable as the coming and going of the rains. It had come sooner than expected, which meant her plans were more transparent than she hoped. Still, the wheel was in motion. No one could stop it now.

Inaamdura unrolled the scroll and handed it back to the messenger.

"Read it," she commanded.

"Inkosa, I thought..."

Inaamdura's smile calmed the worried herald. "Of course, I can read. I would prefer you to read it, my brother. It has been a long time since I heard the words of my homeland spoken by someone other than myself."

The messenger bowed and opened the scroll.

"My dearest daughter," he read. "It has been five dry seasons since you left us, and my heart still aches when I visit my garden. The days are colder without your company and council. It is time you visited your mother. We have much to discuss."

Dingane shrugged his shoulders. "Is that all? That was a waste of good paper. The damn messenger could have memorized it."

"Please, Dingane. This is a letter from my mother. She deserves your respect."

Dingane laughed. "She is not my wife or my mother. She deserves nothing from me."

He lifted his bulk and left. Inaamdura watched him, admiring his firm form. She had been right when she advised her mother on the Sesu Inkosi years ago. Her sister could not have controlled this man. But she was also wrong that day as well. Inaamdura, her mother's greatest pupil, could not control him, either.

She took the scroll and read it silently. The words forming in her head were different from the words the messenger read. It was the hidden meaning behind the obvious, the true intent of the message far from innocuous.

"I know what you are up to," the words said to Inaamdura. "Meet me immediately if you wish to avoid a war."

She rolled the scroll and handed it back to the messenger.

"Thank you for your loyalty to my father and mother. I will give you a message for them and I pray for your safe return.

"When shall I return with your reply, Great Mother?"

"The rainy season will be over soon," Inaamdura mused. "I insist you wait as our guest until then."

The messenger didn't try to hide his disappointment.

"Inkosa, the journey from Shamfa was long and dangerous. It's been months since I've seen my family. If it is not too much to ask, I wish to leave as soon as possible. I have performed my duty. I wish only to return home."

Inaamdura kept her smile despite the anger seething beneath her flawless brown skin. This fool was probably some noble's son, someone who thought his rank gave him the privilege to speak to her in such a way.

"I am aware of your discomfort, but my decision is final. You will remain with us until the dry season, and then you will accompany us to Shamfa. You can, of course, disregard my command and leave on your own accord. I must warn you that although the Sesu are not well versed in Shamfa protocol, they know an insult when they see it. You may not survive the trip home."

The messenger's eyes narrowed. "I am a messenger! My position grants me immunity."

Inaamdura frowned, allowing her true emotions to the surface. "This is not Shamfa. This is Sesuland."

Her guards grasped the messenger under his arms, lifted him from the ground and carried him from the courtyard. Inaamdura remained composed until he disappeared then slumped into the soft kapok cushions of her throne. The messenger was right; he did have immunity. Among the cities of the north protocol was important, a necessity that always allowed an opportunity for rival kingdoms to converse in times of peace and war. But she was also right when she stated the obvious. The Sesu had no need of protocol. Dingane once told her that negotiations are for the weak. The strong made demands and the weak acquiesced. Sesu way had seeped into her pores, molding her way of thinking and way of living. Though she exerted great influence over the inkosi, she did not control him. He remained his own man, listening to her council but not always following her advice. Every decision she made had to be confirmed by him. He made it obvious to her; she was his Great Wife, but she was not his equal.

Still, she could bask in her accomplishments. Under her guidance the Sesu had transformed from a powerful clan depended on plundering their weaker neighbors to a kingdom that controlled the ebb and flow of life in the grasslands. The constant raids acquiring tribute had been replaced by a series of fortified towns positioned strategically near major trade routes to collect tariffs for safe passage. The accumulated wealth allowed Dingane to form a standing army, one that was well fed, well-armed and well trained. A farming class developed, focusing its energy on the rich soil along the Kojo. Selike became a permanent city, grass huts replaced by wood and stone homes, weak thorn fences transforming into stone enclosures holding each clans' cattle.

Sesuland's prosperity sparked the message from her mother. There was no way it would go unnoticed in the north, since most of the merchants taxed by the Sesu were headed to Shamfa. The caravans arriving in the northern reaches carried less goods, driving up the prices of the little they were allowed to keep. The caravans were also less frequent as the southern merchants realized they could seek their fortunes among the Sesu and take advantage of the relative peace Sesu domination had imposed upon the grasslands. Shamfa would not sit by and watch its wealth be siphoned away by a people they considered beneath them.

She went in search of her husband. She recalled the first time she saw Dingane. She was overwhelmed by his vitality and seduced by his presence. He was a man born to lead, a warrior who gained his position by proving his fitness to his people and his ancestors by bringing victory and prosperity long before their marriage. The Sesu were not a people that valued politics; their way was straightforward and brutal. If an induna wished to challenge Dingane's authority he would gather his warriors and attack him. There was never a doubt in Dingane's intentions.

She found him in the Royal Umuzi, standing under the acacia wearing only his loincloth and headring. Inaamdura frowned; the years had not softened her feelings on Sesu attire. Nakedness was tolerated among common folk, but nobles must display their rank.

"So, you will go visit your mother?" he asked.

Inaamdura knelt at his feet. "If you allow it, my husband."

Dingane laughed. "I couldn't stop you if I tried. Your attempt at being a good Sesu wife is admirable, but I know you suffer. Bongo men are weak. They need their women to give them counsel. We Sesu are a different breed."

"You are, indeed."

Dingane studied her face then smiled. "I don't think you meant that as a compliment. Of course, you can visit your mother. It has been a long time since you've seen your family."

"She expects gifts," Inaamdura warned.

"And she shall have them," her husband replied. "Take what you think will make her happy."

Inaamdura looked up at her husband in wonder. Was he agreeing with her? She expected an argument or at least a lively exchange. Her eyes focused on him, studying his expressions, his body movements, his breathing, all the signs a Bongo wife was taught to understand the mood of her husband as so to manipulate him. She jumped as she realized what Dingane was doing.

"You know, don't you?" she said.

Dingane smiled. "I can't read that mountain scribble, but the words spoken by your messenger carried many meanings. Go to your mother with her tribute. But let her know it is only a gift from a daughter to a mother, not a tribute from the Sesu to the Shamfa."

"She won't accept anything but tribute. We are strong, Dingane, but we are not ready for war with Shamfa. The tribes we defeated in the grasslands are ants compared to the northern nations. They will not balk at the sight of your warriors. They are well-armed, and their walls are made of stone, not branches. If we don't offer tribute their armies will come the moment the rainy season ends."

"Walls are only as strong as their weakest gate," Dingane answered. "As I said, take you mother her gifts. You decide what you will need. I will organize your escort."

"My escort?"

"Of course," Dingane said smiling. "You are my Great Wife. I cannot let you go into the wilderness with such a treasure alone."

Inaamdura felt coldness in her throat. "It is not necessary, my husband. Who would dare threaten the wife of Inkosi Dingane?"

In a sudden motion he lifted her off her feet, cradling her in his massive arms like a child. "Come inkosa, let us talk of other things. His fierce kiss doused her protest and she wrapped her arms around his shoulders. As he carried her to their bedchamber she realized she would never control this man. She never wanted to.

Small hands played with Inaamdura's face, dragging her from pleasant slumber to muted daylight. She grabbed the culprit's little wrists and lifted him above her as she opened her eyes. Ligongo stared down at her, a clever smile on his face.

"What are you up to, little zebra?" Ligongo squirmed but Inaamdura's grip was sure.

"You're not as strong as your baba, at least not yet." He squealed when she dropped him, catching him before he hit her chest then holding him tight. Four years ago, the ancestors had finally given her a child. A boy, a true blessing compared to the abomination born to Shani twelve years before. Though she loved her son, she knew he was not the boy Dingane hoped for. There was no trace of Sesu in his face. He resembled her father, the thin cheeks and narrow nose a clear sign of Shamfa blood. Some whispered that he was not Dingane's son, but the child of some long-lost love from her past, some noble who had managed to slip into the royal umuzi and sleep with her, leaving his seed to be raised as the son of Dingane, much like the cuckoo leaves its egg in the nests of others. The words attacked her virtue, but she ignored them. Ligongo was her pride; she loved him as she loved Bikita, unrestrained and uninhibited.

"Momma, are we going on a trip?" he asked.

"Yes, we are. We are going to see your grandmama."

Ligongo looked puzzled.

"Your grandmama is my mother. She is a great queen."

"Is she a greater queen than you?"

Inaamdura laughed as she played with his hair. "Much greater. Come now, we must get ready for our journey."

"I'm ready!" he proclaimed, throwing his arms into the air.

"Not quite, little zebra. Let's go to your room and find you some decent garments."

Ligongo broke free and ran ahead. Inaamdura watched him go, fighting the fear that crept into her heart. In Shamfa he would be celebrated; gifts piled at the foot of his cradle, hordes of people lined outside the inner walls to catch a glimpse of their new prince. In Sesuland a shadow loomed over him, an obstruction named Ndoro. By Sesu law Ndoro's ascension to the stool was impossible due to the shunning imposed on him by Mulugo. The ancestors seemed to have ignored their own curse, for Ndoro was growing up to be more than anyone could have imagined. At sixteen he was an accomplished warrior, tall and broad of shoulder with agility none could match. People still told the story of Shange's honor, whispering among themselves that maybe Mulugo was wrong. Ndoro was Dingane's son in every way; the elders must surely see the obvious.

Such talk had not bothered Inaamdura until Ligongo was born. He deserved to be Dingane's heir. Everything the Sesu had become was because of her tireless work. She would not let the son of a disgraced wife claim what her son deserved. Mulugo had done a fair job keeping Ndoro down, but his influence was wavering. Dingane was noticing the boy more of late, giving him long glances and an occasional smile when he thought no one looked. Inaamdura always looked and she always saw.

Ligongo broke her trance, pulling on her hem.

"Look, mamma. I'm ready to go!"

Inaamdura looked at her boy and tried to keep a smile on her face. Ligongo was dressed in Sesu regalia, a leopard headring round his head, a necklace of brushed cowtails cascading over his chest and back. Another ring of cowtails encircled his waist, the ends brushing the tops of more cowtails around his ankles. He held a white shield in his left hand, a small assegai in his right. Dingane's youngest wife, Ntozake stood behind him, a smug smile on her face.

"You look wonderful," she said. "Now go outside and wait for me. I must speak to Ntozake. Ligongo skipped out into the courtyard, jabbing his assegai at imaginary opponents.

Inaamdura waited until her son was at the opposite side of the courtyard before slapping Ntozake, knocking her to the ground. She dropped her knee into the young wife's stomach and grabbed her hair, pushing her head into the ground.

"Who do you think you are?" Inaamdura hissed. "You wish to play games with my son?"

Ntozake tried to answer but Inaamdura slapped her again.

"I am tired of you Sesu and your damned insults. You can attack me, but you will not use my son against me."

Inaamdura pushed Ntozake's head into the floor as she stood. "If I killed you today Dingane wouldn't care. If you wish to live long enough to bear him sons, you will do well not to cross me."

Inaamdura stormed from the room full of anger and shock. What had she done? Whatever possessed her rushed through her like a wildfire. Ligongo's innocent face triggered her rage, the boy oblivious to the insult his outfit represented to her. This emotion was new to her; she would have to learn to recognize it and control it. Control was essential for a Bongo wife. If she could not harness her emotions she stood no chance controlling the emotions of others. She repeated the incident over and over in her mind as she went to the stables, analyzing and memorizing each moment for signs of weakness.

Her porters waited, wagons filled with precious objects and provisions for the journey. The wagons were hitched to a team of oxen, a driver assigned to each one. Ramosa, a small man with a muscular build and a speckled beard approached, falling to his knees and touching his head to the ground.

"Inkosa Inaamdura, we are ready," he announced.

"Good, Ramosa. Where is my escort?"

"I do not know inkosa."

"Didn't the inkosi send them?"

"I have seen no one, inkosa."

Inaamdura sighed. "I will not wait for them. Prepare my wagon. I will fetch Ligongo."

Inaamdura found Ligongo chasing his younger brothers with his shield and spear. She grabbed him and dragged him away, her patience growing shorter and shorter as her departure neared. Dingane's escort had not arrived when she returned. She pushed Ligongo into the wagon then signaled Ramosa.

"We leave now," she shouted.

Ramosa's worried face angered her more.

"Inkosa, we must wait for the escort."

"Ramosa, get these wagons moving now!"

Warrior chants spilled into the stable yard. The escort arrived, fifty warriors dressed like Ligongo, their cowtails bouncing as they ran to surround the escort. Induna Kotsi approached her wagon, bowing with exaggerated motions.

"Inkosa, I apologize our tardiness. Inkosi Dingane insisted we visit Mulugo for his blessings before we came. We wished the ancestors' sanction for this special journey."

Inaamdura scrutinized the escort and was disappointed. They were Dingane's best, she was sure, but there were so few of them. Her mother would not be impressed.

"Is this all?"

Kotsi bowed again. "I am sorry, inkosi. Mulugo is slow. The others will catch up to us later."

Inaamdura looked at the man, letting her rage trickle away. She was weary of reacting to every situation without thought. A fly landed on Kotsi's head and she focused on it, watching the insect attempt to burrow into his dense hair. The fly wandered to his head ring, crawling and buzzing around the warrior's dome. The humor drenched her rage; she now stood before him trying not to laugh.

"You are here now, Kotsi," she said with a grim. "There is no need to discuss your lateness. Take your place. We leave now."

Inaamdura climbed into her wagon. Ligongo slept, his lean body stretched across two pillows at the head of the wagon. Inaamdura went to the rear, reclining on rugs of leopard and lion, an ivory head rest covered with a navy silk pillow placed at the edge of the rugs. She laid her throbbing head onto the headrest and the tension of the day seeped away. Ramosa cracked his whip and the wagon lurched. They were on their way, the oxen keeping time with the cadence chant of the escort. Inaamdura closed her eyes and let the intonation and rocking coax her to sleep.

She chose to meet her mother close to Nontuluzelo, the lush valley that served as a boundary between Shamfa and Sesuland. It was once the home of the Shamfa before frequent Sesu raids pushed them north into the foothills of the Urowo Mountains, homeland of the Bonga. The Sesu chose not to settle the area because of its lack of good grazing but attacked the Shamfa whenever they attempted to reclaim it. Eventually both tribes abandoned the valley, accepting it as an unofficial buffer zone. The journey would take ten days, too long a time for Inaamdura to worry herself over meeting with her mother. Instead she immersed herself in the amusement of Ligongo, playing countless games of oware and naming the endless procession of animals they saw along the way. The warriors insisted on taking the prince with them on their daily hunts, but Inaamdura only permitted him to go every other day. He needed to develop a kinship with the men he would one day lead, but he also needed to keep a respectful distance. This was her advantage over Ndoro and his mother. They could admire the ostracized boy, but they would never bond to him like they would Ligongo. She would see to that.

One night away from the rendezvous Inaamdura awoke to darkness. The day had long passed, the sky sparkling with dry season constellations, the full moon casting a strong light across the fields. She climbed out of the wagon, pulling her cloak close as a chilly wind swirled about her. She smiled as the familiar breath from the distant mountains danced about the camp, teasing the withering fires and agitating the smoldering embers of earlier flames gone dead. The air was sweet, tinged with the moisture of the nearby river and seasoned with the musky fragrance of constantly blooming shrubs. The image of her mother's garden appeared in her thoughts and the wind suddenly became cold, shaking her limbs and raising bumps on her soft skin. She pulled her cloak tighter, protecting herself from the fear that drifted on the wind and touched her soul. Was this some sort of spell? Was her mother making sure she would not be ready to face her? Inaamdura turned to run back into her wagon when she saw the silhouette of a warrior against the horizon, a chagga pipe dangling from his lips as he leaned on his assegai. His shield lay at his feet, serving as a makeshift bed while on the march. He displayed no fear, though he was miles away from home near the land of his enemy. He was a Sesu; no man could defeat him. Death could only claim him if he allowed. She calmed, the wind's frigid grip subsiding. She looked at the warrior a moment longer before retiring to her wagon, her mind clear.

Morning had long passed when the Shamfa party came into view. It was a grand spectacle, an arrival designed to impress and awe. Inaamdura stood before her tribute wagon, a smirk marring her perfect countenance. The Imperial Wagon lumbered forward, pulled by ten oxen and guided by five drivers. Two hundred Shamfa cavalrymen flanked the wagon, covered in yellow kapok quilts, red cylindrical caps rising high from their heads. Each rider carried a lance flying the yellow banner of the royal family. Their mounts were covered as well in yellow kapok quilts with red piping. Drummers played, and dancers performed, singing a song that Inaamdura knew by heart but for some reason struck her as unfamiliar.

Lingongo clapped to the rhythm, a joyous smile on his face.

"You were right, mama," he squealed. "Grandma is a greater queen than you!"

Inaamdura ignored the naïve enthusiasm of her son. Kotsi, standing on her right, was not as forgiving.

"It is a dance of fools," he said. "Only the weak would be impressed. A man still bleeds when he is stabbed by an assegai, no matter how pretty his clothes."

"Whenever you are ready," Inaamdura said to Kotsi.

Kotsi barked and a young warrior ran forward, a throwing spear gripped in his hand. The induna nodded, and the man took a running start then let the spear fly. It soared in a perfect arc, landing over a hundred paces from where they stood.

The Shamfa stopped. One of the riders dismounted, pulling a spear from his quiver. He ran and threw as well, his spear landing a good fifteen paces away.

"It will be a long walk, inkosi," Kotsi commented. "You should ride on the wagon."

"I'll walk," Inaamdura replied. She grasped the nose ring of the ox harnessed to the tribute wagon and led him away, her firm grip quickly subduing the protests of the beast. She watched as the door opened to the Imperial Wagon and her mother emerged. From a distance she looked the same, but Inaamdura had readied herself for the changes time may have visited on her. Another woman emerged from the wagon and stood beside her mother. She was too tall to be Amadika; it was possible her mother had acquired a servant. The duo came forward alone, walking with the graceful dignity of Bonga women. Halfway across the field the woman with her mother broke away and ran towards her, her arms outstretched.

"Rah-rah!" she shouted.

"Bikita?" Inaamdura focused on the woman's face as he came closer. It was her; the woman running to her was Bikita. She succumbed to a rush of joy, releasing the ox and running to her little sister. They hugged, Inaamdura comforted by the willowy arms of her sister.

"I missed you so much," Bikita confessed. "I wanted to visit, but mama said it wouldn't be proper."

Inaamdura forced her arms to let go of Bikita, her hands sliding down into her sister's.

"You have been to the garden, I see."

Bikita's face became solemn. "Yes I have."

Inaamdura nodded in understanding. Her little sister was gone, her innocence lost once she ventured beyond the wooden gate of Azana's garden.

"She's headstrong just like you," Azana said. Inaamdura had not noticed her mother's approach. She looked older but still beautiful, the lines on her face adding wisdom to her presence. Inaamdura knelt at her mother's feet.

"Forgive me if my time with Bikita poisoned her with my bad habits."

Azana touched her shoulder, giving her permission to rise. "Bikita was destined to behave the way she does. You have no fault here."

Inaamdura stepped aside, displaying the wagon. "I can never hope to repay you for all you have given me, mama. I hope you accept my offering in the spirit in which it is given."

Azana glanced at the wagon and stared at Inaamdura. "My love knows no price, daughter. It is given freely. The Shamfa, however, require something more."

Inaamdura pushed the emotions stirred by Bikita's presence aside. Her mother was ready to talk. There would be no more indirect banter.

"Inkosi Dingane respects my wish to honor my mother. He does not understand why he should send tribute to the Shamfa."

"The Shamfa have allowed the Sesu to establish themselves as protectors of the trade routes leading north," Azana replied. "This has caused some discomfort among our people which can be reconciled by the proper tribute for our generosity."

"Sesu warriors subdued the tribes of the grasslands," Inaamdura said. "Sesu servants built the roads that cross the grasslands. Sesu elders administer the peace impartially, allowing the trade north to prosper more than anyone has seen. We see no Shamfa hand in this."

Azana's eyebrows rose when Inaamdura used the term "we". She came at Inaamdura quickly, stopping so close their noses almost met.

"Is this the best you could accomplish?" she asked. "Your husband careens around the grasslands like a drunken child, claiming to be the master of it all. I knew Amadika would fail as soon as I saw him, but I thought you had a chance. No, I knew you could do it. Instead you stand before me insulting me with this nonsense of Sesu control."

"You underestimated them," Inaamdura argued. "You did then, and you do now. My council has played a part in this, but Dingane is more than just an ambitious barbarian. He leads a people that believe the world belongs to them and they will not stop until they claim it all. They don't bog themselves down with the intrigues of politics. Their actions are simple, direct and effective."

Azana seemed to listen to Inaamdura's words. She stood silent, her face emotionless. It was Bikita that warned her something was wrong. Her younger sister's expression was one of puzzlement and fear. The inkosa turned to see Kotsi running towards her, shield and assegai in his hands.

Go back, she said silently. *Go back or the Shamfa riders will attack!*

"Inkosa! Inkosa!" he shouted. "Your escort has arrived!"

Bikita was terrified. "Rah-rah, what is he talking about? What is happening?"

Inaamdura couldn't answer. She could hear the chanting, the beating of thousands of assegais against thousands of shields, the thumping of countless of feet against the ground. The Sesu warriors emerged from the horizon running full speed toward the inkosa and her family. Inaamdura feigned shock, but she knew something was about to happen. Her surprise came from the number of warriors Dingane sent and how quickly they covered the distance. Dingane had planned this march the moment Inaamdura received the Shamfa messenger, she was sure. He had no intentions of offering any tributes to the Bonga. War with the Shamfa was inevitable.

Bikita staggered away, her hand over her mouth.

"Come to me, Kita," Inaamdura urged. "They will not harm you if you are close to me."

Bikita's terror could not overcome her fear.

Inaamdura looked to her mother for help and found an expression no child should see. Her eyes seethed with hatred, her teeth bared like a cornered wolf.

"This is your doing!" she hissed. "You have violated every rule I taught you. You have taken all that I gave you and smashed it into the mud."

Inaamdura ignored her mother's insult. Her attention was focused on the Shamfa cavalry. They charged not to confront the approaching Sesu horde but to protect Azana and Bikita. The Sesu wave surged past the women, surrounding the horsemen and bringing them down under a barrage of assegais and orinkas. Moments later the slayers danced among the dead, draped in blood stained kapok armor.

Azana's rant penetrated her trance. She looked at her mother, a solemn smile on her face.

"You have betrayed your family, your honor and your heritage! You've done it for this...this horde!"

Inaamdura reached out to her little sister and pulled her close, burying her head into her shoulder to comfort her. Her words for her mother were far from kind.

"Look at them, mother. This is the future. This is the Shamfa's future. They are no more than the Shamfa and no less. Shamfaland will be ours."

A group of warriors approached, leading the royal wagon. Inaamdura flinched as she recognized Ndoro, his bloody assegai dangling from his hand, his shield blocking his left side. His grim face contrasted with the warriors surrounding him, each one smiling with pride, their eyes on the ostracized son of Dingane. He was their leader, not by title but by deeds. She felt a nudge at her hip and looked down to see Ligongo, his young face locked in admiration of his courageous half-brother.

Ndoro and the warriors dropped at her feet. "Great Mother, what do you wish?"

Though his words were respectful, Inaamdura felt the scorn in his voice. Her tone was no less threatening.

"I have no use for you," she replied. "Take your place among the warriors."

Ndoro turned away and led his warriors back to the ranks.

"Kotsi!" she yelled. The induna came to her side.

"Escort my mother and sister back to Shamfa. Take them close enough to the walls to be seen, but don't endanger the lives of your men."

She turned to Ndoro.

"Your ibuthu will escort me back to Selike."

Ndoro's eyes narrowed. "As you wish, Great Mother."

It was a petty gesture, but it made her feel better. She could not stop all Ndoro's efforts to raise his status among the warriors, but she would at least squelch this legend unraveling before her eyes.

Bikita clutched her tighter. "I want to stay with you, Rah."

Inaamdura's hardness melted away. She patted her sister's head and pressed her lips close to her ear.

"You must go with mama," she whispered. "She has lost me; she wouldn't be able to go on if she loses you. She needs you more than you know."

Bikita pulled away, her glistening eyes bewildered. Inaamdura smiled as her heart broke to pieces.

"Go, Kita. Take mama back to Shamfaland."

Bikita walked to Azana, placing her hands on her mother's wet cheeks. Inaamdura watched her gestures and smiled. She learned that from me, she thought. I taught her to be kind.

"Come, mama," Bikita whispered. "It's time to go home."

Azana looked up at Inaamdura. Age had conquered her face in those brief moments. Her face seems drawn, like all the energy had seeped away into the grass. Inaamdura realized the words she spoke to Bikita were true. Her mother's spirit was broken. She saw it in her tired eyes.

"You have killed me," she whispered. "You have stabbed my soul."

Inaamdura took her mother's cheeks between her hands and kissed her.

"I am what you made me, momma. Farewell."

Bikita guided her mother to the wagon and helped her inside. She climbed in behind her, stopping to take one last look at Inaamdura then disappeared.

Kotsi took control of the oxen, guiding them around and leading them away, his ibuthu chanting as they headed for Shamfaland. Inaamdura watched until they disappeared into undulating horizon. It was done; she was free. She gave Ndoro the order and the Sesu party set a brisk pace across the grasses to their home, no, her home. She was no longer Shamfa. From this day on she was Sesu. She was the Great Wife of Dingane and her son, not Ndoro, would be his heir. She would make sure of it.

9

Ndoro placed the antelope carcass downwind of the pride, careful that he was not seen. He smeared himself with the animal's blood to cover his scent and made certain the females were hunting before approaching the ancient baobab tree under which the males and young ones rested. They were all there. The three young males, their manes barely visible from his distance, cavorted under the tangled tree branches. Ndoro was not concerned with them. He watched the old one, the full, dark mane beast languishing near the tree trunk, the other simbas keeping a respectful distance. The pride belonged to him, and he ruled with quiet strength.

Old Simba raised his head, his nostrils flaring as he caught the antelope's scent. He was an opportunist; Ndoro had watched him chase hyenas and jackals from their kills and indulge himself on their hard-earned rewards. He knew Old Simba would come for the kill. He had no doubt in this part of his plan.

Old Simba yawned, stretched, and then came to his paws. Looking at his magnificence, Ndoro began to have second thoughts. This massive beast could break a bull's neck with one bite; one swipe of his paw would break Ndoro's limbs. Maybe there was something else he could do to prove his bravery, some other task that would break the silence between him and Dingane. Ndoro bit his lip until blood came, the anger welling up in his chest as he thought of his father. He was the best, the smartest, the strongest and the fastest of all the young men in his induna. But he was disowned. No bravery he committed thus far dispelled this condition. He and his mother existed in the last hut of the royal umuzi, their lives a pale reflection of that of the Great Wife Inaamdura, a position his mother once held. Ndoro was tired of being an outcast. No longer would he suffer the taunts and insults of the villagers, people less than cattle in his eyes. His suffering would come to an end this day.

Old Simba looked his way. He sauntered to the kill, his stride confident and deliberate. The younger ones attempted to follow; Old Simba turned and roared, swiping at the closest of the three. They roared back feebly then sulked back to the shade. Old Simba turned and continued to follow the scent. Ndoro's hands clenched about his assegai, his chest pounding. His plan was simple. He would take the simba the old way, the way the elders talked about in their stories of the first Sesu. Then he would cut the simba's throat with his knife. He practiced the maneuver on lesser animals, but now as his true target came closer Ndoro was in awe. He did not realize Old Simba was so big. His plan would not work. He wanted to run away in shame, but it was too late. Old Simba was almost upon him.

Old Simba halted before the antelope and tilted its head to the side, his eyes distant. Ndoro stumbled into view and Old Simba's eyes focused on him, a low growl escaping between his bared teeth. Ndoro could not run now even if he wished. He crouched and waited.

Old Simba sprang. Ndoro waited until Old Simba was almost upon him, his mouth wide. Ndoro shoved the mouth spike he gripped in his right hand straight into Old Simba's mouth. The simba's head slammed into Ndoro's chest, knocking the wind from him. He crashed on his back into the grass gasping for breath, sightless with pain, waiting for Old Simba's bite. Moments passed, and nothing happened. When his sight returned he saw Old Simba hovering over him, his mouth locked open by the spike. The simba stood frozen, just as the elders said. Ndoro seized his knife and slashed across the simba's throat. A roar of pain came from its gaped mouth and it swung its paws in reflex, raking its claws across Ndoro's chest and tearing at his flesh. Before he could scream, Old Simba collapsed on him, again knocking him breathless, this time covered in blood.

Ndoro lay trapped under the dead simba, blood oozing over him. Slowly and painfully, he brought his legs up one at a time until he could press the bottom of his calloused feet against the simba's torso. He stopped, his breath heavy, his entire body throbbing in pain. He looked into the sky, the vultures already beginning to circle. The sight fueled his limbs and he pushed the body up and dropped it to the side, his exhausted body turning in the same direction. Old Simba lay on its side, the blood still flowing from his neck, his mouth open in a silent roar. The young males were halfway between the baobab and Ndoro, looking at the warrior with penetrating eyes. Ndoro bent over and jerked the mouth spike from Old Simba's throat. He spun in the direction of the young simbas, crouching low. The young males turned away. This beast had done something they could not do, and they were in no mood to challenge him.

Seeing the simbas retreat, Ndoro set about his next task. He staggered to where he'd hidden the harness and dragged it back to the body. Securing the carcass, he positioned the yoke across his shoulders. The wood bit into his neck, but it was a good pain, a trophy he relished as he did the wounds Old Simba had inflicted on him. There would be no denying him his place any longer.

* * *

The celebration began the night before with the return of the ibuthu. The raid went well, securing many cattle, slaves and the assurance that the Komo would never again be a threat to the Sesu. The southern grasslands were now open to Sesu expansion, giving Dingane a kingdom larger than any inkosi before him. There was a ceremony on the Royal Umuzi ground, with Dingane granting a stork feather to the ibuthu leader and two of his prized white cattle.

Daylight brought the festivity to full scale. The Sesu awoke to the sound of the royal drummers, their jubilant rumbling echoing throughout the city. Dingane did well imitating the grandeur of Abo; his city of Selike was the greatest known to the grasslands. Stone huts, gaily painted, lined the wide avenues of pounded mud. Each road led to the center of the city, terminating at the Royal Umuzi. Here the Sesu inkosi concentrated most of his work, building a palace unlike any other. The main building loomed over the city, constructed of stone carved in the Kijaru Mountains and transported by oxen and slaves to

Sesuland. The palace rested in the center of a wide pasture surrounded by the royal cattle, magnificent white bovines marked with the brand of Dingane family. A road lined with cowry shells and filled with marble brick descended from the palace then merged into the mud-packed wheel circling the Royal Umuzi. Bordering the wheel was the white wall, and within these walls were the homes of Dingane wives. They numbered twelve, from the grand residence of Inaamdura, his Great wife, to the plain brick hut of Shani, the once great wife now fallen from grace.

Drummers stood upon the royal wall, their muscular arms beating a triumphant rhythm. Down the avenues came the celebrants following brightly-dressed dancers. They all sang the same song, a song which had become common in the city, a song of triumph and greatness.

The dancers converged in the royal courtyard, a wide area outside the royal wall where the gilded stools had been placed that morning. Dingane's wives sat in their places of honor, each dressed in the cloth of Dingane clan, the Imbubesi. Flanking Dingane Royal Stool were Inaamdura and Mulugo. The medicine-priest seemed as ageless as ever, a permanent scowl on his face, his frail body wrapped in his own print. He held his staff as always, his herb bag hung loose about his waist. The look on his face made it obvious he was in no mood for celebration; he'd spent all night performing the necessary spells to ward off the spirits of enemy slain by the Sesu in addition to his ever-constant vigil against the evil instigated by the presence of the abomination, Ndoro.

Inaamdura was in a more festive mood. Her precious son Ligongo stood at her side pretending to be as serious as his father. She stroked his head and he turned and smiled, his grin brighter that the sun above drenching them with its heat. The inkosa wore her hair in the style of her people, the Shamfa, long braids tipped with brightly colored beads. She wore the yellow cloth of her people, a symbol of the strength of the alliance between the tribes. She smiled as the dancers approached the courtyard, her ivory smile like a crescent moon against a night sky.

Shani sat on the stool at the end, Jelani standing nearby. Her face was a picture of worry, her eyes searching frantically among the children sitting before them. Where was Ndoro? He left the hut before she woke days ago. She did not know where he had gone, nor did anyone else in the city. Not that anyone cared. There were many who agreed with Mulugo, wishing both she and her son would disappear. Inaamdura only made matters worse. Although Inaamdura had succeeded in pushing Shani to the lowest wife status, she failed in banishing her altogether. Dingane would not go that far. For reasons of his own, Shani remained with the Sesu, which for her and Ndoro was no great favor.

"Jelani," she said. "Where is Ndoro?"

"I don't know," Jelani replied. "I haven't seen him in two days."

"Did he tell you where he was going?"

"No. He seemed preoccupied when we last spoke."

Jelani was cut off by the rumble of the elephant drums. Everyone's attention turned toward the royal palace. The ebony wood doors swung wide and the procession began. First to appear were the indunas, each bearing a staff topped with the symbol of his impi. Behind them came the tribal council, men and women representing the royal families. Each wore the cloth robe, a pure white garment clinched at the waist by a broad beaded belt. Each belt was meticulously crafted in the pattern of each honored family. Those on the council carried staffs as well, but unlike the indunas, the council staffs were made of gold and ivory, a symbol of each family's wealth.

The Blood Men came next. They were Dingane's bodyguard, each a member of the Imbubesi clan. They marched with cold precision, garbed in traditional Sesu warrior clothing, barechested with a leather loincloth wrapped around the waist, a single black stork feather extending from their headbands. In their left hands they carried white shields made from the hides of the royal herd, each shield scribed with symbols to ward off evil spirits and to make them invulnerable in battle. The Blood Men carried no assegais; their weapons were the dagger, the wrist knife and the orinka. They chanted as they ran, their deep voices reverberating like the elephant drums that summoned them. The crowd took up the chant as the litter of Dingane emerged from the palace. He sat cross-legged, his gray head encircled by a bejeweled head ring. Braided cowtails surrounded his neck, a leopard robe draped over his broad shoulders. The excess of rule showed in his form, his once lean face rounded, his paunch clearly visible beneath his clothing. Dingane held a gilded orinka carved with intricate hieroglyphics, each symbol a chronicle of his reign. When the celebration was complete its symbol would be added to the long list of his accomplishments. What had begun as a dream of an ambitious chief had become the reality of a king.

The procession made its way down the hill to the courtyard. The marchers took their places as Dingane's litter was placed between Mulugo and Inaamdura. Dingane nodded to Mulugo, and then turned his full attention to his beautiful wife.

"Unkulunkulu smiles on us," she said. "Once again we celebrate victory."

"Victory is not new to me," Dingane replied. "It is you who are the true prize."

Inaamdura gave Dingane a coy smile.
"I await your attention," she answered.

Fire blazed in Dingane's eyes. Inaamdura was his jewel, the best thing to happen to him since Shani. The thought of his former Great Wife doused his passionate musing and he turned his attention back to the celebration.

The dancers began again, their vigorous movements repeating the victories of the impi. The drummers picked up the pace and soon the entire city danced. Dingane was filled with pride; he'd taken a village and built it into a city on the verge of becoming an empire.

As those before his stool danced, Dingane noticed discordant sounds emanating from further away. Something was happening in the distance. The throng parted, and the din of celebration subsided as that something moved closer, dividing the Sesu like an invisible knife. Without thinking Shani stood, and others of Dingane's entourage did also. Dingane and Inaamdura remained on their stools, stretching their necks as much as they could toward the approaching commotion. The dancers stopped, they too caught in the curiosity of the crowd. The palace drummers played on, too far away to see or hear the strange interruption to the celebration.

The crowd pulled away to the edges of the avenue. Ndoro staggered up the road, wooden yoke on his shoulders, blood running from his arm and splattered on his chest and stomach. Behind him, dragging across the packed mud was the body of Old Simba. Shani jumped to her feet, but Jelani grabbed her arm.

"No, Shani," Jelani advised. "This is his moment."

Shani looked into Jelani's eyes then slowly sat down.

"You can do this, Ndoro," she whispered. "You must."

Ndoro dragged the simba a few more steps then stopped. He dropped the yoke, untied the carcass and knelt before it. He worked his hands under the body and lifted the hind quarters. He ducked his head as lifted the body, his arms quaking. Ndoro eased the simba onto his shoulders. Drawing his legs close, he struggled to push himself erect.

Jelani's grip tightened around his assegai.
"Stand boy! Stand!" he whispered.

Ndoro let out a deep grunt and sprang tall, his legs straight. He wavered, shaking from the effort of lifting such an enormous burden. Strength seeped from his body like the blood from his wounds. But he saw his father and anger fueled his limbs. He steadied and began to walk.

Jelani leaped from the platform with his assegai and shield then ran to the courtyard, halting in plain sight of Ndoro. His face stern, he hit his shield with his spear, again and again, setting a steady pace for the boy.

"Show them your Mawena blood, Ndoro!" he shouted. "Show them a true warrior!"

Others joined in with Jelani, beating against their breasts, stomping their feet, whatever they could do. The same people who had once shunned Ndoro now encouraged him. Even the Blood Men were overwhelmed. They stood in unison, beating their gilded clubs against their shields.

Ndoro's world was silent. His father's face filled his vision, the bewildered countenance growing larger with each step. Flashes of fatigue ripped the image away and replaced it with blackness, but the image always returned. Finally, he could walk no longer. Anger could push the body only so far. Each beat of his heart stabbed him; each breath burned. With his last effort Ndoro lifted the simba's body over his head. The crowd fell silent.

"I . . . am . . . your . . . son!" Ndoro boomed. He dropped the simba at his father's feet. Dingane looked down at the slain beast, then to Ndoro. Inaamdura leaned toward the inkosi with Mulugo, anxious to hear Dingane's response. But before he could speak, Ndoro collapsed.

Shani sprang from her seat then ran to her son, laying over his body as she sobbed. She looked up at his father; Dingane gazed up Shani with a kindness she had not seen in many years.

"Take him to my palace," he said. "Your face is the first he should see when he revives."

Shani smiled brightly. "Thank you, my husband." Jelani and members of the Blood Men lifted Ndoro onto their shoulders and carried him away. A chant began somewhere in the crowd and raced throughout like wildfire. The chant was for Ndoro, and the drummers and dancers joined in. The Sesu continued to sing until Ndoro and his bearers disappeared behind the gates of the Royal Umuzi.

* * *

Inaamdura waited alone beside the trickling stream. She sat on the ground, her legs folded to the side, her hands resting in her lap. In such a pose she resembled a sculpture carved from ebony wood, her features artistic perfection. Her eyes looked westward, toward Shamfaland.

She longed for her mother's council but Azana had separated herself from the world, locked away in her precious garden refusing all visitors. The task of advisor had fallen on Bikita's callow shoulders. Her first act was to establish an alliance between Shamfaland and Sesuland, a decision that split the kingdom. Shamfa and Bonga became enemies, dividing the royal family as well. Amadika fled to Bongaland and married Twaambo. Twaambo then claimed himself ruler of both lands by marriage, which her father quickly denounced. Both sides declared war, but not a sword was unsheathed, nor a spear thrown before the factions fell into a tangle of procedure and protocol. Bikita, overwhelmed by the responsibility, sent word to Inaamdura for help. Her answer came in the form of twenty thousand Sesu warriors who swept through Bongaland like a dry season grass fire. They drove the Bonga out of the foothills and over the mountains into the Barrens. Dingane declared Shamfaland under his protection, annexing the kingdom and doubling the size of his empire in one swift stroke. Muchese became a vassal of the man he once called a savage and Bikita remained his advisor. Azana remained in her garden.

She heard shuffling in the grass and stood. The person approaching took his time, stopping once to curse the darkness and the thorn lodged in his calf. Although she knew who he was, waiting in the darkness made her nervous and wary.

"Mulugo?" she called out.

The medicine priest responded with a grunt as he stepped into the torchlight.

"Are you alone?" she asked.

"I am," Mulugo replied. He sat, laying his staff beside him. "Why have I been summoned here?"

"What I wish to discuss is of the utmost privacy," Inaamdura replied.

Mulugo laughed. "You are full of secrets, Great Wife of Dingane. Which one will you share with me tonight?

Inaamdura ignored Mulugo's disrespect. "I wish to discuss Ndoro."

Mulugo's face turned grim. "I will not speak about it."

"It?"

"Yes, it. The demon you call Ndoro."

Inaamdura was surprised by Mulugo's response. "I see no demon, only a troublesome man-child."

"You see with normal eyes," Mulugo replied. "Ndoro was one of twins, an abomination. His twin was killed according to tradition, but he was spared to satisfy Dingane's lust for a son. Ever since then I have spent my entire life appeasing the ancestors and driving off evil omens summoned by that demon's presence. I have good reason to hate this thing."

Inaamdura smiled. This would be easier than she thought. "I understand. It would be best that Ndoro was driven away."

Mulugo let out a dry cackle. "Ndoro will stay, Great Wife. Even you cannot change that fact."

"Why?" Inaamdura asked.

"Because Dingane loves the thing. Oh yes, he shuns it, never speaks to it or acknowledges it, but he loves it and has ever since it was born."

Mulugo did not tell Inaamdura anything she did not already know, but it was in her own interest to act otherwise.

"If that is true, yesterday's display might overcome Dingane's shunning," she said. "For the sake of the Sesu we must not let this happen."

Mulugo took on a venomous look. "Do not mock me with your false concerns for the Sesu, Great Wife."

"You take your liberties too far, medicine-priest," Inaamdura retorted.

"It was you who asked for this meeting," Mulugo shot back. "I detest Dingane's habit of marrying outside the tribe. There are Sesu women of strong lineage more suited for Great Wife than you or Shani. You care only for yourself and your son, and Ndoro stands in your way. The only thing you and I need to discuss is why you think I should listen to your plan."

Inaamdura grinned. She had underestimated Mulugo. "We both have our reasons to be rid of Ndoro. The servants say the day Ndoro was born was the day Mulugo lost his nyama. They say the longer he lives the weaker you become. That is why you cannot get rid of him. Some even say you see your death in his eyes."

"They are all fools!" he exclaimed. "I have lost nothing! They forget who drives the spirits from their homes and who keeps the ancestors placated. They run to the warrens now, spending their cowries on that fool from the east."

Inaamdura's eyes widened. This was something new.

"What fool?"

"Cacanja," Mulugo spat. "He's a blind man who lives in a hovel spouting nonsense and selling poison."

Inaamdura stood. She needed nothing else from Mulugo.

"We are finished. I will contact you when we need to speak again."

Mulugo struggled to his feet. "Cacanja cannot help you and neither can I. I doubt you'll send for me again."

"We'll see, Mulugo. We will see."

She hurried back to the royal umuzi, changing from her royal clothes to a plain sand colored robe and hood like the desert nomads. There were only a few hours of darkness left and she had to make the best of her time alone. Dingane was amusing himself with one of his younger wives, giving her all the time she needed. The Bonga guards flanking the doorway to her house recognized the disguise and followed, careful to keep a respectful distance but close enough to respond to any threat. The Great Wife was on an adventure; they would follow and obey.

She had no idea where to find this Cacanja. Mulugo mentioned the
warrens so she made her way there. The Warrens was a jumble of makeshift buildings and cluttered streets, a part of the city as unpredictable as its inhabitants, home of those people not nu-

merous enough to petition Dingane for a city compound. Inaamdura wandered about, hoping to find someone who could tell her where to find the sorcerer. To her dismay the streets were empty. She was about to turn back when some force held her in place then guided her down a winding, muddy street. She let herself heed the pull until she stood before a small mud shack embellished with an intricately carved door incongruous to the dilapidated structure. Smoke seeped from gaps at the bottom and sides. Inaamdura turned and peered into the darkness behind her. Her bodyguards were still with her though she sensed their uneasiness. She took a deep breath and knocked on the door.

The door creaked open and blinding smoked billowed out, swallowing her with pungent confusion. A pair of calloused hands grabbed her wrists and pulled her inside, the door slamming shut behind her. Inaamdura rubbed her eyes frantically as her bodyguards pounded the door. Someone laughed before her and dread coursed through her. She had made a mistake.

"No, inkosa, you have made no mistake," Cacanja cackled. "You are where you wished to be."

The sorcerer emerged from the smoke, a tall, thin man with deep brown skin. A wide grin creased his gaunt face as he stared at Inaamdura with white dead eyes. A leather cloak covered with gris-gris hid his body, heavy with the smell of smoke and decay.

Inaamdura did her best to stay composed despite her fear.

"Let my men in," she insisted.

"You need no protection here," Cacanja replied. "You are in the safest place in Selike."

Cacanja shuffled to the iron pot in the center of his home, the source of the enveloping smoke.

"You are just in time," he said. "It is ready."

"Just in time for what?"

Cacanja pulled a pouch from his cloak and opened it. He dipped the pouch into the pot then closed it.

"There are no secrets to me. I see with eyes not of this world."

He extended the pouch to Inaamdura. As she reached for it he pulled it away.

"Consider what you are about to do, inkosa. The spirits will grant your desire, but they demand a price."

"If this will rid me of Ndoro it is worth any price."

Inaamdura took the pouch.

Cacanja returned to his pot. "Take it to the hill overlooking the Royal Herd. Raise it over your head and open it. The wind shall do the rest."

"Is that all?"

Cacanja grinned. "Sleep with Dingane tonight. He should be with you when it happens."

Inaamdura's throat tightened. "What will happen?"

"You shouldn't know. You must be just as surprised."

Inaamdura nodded. It was sound advice. "What do I owe you?"

Cacanja looked away. "You have already paid a great price."

The door swung open and her bodyguards tumbled inside. They made their way to Cacanja, assegais lowered. Inaamdura stopped them.

"Leave him be. We're done here."

She led them back into the streets, the pouch clutched in her hand. She loosened the strings and opened it, revealing an innocuous looking white powder. She closed it quickly and tucked it away in her robe. She had no idea what Cacanja had given her or why she accepted it, but she sensed she had crossed a river where there was no turning back. As she followed the winding roads back to the Royal Compound, the last words of Cacanja echoed in her mind.

"You have already paid a great price."

* * *

Ndoro awoke in an unfamiliar place. The roof above him revealed no gaps like those of his home, the thatch woven by expert hands. The bed on which he rested was soft and comfortable, entirely different from the cot he slept upon each night. He ached, but there was no deep pain. A bandage covered his wrist; he felt wet poultice against his skin. The walls of the room were covered with mud cloth and expertly carved masks. Ndoro was overwhelmed by the room's opulence.

"Well, well, the simba is not dead after all." Jelani strode into the room, a wide smile splitting his grizzled face. "I have something for you."

He handed Ndoro a small leather pouch. Ndoro opened it, revealing the hair balls from the old simba's stomach.

"The elders asked me to give these to you," Jelani said. "They are a symbol of the courage you showed by taking the simba the old way."

Ndoro was honored, but his mind was on more pressing matters.

"Jelani, where am I?"

"You are in Dingane's umuzi."

Ndoro jumped at the sound of his mother's voice. She sat beside the bed, her tired eyes emitting a mother's joy.

"Unkulunkulu brought you back to me," she said. They hugged for a moment; Ndoro felt awkward showing such emotion before Jelani and gently pushed his mother away.

"This is my father's house, mama," Ndoro said, "your husband's house."

"You should know better by now. Dingane stopped being my husband the day you were born," Shani snapped. "He was never your father. You wouldn't be alive if not..."

"Shani," Jelani interjected, "this is not the time."

Shani's eyes went wide. She plunged her face into the palms of her open hands and sobbed.

Ndoro was driven by curiosity. "It is not for what, mama?"

"If not for your grandfather," Dingane replied. He stood in the entryway, draped in his royal robe, his hair braided Shamfa fashion. Shani's head jerked up, a poisonous look aimed at her husband. Ndoro stood to face his father. It was the first time Dingane spoke to him directly.

"I see you are well," Dingane continued. "I am happy." He looked at Shani and smiled, oblivious to the tension he created.

"You did a good job, Shani. Maybe you should be a healer."

"Don't tell him, Dingane," Shani demanded.

"It's time he knew," Dingane answered.

"I am his mother. I decide what he should or should not know."

"I want to know, mama," Ndoro interjected. "I want to know why we are shunned. I want to know why my own father rules Sesuland but can't speak to his son. I want to know why I have been denied my place beside him."

Dingane stared at Ndoro for a moment, and then motioned to him. "Come with me," he said.

Ndoro followed his father out of the room, through the palace and outside to the umuzi. The sunset painted the rolling grasslands red as the sounds of a city preparing for rest climbed the umuzi walls. Dingane walked to the meeting tree and sat, motioning Ndoro to sit beside him.

"Do not be fooled by my appearance of power," Dingane said. "It is not truly mine. The power belongs to those you see below you, the Sesu. It was our elders who selected me to serve as inkosi, and that power can be taken away just as easily."

"But they would not do such a thing," Ndoro replied. "You have a made us a great people."

Dingane gave Ndoro a weary smile. "That's not important. What's important is I rule without violating Sesu traditions. I have done so only once, when I let you live."

Ndoro was puzzled. "Let me live?"

Dingane told Ndoro the story of his birth. The young warrior was stunned, his mind a tempest. Tradition said he should be dead, but since that had not been allowed, a living death had been imposed. In Ndoro's mind his brother suffered a kinder fate. But nothing changed his right to claim what was his.

"Can you break the rules again?" Ndoro asked.

"I may not have to," Dingane replied. "Yesterday's show was enough to change the minds of many, although there were those who saw what you did normal for an athakathi."

Ndoro's blood burned. "I am no demon!"

"Of course you aren't," Dingane replied. "On the day you were born I vowed my son would be inkosi. Shani's mistake put an end to that dream for a time, but you have given it to me again."

"But what of my brothers?" Ndoro asked. "What of Inaamdura's son?"

"Inaamdura's son is not Sesu," Dingane replied. "As for your other brothers, none of them can hold a shield to you. It is what hurt me so, seeing you grow into a proud warrior and not being able to say one thing to you. You are a son that any man would be proud."

Dingane grasped Ndoro's shoulders, his eyes intense. "The next few days are crucial to your future, Ndoro. You must avoid doing anything that would offend the elders and the spirits. Be humble and obey your mother, and above all, avoid Mulugo. Anything you do around him will be used as judgment against you."

"What will this change?" Ndoro asked.

"It will give me time to talk to the elders and convince them it is time you took your rightful place at my side," Dingane replied.

"No matter what the elders decide, I will still be shunned. I will still be thought of as a demon."

"I can do nothing to change the minds of people," Dingane said. "That will be up to you."

"I will do as you say," Ndoro said. "Must we leave the Royal Umuzi?"

"You must, for now." Dingane took off his cowry necklace and placed it around Ndoro's neck.

"My promise to you," he said. He smiled, stood, and then walked away, leaving Ndoro alone among the royal herd.

Ndoro stood. If he were the sun, Sesuland would burn under his brilliance. The time had come for him to take his rightful place beside his father as heir to the stool. There would be many to oppose him, but he knew what the outcome would be. It was his destiny, and he would accept nothing less.

* * *

The wail echoed throughout the royal umuzi. Dingane jumped from his bed then ran to the window, snatching aside the cowhide and staring into the dark. Kefi, his royal herdsman, dashed up the hill, his heavy arms spread wide.

Inaamdura rose from her headrest, cotton sheets falling from her nude body. "What is it?" she asked.

"I don't know." The inkosi dressed quickly and left the room.

The Blood Men waited for him, armed and ready. Dingane trotted through the gauntlet and down to the ground level where Kefi waited, his head buried in the grass.

Get up, man!" Dingane ordered. "What is the matter?"

Kefi struggled to his feet but could say nothing. He grabbed Dingane's arm; the Blood Men jumped toward him, but Dingane waved them back. A sense of dread gripped him. He'd never seen Kefi so distraught. Something terrible must have happened; something more than the loss of a calf to a hyena or simba.

Kefi towed him to the edge of the hill. Strewn across the fields of green grass were the white bodies of the royal herd. There was no bovine standing, just white humps of flesh motionless in the verdant grass.

"What...," Dingane said.

"I don't know, my inkosi, I don't know!" Kefi replied. "Nothing was done wrong, nothing!"

Dingane stared at his wealth scattered across the hillside. Something more foreboding was growing in his mind, something which the evidence was too powerful to deny. He turned slowly, eventually facing the Blood Men.

"Bring Mulugo here," he ordered.

The medicine priest came to the royal umuzi immediately. Upon seeing the dead cattle he fell into a fit. For what seemed like hours he was unintelligible, running and rolling about the field touching each of the corpses with his staff. He finally ended his gesticulations at Dingane's feet, spread eagle on his back, his eyes staring into the cloudless sky.

"A powerful evil is among us," Mulugo moaned, "an evil that has festered among us for many seasons."

Dingane took on a harsh look. "What are you leading to, Mulugo? Are you saying Ndoro caused this?"

Mulugo came to his feet. "I am not accusing anyone. There is a demon wearing the skin of a man in this city, and it has demonstrated its power. We must have a smelling out."

Dingane felt the hairs on the nape of his neck raise. No one knew if they were possessed; only Mulugo could determine so. The demon could be in anyone; only impalement could drive it away. But death was a small price to pay to rid the Sesu of a demon powerful enough to cause such carnage.

The darkness that filled Sesuland that night seemed alive, touching every man and woman with an evil cold. The moon fled the night sky, giving up the heavens to the palpable blackness. The only visible light came from the royal umuzi, its source a huge bonfire made from selected branches of the meeting tree. A ring circled the fire, a ring made of the inhabitants of Selike. The firelight danced across their faces, revealing glimpses of the fear that gripped everyone. Ndoro was part of the ring, his rigid face hiding his turmoil inside. He remembered his father's words and fought to keep from shuddering. Mulugo thought he was a demon. What if he was? It was said a man did not know if a demon rode his back. Only a smelling out can reveal the spirit and only impalement of the host could drive the vile creature away. Ndoro clinched his hands, his nails cutting into his palms. No, he convinced himself. The demon was not in him.

Mulugo occupied the center of the circle. He sat cross-legged, his small chest bare, his groin covered with a loincloth. In his hand he held his staff, his face covered with the demon mask. The mask was decorated with inhuman perfection, its fierce expression fitting for a smelling out. Mulugo sat stiff, his gaze unsettling to those brave enough to look directly into his burning eyes.

Mulugo jumped to his feet, yelling into the night sky. He fell into an energetic, foreboding dance that attracted as much as it repelled. The medicine priest chanted a litany Ndoro knew well. It was a prayer of protection every Sesu learned as a child.

Unkulunkulu! We are your children!
We pray for your protection!
Give us your shield!
Drive the evil away!

The Sesu took up the chant, falling into the rhythm of Mulugo's steps. The medicine priest's dancing became more vigorous, the chanting stronger. Suddenly the chant changed. Mulugo ranted, his words streaming from his mouth so rapidly they were unintelligible. His dance transformed into a struggle against an unseen foe, his arms reaching and grasping the night. He fell to the ground, writhing in the dust and grass, the Sesu falling into a deadly silence as they watched the spiritual struggle.

Mulugo sprang to his feet, running as fast as his old legs could manage towards Ndoro. Ndoro tried to back away but the ring held him firm. He looked to either side and was met with hateful eyes. Mulugo finally confirmed what many Sesu suspected. He was possessed with a demon.

"No!" Ndoro protested. He broke away from the ring, backing away from the babbling Mulugo. He searched desperately for his father but he was nowhere to be seen. The realization transformed Ndoro's shock into anger. He stopped, his eyes narrowing as he looked into Mulugo's crazed face.

"I am not a demon, medicine priest!" Ndoro shouted. Mulugo fell silent, and then with a shriek raised his staff over his head with both hands. Ndoro grabbed the staff, wrenching it from the old man's hands, and, as if continuing Mulugo's motion, crashing the staff down on the priest's head. There was a sickening crack and Mulugo fell to a heap at Ndoro's feet. The circle was silent, stunned by what had occurred. Ndoro took advantage of the inaction, breaking away and running down the hill, back to the city. He was almost among the buildings when he heard a deafening roar. The spell was broken; the Sesu rushed down the hill, each one determined to rid their city of the demon.

Ndoro ran on, his mind a jumble of anger and fear. He became lost, scampering back and forth through the streets, the din of his pursuers growing louder with each moment. He stumbled deeper into the city, despair beginning to settle into his mind. He should stop and let them take him, he thought. This torture which has passed for his life for eighteen years was no longer worth the struggle. He had been cursed at birth, and Mulugo sealed his fate. If he was to die, then so be it.

"Ndoro!" Someone called out his name. He jerked his head in the direction of voice and saw Jelani running towards him, spear and shield in hand.

"You've got to get out of here now," Jelani said.

"Why?" Ndoro asked. "Mulugo wants me dead, so here I am."

Jelani threw down his spear and shield. "That old crow will never see that day. You killed him."

Ndoro smiled, but it was like closing his eyes before the gods. He'd sealed his fate.

Jelani had stripped down to his loincloth. "Give me the simba hide."

Ndoro removed the hide and gave it to Jelani.

"Take my clothes and put them on now," Jelani instructed.

"You don't have to do this," Ndoro said.

"You don't have much time," Jelani replied. "They will find us soon."

Ndoro donned Jelani's garments. Jelani gave him a quick inspection and smiled approvingly.

"You'll make a fine Mawena warrior," he said. "Now chase me out into the open. Once they see us, you stop and point them to me."

"This is my fight, Jelani," Ndoro said.

"But you cannot win it now," Jelani replied. "Go to the Mawena, to your grandfather. They will welcome you, and you will meet your . . ."

The pair heard voices and saw flickering torch lights in the distance. Jelani turned and ran towards the light. Ndoro went after him, shield and spear in hand. Jelani disappeared down a side alley; before Ndoro could follow he found himself standing before the Blood Men. Ndoro raised the shield to obscure his face.

One of the Blood Men stepped forward. "Was that him? Answer me, Mawena!"

Ndoro nodded and the Blood Men took flight, yelling for the others to follow them. Ndoro watched and waited until the crowd disappeared. But still he did not go. He walked slowly as he played with the cowry necklace giving to him by Dingane, savoring the image of the city which had been his home and his prison. As he neared the outskirts, he trotted, leaving the memories that haunted his life, fleeing the revelations the past few days had heaped upon him. His hand clenched around the necklace, and with a sudden jerk he ripped it from him neck and flung it into the darkness. By the time he reached the grasslands he was running, tears streaming down his cheeks, a vow forming in his mind and his heart. He would return and Selike would burn.

10

The harvest season was upon Abo. Farmers labored in the small fields surrounding the city, collecting the bounty of a successful season. It was good that the crop was abundant, for Abo was a growing city. Mawena tradesmen traversed the grasslands, deserts and forests, trading goods with distant cities and returning with the bounties of other nations. All around him Oba Noncemba watched his people prosper, the forest giving way to new homes and new problems. But it was one growth that was the most perplexing to the wise oba, one problem he never seemed able to solve.

Noncemba sat on his gilded stool flanked by his guards. His graying head rested in his palm, his eyes following Kumba as he paced across the floor.

"I tell you my oba; this boy ties me in knots! No matter what I do, he responds with total indifference!"

"Maybe it is because he is indifferent," Noncemba responded.

Kumba stopped his pacing and glared at the oba, an expression Noncemba dismissed. Kumba was allowed a certain leeway because of his family rank, a privilege he used at every opportunity.

"It doesn't matter how he feels," Kumba said. "What matters is his duty as a Mawena and as a member of the royal house."

"Don't explain duty to me," Noncemba replied. "Obaseki is well aware of his responsibility. His interests at the moment lie elsewhere."

"And that's another thing," Kumba continued. "He spends too much time with Fuluke. The boy should be training as a warrior, not as a medicine priest."

"We cannot deny Obaseki his calling or his wishes," Noncemba reminded Kumba. "Remember, he is one of twins, a meji, and we cannot displease him lest bad luck befalls our clan. He has special talents that only Fuluke can develop."

Noncemba paused to scratch his beard. "Meji or not, Obaseki should spend more time with you. When he returns, I will discuss this matter with him."

Kumba almost smiled, the closest Noncemba had seen him happy in months. He turned to leave the room. "I will expect him in the morning."

* * *

Obaseki was far away from the conversation deciding his fate. He had grown into a tall, broad-shouldered man, resembling his grandfather in many ways. He was deep in the forest, close to the area known to the Mawena as Tepula, the land of the hidden ones. He moved with the grace of a gazelle, walking the narrow, wet path as if he'd walked it for many years. In a way, he had. These woods were filled with spirits, and Obaseki had a way with spirits.

Fuluke raised his hand and Obaseki obeyed, halting in the middle of the path. This was dense forest; the sun's light barely penetrating the green canopy of leaves overhead. The glade was alive with sound, a natural symphony that comforted both men.

"I think this is the place," Fuluke said. "It has been many years." He turned to Obaseki. "What do you see?"

Obaseki looked into the forest to a clearing off to his right. "There," he said. He entered the underbrush, clearing a path for Fuluke with his machete. They halted at the edge of the clearing.

"It is a small village," Obaseki remarked. "There are at least twenty huts. I don't recognize the people. They are not Mawena."

"They called themselves Noke," Fuluke replied. "Do you recognize the chief's hut?"

"Yes," Obaseki replied, "near the center."

Obaseki saw a spectral outline of the hut. "I see something near the fireplace. It glows like a spirit, but it is not."

Fuluke nodded. "So, the mayembe has not been discovered."

"Mayembe? What is a mayembe?" Obaseki asked.

"Go see," Fuluke replied.

Obaseki hesitated. This place was powerful. The spirits were clearly defined, as if they'd all just passed into the Zamani, though he knew this not to be true. Never had he encountered such a thing and it frightened him. He looked back to Fuluke.

"Go on, Seki," Fuluke urged. "You of all people should have no fear of this place.

Obaseki entered the site with respect, aware he violated sacred ground. The spirits made way for him as if it was a normal day. Obaseki entered the spectral home. Crouching above the fireplace, he dug with his spade, each shovel revealing more and more of the mystery. The spirits turned toward him, ceasing their empty chores to watch the stranger among them. Obaseki didn't notice; he was submerged in discovering this strange energy.

Obaseki was suddenly overwhelmed by a searing white light. He plummeted past angry faces shouting at him in unknown tongues. Terror swallowed him as he fell faster and faster, the burning brightness usurped by a numbing darkness that penetrated him like a thousand spears. But then he stopped, hovering in darkness over a single object. It was a horn; it's wide base encircled with a gold and cowry shell ring. At the point was a ringlet of emeralds. Obaseki gazed at the horn, his sight penetrating its surface into its core. The gilded horn held an orisha, the most powerful of all spirits, a messenger between ordinary men and Olodumare. Obaseki expected to feel anger emanating from the spirit; he instead felt contentment. This orisha was apparently where it wanted to be.

Obaseki reached out to the mayembe; to his surprise it rose from its resting place and glided to his hand. It touched his flesh and darkness engulfed him again. He spun as a rush of images passed before his eyes, sights that seemed incomprehensible and yet so familiar. His eyesight returned as suddenly as it fled. He sat on the back of his legs, the back of his hands resting on his thighs, the mayembe warm and pulsing against his palms. Hundreds of tiny lacerations covered his body, blood mixed with sweat forming rivulets all over his body.

Obaseki looked up to see Fuluke. The medicine-priest smiled and nodded his head in approval.

"What happened?" Obaseki asked.

"You have been tested," Fuluke replied. "And the fact that you are still alive means you passed."

Obaseki struggled to his feet, surprised at his weakness. "I don't understand," he said.

"You will, Seki, you will," Fuluke replied. "Come, we have what we came for."

Fuluke grabbed Obaseki by the arm and helped him walk. They made their way back to their horses as nightfall crept slowly across the forest, sealing off the light that filled the gap between the leaves. Fuluke and Obaseki made camp in a clearing not far from the road they traveled, preparing themselves for the night ahead. Their journey to the Noke settlement had taken only half a day; because of Obaseki's condition it would take much longer to return to Abo.

Fuluke gathered medicinal herbs the nearby woods then prepared a healing broth for Obaseki. The bleeding had stopped, but the young apprentice was still weak. He sipped Fuluke's concoction and felt momentarily refreshed, strong enough to raise himself to a sitting position.

"You said you would tell me about the mayembe," he said to Fuluke.

"Moyo," Fuluke answered. "The mayembe you possess is called Moyo, the Noke word for heart."

"How did it come to be?" Obaseki inquired. "The medicine-priest who created it must have been very powerful."

"Moyo was not made by a medicine priest," Fuluke responded. "No one knows how it was created. Some say Moyo was cast down from the heavens, that the orisha trapped inside offended the One and was sentenced to eternity within the horn. Jakobi of the Noke was the first to stumble upon Moyo and gained the orisha's favor by promising to find a way to free it from the horn. He used Moyo's power to make his people great, but soon Moyo realized that Jakobi did not intend to keep his bargain. Jakobi was oba of the Noke by then, holding council over his people and many surrounding tribes. But Moyo set a chain of misfortunes upon the Noke, circumstances that ended with Jakobi and his followers being driven from Nokeland. They ended at this site, Jakobi spending the rest of his days trying to free Moyo from the horn."

"If Moyo does not trust men, why am I allowed to possess it?" Obaseki asked.

"Moyo no longer dwells in the horn," Fuluke replied. "When he was cast from the heavens, Moyo became mortal. What is left of Moyo, his ka, inhabits the horn. And you know the ka well."

Obaseki understood. Ka was pure essence, that elemental part of every being closest to Olodumare, responding instinctively to the powers surrounding it.

"I still don't understand why I have been chosen," Obaseki asked.

Fuluke yawned and rubbed his gray-brown eyes. "You won't understand any better tonight than you will tomorrow. Now sleep and rest. We must go back to Mawenaland tomorrow for I have matters to attend to."

Thin threads of light stole through dense leaves, making splotches of light on the forest floor. The canopy rustled with the movement and sounds of birds and monkeys. Obaseki and Fuluke rose early, breaking camp and setting a good pace. By afternoon they entered Mawenaland and Obaseki relaxed. This was familiar ground; the spirits surrounding him were welcomed.

The road became a series of crest and troughs as they approached the highlands encircling Abo. Fuluke's home rested atop a hill about three miles from the city, overlooking the farmland surrounding Abo like a cultivated moat. Their pack horses seemed to sense the nearness to home for they climbed the steep path leading to Fuluke's house eagerly despite the long journey behind them. Fuluke and Obaseki were happy to see the old stone building, looking abandoned despite Fuluke's presence. Herbs grew in profusion; some even grew from the cracks in the stone wall. Unlike the farmer who fought constantly to stead nature's chaos, Fuluke welcomed it, for the morass of flora possessed the magic that healed the sick, changed fortunes and summoned the spirits.

Someone awaited the duo as they neared the house. Obaseki recognized him as one of his grandfather's messengers. The man slept, his head resting on his knees which were drawn to his chest, his arms languishing at his sides. His right hand barely held the royal symbol, a ceremonial sword carved with the shape of a leopard. Obaseki rode up to the man, dismounted and knelt close to his ear.

"Jambo!" he shouted. The messenger yelped and tumbled into the shrubs. Fuluke and Obaseki laughed.

"Calm down, Jela," Obaseki said. "The spirits have not come for you yet."

Jela stood quickly, dusting himself off in an attempt to reclaim his dignity. "My prince, Oba Noncemba requests your presence at the palace immediately."

Obaseki frowned. He'd long tired of the mindless intrigues of the royal court. And then there was Kumba, constantly droning about his duty and continuously attempting to make him an outstanding killer.

"I will be along, Jela," Obaseki replied.

Jela stepped out of the shrubs. "I'm sorry, but I must insist that you return with me at this instant. Your grandfather made it clear that you must not delay. A day has already past."

"Go on, Seki," Fuluke said. "I have wasted enough of your time."

"My time with you is never a waste, Fuluke. I will see you soon." Obaseki turned to Jela. "Let's go."

Jela bowed, and then set off down the trail. Obaseki followed on horseback, his mood shattered by the summons. He enjoyed his grandfather's company, but lately his time was occupied with various complications affecting a city like Abo. As they passed through the farmlands Obaseki watched the farmers working the fields. To his right the construction of the outer wall continued, his grandfather's latest effort to protect his people. So much had changed so fast, too fast for many of the tribal elders. Though Abo was still Mawena, many other people now lived in the city. They were drawn by the stability and safety of Mawenaland and they brought commerce and growth with them. Prosperity also brought jealousy; Mawenaland was under constant threat from nearby tribes anxious to usurp Abo's position as dominant trade city between the forest and the savannah. It was obvious that Noncemba did not need the added aggravation of a truant grandson.

They reached the outskirts of Abo at dusk. Obaseki and Jela crossed the thorn bush moat encircling the inner wall of the main city. The Breast of Mawenaland, as it was called, radiated the energy of an anthill. People rushed about, closing deals and gaining profits with every step. Though most were Mawena, the collage of costumes revealed many different tribes, all merchants hoping to bring wealth and prestige back to their homelands.

Obaseki rarely saw spirits in the inner city. Abo was not built on ancestral ground; the elders would not allow it. The city was constructed to the east of Mawena tribal land, so as not to draw foreigners to sacred ground. Obaseki felt cold in Abo. There was something unnatural about a land with no ancestors. Fuluke had likened it to an empty vessel waiting to be filled. The city teemed with people; still the young prince doubted if his grandfather had filled it with the right water.

Jela and Obaseki walked the wide avenue leading to the center of the city, the ward of the Mawena. The compound was surrounded by the tallest and widest of the three walls. Atuegbu patrolled the mud brick ramparts. Jela and Obaseki were recognized and the iron gates opened. They shut quickly once the duo passed through, the heavy thud chilling to Obaseki's ears.

Within the walls of the ward the wealth of the Mawena was clear. Wide brick streets separated well-tended gardens crowded with the fruits and vegetables. Beyond them were the houses of the tenders, neat and tiny structures of a much better quality than those on the outside. The homes beyond these belonged to the ancestral families, those who tradition had passed down the privilege of eldership. In the center of it all, resting on a hill constructed by hand was the palace of Oba Noncemba. Jela stabled Obaseki's mount and the young prince passed quickly through the palace oblivious to the numerous servants and relatives that greeted him as he passed. He deposited his belongings in his room paying little attention where, with the exception of the mayembe. That he placed in a special compartment beneath his bed, making sure no one watched as he did so. He was leaving his room when he spotted Azikiwe, his uncle. There was a serious look on his face, a look that disturbed Obaseki.

"Uncle!" Obaseki called.

Azikiwe jerked his head towards Obaseki. "What? Oh, hello Seki." He spun about and hurried down the hallway. Obaseki was even more perplexed. Azikiwe was always ready for a conversation.

"Uncle, wait!" he called out, but Azikiwe did not heed his call. In fact, he seemed to walk faster. Obaseki stopped his pursuit, watching his uncle mount his horse and gallop away. Something fell from the horse as he rode off and Obaseki retrieved it. It was a gold coin. Not the kind produced in Mawenaland, but a coin unlike any Obaseki had ever seen. He put the coin in his pouch and went on to see his grandfather.

Noncemba was in his chambers, looking very unlike a powerful oba. He was dressed in the fashion of a desert nomad, his body covered with a white robe, his head topped with a checkered turban which hid his face. It was close to evening and Noncemba was preparing to fulfill one of his many obligations as oba.

"Grandfather," Obaseki said. I have come as you requested."

Noncemba turned to the young man, his eyes stern. "You are a day late. Explain yourself."

"Fuluke and I were gathering herbs," Obaseki replied, his voice timid. Although he hated court life, he hated disappointing his grandfather more. "Jela was waiting when we returned, and I came as soon as I received you summons."

Noncemba continued to dress. "Kumba was here two days ago. He said you are neglecting your studies. He also said you haven't paid much attention to weapon training."

Obaseki felt like a trapped bull. "It's true haven't been attentive to my studies. I..."

"And that is the problem, Seki," Noncemba interjected. He gestured for Obaseki to sit. He sat beside him.

"I have tried not to interfere while you pursue your way. But you are part of the royal house and you have obligations that must be fulfilled. It's time you started learning your role."

"Why?" Obaseki replied. "Azikiwe has returned and made you proud."

"Azikiwe's situation has not changed. He's accomplished much against the Kossi, but the elders are still not convinced. Neither am I, but we're not discussing your uncle.

'You are my daughter's son. You of all people should know the importance of tradition and the roles we play. We all have a duty to the survival of the Mawena and we must fulfill them. No one is exempt, not even I."

Noncemba stood. Even in the common robes of a merchant he took on a regal bearing. He went to his clothes chest and removed a similar outfit.

"Put this on," he commanded. "You will come with me tonight. It's time you caught up on your lessons."

Obaseki was startled. He dressed, his mind swirling with a mix of apprehension and excitement. The oba was required to go on a daily procession, touring the confines of the city and settling any disputes presented to him. But the oba was also obligated to go out secretly among his people to hear the grievances of those too timid or pessimistic to talk to him publicly. To Obaseki's knowledge, no one had ever accompanied Noncemba on this most secret aspect of his rank.

Noncemba looked him over. "You'd make a fine Bedouin," he said. "Come, we have many stops to make tonight."

Obaseki followed his grandfather out of the room and into the empty walkway. Halfway down the corridor Noncemba pushed against the wall, revealing a passageway Obaseki never knew existed. At the end of the passageway was a hatch door in the floor. Noncemba took out a key, unlocked and lifted the door, then descended through the opening. Obaseki followed, clamoring down the ladder into a narrow tunnel. They walked for a good distance before finally coming to a halt. Noncemba opened another door, and then motioned for Obaseki to follow. Obaseki stepped from the darkness into more darkness, emerging into the forest outside the farmlands of Abo. Before him was a stable holding two camels and a pair of pack donkeys.

"Our disguise is now complete," Noncemba announced. He strode over to his camel and mounted, signaling the reluctant Obaseki to follow. Obaseki climbed onto his mount and the two set out for Abo.

The first stop was the outer wall. Each person bringing goods to the city was stopped while the value of his goods was assessed and the appropriate tax levied. Obaseki was impressed with how his grandfather handled the minor obstacle, going as far as to argue with the tax assessor about the amount of tax required for his goods.

After they'd passed through the gate, Noncemba gave the tax collector a long look. "He charges more than the law dictates. I will be sure to have a meeting with him soon."

They continued to the section of the city where the foreign merchants lived. There was an inn there, and after they secured their animals they went inside. Noncemba sat close to a group of Kossi merchants engrossed in animated conversation.

"The Kossi are well-traveled," he whispered to his grandson. "They are the best source of information on other cities that might threaten Abo."

They listened while the Kossi traders went on about prices and taxes and other mundane business. Obaseki tired of this conversation quickly, his mind wandering back to his encounter with the mayembe. Images that were blurred during his ordeal were clearer as he thought back on the moment. He remembered a parade of faces as he plummeted, two which stood out prominently. One was the face of a woman weeping, consumed with grief so deep Obaseki found his eyes watering as he recalled her. The other was a face that unnerved him. It was his own face, but not his. This Obaseki wore a hard countenance; the deep creases on his face making him seem much older. But his eyes were what shook Obaseki the most. The brown orbs smoldered with revenge. His lips moved, seeming to repeat the same word over and over, a word the young prince could not decipher. The image scattered suddenly, replaced by the Kossi traders still engaged in tepid conversation.

"Not much today," Noncemba finally said. "I think we . . ."

Noncemba fell silent, his eyes transfixed on the entrance of the inn. Azikiwe entered and was immediately approached by the Kossi traders. Words they could not hear were exchanged and the men followed Azikiwe outside.

Noncemba waited a moment then followed, Obaseki close behind. They exited nonchalantly then walked to their camels. Obaseki searched for his uncle as well as he could in the darkness without seeming obvious. He found him standing with the Kossi before a well. A bukra man had joined them, a white man from across the sea. They talked by the well for a moment, and then moved into the shadows of the nearby buildings. Obaseki saw them approach a cart in the darkness where the bukra lifted a sheet covering the contents. Both his uncle and the Kossi trader nodded in approval.

"Our night is finished," Noncemba said.

"What is going on?" Obaseki asked. "What is uncle doing with those men?"

Noncemba gave Obaseki a stern look. "What you see tonight must stay with you. No one must know, not even Fuluke. Do you understand?"

Obaseki had never seen his grandfather so serious. This was something dangerous, so much so his grandfather seemed to be threatening his life.

"I understand," he replied.

Noncemba grasped his shoulders. "Go back to Fuluke's and stay there until you are summoned by me and me alone. Make sure no one sees you."

"Yes grandfather."

"You must go tonight." Noncemba's eyes had a distant look to them, his mind apparently dealing with the mysterious events of the night. Obaseki hoped for some sign of weakness, but his grandfather's eyes held none. He reined his camel and galloped away, his grandfather headed silently for the hidden corridor. Obaseki got what he wished for, but as he rode through the shadowy streets of Abo, he sensed that the trade-off would be devastating.

* * *

Fuluke put the seeds in the earthen bowl and ground them to a thick paste. He added leaves from the spirit tree, ashes from the bones of a freshly killed goat and a small amount of spittle. After a short chant, he began to grind the mixture.

"This is what works for me," he told Obaseki. "You will discover the same medicines do not always work for every priest. The power of one's ka and his mayembe has much to do with the power to heal."

Obaseki nodded, locked in deep concentration. The two weeks he'd spent with Fuluke was more than he could have dreamed. The time of running errands and gathering herbs was past; Fuluke now taught him the true ways of the medicine-priest. Most of all, Fuluke was schooling him in the powers of his mayembe. He held Moyo in his right hand, the horn pulsating with his body rhythm. It was a living thing, far different from Fuluke's cold and lifeless buffalo horn. He was sure his teacher's horn contained a spirit; Obaseki had seen it in use enough to be respectful of its power. But it was nothing like Moyo.

"This should be applied to the sick person's chest," Fuluke continued. "Your mayembe will do the rest." The old priest scooped the paste from the stone gourd and put it into a smaller gourd, closing it tightly.

"Now, are you ready, Seki?" Fuluke grinned.

Obaseki stood with Moyo in his hand. "I am, teacher."

Fuluke chuckled. "Bring the horses about and we'll be off."

Their destination was the home of Ayinde Duruji, a farmer and friend of Fuluke. Ayinde's wife, Halina, had fallen ill three days ago. What Fuluke thought to be a minor sickness grew more serious, causing the medicine priest to believe unsettled spirits were involved. Ayinde performed the proper libations, but Halina's condition remained the same. It was time for more drastic actions.

Ayinde was a prosperous farmer and it reflected in the size of his farm. His fields were filled with yams and millet; just beyond the hills cattle and goats grazed upon dense grasses. The farm was tended by young bachelors from Abo working to earn enough cowries for a decent dowry for marriage. A group of such men met Fuluke and Obaseki and led them to Ayinde's house.

When the duo entered the house, Ayinde was kneeling before his ancestors shrine performing libations. They remained quiet until he finished. When Ayinde finally greeted them, his smile was one of relief tinged with fear.

"I thank you for returning," he said. Worry lines etched Ayinde's broad forehead. "She's worse. I think she is going to die."

"Don't give up yet," Fuluke replied, patting his old friend on the shoulder. "A spirit sits on your wife's head, and we are here to remove it."

"A spirit?" Ayinde wrung his hands. "That is possible. A man like me is bound to have enemies. I am not an easy person."

"It's not your fault," Fuluke advised. "The reason such things happen are not important." He looked at Obaseki. "Come, let us begin."

They followed Ayinde to the adjoining room. Halina lay on the bed, tended by their daughters, Eshe and Nafuma. Nafuma resembled her father, tall and thin with a face too bird-like to be considered attractive but still pleasant enough. Eshe resembled her mother; soft, brown eyes with a delicate face almost regal in appearance if not for the creases on her forehead from hard work in the fields. Obaseki didn't notice himself staring at her. She did, and she turned away.

Halina was bound to the bed. At the moment her face was solemn, as if she slept. Obaseki went to her side. Her eyes opened suddenly in a blank stare and Obaseki felt Moyo stir in his pouch. He reached for it and Fuluke grabbed his wrist.

"Not yet," he said. "The poultice will ease the removal of the spirit. If you use your mayembe now it might tear her ka free as well."

Obaseki nodded and removed the poultice pouch instead. He spoke to the sisters, but his eyes fell on Eshe.

"Pull her shirt back so I can apply this poultice to her chest." The sisters did as he asked, gently pulling back their mother's shirt. With nervous hands Obaseki applied the poultice, following Fuluke's instructions. As he did so an image began to appear, one he knew only he could see. A white aura outlined Halina's form, the sign of the spirit intruding upon her. The spirit took form as the poultice did its work, the aura expanding from outline to coherent form across Halina. Obaseki watched, fascinated at the transformation.

"Do you see it?" Fuluke asked.

"Yes, I do." Obaseki's voice shook with excitement. "I know him."

Everyone looked at each other nervously.

"It is Kafele Gamba, Ayinde's great grandfather."

Ayinde stepped back, his hand against his chest. "Great grandfather, what have I done to offend your memory?"

Fuluke went to Ayinde and placed a hand on his shoulder. "Spirits are like us, my friend. Who knows what might cross them?"

Fuluke looked at Obaseki. "It is time."

Obaseki removed Moyo from the pouch. The horn was hot in his hands, but he dared not drop it. He held it directly over Halina then moved it back and forth over her body. Kafele followed the horn with his eyes, a smile slowly forming on his face. His form shimmered and became incoherent again, reduced to the glow of the spirit. The glow lifted from Halina, her chest heaving with its exit. It hovered over her body for a moment then settle into Moyo. The heat subsided and Obaseki felt suddenly tired. He slumped to the floor. Every cell in his body ached from what seemed like an easy effort.

"It is done," he said, his voice weak. It took every effort to put Moyo back into his pouch, draining what little energy he had left. Turning to Fuluke, he was swallowed by blackness and fell to the floor.

When his eyes opened, Obaseki rested in Halina's bed. He heard the sound of dripping water and turned to its source. Eshe stood there, wringing out a wet cloth over a gourd. She turned to him and smiled.

"You have come back to us," she said.

Obaseki managed to sit up. His head ached and his stomach cramped with hunger.

"How long have I been here?"

"A week," Eshe replied. She came to him, placing the cloth on his forehead and gently forced him back down on the bed.

"You passed out after releasing mama from Kafele."

"How is she?"

"She is much better," Eshe answered. She dipped the cloth in the water gourd. "She is back to bossing baba around." She laughed and Obaseki found himself laughing also. She was a beautiful woman with radiance from within. It was like seeing a spirit.

"The medicine priest returned to his home," Eshe told him. "Baba will send a man to tell him you are well."

"I thank you for your kindness," Obaseki replied.

Eshe smiled and turned away. "I will get you something to eat. I know you are hungry."

Obaseki spent the next few days under Eshe's watchful eye. His strength increased rapidly; soon he was about the farm, helping the other workers with daily chores. He should have been spending more time with his herbs but he'd not gone near his bags since raising the spirit from Halina. He was terrified, not of the herbs, but of his mayembe. Fuluke said he was ready, but he was not. He found himself lost in its vastness, drowning in the essence of a spirit over which he had no control. The horn was too powerful. When Fuluke returned, they would go back to the old village and bury Moyo, leaving it for another medicine priest more worthy.

On the sixth day of his recovery, Fuluke returned. Obaseki had gone to the pasture with the young boys, watching over the grazing bovine. The rainy season was coming to an end, the clearing sky and rising temperature heralding the change. Fuluke found the young prince leaning against a tree, his hands wrapped around a herding staff.

"Teacher! It is good to see you."

"You look well, Seki," Fuluke said. "Eshe has done well."

Fuluke's mention of Eshe embarrassed Obaseki. "Is it so obvious?"

"Only to me," Fuluke replied, "And probably to Eshe."

"She is a special woman," Obaseki said. They sat beneath the shady tree branches. "I've spent so much time learning the ways; I haven't had the time to notice many women."

"Take the time," Fuluke advised. "Otherwise you'll end up old and mean like me." The old man looked at Obaseki more seriously. "Where is Moyo?"

"Back in the hut," Obaseki replied.

"You left it alone?"

Obaseki saw the concern in Fuluke's expression and looked away. "Teacher, I am not worthy of such a thing. When I used it to raise the spirit from Halina, I was totally lost within it. I had no control over it."

"No one can completely control Moyo," Fuluke answered. "You must remember you possess the ka of an orisha. Even though its state is elemental, it still has its own will." Fuluke laid a hand on his shoulder. "You have the gift of a meji. If anyone can handle Moyo, it is you. Doing so could mean great things for the Mawena."

Obaseki was not sure of Fuluke's last statement. What could a medicine priest do to create greatness among a people? The arts of healing and appeasement were essential to any tribe but paled to the power held by the oba and his council of lineage elders. Fuluke must be showing his age, he thought.

A horse and rider appeared over the hill from the direction of the farmhouse, galloping frantically towards the herd. Obaseki came to his feet, straining to make out the rider's identity. A group of horsemen appeared soon afterwards, bearing shields had lances. Obaseki recognized the white turbans and uniforms and his heart raced. They were Kossi warriors, and they were pursuing Eshe.

"Everyone to the forest!" Obaseki shouted. Fuluke was on his feet, his herb knife in hand.

"Come, Seki," he urged.

Obaseki ignored him, running for Eshe. The world went silent around him, his senses filled by the sights and sounds of Eshe riding towards him, her pursuers closing the gap with every second. Some of the riders broke away, chasing the herdsmen or going after untended cattle. Three warriors continued to pursue Eshe, their lances lowered towards her horse.

Eshe reached him, slowing her horse just enough for him to leap on it. They galloped to the forest edge and Eshe jumped off. She looked at Obaseki in terror.

"Go!" he said. Obaseki reined the horse about and charged towards the Kossi. He veered his mount to his closest attacker, deflecting his lance thrust with his staff and striking across the face in one motion, toppling the Kossi from his mount. The others tried to converge on Obaseki simultaneously, but the young prince darted between them. It was not his intention to fight, only to draw the raiders away from the others hiding in the woods. Riding erratically across the fields, he harassed other groups of Kossi until they all pursed him. Obaseki led them away from the fields and toward the road. As he fled he saw plumes of smoke rising throughout the farmlands. This was not just a raid. A battle was taking place around Abo, he was sure, and the Kossi pursuing him were just a glimpse of what was occurring in the city.

Obaseki saw Ayinde and the rest of the workers running towards him, each man armed with spears and bows. The Kossi broke off their pursuit, galloping across the yam fields to the main road.

Ayinde ran up to him. "Where is my daughter? Where is Eshe?"

"She is safe," Obaseki assured him. "She hides in the woods with Fuluke and the herdsmen."

Ayinde relaxed for a moment, but his anxiety quickly turned to anger. "Kossi bastards!" he shouted. "Oba Noncemba will kill you all!"

The mention of his grandfather spurred Obaseki into action. "Ayinde, I need to use this horse."

"Take it," Ayinde replied. "Do what you must."

Obaseki rode to his house and quickly gathered his belongings, hesitating as he reached for his herb bag. He could feel Moyo from a distance, the green glow radiating from the seams of the bag. He finally grabbed the bag, mounted his horse and set out for Abo.

Obaseki knew better than to ride the main roads. They would be filled with warriors charging the city. Instead he cut through the forest searching for the glade hiding the secret passage to the palace. He passed burned homes and trampled fields, frantic farmers racing back and forth with buckets of water, trying desperately to quench the fires that seemed endless across the horizon.

He finally reached the glade. He wandered about for a moment, making sure he had not been followed. Pushing aside the thicket hiding the entrance, Obaseki charged into the tunnel like a madman, running until he reached the main tunnel that angled upward to the palace. He heard commotion above him and his hands began to sweat. Pushing the iron door under the hall chest open, he climbed into the palace, crept across the room and peered into the hallway. Servants darted about, carrying valuables to load in royal wagons waiting in the courtyard. Obaseki stepped into the hallway and was almost ran over by Jela. The guard went for his sword.

"Fool! Get out of my way! Can't you see..."

Jela's words froze in his throat as he recognized Obaseki and fell to his knees.

"My prince, I am so sorry! Forgive me." The guards shocked expression transformed to puzzlement. "How did you get into the palace?"

Obaseki ignored the question.

"Where is my grandfather?" Obaseki asked.

"He is at the gate. I will take you to him."

The two men ran through the palace. The building was in chaos as servants dashed about amid the babble of panicked voices. They hurried to the stables, mounted and galloped to the gates. The roads of Abo swelled with refugees, people who had entered the city before the gates were shut. Obaseki worked his way through the horde the best he could. He cursed, frustrated with his slow progress, and jumped from the horse. He surmised he could make more time on foot, and he was right. Pushing his way through the mass he soon heard the clamor of battle before him and stopped. He was afraid, far more than he'd ever been in his entire life. It was the true reason he avoided Kumba's instruction, why he never wanted to fight. Obaseki did not want to die. He'd seen all his life what death meant, wandering as an aimless spirit, slowly becoming nothing more than a speck of life. Other men must know what he knew, but still they sang songs of battle and sought its glory. To Obaseki, war was a sinister wall which he wished not to climb.

His hand found Moyo. The mayembe pulsed in his palm it's heat seeping into his arms then moving through him like a lazy stream of awareness. This was not the possession he feared, nor was it the fall into blackness he experienced before. This was a union, a bond that filled the void of fear in Obaseki's heart. All his senses sharpened, his mind moving in a blur as he watched the chaotic scenes around him. He moved forward again, not with the timidity of fear, but with the confidence of experience.

Mawena archers lined the ramparts of the third wall, delivering their poison arrows with lethal precision. The Kossi screamed and fell in scores but more stepped forward to take their place. Obaseki wondered how their attackers had breached the first two walls. Then he remembered the night in the tavern, the meeting of his uncle Azikiwe, the Kossi and the bukra man. Could his uncle have conspired so? Obaseki pushed the thought from his mind. He had to find his grandfather first. The answers would come later.

The battle raged with unrelenting fury. Women dragged the wounded and dead away from the walls, tending the injured the best they could. Obaseki searched for his grandfather among them.

"Obaseki!" someone shouted. The young prince looked to see one of the palace guards running to him. He was Zubeki, smiling despite the carnage around him.

"My prince, the oba will be happy to see you! We thought the Kossi killed you!"

Obaseki ignored Zubeki's remark. "Where is my grandfather?"

"Follow me."

The duo worked through the confusion to the western section of the wall. Horsemen gathered there, mostly Mawena but also a large number of warriors from the surrounding tribes. They all knew the value of Abo to the stability of the entire region and were ready to give their lives to preserve it. The horsemen surrounded a score of Atuegbu resplendent in their green kapok uniforms and golden trimmed helmets. They held double-headed lances in their hands, gold pommel swords at their sides. At the center were Kumba and Oba Noncemba.

Zubeki yelled over the commotion and waved his lance. The group parted and Noncemba rode up and dismounted, a broad smile on his face.

"My grandson returns," he shouted. "How to you like the celebration?"

"I don't think this is the time for jokes," Obaseki replied as he hugged his grandfather.

"Then maybe you should sit on the royal stool," Noncemba said.

Obaseki turned to Zubeki. "Get me a horse and a lance."

"No," Noncemba said. "You will stay inside until this is over."

"My place is with you," Obaseki protested.

"You don't have the training," Noncemba countered. "This is no game, Seki."

Kumba interrupted their argument. "My Oba, we must strike now. The Kossi are massing a final assault."

"Stay here," Noncemba ordered.

"I'm going with you," Obaseki said.

"Let him come," Kumba agreed. "If he does not live, he never deserved to take your place."

Noncemba glared at Kumba. "Come."

Zubeki returned with a fine roan stallion and a chain mail breast plate for Obaseki. The prince tied Moyo around his waist then donned the mail, covering it with his traditional kapok padding. Zubeki gave him a lance and a sword. Obaseki mounted then rode to join the cavalry.

Obaseki joined the warriors as his grandfather made a final inspection of his remaining forces. Nodding his approval, he signaled for them to gather around him. Obaseki rode beside him, with Kumba flanking the Oba's opposite side. The guard fell in behind them, followed closely by the rest of the cavalry. The men on the ramparts watched, waiting for the horsemen to reach the gate. On the Oba's signal they raised the gate. A deep drum sounded and the cavalry charged.

The horsemen wheeled left to confront the main group of Kossi scaling the walls under the cover of archers. Noncemba attacked the left flank, threatening to pin the Kossi between his cavalry and the wall. The Kossi would have no choice but to retreat. Surprise was the key; despite their valor the Abo's elite cavalry was small. If the Kossi did not falter in the initial engagement they would all be killed. Noncemba knew this, Obaseki realized. As Oba, he could only survive with victory. Defeat meant he was no longer the strongest link between the Mawena and Olodumare, that he was not strong enough to protect the tribe from its spiritual and physical foes.

They lowered their lances, galloping over the last strides between them and the marauding Kossi. Obaseki felt detached; the scene before him some sort of morbid dream over which he had no control. The bravery was not his but Moyo's, fueled by what he felt as a sense of pleasure. This was what made Obaseki fear the mayembe. Moyo thrived in what he feared the most.

They were almost upon the horde when it began to rain Kossi arrows. Obaseki flinched as a projectile raked his cheek, leaving a thin, red welt in its wake. He rode on, bending low against his horse and urged it on. He managed to glance back and witnessed a terrible sight. The Atuegbu still rode with him, but the remaining cavalry faltered under the onslaught. The Kossi took advantage, leaping down from the roofs with swords held high. Ahead more Kossi broke away from the assaulting mass to meet the charge. The element of surprise was lost. They were no longer fighting for Abo; they were fighting for their lives.

The Mawena cavalry crashed into the Kossi, Obaseki driving his lance into a man before him. He rode past letting the lance trail behind him before pulling it from the man's body and returning it level. He had no time to think, no time to realize that this was the first time he'd taken a life.

Another Kossi appeared before him, this one on horseback. Obaseki charged forward; the Kossi knocked the lance down with his sword. The lance went into the horse instead; the beast screeched in pain and collapsed under its rider. The Kossi leapt from the horse and slammed against Obaseki and they both fell to the ground. The impact stunned them for a moment; Obaseki was the first to regain his composure. He pulled his sword and brought the hilt down hard on the Kossi's head, knocking him senseless. He stepped away with a moment's respite, the battle swirling around him in a haze of dust, blood and smoke. Someone called his name; he and saw the Atuegbu making a final stand. They formed a semi-circle against a section of the second wall that still stood. Kumba stood in the center, his shield and sword working furiously against the endless Kossi onslaught. Obaseki could barely see Noncemba in the center of the circle, his sword at the ready. He ran to his grandfather, knowing that he would not make much difference, but feeling he had to be at his side. As he ran to his grandfather, Obaseki spotted a group of ten Kossi warriors charging in his direction on horseback. The lead horseman he recognized as his uncle Azikiwe draped in Kossi robes. A group of Atuegbu broke ranks and charged the horsemen, shields and lances at the ready. The horsemen pulled short of lance range and lifted what seemed to be some type of club to their shoulders in unison. Azikiwe raised his sword, his eyes on the advancing Atuegbu.

He sliced his arm downward and Obaseki's ears exploded with a deafening roar. He blinked with pain, his eyes opening to a confusing scene. The horsemen were shrouded in a gray blue haze as they worked the sinister clubs that caused the terrible sound. Before them the Atuegbu lay broken, some not moving while others cried in pain. The Mawena were stunned, frozen wide-eyed by the scene. Worst of all to Obaseki his grandfather and Kumba stood alone, their faces solemn to what they realized what would happen next once the Kossi horsemen raised the clubs to their shoulders again.

Obaseki reached for Moyo, extracting the horn from the pouch. Maybe there was something the spirit could do that he could not. Until this point he had used the mayembe only to heal, but he knew the horn could kill. He knew the killing chant, the words that transformed the mayembe into a kifaalu, a death spirit. As he ran to his grandfather, he let the words escape his lips. If Moyo was truly the spirit of a fallen god, he was about to learn the extent of its power.

Moyo erupted. Obaseki was consumed in blinding whiteness, no longer feeling his body. The kifaalu became a ball of white fire with Obaseki in the center, fiery tendrils lashing out indiscriminately at the warriors surrounding him. A tendril struck Azikiwe, lifting him off his horse, his wide eyes filled with terror. The tendril jerked away and his ka was ripped from him, his body falling lifeless to the ground as his spirit was consumed by the burning light. Moyo the kifaalu cared not who became its victim. Mawena fell as quickly as Kossi. Obaseki realized the horror he'd unleashed and struggled to control it, shouting the words to return the kifaalu to the docile mayembe. But Moyo fought back, moving slowly towards the Atuegbu, striking down all in its path. The Kossi fled in terror, screaming to their cohorts of the terrible death approaching. The onslaught became a confused retreat. But the Mawena behind the ramparts did not pursue. They were just as terrified; many praying that whatever this thing might be would not be able to breach the inner wall of Abo.

Obaseki battled to wrest control from Moyo, slowing its advance toward the Atuegbu and his grandfather. One bodyguard jumped from the ranks, his sword high, most of his body hidden by his leaf shield. Moyo lashed out just as quickly and the man fell dead to the ground. Obaseki watched as the man's soul was dragged towards him, the face screaming in silent pain as it was consumed. Obaseki could take no more. He yelled, concentrating everything he could muster into a final grasp for control. The light dissipated and Moyo receded into its material form, clasped tightly in Obaseki's right hand. The prince fell to his knees only a few steps away from the Atuegbu. He tasted blood; his face drenched with sweat, the pain in his body all consuming. He looked up to his grandfather's face. He expected a grateful smile; instead he saw the same fear he'd seen in the face of the Kossi. Obaseki swayed and fell forward, his head crashing into the dirt.

The pungent smell of healing herbs stirred Obaseki from unconsciousness. He could feel pain, but it was dulled by whatever had been applied to him. He opened his eyes, thankful for the darkness. Torchlight flickered in the distance, illuminating uneven shelves packed with countless gourds. He lay in Fuluke's hut, but he did not know how he arrived.

Fuluke appeared above him, a grim look on his face as he checked Obaseki's wounds. His expression changed when he noticed Obaseki was conscious.

"Seki, always in a hurry," he said. "You are not well enough yet."

Obaseki opened his mouth and blacked out for a second. When he focused on Fuluke again, his mentor gave him a sympathetic smile.

"Close your eyes," he said. "The herbs will calm you if you let them."

Obaseki knew better than to talk again, so he closed his eyes and settled into darkness. He dreamed he stood on a grassy plain, a violent wind pressing hot against his skin. A figure appeared in the distance, running toward him at incredible speed. The man carried a shield and an assegai, the spear held high as if to attack. He tried to run, but his feet were fused into the ground. The man stopped before him and Obaseki gazed in horror. He looked at himself, a malevolent version of himself. The grass surrounding them began to burn, and the false Obaseki uttered one word as the flames consumed them: Shumba.

Sunlight breached the cracks in Fuluke's walls and pulled Obaseki from his disturbing vision. It was a message he was sure, but of what he didn't know. He fought his first battle but showed none of the bravery the Obaseki of his dream possessed. He tried to decipher the image but the details faded rapidly. In moments he could barely remember any detail. Only one word remained in his mind; Shumba. He had no idea what it meant.

He was alone. His clothes rested at the end of the cot and he put them on, feeling better the more he moved about. Gingerly he stood and his legs held firm. Standing alone in good health, it was hard to imagine he'd experienced the terror of battle.

He heard footsteps and turned to the door. Fuluke entered with a smile on his face. Obaseki was pleasantly surprised to see Eshe with him.

"Again, I amaze myself," Fuluke bragged. "How does it feel to be back from the dead?"

"Good," Obaseki replied. "Hello, Eshe."

Eshe turned away slightly, her smile like the sun. "My father sent me when he heard of your condition. I brought you food and fresh milk."

"Thank you and your family," Obaseki replied. "I will mention your kindness to my grandfather when I return to Abo."

"You cannot go back," Fuluke said.

"I feel fine, really I do," Obaseki replied.

Fuluke and Eshe glanced at each other. "That is not the reason, Seki", Fuluke said. "The council has forbidden your presence in the city."

Obaseki sat slowly on the cot. "Why?"

"You unleashed a power never seen before, and it terrified them."

"I was trying to save my grandfather," Obaseki defended.

"You killed many men, Seki, Kossi and Mawena. You killed your uncle."

"My uncle deserved to die," Obaseki spat. "He betrayed us. He led the Kossi against us and tried to kill Grandfather!"

Fuluke nodded in understanding. "You also killed the son of Abasi Kanata."

Obaseki stiffened at the mention of the elder's name. Abasi held the highest position on the tribal council. His family was the oldest of the Mawena, and the most powerful.

"I...I didn't mean to." Obaseki dropped his head to hide his watery eyes. "I couldn't save grandfather alone. I thought I could control Moyo, but it was too strong. By the time I had it under control..."

"You don't have to explain anything to me," Fuluke said.

"Or to me," Eshe agreed.

Fuluke sat beside Obaseki on the cot. "You must understand what you possess, Seki. A medicine priest holds the power of life and death in his hands. We heal the sick and placate the ancestors. We are responsible for the harmony between Mawena and the Zamani. We are not obas because our lineage does not allow it. But you are special. You have the power of a medicine-priest and the lineage of an oba. Most of all, you have Moyo."

Fuluke placed his hand on Obaseki's shoulder. He calmed as he looked in his mentor's eyes.

"You threaten the hierarchy of the tribe, and the elders know this. When you unleashed the power of Moyo on the Kossi, you also unleashed the power of the elders on yourself. This is a flood not even your grandfather can stem."

"I don't want to be oba," Obaseki replied. "You know that."

"I know, I know," Fuluke replied. "But the elders do not."

Obaseki asked the question that mattered to him the most. "What does my grandfather think?"

Fuluke's face looked grave. "Your grandfather loves you, but he fears for you. He doesn't understand the power you possess."

"So, I must be judged," Obaseki concluded. "I could save everyone the trouble and leave."

Eshe's eyes went wide on hearing Obaseki's words, but Fuluke remained calm. Obaseki knew his decision was rash, but he was angry. Not at the elders, but at his grandfather. He unleashed Moyo to save him! What was so hard to understand?

"What should I do?" Obaseki asked his teacher.

"You must answer that question," Fuluke replied. "You have taken the first step to learning your place in this world. You will never be the priest you can be if you stay in Abo. You can't learn here what you must to control Moyo while appeasing the local spirits. You have destiny that began the day you were born a meji. You must go out into the world to discover you path."

Obaseki could not believe what Fuluke suggested. Abo was his home!

"But where would I go?" Obaseki asked.

"Moyo will lead you," Fuluke answered.

"Forgive me, Teacher, but I think you are wrong," he finally said. "I know the elders well. They are all my uncles. They have no reason to think I would harm them. I made a terrible mistake be releasing the kifaalu. I know I need time to master Moyo, but when that day comes, I will use my power to help, not harm."

"It is your decision," Fuluke replied. "You are Mawena. But think long on it, Seki."

Fuluke left Obaseki alone with Eshe. He wished she'd not been present to hear what was said, but he was pleased she stayed. Seeing her was comforting and she seemed to sense it. He lay back on the cot and closed his eyes, his mind spinning with decisions to make. The jumble of questions was dashed aside by Eshe's sweet humming. She looked at him, smiling as she hummed. She was preparing a meal for him.

He moved closer to her. "Eshe, why did you come?"

"Because my father sent me," she replied

"Why did you come?" Obaseki asked again, his voice firm.

Eshe looked at him directly. "I came because I am interested in you. You are a strange man."

Obaseki was offended and turned away. "So you see me as a spectacle?"

"No, I did not mean strange in a bad way. You are not like most men. I sense the spirits about you, like I did with my mother. But they do not harm you."

Obaseki did not understand at first why he was having this conversation. His mind should have been on the council and his impending banishment. But that situation was beyond his control, firmly in the hands of Olodumare. This, however, was something he could deal with, and he needed it desperately.

"You wished to see the odd one," he said.

"At first, yes. But I sensed your ka, and I see you are a man full of kindness and I became sad."

"Why?"

"Because I sense your ka is not whole. Every man has evil within him, whether it manifests itself or not. The good and evil constantly struggle but neither wins, for both are useful in one's life. But you have no evil. Your ka only knows one way. That is why Fuluke took you to the mayembe, I think, and that is why he feels you should leave Abo."

"I dreamed of my evil," he said. "I saw a man with my face, but with a different ka. He is a warrior, ruthless and terrible. He said Shumba. I don't want to find Shumba, Eshe. I am terrified of what would happen if I did."

Obaseki looked into her soothing eyes.

"Will you go with me?" he asked

Eshe smiled with the glow of sunshine. She moved her mouth as if to answer him, then abruptly handed him his meal.

"This will make you better," she said, then quickly exited the hut.

Obaseki ate slowly as he contemplated his decision. Abo was his home, a sanctuary of wealth, power and spirit. He had enemies among the elders now, but he felt he could convince them he meant no harm. Abasi Kanata had always been stern to him, but his grandfather was very close to Abasi and could sway him. He finished his meal, dressed and left the hut.

Fuluke and Eshe sat outside, their conversation halting when they noticed him.

"I'm going to Abo," he announced.

"You should wait," Fuluke advised. "Let the memory of what happened grow cold in their minds before you confront them. A boiling pot does not cook any meat."

"No," Obaseki replied. "If the council wishes to exile me let them do it now. The pain will be no less now than tomorrow."

"The guards at the gate may not let you pass," Fuluke said.

"They don't have to," Obaseki replied. He turned his attention to Eshe. "Are you going with me?"

Eshe nodded.

"Good, then let us go." Eshe went to the tie post for the horse. Obaseki followed but was stopped by Fuluke's hand resting firmly on his shoulder.

"Be careful, my son," he said. "Whatever happens, it is not worth your life."

Eshe returned and Obaseki mounted the horse. Eshe wrapped her arms around his waist and they trotted down the steep path leading towards the city.

They rode for a day, covering as much ground as they could before nightfall. Obaseki discovered he was not as well as he thought; the jostling of the trail wore him down quickly, forcing them to set up camp long before dark. They stopped at the forest's edge, only a few strides from the beginning of the farmland that surrounded Abo. Once they entered the obadom, a confrontation was imminent. He wanted to be strong when that happened, and the only way to ensure that was to stop and rest.

Obaseki began to build a fire but Eshe stopped him.

"You must rest," she said. "Take this cot and find a place with many leaves. It will be the most comfortable. I will start a fire."

Obaseki obeyed eagerly. He found a spot like Eshe described and quickly fell asleep, the first dreamless slumber he'd experienced in days. When he awoke Eshe lay beside him, her warm body pressed against him. Carnal thoughts rushed in his head but he pushed them away. He admonished himself for thinking in such a way, struggling against his urges until he worried himself to sleep.

They broke camp at sunrise and headed for the glade that hid the secret entrance to the palace. The duo arrived about midday, thankful for the shade of the ironwoods standing guard. Obaseki searched for and found the entrance buried under the leaves. He cleared the brush away and called Eshe to him. She hesitated, fear in her eyes.

"Don't be afraid," he said. "This tunnel will take us directly to the palace."

He took her trembling hand and they descended into the tunnel, making good time in total darkness. The ground angled upward through the layers of rock and soil, pierced by the tunnel that eventually led to Oba Noncemba's bedroom. Obaseki pushed against the hatch sealing the door and slid it open. His grandfather's room was empty. No sounds emanated from the other rooms close by. Confident they were alone; Obaseki helped Eshe out to the tunnel and into the room. She seemed awed by the opulence, her eyes wide and watery as she scanned the room's treasures of gold, ivory, cowry shells and precious stones.

"What do we do now?" Eshe asked.

"We wait." Obaseki walked over to the stool at the foot of Noncemba's bed and sat. Eshe sat on the floor beside him, laying her head on his thigh. No sooner had they settled did they fall asleep. The arduous journey had left their bodies drained.

They awoke to the clamor of footsteps. The door to the room swung wide and Noncemba strode in followed by two Atuegbu. He wore his riding clothes, the dust from the trail still heavy on his garments. His sword hung loosely from his shoulder, its golden scabbard beating against his waist. Noncemba stumbled back into his bodyguards when he saw Obaseki and Eshe. He raised his hand just in time, halting the mortal assault of his bodyguards.

"Leave us," he commanded. The guards left, glancing malevolently over their shoulders.

Noncemba's face remained stern until the Atuegbu were gone. A broad, joyous smile broke across his face and his arms went wide. Obaseki ran to his grandfather and they embraced like father and long lost son.

"Seki, it is dangerous for you here," Noncemba admonished.

"It is dangerous for me not to be here," Obaseki countered.

His grandfather held him at arm's length. "You look well. That is good." He turned to Eshe who was kneeling, her head touching the floor.

"This is Eshe, daughter of Ayinde," Obaseki said.

"Stand up, woman," Noncemba commanded. "You have taken care of my grandson and I am grateful."

"Thank you, oba," Eshe replied.

"Grandfather," Obaseki interrupted. "Why was I banished?"

Noncemba's face took on a gloomy shadow. He sat heavily on his stool.

"Abasi wants it, and you know he is a powerful elder. Your mayembe killed his son, a loss that even our years of friendship cannot heal. He has bent the judgment of the elders, using your uncle's betrayal against our family. He has even gone so far as to question my rule. He cannot usurp me; I have done the Mawena well as oba and our lineage gives us the right to rule. So he has gone after you."

"I must speak to the elders," Obaseki said. "I will not be banished without the chance to defend myself."

"You are right, Seki, but now is not the time. We must wait until wounds have healed. Abasi was not the only one in the city to lose a loved one to your magic. That is why he wields so much power at the moment."

"No, it must be now," Obaseki retorted. He saw the look of disapproval on his grandfather's face and felt sorrow. It was never his wish to defy him, but this had to be. If what Fuluke said was true, then the outcome was already known. But even if he did not change the minds of the elders, he would be satisfied if he said how he felt.

"You are too old to be so impatient," Noncemba replied. "Give it time before you make any rash decisions."

Obaseki was not to be swayed. "Grandfather, I need to see the council. Will you grant me this?"

Noncemba sighed and slumped in his stool. "I will convene the elders. I will not, however, let them know you will be at this meeting. They would refuse to come."

"Thank you, Grandfather."

Noncemba rose. "Wait here until I send for you. The servants will bring you and Eshe food. Eat well and rest. You will need all your strength."

The servants brought a feast to the room, all of them happy to see him back at the palace. They were enchanted by Eshe, and the women fell upon her like joyful captors, dressing her in the finest of Abo and reworking her braids in a fresh and attractive pattern. Obaseki was never in doubt of Eshe's beauty, but seeing her refreshed by skilled hands affected him more than he could imagine. She was truly a special woman, worth the dowry he was contemplating if he was allowed to stay in Abo. He realized with those thoughts that he really wanted to stay. Despite Fuluke's prophesy, he was afraid to leave home. Fuluke would one day give up his responsibilities as medicine-priest, and who better to take his place than Obaseki? Fuluke himself said that he would never be allowed to be oba. Even without the fear of too much power in one hand, the stigma of Moyo's slaughter had done enough to eliminate that option. If he convinced the elders that the terrible power they witnessed could be used for the good of the city, Obaseki believed there would be no banishment.

His thoughts were broken by the entrance of the royal messenger to the room. He looked at Obaseki intensely; his true feelings clear despite his submissive tone.

"My prince, Oba Noncemba requests your presence at the meeting tree," he said curtly.

Obaseki stood and turned to Eshe, extending his hand. Eshe eyes flashed with curiosity.

"What do you want?" she asked.

"I wish you to come with me."

A collective gasp filled the room. Eshe hand came to her chest as it heaved with heavy breath.

"I cannot go to a council!" she shrieked. "I was not summoned."

"I am asking you now," Obaseki replied. "You have helped me unselfishly, and I would feel much better before these great men with you beside me."

Eshe smiled broadly. "I will be with you as long as you wish."

Obaseki turned to the messenger, his resolve strengthened knowing that Eshe would accompany him. "We are ready," he said.

They followed the messenger out of the palace and into the streets.

A human fence bordered the avenue leading to the center of the city and the meeting tree. The city was void of sound with the exception of the whistle, moans and calls of animals. Mawena eyes focused on the duo, showing a mix of fear, admiration and hate. Obaseki tried his best not to ignore them, clutching Moyo under his shirt as it pulsed with heat. Grasping Eshe's hand, he looked toward the tree, striding regally like the son of the oba. They walked for an eternity, the streets he grew up to know suddenly alien and hostile to him. As they neared the tree, he saw the elders sitting around its base with Noncemba seated in the gilded stool. Abasi sat nearby, his face showing none of the emotion of which his grandfather warned him. The other elders were just as stoic. He approached until he was among them, his grandfather stepping forward with the ceremonial sword gripped in his right hand.

"I have called you together to hear the plea of Obaseki of the Buhari. He has come to address his issue of banishment before your sacred council to explain his actions and beg for reconsideration of his sentence. Will you grant his request?"

Abasi looked directly into Obaseki's eyes. "We grant his request."

Obaseki watched as his grandfather took his place on the stool. "You may begin," he said.

Obaseki fell to his knees, his arms outstretched and finger spread wide.

"Great elders, I humble myself before you to ask for reconsideration of my sentence. On the day of my discretion, our city swarmed with Kossi, a scheme devised and aided by my uncle. Their numbers seemed vast, and with the weapons they possessed our situation seemed dire."

Obaseki paused a moment to study the elders' faces. Some nodded in agreement, while others frowned. Abasi remained unreadable, staring at his folded hands resting in his lap. Obaseki glanced at his uncle, who motioned for him to continue.

"The pain and anger in my heart was great, but it became greater still when I saw my grandfather and his warriors surrounded by Kossi. Having no other choice, I summoned the spirit of my mayembe to protect my grandfather and Abo."

"There was another choice," Abasi countered. "That choice was to raise your sword like the warrior you were trained to be, a warrior like my son." The elder had raised his head, his eyes on Obaseki. Though his face remained calm, Obaseki saw the malice in his stare.

"That is true, Elder Abasi," Obaseki acknowledged. "But my sword would not save my grandfather or our city. It was my hope that my mayembe would."

"So, you unleashed a power that you could not control, costing us many warriors," Abasi finished. "Better that you die a warrior's death at your grandfather's side than to foul this city with evil."

"The boy meant no harm," Abegunde interjected. "Any one of us would have done the same if we possessed such an item." He turned to face Obaseki. "Your failing was you tried to use the mayembe before you mastered it."

"Which is why he must be banished," Abasi said. "This boy must learn the penalty for immaturity. He caused the death of many that day. Granting him leniency disgraces the memory of those who died for nothing."

"You are an elder," Chinzira replied. "Though the loss of your son is one I can only imagine, you cannot let it influence your judgment at this council. Obaseki attempted to save his grandfather and this city, which none of us here can deny. He succeeded, but at a great cost." Chinzira stood, a tall, powerfully built man whose word usually swayed the vote of the majority of the elders. "Obaseki should suffer banishment, but only for a time. Hopefully he will use this time to master his abilities for the betterment of our people. This should please the spirits of those wrongly slain."

"My spirit still burns!" Abasi hissed. "If this is the judgment of the elders, then I renounce my place among you. The Chuma family will not live among those who condone murder!"

The scene was engulfed in an explosion of noise. Elders leapt to their feet in protest of Abasi's words. Others joined in with Abasi's demands, threatening to bring about the fall of Mawenaland. His grandfather stood, yelling for order. In trying to save Abo Obaseki had done more damage than the Kossi could ever imagine.

"Elders, elders, please listen to me!" he shouted. The ruckus went on unabated. Obaseki extracted Moyo and held it high over his head.

"LISTEN TO ME!" His voice thundered throughout the city like the roar of a thousand storms. The elders stumbled away, eyes wide in shock. Even Noncemba cowered as he looked at his grandson. Obaseki gazed at them all, elders and citizens alike and finally saw the truth in Fuluke's words. What he possessed was beyond their comprehension as well as his own. He would find no understanding here, only suspicion and fear.

"I never meant to harm anyone. Abo is my home, but if staying causes the separation of the families that make the Mawena great I have no choice."

He looked at Abasi directly, trying his best to project the sympathy he felt. "I accept the council's first judgment of banishment. I will be gone before first daylight."

Obaseki didn't allow for any further words. He turned quickly and strode away, Eshe trotting to catch up with him and join his side.

"Are you sure this is what you want?" she asked.

"It's not want I want. It is what I must do."

"Then you are the man your grandfather wished you to be," Eshe replied.

Obaseki looked into Eshe's eyes and grasped her hand. Together they walked to the palace between the silent throng, disappearing behind the gilded walls.

Meji

Dingane

Noncemba

Shani

Mulugo

Ndoro

Obaseki

Book Two

11

The quiet village nestled on the banks of the Nyoka River was nothing special; it was a simple community that ebbed and flowed with the rhythm of the river. Its people labored under gray rainy season skies, their easy voices in contrast to their labors. The women and children worked expansive fields of sorghum and yams while the men tended the cattle and goats, sitting in groups to discuss the village business as men do. They called themselves Diaka, which in their language meant 'the good people.' Anyone observing them would agree with the claim.

Ndoro peered down at the village from his hiding place in the nearby hills. For days he'd watched the Diaka go on about their lives, trying to decide the best way to approach them. He had no doubt about meeting them, for he was starving. After fleeing Selike, he wandered about the grasslands, refusing to take the advice of Jelani to head south to Mawenaland, his grandfather's domain. It would be the first place his father would look, and Ndoro was not certain the grandfather he had never met would protect him. Instead he headed east, hunting small game during the day while hiding from simbas and hyenas during the night. He had no purpose or plan; dealing with the events of the past weeks were enough to fill his mind. He had killed a medicine priest. It was a stain on his ego, a blemish that covered the triumph of bringing the old simba to his father. He would have to erase it somehow; when and where, he had no idea. His first task was to stay alive; atonement would come later.

A few weeks from Selike he spotted a Sesu impi running across the grasslands. He spent the night in a baobab, cradled between two large branches like he'd seen leopards do. The impi did not see him, but throughout the day he was wary, keeping his journey close to areas where he could escape to cover quickly if seen. The next day confirmed his suspicions; Sesu impis crisscrossed the area, some running, others creeping about looking for his sign. His days of wandering were over. He had to set out in any direction that took him away from Sesuland. He'd wandered too far away from Selike to get his bearings toward Mawenaland and the supposed safety of his grandfather, so after a long sleepless day, he decided to follow the Kojo River. It was said the river ran through the bordering hills and into the forest. Stories told to him as a boy spoke of trees so dense, a man would have to cut himself in half to pass between them. It was said to be the home of lost spirits, the place where the souls of those forgotten by their descendants fled to suffer, torturing others that came across their path.

Waiting for the cover of darkness, Ndoro slept in his wooded sanctuary invisible to the wandering Sesu. The absence of heat was his awakening; he opened his eyes to the reddish sky of a setting sun. He also spied a frightening sight in the branches below him. A leopard lounged, gnawing on the leg of an antelope. The smell of fresh kill covered Ndoro's scent, making him invisible. The leopard finished its meal then proceeded to fall asleep. Ndoro had been patient enough. He jumped up and down on the branches, startling the drowsy leopard. It growled and scrambled out of the tree, disappearing into the darkness. Ndoro waited to be sure the feline was gone before climbing down and heading for the river's edge.

The savannah was unveiled by the luminescence of a full moon. For Ndoro, it was a blessing and a curse. The light made it easier for him to see the river and the animals that made the riverbank treacherous. It also made him more visible to anything or anyone searching for him, but he had to take the risk.

The river's edge bristled with movement. Crocodiles dragged themselves in and out of the murky liquid while hippopotami waded among the reptiles with little interest. Both were dangerous to Ndoro, so he stayed away from the edges unless the shoreline proved desolate enough that he could move closer without harm.

Ndoro did not realize the monumental task he was undertaking until it was too late to turn back. The river he assumed was the Kojo did not lead to Mawenaland. This was the Nyoka, which wound its way across the grasslands then turned south into the savannah. It was there, after two weeks of night-trekking, that he found himself staring down into the village below.

He could wait no longer. Leaving his weapons in the bush, he emerged from the dense foliage and clamored down the hill onto the road leading into the village. He timed his appearance to meet the old man he'd seen coming down the path every day, driving a herd of goats from the grassland to the village. Ndoro lost his balance and stumbled, falling on the road at the old man's feet. The old man looked down at him, smiling with broken teeth.

"So you finally decided to show yourself."

Ndoro could say nothing, the wind knocked out of him.

"You must be weak if a little fall like that hurts," the old man said. He reached out, grabbing Ndoro's arm with surprising strength and lifting him to a sitting position.

"My name is Jabulani. Who are you?"

Ndoro coughed, eyes downcast. "Ndoro kaDingane."

"Hmm...are you Sesu?"

Ndoro looked up at the elder, feeling slight comfort in the fact that Jabulani knew his origins.

"Yes, baba, I am Sesu."

Jabulani nodded his head, reaching into his waist pouch. He handed Ndoro a yam.

"Here. You are very hungry. I will take you to my home."

The sight of the yam brought the pain of hunger back to Ndoro. He took it as politely as he could then bit into it voraciously. The firm sweetness made him close his eyes with joy.

Jabulani laughed. "Slow down, son. That's your yam. No one's going to take it from you."

When Ndoro finished, Jabulani helped him stand and gave him another yam as they walked down the narrow path to the village. It was larger than Ndoro expected, occupying a large field at the edge of a stand of trees. As they passed curious onlookers, Ndoro got the impression that Jabulani was more than a goat herder. Intense stares at him were followed by respectful nods to Jabulani.

"It seems I am in noble company," Ndoro commented.

"The worm cannot tell the difference between a rich dead man and a poor dead man," Jabulani replied.

Two young men pushed their way through the crowd toward them. One was as tall as Ndoro, but with a heavy muscular frame. The second man was a mirror image of the other, but a head shorter. The resemblance to Jabulani was unmistakable.

"Baba, where have you been?" the taller one asked. There was a hint of anger in his respectful tone.

"I took my goats to the hill pastures, Jawanza."

"The hills are not safe with the man-killer about," the other son said.

Jabulani frowned at his son. "Kamau, you're afraid of a donkey's horns."

The two looked at their father with exasperation, and then turned their attention to his companion. Ndoro lowered the yam from his face, standing straighter as his eyes met those of the brothers.

"This is Ndoro," Jabulani said. "He is a lost Sesu. He will be staying with us for a while."

The brothers' expressions transformed from distrust to awe.

"A Sesu?" Jawanza replied. "Then you were in no danger."

"A simba hunter," Kamau whispered. "You found a simba hunter!"

"Your baba didn't find me," Ndoro corrected. "I came here on my own."

"You must admit, you presence is good for the Diaka," Jabulani said. "A shumba stalks our village and has killed two, both of them children. We are not hunters, but I remember stories of the Sesu and their skill at hunting. Now come, you will rest and build up your strength, and then you will kill the shumba."

Ndoro's anger was not tempered by the old man's generous smile. He'd been tricked, but he could not refuse after accepting Diaka hospitality.

"What is this shumba, baba?" Ndoro asked. "Is it a simba?"

Jabulani shook his head. "I wish it was so. A shumba looks like a simba, but it is much different. It hunts alone and prefers the forest to the savannah. Some say they are spirits of the old gods, forced to roam the earth for some transgression no one remembers. They are very dangerous, and they have no fear of men. In fact, they prefer us as food."

Hunting the shumba would be difficult even with experienced Sesu hunters. Of course he'd killed Old Simba alone, but it was something he didn't wish to do again. Simbas were obvious in their ways; this shumba seemed more like a leopard in habits. This would be a far more dangerous hunt.

As they approached Jabulani's home, Ndoro pushed back his concerns. A low stone wall surrounded the group of wooden homes inside. Outside the entrance, two women surrounded by a group of children stopped their basket-weaving and jumped to their feet.

"Baba!" They rushed Jabulani with hugs and cries, followed by the children. From inside the compound others came, their joy just as passionate. Somewhere a drummer began to play, and the family sang and danced. Ndoro stepped aside as Jabulani's family celebrated their patriarch's return.

A shrill scream pierced the singing, emanating from within the compound. The drumming and singing ceased. Jabulani's children turned in the direction of the compound, whispering among themselves. Jabulani let out a sigh and rolled his eyes as Jawanza and Kamau snickered.

"What's wrong?" Ndoro asked.

"Mama is coming." Jawanza smiled.

The woman was as tall as Jabulani and almost as wide. Her chubby face was contorted into a frown as she marched toward her husband, a narrow tree branch in her hand.

"Talana," Jabulani began, "I..."

Talana swatted Jabulani across the arm.

"Woman, what is wrong with you?"

"If you wish to act like a child, I will treat you like one!" Talana retorted.

"I was gone for only a week."

Talana's anger subsided. "No one knew where you were. I thought the shumba killed you."

Jabulani touched his wife's shoulder and she smiled. "I went to the temple on the lake to ask Kikuba for help. He accepted my gift of goats and sent this man to help us." Jabulani put his hand on Ndoro's shoulder. "He is a shumba hunter."

"I was not sent by any god to help you," Ndoro explained.

"If Jabulani asked Kikuba to send help, then it is why you are here, whether you know it or not." Talana looked him up and down. "You need to eat. Come."

She took a step then turned back to Jabulani, hitting him again with the branch. "I don't care if you did talk to Kikuba. You tell me where you're going the next time."

Ndoro covered his mouth to hide his smile. Jabulani's grandchildren were not as modest, laughing at their grandfather out loud. Even Jabulani smiled, despite his best efforts to appear angry.

Talana led Ndoro through the gates of the family compound and into her house. His eyes burned from the smoke, but the smell of the stew simmering on the pot over the fire was worth the pain.

"Sit here." Talana pointed at a woven straw mat on the floor. Ndoro sat and Talana handed him a bowl of stew and a spoon.

"Thank you, mama," Ndoro said respectfully. The stew was the best food he'd eaten since fleeing Selike. A wave of serenity passed through him as he ate, followed by a sudden tiredness. He barely finished the stew before the bowl dropped from his hand, Talana catching it before it hit the ground. He was sound asleep before he collapsed on the mat.

When he awoke, he felt better than he had in days. Strips of sunlight penetrated the thatch roof of the hut, illuminating the inside. Talana and Jabulani sat opposite each other, enjoying a meal that smelled as delicious as the stew he ate before sleeping.

Jabulani looked at him and smiled. "Good, you are awake. I thought Talana killed you."

Talana punched Jabulani's shoulder. "I don't know anything about Sesu. The potion was just right for a Diaka man his size."

"You drugged me?" Ndoro asked.

"You needed to rest. You feel better now, don't you?"

"Yes, I do," Ndoro admitted. "But from now on, I would like to know if I'm about to be helped."

Jabulani nodded, and then handed Ndoro a plate. "Eat now. We must meet the elders today to discuss the shumba. It killed Shuka yesterday in his millet field. It is growing bolder every day."

Ndoro nodded. “It has become used to man-flesh and it senses your fear. We must kill it as soon as possible.”

Jabulani smiled. “So you will help us?”

“Of course,” Ndoro replied. “It is true we Sesu hunt simbas. But it is no easy thing. Many warriors have died during simba hunts. Planning and experience are very important. This shumba seems much more dangerous”

“Have you killed a simba?” Talana inquired

“Yes,” Ndoro answered.

“How many warriors did it take?”

Ndoro hesitated, not wanting to seem boastful, but refusing to lie to his hosts.

“I killed him alone.”

Jabulani sprang to his feet, clapping his hands. “Kikuba has truly blessed us! He sent us a great simba hunter.”

Ndoro raised his hand. “Baba, please listen to me. What I did was stupid. I was trying to prove myself to gain my father’s respect and almost died doing so.”

“But you did not die, and your wisdom will help us succeed,” Talana finished.

Ndoro sighed, giving up his attempts to dampen the couple’s expectations.

Jabulani finished his food then stood. “Come, Ndoro, it is time to see the elders.”

Ndoro and Jabulani exited the house into the bright sun. Jawanza and Kamau waited for them by the compound gate. Ndoro smiled when he saw Jawanza carrying his assegai, sword, and shield.

“I brought these for you,” he said. “You will need them.”

“Thank you.” The four men set out to meet the elders. They walked through the twisting crowded streets, following the narrow alleyways separating family compounds until they emerged on the wide avenue leading to the center of town. Everyone they passed stared at Ndoro hopefully, and he was embarrassed by all the attention. It was odd how bold and confident he had been in Selike when nothing was expected of him. Now that he was getting the respect he deserved, he was nervous and unsure. Maybe this was a spell of Mulugo’s doing, even though medicine priest was dead. Could his spirit be following him? He would ask Talana once he returned from his meeting with the elders.

They made their way to a grove of trees in the center of the village. Under the huge canopy of the largest tree sat eight elderly men deep in discussion. As they walked closer, the men halted their conversation. They all stared at Ndoro, their faces a patchwork of emotions.

They halted before the elders and sat. Ndoro watched his companions for any sign of ceremony, waiting to follow their movements. But there were none, only the simple head-nod of acknowledgement. Ndoro nodded his head as well.

"Elders, I bring you Ndoro kaDingane of the Sesu, the Shumba hunter," Jabulani announced.

"Your influence on Kikuba is impressive, Jabulani," one of the elders said. "There has never been a time you have visited the oracle and not succeeded."

The elder stood. "I am Shaihi, chosen to speak for the elders. Your coming is a true blessing, for the shumba is killing every day. I see you have your weapons."

Ndoro nodded.

"Good. Once you kill the shumba, you must hide them. The fari does not allow weapons in the village unless issued by him."

"Excuse me, but who is this fari?"

Shaihi cut his eyes at Jabulani, who looked away. "The fari is our master."

Ndoro's eyes went wide. "You are slaves?"

"Our village belongs to the fari of Galadima, servant of Askia Diallo."

Ndoro could not stay among these people. If the fari appeared while he was present, he might be considered a slave as well. However, he was obligated to help them when he accepted their hospitality.

"If shumba's are like simbas, he hunts you because he is old," Ndoro said. "I need help tracking him; I am not familiar with the signs of the forest. Once we know its hunting pattern, we can plan where to bait him."

The elders nodded.

"How many men will you need?" Shaihi asked.

"As many as possible."

"We will ask our families for volunteers. We will meet again this evening to discuss our plans for hunting the shumba."

Ndoro looked puzzled. "Volunteers?"

"We are elders, not Askia. We can only ask."

"I will help," Jawanza announced.

"I will, too," Kamau said, although his voice betrayed his uncertainty.

Shaihi smiled. "You have two so far."

Ndoro shrugged his shoulders. The Diaka were definitely not warriors. Sesu men and boys fought for the chance to join the simba hunts, the highest praise going to the warrior that struck the first blow. Among the Sesu, killing a simba was the highest form of bravery.

The groups dispersed to their clans. Ndoro said nothing as they walked back to the family compound. He went straight to Talana's hut, Mulugo's spirit still on his mind despite his situation. The matriarch of the Osseni clan was tending her yams, humming a song as she weeded the rows.

"Mama Talana, I must tell you something."

Talana ceased her gardening. "What is the matter, Ndoro?"

"I think a spirit is haunting me."

Talana put down her hoe and approached him. She traced his body with her palms, keeping her hands a few inches from his skin.

"I sense no spirits about you."

Ndoro sat before Talana. "You must understand how I came to be here. It had nothing to do with Baba Jabulani's prayers." Ndoro told Talana his story. After he finished, she sat beside him.

"You've caused a lot of trouble for one so young, boh-boh. Let me tell you a secret. Spirits exist among us. Some are peaceful, yet some are angry and use their second lives to seek revenge on those that harmed them while they were alive. This Mulugo was a medicine-priest, so he could be especially dangerous. Pray to your ancestors for protection, Ndoro."

Ndoro smiled. "The ancestors have done nothing but cause trouble for me. I have chosen not to listen to them."

"That is your decision," Talana replied. "But remember, if you choose to live your life without respecting the ancestors; do not expect them to respect you."

Talana handed him a yam. "Now eat. You will need your strength for the days ahead. I think you will find the Diaka are not the bravest of men."

Talana's prediction was sadly true. When the elders met again that afternoon, no clan had sent men to join the hunt. It would be Jawanza, Kamau and himself.

Shaihi's face was a portrait of disappointment. "I am sorry, Ndoro. It seems our young men have no taste for shumba-hunting."

"But the shumba has a taste for them," Ndoro snapped. "Jawanza, Kamau, and I will kill the shumba." With that Ndoro stalked away. Jawanza and Kamau ran to catch him. Jawanza was excited, but Kamau's face drooped with worry.

"What do we do first, Ndoro?" Jawanza asked.

"We bait him before he attacks again," Ndoro replied.

They returned to the compound, discussing their plan along the way. They found Jabulani sitting before Talana's hut, enjoying a snack of kola nuts.

"Baba," Jawanza said, "we need a goat."

Jabulani frowned but didn't argue, leading the trio to his herd and giving them a sickly grey animal. They led the goat through town, a parade of children and adults trailing them. Ndoro scowled at them all, still ill-tempered from the Diaka reaction to the call for help.

The impromptu parade ended as they left the village and entered the surrounding clearing.

"Jawanza, where have the attacks taken place?" Ndoro asked.

"There, there and there," Jawanza answered, pointing out the directions.

"He is hunting along the river's edge," Ndoro commented. "Animals are distracted when they drink, or people when they fill their calabashes."

Ndoro walked to the river, searching for crocodile sign.

"The trees come close to the river on the south," he said. "If we leave the goat too near the shore, crocodiles will surely make a meal of it."

"There is a trail that leads from the bush to the river there," Kamau said. "Elephants use it when they come to drink."

He led them to the trail. "This is an excellent ambush spot," Ndoro said. He pulled his knife, grabbed the goat and slit its throat.

Kamau was not happy. "You killed baba's goat!"

"What did you think I was going to do?" Ndoro asked. "Simbas kill only when they have to. He will take an easy meal over a difficult one. That's why he hunts you."

Ndoro placed the goat's carcass downwind from where he thought the shumba might approach.

"We will wait in the trees. Jawanza, we need bows and poison arrows."

Jawanza ran immediately to the village. Ndoro looked at Kamau, sensing his uncertainty. He placed his hand gently on his shoulder.

"Kamau, a simba is no different from any other animal. If you stand your ground and show no fear, he will respect you and give way. Maybe shumbas are the same."

Kamau nodded but still looked worried.

"Come," Ndoro said. "We will sit here until Jawanza returns."

Jawanza returned an hour later with the weapons. The three men separated, Jawanza and Kamau positioned on either side of the goat. Ndoro sat across the path opposite the goat. When the shumba approached, Ndoro would draw it into the path, giving the brothers a clean shot. Sesu hunters would have taken the shumba with spears, but Ndoro did not trust his raw companions at close quarters with such a beast. Jawanza was too eager, which would make him careless, and Kamau was afraid. The men went to their stations and prepared for a long night, with Jawanza taking the first watch.

Ndoro jumped from sleep, a sense of dread in his mind. Rain had come unexpected, drenching him. He grabbed his assegai and shield and sprang to his feet, looking about desperately for Jawanza and Kamau. A scream cut through the rainy night, a sound Ndoro felt in his bones. Jawanza and Kamau emerged from their hiding places.

"What was that?" Kamau asked.

"I don't know," Ndoro replied.

"Baba Keffi!" Jawanza shouted. "His farm is near." Jawanza sprang from the brush and ran down the road toward the sound. Ndoro and Kamau went after him, catching him moments later. The three splashed down the muddy path until Ndoro spotted movement in the distance through the sheets of rain.

"Jawanza, Kamau, go to the woods quickly. Remember our plan!"

The brothers disappeared into the wet trees. Ndoro raised his shield, his assegai braced in his right hand, his eyes focused on the image as it drew nearer. It was the largest simba he'd ever seen. The beast carried something in his jaws; as it came closer Ndoro saw it was a man, probably Baba Keffi. With a jerk of its massive head, it tossed the body aside and fixed its eyes on Ndoro. Ndoro realized he was not confronting a normal simba. It seemed to smile, then rose up on its hind legs.

"Ndoro," it growled. "You did not think you would escape me so easily, did you?"

Ndoro was startled. "Mulugo!"

The shumba laughed. "I have followed you since the day you struck me down, waiting for my chance for revenge. It is time for you to die, abomination!"

Shumba Mulugo stepped toward Ndoro then roared in pain, an arrow protruding from its right shoulder. The beast reached for the arrow as if its paw was a hand. Another arrow whizzed by, missing it by inches. A third arrow struck the beast in its left paw. The beast roared again, turning his head toward Jawanza's hiding place.

Ndoro shifted his assegai and threw it as hard and as straight as he could. The projectile struck the beast in the chest and it yelped. It grasped the shaft with both paws as it stumbled away. Ndoro charged, raising his sword over his head for the killing blow. He stopped as he felt a hard blow to his jaw, the world turning dark as he flew backward and smacked into the hard mud path.

No sooner had he hit the ground was he lifted again, his shoulder on fire. The Mulugo-beast had his shoulder in its jaws, raising him from the mud. Ndoro slammed his wrist-knife from his free arm against the beast's head, but it only tightened its grip. He struck again and Mulugo dropped him. He blacked out for a moment, and then opened his eyes to see Jawanza on the creature's back, stabbing frantically with his knife.

"Kamau!" he called out. "Help us!"

Ndoro tried to lift his left arm, but it would not respond. He pushed himself up with his right arm and crawled to his assegai and shield. As he turned, Kamau stepped out onto the trail. He looked at Ndoro, at his brother struggling with the beast, and then turned and ran away down the road. Ndoro shook his head, disappointed but not surprised. He struggled to his feet, assegai in hand and staggered back into the battle.

The Mulugo beast managed to grab hold of Jawanza and threw him into the bush. He was about to follow and finish off the Diaka when Ndoro blocked his path.

"Is this all?" he shouted. "Is the spirit of a great medicine priest weaker in death than in life? Come so I can kill you again!"

The beast let loose a roar that shook the trees. It half-ran, half-stumbled toward Ndoro, apparently weakened by the poison. Ndoro crouched low, bracing himself for the attack.

"Die, abomination!" it roared. The creature leapt at Ndoro, who rolled backward onto his back. As the Mulugo-beast filled his vision, Ndoro raised his assegai, bracing it as well as he could in the mud. The blade cut a path through the creature's lower jaw, tearing through the roof of its mouth and penetrating the skull to the brain. Its weight fell full on Ndoro, and his right arm snapped as the breath was knocked out of his lungs. Blood and rain flowed over him as he gasped for air.

"Forget about me!" he heard Jawanza say. "Ndoro is under the shumba!"

The pressure of the shumba's body eased then was no more. Above him, a circle of Diaka men stared down at him.

"Is he alive?" one asked.

Ndoro nodded his head and saw stars.

"Put him in the cart with Jawanza. The rest of you get the shumba's body. Mama Talana said we must bring it, too."

The voice giving the orders was that of Kamau. The men tried to be gentle, but Ndoro experienced less pain fighting the Mulugo-beast. They laid him down in the cart, beside Jawanza.

"You killed him," Jawanza said.

"No, we killed him," Ndoro replied.

Jawanza smiled, and then passed out. Ndoro wished he'd been so lucky. The cart ride back to the village was a terrible affair; the jostling of the cart amplified the shooting pain of his injuries. His rescuers were just as rough removing him from the cart and carrying him to Mama Talana's house. Two beds waited for him and Jawanza. As soon as they were eased into the beds, the room crowded with the curious. Ndoro was in so much pain, he was beginning to wish the shumba had killed him.

There was a sudden commotion followed by smacks, yelps and curses. The crowd fled and Talana stood alone before them, breathing heavily with an old, dented orinka in her hand.

"Damn fools!" she said. "What do they think this is?" Her expression softened as she looked at Ndoro and Jawanza.

"It looks as though Kamau was the smartest of the three of you."

She pulled up a stool and sat between the beds. "Well, shumba slayers, let's get on with it."

She shoved a foul-smelling ball of fat into each of their mouths and ordered them to chew. Ndoro was on his second chew when the pain in his body disappeared with his consciousness. He fell into a deep, restful sleep briefly interrupted by questions and answers he couldn't remember. When he finally awoke, his wounds were bandaged and his broken bones set. Jawanza lay beside him, still unconscious. Ndoro struggled to sit on the edge of the bed and was pleased. There was pain, but nothing he could not handle.

"What are you doing?" Talana shouted.

"Sitting."

Talana pushed him back down on the bed and he winced.

"You shouldn't be awake," she complained. "You should still be asleep. It's been only three days and the poultice was made for one week."

"I've been asleep for three days?"

Talana lifted his bandages. "Your wounds are healed?"

She removed the remainder of the bandages but left the splint on his arm.

"You have a magic about you, boy. Your wounds have healed too quickly for a normal man."

"I am Sesu," Ndoro boasted.

Talana moved the shoulder of his broken right arm and he grimaced.

"Your arm is still broken, O Great Sesu. You will be with us for a while yet. Besides, you are a hero now. There are many people waiting to celebrate you and to offer their daughters for marriage."

"I can't stay," Ndoro said.

"Is it time to leave the company of slaves?"

Ndoro fell silent, embarrassed by Talana's question.

She inspected Jawanza's wounds, her back turned to Ndoro. "No need to be ashamed. You are a free man from a noble people. You should not be here. Jok created a place for everyone in this world; the Diaka are here to serve. But I feel a change coming for us. I think you are at the center of this change."

"I respect your words, Mama Talana, though I don't put much trust in feelings."

"It doesn't matter. Your bones will heal slowly. You will have to stay until the dry season."

As Talana predicted, Ndoro's rehabilitation lasted the length of the rainy season. During those damp days Ndoro gradually became a part of Jabulani's family, taking on the chores he could manage with his injured arm. He became the buffer between Jawanza and Kamau, easing the tension that developed between the brothers after the shumba hunt. Ndoro had no doubt Kamau fled in fear, but he had at least gathered himself enough to bring help, however late it had been. By the end of season, the brothers were speaking to each other again, much to the joy of the entire family.

That joy ended during the beginning of the dry season. The rains dwindled as the days grew shorter; soon the cloudless skies dominated the Diaka lands. Ndoro sensed a change in the attitude of the village with the season. Uneasiness replaced the joy of the rainy season; the villagers seemed agitated.

Ndoro sat with Jabulani in front of the walls of the compound, enjoying a snack of kola nuts.

"Baba, the village has changed since the rains. Everyone seems nervous."

"It's dry season," Jabulani replied. "The fari will come soon."

"Is there a problem with the harvest?"

Jabulani took the kola nut from his mouth. "No, the harvest will be fine. Dry season is war season, and the fari is always at war."

"That should be no concern to you," Ndoro said. "Your people are not warriors."

Jabulani stared at Ndoro. "We are whatever the fari wants us to be." The old man rose and shuffled into the compound. The reason for the change in mood was obvious now; if the Diaka were called to fight, they would be slaughtered.

The fari arrived the next day during the afternoon. Ndoro was helping Mama Talana dig yams when a commotion caught their attention. Kamau came running up to them, stumbling to a stop and resting his hands on his knees, his mouth wide and gasping for air.

"What's wrong, boy?" Talana asked.

Kamau looked up. "The fari...the fari is here. I saw his camp near the river when I went to check the fish traps."

Talana froze, dropping the yam she held. Ndoro watched her trudge to the bell hanging near the front of her home. She struck the bell with a mournful rhythm, its shallow sound calling all the family members to the compound. Despite its size, the courtyard filled in moments with extended family. They gathered about Jabulani's home, waiting for their patriarch to appear. But Jabulani was nowhere to be found.

"Ndoro, Jawanza," Talana called. "Go find your father."

The two set off immediately. The village streets emptied as other families were called to their compounds to prepare for the fari's arrival. Ndoro and Jawanza ventured outside the village and found Jabulani tending his goats at the village pasture.

"Baba!" Ndoro called, "Mama sends for you."

Jabulani turned to look at the two, his face sad. "The fari is here?"

"Yes, he is, baba," Jawanza replied.

Jabulani followed Ndoro and Jawanza back to the compound. The family was gone, so they made their way to the meeting tree.

"You don't have to come," Jabulani said to Ndoro.

"You have accepted me as your son. I will respect you as a father," Ndoro replied.

They hurried along, joining the family and the others as they gathered in the grove surrounding the meeting tree. Ndoro looked over the crowd and saw the fari sitting on a gilded stool. He stood and the Diaka fell to their knees in unison, sprinkling their heads with dirt. Ndoro remained standing, staring at the fari. The master of the Diaka was a tall, strongly-built man with intelligent brown eyes that focused on Ndoro. Multiple *topes* covered his upper body to increase his girth, the outer garment a deep blue robe decorated with finely woven white patterns. Two servants stood beside him, one holding an elegant ebonywood staff capped with ivory and gold, the other a wide umbrella over the fari. Behind him his warriors posed, fierce men covered in dark robes and leather helmets, armed with studded shields and tall lances.

"You have his attention," Jabulani whispered. "That is not a good thing. Be careful, my Sesu son."

The Diaka were all present. Without hesitation, the fari stepped to the edge of the gathering, standing before the elders crouched at his feet.

"The Diaka have served my family faithfully for many years, and I have done my best to answer your service with kindness. We accept your gifts of the harvest, the abundance a sure sign that the ancestors are content."

The fari's face changed from benevolent to serious. "As you know, I am a proud servant of the Askia and as his servant I am subject to his will. So it is with gratitude that I respond to his call in time of peril. As we speak the enemies of the High One conspire to do him harm within the borders of Bordu. The Askia has asked that I serve him by raising an army to deal with this threat and, as his servant, I have agreed. Today I ask the Diaka to do the same for me. The time of farmers has ended; as you rose to slay the shumba that hunted your own, you must rise to slay those that hunt your Askia."

The Diaka responded with utter silence. They clutched each other, their mouths moving in silent prayer. The fari paused for a moment, letting his words sink in.

"In a month's time, Sanafaran Otuhu will come to accept our Diaka brothers into his ranks. We will dance together in victory when the Bordubu are destroyed."

The fari remained standing as his servants gathered his stool, placing it in its gilded chest. The Diaka dispersed; many mumbling about the misfortune the fari had placed upon them. Ndoro remained where he stood. The warriors approached him, their swords in hand. They walked up to him, forming a semicircle about him.

"Who are you?" the closest man asked.

"I will give my answer only to the fari," Ndoro replied. "Men of equal status must speak face to face."

The warrior frowned and motioned for Ndoro to follow him. They escorted him to the fari, who stood between his servants with a curious smile on his face.

"Who is this free man living among my slaves?" he asked.

"I am Ndoro kaDingane."

The fari's eyes widened with his smile. "A Sesu!" He circled Ndoro, looking him up and down. "Ndoro son of Dingane, is it? You seem to be a true warrior of the grasslands. But I ask myself, what is the son of an inkosi doing among my slaves?"

The warriors laughed at the fari's insult. Though his throat burned in anger, Ndoro held his posture. He would not lose his temper or his life because of an insult. The fari seemed to be waiting for a response, for a disappointed frown came to his face.

"You need not answer my question," the fari finally said. "No one knows the changing favors of nobles better than I. A trusted brother one day becomes a hated enemy the next."

The male servants arrived with the fari's litter.

"I am Biton Sangare, fari of the Diaka. You may stay among them if you wish, although I think you would find the hospitality of free men more comfortable."

"I am Sesu," Ndoro replied. "The simple life suits me fine. Besides, I will be on my way soon."

Biton raised an eyebrow. "Really? I wish to ask you a favor before you leave us, young Sesu." He stepped closer to Ndoro, looking about as if concerned about being heard. "I do your friends a great wrong by asking them to fight. They are not warriors and I fear the only benefit they will be is to catch the arrows and spears of the Bordubu. I need fighting men."

"There are brave men among them," Ndoro replied.

Biton smiled. "True, but bravery cannot stop a spear. The Sesu are trained from birth to be warriors, is that not so?"

Ndoro didn't like where this conversation was going. He nodded in response.

Biton's smile grew wider. "I have a proposal. Stay here as my representative, my koi for the Diaka. Train them in the warrior ways of the Sesu. You will be paid well, of course."

"There is no time to train them," Ndoro replied.

"I give you till next dry season. The Diaka will be spared this season's campaign if you agree to train them for next season. I can wait for trained warriors."

"That is still not enough time," Ndoro explained. "Sesu are trained from birth. No one can learn so much in so little time."

Biton's smile faded. "My Sesu friend, you must do this. Every season I raise an army in hopes of defeating the Bordubu and every season I fail. The nobles are more concerned in duels and praise-songs, and the foot soldiers are no better than the Diaka. They break like twigs against the shields of the Bordubu army. The only reason that the Bordubu are not our masters is that they have no interest in subduing us. But with a trained army, victory could be ours. Besides, the lives of your friends depend on your decision. Whether you agree or not, the Diaka will fight. They have a better chance of surviving if they had the skills of a Sesu."

Biton climbed into his litter. "Please consider my request. If you decide train them, send a runner to me. The Diaka know where to find me."

Biton waved a hand and the litter-bearers set off down the main avenue followed by his bodyguard. Villagers prostrated as the litter passed, remaining on the ground until the entourage disappeared into the surrounding brush.

Ndoro watched the fari leave and contemplated his words. Training the Diaka to fight was a tremendous burden to place on his young shoulders, no matter what his heritage. Though he was the son of an inkosi, he had never been trained to be an induna because of the stigma placed on him and his mother. The responsibility he craved as a Sesu had been granted to him among strangers.

Jabulani interrupted his thoughts. "The fari spoke to you. What were his words?"

Ndoro looked at his adopted father and realized the wisdom of the fari. He knew Ndoro would help the Diaka not because he was asked, but because he truly cared for them.

"I have until next dry season to make you fighting men."

Jabulani fell to his knees then raised his hands to the sky.

"Ayha! Ayha! I praise the spirits for sending you!"

Diaka ran to them upon hearing Jabulani's shouting. Ndoro attempted to calm him down. "Baba, listen to me! You still have to fight."

"But we will fight like warriors and bring honor to our families," Jabulani sang.

Jawanza and Kamau were the first to reach them. Before they said a word, Jabulani raised his hand to silence them.

"Gather the elders and bring them to the grove," he ordered. "Come, Ndoro. We will wait for them."

Jabulani grasped his arm and almost dragged him back to the meeting tree. Ndoro sat under the heavy branches, his head reeling as the crowd gathered again, but this time in optimistic expectation. The elders appeared soon afterward. There was not a happy face among them. Shaihi's voice was tense when he spoke.

"What is going on, Jabulani?"

"The fari has postponed our service until next dry season. He has made Ndoro our koi. He is to train our men in the Sesu warrior way.

Shaihi's eyebrows rose as he looked to Ndoro. "Is this true?"

"Yes," Ndoro answered.

Shaihi exhaled. "The ancestors truly listen to you, Jabulani." Shaihi prostrated before Ndoro and sprinkled dirt on his head. The other elders repeated the gesture; Ndoro reached down to pick each man up.

"Please, don't do this. I agreed to train you, nothing more."

"You are the son of a chief, are you not?" Shaihi asked.

Ndoro nodded.

"Then you were born for this responsibility."

Jabulani touched Ndoro's shoulder.

"Shaihi and I are old enough to remember the last time the Diaka marched off to war for the fari. We watched our fathers and brothers leave this village, never to return. They, like us, were farmers, not warriors. They were never trained to fight. Your knowledge will give us a chance at least to come home."

"I can't promise you that," Ndoro said.

"With your training, we can at least hope," Shaihi replied.

Ndoro felt trapped. The Diaka and the fari were depending on him. Maybe what little he knew might help his adopted tribe, but he doubted it. Still, there was hope among the Diaka and he would not rob them of that.

"We don't have much time," Shaihi warned. "The seasons will pass like a cheetah. Koi Ndoro, what do you wish us to do?"

Ndoro was speechless. This was happening too fast. He needed time to understand this sudden change in status.

"Everyone, return to your homes," he finally said. "I need time to organize. Shaihi, Jabulani, can I depend on the wisdom of the elders?"

"Of course you can," Jabulani answered.

Drumming erupted in the distance and the city exploded in celebration. Ndoro watched the Diaka dance as the weight of responsibility crashed down on his shoulders. There was so much to do, so much to plan, and he had no experience at all. For the first time in his young life, Ndoro felt like praying.

Jabulani made his way to Ndoro. "There is a house in the compound we will prepare for you until your compound is complete."

"I don't need a compound!"

"Yes, you do. You are a koi now. You will need a compound for your personal needs and to hold the homes of your officers."

There was no stopping Jabulani. Ndoro nodded and followed his family in a jubilant parade back to the compound.

The house Jabulani gave him had belonged to one of his daughters who married Shaihi's eldest son two years before Ndoro's arrival. Talana had kept it in good shape, the conical thatch roof recently rewoven with fresh grass and the interior floor swept smooth. Ndoro had nothing except his weapons, but that was soon remedied. Gifts came from every family; cooking pots, stools, bed boards, ceremonial masks, and even livestock and grain. Jabulani was right when he said he would need his own compound.

Ndoro had little time to be grateful for his fortune, for his every waking moment was filled with his new duty. Since he had no idea what to do, he began by using his own training as an example. A week after his dubious promotion, he gathered the elders to explain his plan.

"Each family will establish a group of young men, an intanga. The oldest male, the induna, will act as leader of the group," he began. "The group males will be given their own section of the family compound where they will live together. The eldest male will report to me every day for training. When he returns to his compound, he will instruct his group. Once a week, all the males will meet in the village pasture to train together. We begin training today."

The elders returned to their homes to convey the orders. Ndoro walked with Jabulani, his eyes downcast.

"What is wrong, Ndoro?"

"Nothing." Ndoro realized his plan was not the best, but it was the only way he could train every man in time.

His mood lifted when he entered his house. Mama Talana was cooking, the smell of her delicious stew thick in the air. Someone else was with her, a young woman Ndoro did not recognize. She was obviously Talana's daughter, possessing the same intense eyes. Unlike other Diaka women who braided their hair, her hair was short. It reminded him of the women of his homeland.

Talana noticed him staring at the woman and laughed.

"Sit down and eat, boy," she ordered. "These stupid men act as if you've grown ten years in a day."

Ndoro took the bowl from Talana eagerly and ate. The stew was tasty and soothing as always. As he finished, Talana brought the woman to him.

"This is my daughter Sarama. She had come back to us from the Diarra clan. Her husband died of sickness six months ago. We were finally able to return the lobola given for her marriage."

"It had to be a very large lobola for such a beautiful woman," Ndoro said.

Sarama and Talana smiled. "You have a sweet tongue, koi-boy," Talana said. "Be careful how you use it." Talana took his bowl and scooped out more stew. "Sarama will help maintain your compound when it is complete."

Ndoro placed his bowl down. "I accepted this duty because of my debt to your family. Don't look at me as a master. Look at me as your son."

Talana laughed. "Don't worry about that, boh-boh. Mama Talana can still see the child in your eyes. The time will come when you are truly the master of the Diaka, but not now."

Ndoro turned his attention to Sarama. "I thank you for your help."

Sarama shrugged. "It's nothing. You honor my family with your presence, and I can see you are loved by them. It will give me a chance to see if you are worthy of such admiration."

"You are truly your mother's daughter." Ndoro stood. "I must meet the men at the village square. We begin training today."

Ndoro grabbed his weapons and left the house, jogging to the village pasture just outside the walls. All the men and boys were present, including Jawanza and Kamau. The group was a disappointing sight. Their shields and spears were barely sturdy enough for hunting, let alone fighting. Old rusted swords hung at their sides, more useless than the spears they carried. He would have to meet with the elders to see if there was a nearby village or town possessing a blacksmith skilled in weaponry. If not, they would have to ask the fari for help.

The men and boys fell silent as he drew a line with the tip of his assegai in the dirt.

"Take a place at the line," he ordered.

The Diaka formed a ragged line, their eyes wandering. Only Jawanza gave his full attention. Ndoro charged forward, attacking an older man who chatted with a friend. Some of the others yelled, but it was too late. Ndoro slammed his shield into the man, knocking him into the dirt. In a fluid motion, Ndoro stabbed the man in the thigh, not deep enough to maim him but enough to draw blood. The man yelped and grabbed his thigh as he scrambled away. The others, including Jawanza, fell into shocked silence. Ndoro walked back to his place on the opposite side of the line.

"It can happen that quickly," he explained. "One lapse and you are among the ancestors. If you wish to have a chance to live, you will remember everything I teach you today and now on. You will go back to your compounds and teach your brothers, and all of you will practice during every spare moment. If you are lucky, you will learn enough to bring glory upon yourself and your ancestors."

Ndoro began with simple blocking and thrusting drills that lasted until dusk. They trudged back to their compounds, Jawanza, Kamau, and Ndoro returning together in exhausted silence. On his way, he received word that the elders had sent a message to Jehnay requesting new weapons. They did not know when the weapons would arrive. When Ndoro entered his house, Sarama was there, preparing his evening meal. He collapsed on his bed.

"The drill went well?" she asked.

"It went long. They picked up well enough, but this is impossible. I had my entire life to learn what I know."

"A bull grows his ears before his horns," Sarama replied. "Be patient, they will learn."

She handed him his bowl and he ate slowly, watching Sarama as she put away the cooking pots. She had the soothing spirit of her mother, but her body was more than just a distraction. She moved as if she wanted him to notice her, though he also knew it just might be him imagining an invitation. The turmoil of his life had never given him the time to get to know any woman. Had Talana paired them together for just that reason? He looked away from her and into his bowl. Ndoro decided he was reading his own thoughts into Sarama's motions. Besides, despite everything, she was still a slave. He knew Sesu custom well; a clear line separated free men from slaves, a line even the inkosi could not cross. But he was not in Sesuland.

The weeks ran by like the swollen river as Ndoro trained the Diaka. His days were filled with drills, sparring, mock battles, and weapon training, leaving him exhausted by nightfall. Sarama was always there when he returned, preparing his food and listening to him recount the day. Her replies were always encouraging and her advice full of wisdom. Ndoro became more and more impressed with her as time passed.

As Sarama foretold, the bull began to grow its horns. The Diaka took their training to heart and it began to show. Each family's intanga became adept at the drills, impressing Ndoro with their precision. A sense of pride emerged among the groups, each clan creating a family totem that they carried to training displayed atop a staff. Jabulani's clan chose the goat, a gesture of honor to their patriarch and his love of goat herding.

The rains came and the drills continued despite the planting season. With training constantly interrupted, Ndoro spent less time with the men. He occupied his time with the elders, trying to find out as much as possible about the style of fighting in this land. What he heard disturbed him. The Sesu style of the swift mass attack was not done. Instead, large armies met face to face in flat fields of grass, following the ritual of exchanging insults and watching nobles duel in individual combat. Sometimes a battle never occurred, especially if one side realized the magic of its opponents was too strong to overcome. But when a battle did happen it was often brutal and bloody. Ndoro trudged back to his home, his mind heavy with this new revelation. As always, Sarama was waiting.

"What did the elders say?" she asked.

Ndoro collapsed on his stool. "Everything I've done is wrong. It's all wrong!"

Sarama handed him his bowl. "I have waited on you for four months, Koi Ndoro. You have never done anything wrong."

Ndoro shrugged. "How can you be so sure?"

Sarama gave Ndoro one of her gentle smiles. "You are too young to be the man the elders wish you to be. But you did not walk away; you stayed to teach what you could. You did not do anything wrong; you did something different. Now you must change."

"Change to what?" Ndoro fell back onto his cot. "I know nothing of this way of war."

"That is your strength." Sarama sat beside him. "When a people follow a tradition, they never question it. They obey because it is all they know. But you, Koi Ndoro, have the advantage of being free of these traditions. You see our ways from the outside with no care of right or wrong. What is obvious to you is invisible to us. There is strength in our ways, but there may also be weaknesses."

Ndoro sat upright. "Strengths and weaknesses."

Sarama stood. "Eat your stew. It will help you think."

"Thank you, Sarama."

Sarama smiled. "See. A Diaka man would never thank a woman for her advice."

Sarama began to leave when Ndoro stood.

"You don't have to go," he said.

Sarama smiled again. "One change at a time, Koi Ndoro."

Ndoro finished his stew then spent the rest of the night analyzing the words of the elders. He drew diagrams in the floor of his house, trying his best to visualize the patterns explained to him. Look for strengths and weaknesses, Sarama advised. Slowly the patterns emerged. Chaos became coherent; the patterns became clear.

The next morning a sliver of sunshine escaped through the constant clouds and fell on Ndoro's face. He sprang from his cot, gathered his weapons and rushed out of his house to the training field. Splashing to the top hill in the center of the field, he banged the muster drum. The warriors charged the hill moments later.

Ndoro gazed down upon them, barely able to contain himself.

"Diaka, we have trained hard and you have done well. I have given you all I know, and you have honored me by learning with all you have."

"But I have taken you down the wrong path. Today we will begin again not from the very beginning, but taking a different path. When we are done, the word Diaka will strike fear in our enemies and the griots will sing our song for generations!"

The Diaka cheered but Ndoro waved them silent.

"We have a lot to learn in a little time. Our transformation begins today."

* * *

The rainy season ended with a violent storm that damaged crops and destroyed a few homes outside the village. Everyone was involved with repairing the damage when the fari and his entourage entered the village that afternoon. The council drum summoned all to the meeting tree. Ndoro was with Sarama inspecting his new compound when he heard the summons.

"The season passed too quickly," he said.

Sarama place her hand on his shoulder. "We are ready."

Ndoro grabbed her hand. "I don't know how long we will be gone, but when I return, I would like to spend more time with you."

Sarama smiled. "You are a young man, Ndoro. There are many younger women in this village that desire your time."

"My time belongs to you."

Sarama's face became serious. "I won't deny my feelings for you, but I will not be anyone's concubine. As a slave, that is all I can be to you."

Ndoro decided to show Sarama how serious he felt. He kissed her.

"You told me yourself that I could change what I wish. When I return, the Diaka will no longer be slaves."

"A young man's dream," Sarama replied. "Go now. The fari awaits you."

The fari sat on his gilded stool beneath the meeting tree, flanked by his bodyguards and another group of men Ndoro did not recognize. Their rich garments signified noble families, and the presence of griots confirmed his thoughts. The Diaka surrounded them in supplication, their heads covered with dust. Ndoro walked before the fari and assumed the same position.

"So Sesu, you have remained to fulfill your promise," Biton commented. "Rise and show your face."

Ndoro stood. "I gave my word."

One of the noble warriors came forward. He was a head shorter than Ndoro, but powerfully built.

"What good is the word of a Sesu?" he said. "They say your people are cattle thieves with delusions of greatness."

Ndoro looked at this intruder into his conversation and frowned. It was an insult that demanded a response, but Ndoro was not about to kill this man with so much at stake for the Diaka.

Biton raised his staff for their attention. "I see only you, Ndoro. Where are your warriors?"

Ndoro raised his orinka and the muster drums answered. A chant rose in the distance, deep male voices resonating in time with the drums. Down the avenue they trotted, five hundred strong, marching in family groups. Once they reached the plaza, the rhythm changed. The family groups broke into ranks of archers, spearmen and heavy infantry. Ndoro jabbed his orinka in the air and the drumming ceased. He turned slowly to face Biton, cutting a glance at the arrogant nobleman.

"The Diaka await your command."

Biton smiled broadly, apparently pleased. The nobleman stepped forward again.

"They can march, but can they fight?"

"There is only one way to find out," Ndoro replied.

"Koi Ndoro, this skeptic is Otuhu, Sanafaran of my army," Biton explained.

Ndoro was not impressed. He bowed, but did not give Otuhu the same respect he bestowed on Biton.

"Don't assume your claim of Sesu lineage makes you my equal," Otuhu warned.

Biton stepped in before Ndoro was able to reply. "We will spend the night here, and then march to the other villages in the morning."

With that, the fari retired to his litter. Otuhu followed, glaring at Ndoro. Biton's bearers lifted him and carried him to Ndoro.

"Our camp is only a few miles from the village. Join us."

"Thank you for the invitation, but tonight must be for my men and their families."

Biton nodded in agreement. "Celebrate well tonight. I find it is the best way to build courage in men who are about to die. I will send two bulls for your feast."

To a Sesu, it was an expensive gift. Ndoro could barely hide his gratefulness. "Thank you, fari."

Biton waved his flywhisk and the entourage departed. Ndoro needed to say nothing, for all had been heard. The streets filled with jubilant hordes and the warriors broke rank to dance with their families. Ndoro was swamped by Jabulani's clan. He smiled and hugged and kissed them all, but inside he was in turmoil. He searched the throng for Sarama and found her standing too far away, her eyes meeting his, her smile bringing a similar smile to his face.

The feast began immediately. The village center was quickly decorated while cooking pots were rushed from family compounds to prepare the food. A group of excited men attacked the ground with shovels and picks, rushing to dig the cooking pit to roast the bulls. Chickens and goats were slaughtered while Talana, using a special magic just for such an occasion, brought hundreds of fish to the surface of the river for the children to harvest. Two of the fari's guards arrived with the bulls soon afterward as well as the long-awaited shipment of weapons. The only break in the celebrating occurred as Jabulani gave praise to the ancestors and offered the bulls in sacrifice.

By nightfall, everyone sat in a circle around the meeting tree, the area illuminated by dancing torchlight. Drummers played while groups of dancers from different families took turns performing under the broad branches of the meeting tree. Ndoro occupied the honored position closest to the tree with Jabulani, Jawanza, Talana, and the rest of the clan close by. He was served the choicest meat from the bull, as well as given the honor of sampling every item first before it was served to the rest of the celebrants. Never in his life had he eaten so much. His stomach was as tight as a water bag. Sarama was also there, sitting among her sisters. Ndoro saw them talking as they looked at him. Sarama chatted and laughed, keeping her penetrating eyes on him at all times. Ndoro felt his skin warm from the heat of her gaze.

Jabulani slapped his back. "Never have I seen such a feast! The Diaka are truly blessed this night."

"When we return from battle, there will be no other feast grander than this," Ndoro replied.

Jabulani put his fingers to his lips and shushed Ndoro. "Don't dwell on the future. A warrior must live for the day, for it is all he has."

Ndoro laughed. "You talk as if you're the Sesu!"

A swarm of Jabulani's grandchildren appeared, their little hands pulling at Ndoro.

"Dance, dance!" they shouted. "You must dance!"

Ndoro laughed as they pulled him to his feet. "I know no dances. At least not Diaka ones."

"The training dance!" Jawanza chimed. "Show them the cattle raid dance."

Ndoro never imagined the movements taught to all Sesu boys as a dance. As he felt the rhythm of the drummers, he decided to give it a try. He took the dancers spot under the branches. As the drummers played he fell into the movements, his body moving sharp yet fluid as he crouched low, performing the sleeping simba form. He closed his eyes to feel the music while he walked, ran and thrust imaginary spears at empty enemies. The roar of the crowd forced his eyes open to see the indunas, his officers, joining him. They chanted his instructions in time and Ndoro finally heard the music in his words. This was how the Diaka learned what he taught them. Behind the walls of the compounds the training had become a dance, his words a song. As family members joined in, Ndoro saw the effect these new warriors had on the other Diaka. He realized even if all of them died tomorrow, the Diaka would always have this moment. It was the night they stood as men. They would march away the next day not as conscripts, but as warriors.

The celebration did not end until well into the night. Ndoro staggered to his house, more from a full stomach than the insanely potent millet beer served throughout the night. He waved his companions good night as he entered his house. He barely sat on his bed when Sarama entered.

"Sarama? Why are you here?"

Sarama put her finger to her lips. She undid the wrap around her waist and quickly removed her top. Her body was as beautiful as her knowing smile, lighting the room with her aural glow. She moved up to him slowly, placing her hands on his shoulders and pushing him down on the bed.

"I will not be your concubine," she whispered. "Promise me, Ndoro."

"I promise," Ndoro replied, his voice tight with longing.

Sarama disarmed him with another of her smiles. "Now let me show you why my lobola was so generous."

Ndoro awoke alone. If Diaka customs were like the Sesu, it would be an embarrassment for Sarama to have spent the night with him as a single woman. He was glad though; the time had come for the Diaka to march off to war. He dressed carefully, donning the uniform crafted by his adopted sisters. As he placed his plumed helmet on his head Talana entered his house.

"The Great Koi is ready to begin his legend?" she asked.

Ndoro could not match her jovial mood. "Mama, you bless me with your company."

"And what of Sarama's company?"

Ndoro eyes widened as he was flushed with surprise and embarrassment.

Talana shuffled toward him as she spoke. "Do you think I would not find out, boh-boh? Sarama is my favorite; we have no secrets between us. I suggest you begin gathering your lobola. She's very valuable." Talana then reached into her pouch. "It is said we all come into this world possessing a certain amount of magic. Some men possess more than others, which is why some men are faris while others are slaves. But a man can increase his magic by gathering that of other men or animals.

She handed him a necklace of cowry shells with two simba fangs in the center. "I know you have the hairballs of your first simba kill. Add to that the killing teeth of the demon-shumba. They will increase your nyama, your spirit strength."

"Thank you, mama," he replied.

Talana tied the necklace around his neck. "Now, fight and come back home. My daughter need not lose a husband before she marries him." She kissed his cheek, hugged him then opened the door.

Ndoro stepped outside and the muster drums rumbled. He set out at a warrior pace to the village pasture, the warriors of his intanga falling into rank beside and behind him. They ran from compound to compound, other intangas joining them until they all ran together through the town. Very few villagers came out to see them go. Many were still recovering from the night's celebration, while others saw no joy in their leaving. Though Ndoro promised to bring all of the warriors home, no one in the village would hold him to such an impossible vow. Some men would certainly die, but at least these Diaka had the chance to come home. Ndoro had given them skill and by doing so, he gave them a chance to survive.

The fari's camp was five miles north of the village. As Ndoro led the warriors up the steep road leading to the site, he scanned the woods filled with warriors from other villages. They were obviously conscripts, all clothed in whatever they possessed, their spears old and worn, their leather shields ragged.

They looked upon the Diaka as they did the Songhai horsemen. It was a look that did not go unnoticed among the ranks.

Ndoro called the Diaka to a halt before a ring of tents in the center of camp. No sooner had he done so did the flap of the largest tent open and Otuhu emerged.

"You are late," he said.

"I was not told when to arrive," Ndoro replied.

"Don't take Biton's fondness of you as a sign of acceptance, cattle thief," Otuhu warned. "This is the second time you have insulted me. There will not be a third."

Ndoro said nothing, his every effort focused on keeping him from throwing his orinka at Otuhu's head.

Otuhu spun and strode back to the tent. "Come, the others wait."

Biton stood in the center of the tent beside a huge canvas map that hung from the center. The noble leaders of the cavalry sat in front. Behind them sat the leaders of the infantry units. They were less finely dressed, bearing few amulets on their old uniforms.

Biton looked away from the map as Otuhu and Ndoro entered.

"I see you found him," Biton said.

Otuhu said nothing as he took his place among the cavalry. Ndoro sat beside the infantry captains.

"Most of you are not aware of the situation in Jehnay, so let me update you. The interregnum has lasted almost eight months and the city is in chaos. Askia Kasali's death was a great loss. The elders have yet to select a successor among his sons, for they don't think any of them have the strength to lead. The rumor is that they wish to ask Kasali's cousin Jafaru to rule. But Jafaru is not Songhai and does not deserve the title of Askia.

"I have pledged my loyalty to the Askia's eldest son, Sudetu. He has told me that word of the elders' preference has reach Jafaru and that he is preparing an army to march to Jehnay to receive the blessing of the elders. There is only one road from Nala to Jehnay, and that road runs through Galadima. Last season, we attempted to take Jafaru from Bordu and failed. This season, we are charged to keep Jafaru and his army in Bordu until Sudetu has made his claim to the Stool. Once that has been secured, he will send his warriors to aid us."

Otuhu stood and joined Biton. "The Nala road is most narrow here." He pointed at the map. "Jafaru's army is larger than ours, so we must meet them where their size will be at a disadvantage."

"What about the river?" Ndoro asked.

Otuhu glared at him. "As I said, we will position ourselves here, where the road is narrow."

Ndoro stood. "What about the river?"

Otuhu grabbed his sword hilt and advanced toward Ndoro. Biton placed a hand on his shoulder.

"What about the river, Ndoro?" Biton asked.

"If you know he has a larger army, I'm sure he knows as well. He can engage our forces at the gap and send his reserves through the forest to outflank us. If we make a stand at the bridge we lessen the chance of being flanked. If we destroy the bridge, we will force Jafaru's army to ford the river. Our archers could drive them back."

"What you suggest is not honorable!" Otuhu shouted. "I should expect as much from a cow thief."

"It is your decision, Fari. I would follow Otuhu's plan if you wish to die with honor."

The nobles came to their feet and stood beside Otuhu, showing their support.

"We have always trusted the wisdom of Otuhu," Biton replied. "He has led us to many opportunities for honor and praise-songs, but not many victories."

Otuhu looked stunned.

"Fari! You don't mean to listen to the Sesu?"

Biton approached Otuhu and placed a hand on his shoulder. "These are different times, my friend. This is no battle for honor. We must stop Jafaru."

He looked at Ndoro. "Take your Diaka to Ingera. Hold Jafaru at the bridge as long as you can. We will position the remaining warriors at Otuhu's point. When you can hold no longer, send a runner to tell us you are falling back. Jafaru will think we are retreating and drop his guard. Then we will smash him."

Ndoro was impressed with Biton's solution. Not only had he come up with a suitable compromise, he'd combined both tactics into an unbeatable strategy.

"It is a sound plan," Otuhu admitted. "I doubt the cow stealer and his slaves can hold the bridge long enough to make much of a difference."

"If we are not capable of holding the bridge, you won't have to worry about us anymore," Ndoro replied.

Otuhu smiled. "Let them go."

Ndoro bowed to both men as he exited the tent. Otuhu's arrogance challenged his patience. In Selike, a stick fight would have been inevitable, giving him a chance to beat some respect into the haughty Soninke. He pushed that emotion aside as he reached the Diaka camp. His warriors had separated themselves from the other clans, huddling near weak fires. Jawanza and the other indunas gathered around him as he entered the camp.

"What is the word?" Jawanza asked.

"We march to the Ingera Bridge. Our order is to hold the bridge as long as possible."

"We will do this alone?" Kamau asked.

Ndoro felt the uncertainty among them all except Jawanza, who was brave beyond common sense. Jawanza believed in him totally and would do whatever he asked. But Jawanza was not the only Diaka.

"We trained two seasons for this moment," he said to them. "We cannot run away from this responsibility. We must face this battle like men, as Diaka. The others are conscripts, forced to fight by the nobles. They will be no help to us. We stand a better chance standing together at the Ingera Bridge."

"I have no idea how large Jafaru's army is, but I do know the heart of everyone before me. We will make our stand at the bridge and Jafaru's army will not pass."

Ndoro grabbed Kamau by the shoulders. "I need you to take the archers back to the village."

Kamau looked embarrassed. "Why, Koi Ndoro?"

Ndoro knew what Kamau was thinking, what the others thought. "I need you to meet us at the bridge, but I want you to come by the river."

Kamau's eyes brightened. "As you wish, Koi Ndoro." He bowed and left immediately, gathering the archers for the march back to the village.

"The rest of you go back to your units and form ranks. We leave immediately."

The Diaka departure broke the quiet tension of the camp. Kamau and the archers were the first to leave; Ndoro and the remaining Diaka broke camp an hour later. They headed northeast on the Nala road, marching through a gauntlet of Soninke conscripts who yelled insults and laughed. The Diaka showed no response; each man's face was an emotionless mask, eyes locked forward. Ndoro was stoic as well, although inside his mind swirled in a storm of emotions. The excitement in his heart was dampened by uncertainty of what lay ahead and the fear of the battle's outcome. Would the Diaka fight as they had been trained? Would he stand strong as their leader? The questions faded into his mind as he concentrated on the march.

The Ingera Bridge stood fifty miles northeast of the camp, four days' march at a warrior's pace. The road they followed meandered through dense woods, occasionally interrupted by tall grasses and low trees. Ndoro pick a small clearing for the first night's camp, preferring the safety of the open field to the closeness of the forest. They ate and rested that night, rousing before daylight to continue their trek. By nightfall of the second day, they were in forest again, slowed only by a passing herd of elephants sauntering across the path. Another short night and the Diaka were on their feet again, running down the wooded slope to the bridge.

Ndoro ran the last miles of the road cautiously. For three days, the road revealed no signs of life other than the elephant herd and the canopy birds. They'd passed no one traveling the well-used road. To Ndoro it was a sure sign Jafaru knew their plans and might be on the move. He chose not to share his thoughts with the rest of the Diaka. He would get them to the bridge first; after a good rest, he would deal with his misgivings.

That respite was not to be. As they came about the last bend in the highway leading to the bridge, Ndoro saw what he dreaded. Jafaru's army had reached the river first. Tents stood on both banks, the Bordubu warriors going about their daily business. Ndoro raised his hand and the Diaka halted. They moved quietly back out of view. Without his summons, his indunas came forward.

"Jafaru is here," Ndoro stated. "Jawanza, come with me."

Ndoro plunged into the bush with Jawanza close behind. Together they crept through the dense foliage, cutting a straight path to the road's edge. Ndoro peered through the leaves at his enemy.

"They are resting. I believe they've just arrived. Come, we don't have much time."

The duo made their way back to the waiting officers.

"Bring the spearmen forward. Everyone else draw your swords."

Ndoro looked at each induna eye to eye. They were as ready as they would ever be.

"Spearmen advance." The spearmen moved into position, nervous faces on every man. Ndoro smiled, placing a hand of each of their shoulders.

"This is our moment," he said. "Make your ancestors proud."

Ndoro turned and ran into the open. The spearmen followed with spears in hand and across their backs. They reached throwing range undetected, the complacent Bordubu sentries resting on their shields.

The first volley rained down of the Bordubu without warning, the silence destroyed by the cries of wounded and dying men, a sound which caused the spearmen to hesitate with their second volley.

"Your brothers are depending on your actions today," Ndoro scolded. "Don't disappoint them!"

The spearmen threw another volley as the warriors scrambled for cover. Ndoro signaled and the spearmen fell back, making way for the foot soldiers.

Ndoro said nothing as he and his warriors assaulted the bridge. The Bordubu scrambled to form ranks before the attack, but the Diaka charge was too swift. Ndoro met the first man with a push of his shield and thrusting spear. To his relief, the Diaka fell in beside him, fighting with silent efficiency. They drove the Bordubu onto and across the bridge within minutes. With space on the opposite bank, the Diaka formed a solid wall of shields and spears, thrusting the Bordubu back until they faltered and ran down the road to Nala.

A cheer broke loose from the Diaka so loud it startled the birds in the canopy above. Ndoro was swept by a rush of relief and pride, jabbing his assegai in the air as he shouted. But as he turned toward the bridge, the weight of responsibility settled again on his shoulders. There were wounded and dead before him. Many of them were Diaka.

"Come," he ordered. "We must tend to our brothers."

Many of the Diaka were healers and they went to their task immediately. The wounded were treated and bandaged, while the dead were prayed over and covered with their shields. Ndoro sent a patrol down the road toward Nala, and then sent runners back to the bulk of the army waiting at the pass. As he checked the men, he glanced downriver. The archers had not arrived. He began to doubt his decision to send Kamau back to the village for the canoes.

Jawanza came to his side, his face beaming.

"We won, Ndoro, we won!"

Ndoro smiled. "Yes, but this is just the first test. We..."

Shouting came from the trees, the ground trembling under Ndoro's feet. One of the Diaka sent on patrol toward Nala came into view, waving his hands and shouting as loud as possible.

"Horsemen are coming!

The man jumped into the bush as the Bordubu cavalry appeared. They formed a line that stretched from one side of the road to the other. Horses and riders were shrouded in quilted kapok armor, each rider carrying a two-headed heavy lance.

"Form ranks!" Ndoro shouted. The Diaka abandoned the shorter assegais for their longer lances. Ndoro formed the line at the entrance to the bridge, using the narrow way to restrict the number of horsemen that could bear down on them. The sight and sounds of the charging horses became more ominous as they neared. The riders lowered their lances in unison, their wide double blades pointed at the Diaka line. It was more than the neophyte warriors could take. Those in the rear ran back to the forest behind them. Others climbed the sides of the bridge and leapt into the river. Only Jawanza and a handful of warriors remained at the bridge. Ndoro had no choice but to pull back. They fled across the bridge, following the other Diaka into the bush. As he jumped into the temporary safety of the foliage, a second plan formed in his mind. The Diaka had to retake the bridge; he would not give Otuhu the satisfaction of being the predictor of their defeat. If he had just a little time to regroup, he could turn this retreat into an advantage.

A hail of arrows stopped the charge of the Bordubu midway across the bridge. Ndoro ran to the edge of the road to see a magnificent sight. Canoes filled with Diaka archers spanned the river from bank to bank, the archers firing with uncanny accuracy considering the constant swaying of the boats. Their missiles ripped through the Bordubu's protective kapok, driving the warriors into confusion. It was all the time Ndoro needed. With his intanga surrounding him, he made his way back to the road. The Bordubu cavalry milled about on the bridge, some throwing spears at the archers while others attempted to regroup to start the charge again.

Ndoro ran into the muddle, throwing his spear into the nearest horseman. He pulled his sword as he grabbed another rider and toppled him from his mount. The other Diaka followed his technique, swarming around the cavalrymen and dismounting them. The riders on the opposite side of the bridge turned and rode away.

Again the Diaka celebrated and again Ndoro checked their enthusiasm.

"Regroup!" he shouted. Ndoro sprinted to the edge of the bridge and called for the archers. Kamau was the first to the bridge.

"Well done, brother," Ndoro said. Jawanza ran to his true brother and hugged him.

"Fall in with the others. We must pursue the Bordubu immediately."

"Biton ordered us only to hold the bridge," Kamau said.

"The Bordubu are broken," Ndoro replied, annoyed that Kamau mentioned Biton's name. "If we wait for Otuhu we will lose our advantage. We must move now."

The Diaka chased the Bordubu, leaving a few warriors behind to tend to the wounded and the dead. Ndoro was wary of ambushes along the way, but the Bordubu seemed to be in full retreat. They came across scattered bodies; the Bordubu were abandoning their wounded to increase their pace. The cruel tactic did not work. By dusk, the Diaka saw Bordubu stragglers before them.

The highway widened as they advanced on Nala, the thick brush along its edges giving way to grasslands and small abandoned farms. By nightfall, Ndoro could see the outer walls of Nala. The Bordubu flew across the field surrounding the city, rushing through the city gates which closed quickly behind them.

Ndoro stopped then waved his shield. The Diaka halted before the bleached stone walls, breathing heavy but maintaining formation as they awaited orders. Though they proved themselves in open combat, they had no experience in siege warfare. Ndoro himself had no knowledge of such fighting. As much as he hated to admit, they would have to wait for Otuhu and the rest of the Soninke army.

The Diaka put on a belligerent display, beating their shields and yelling insults before retreating to the safety of the woods to set up camp. Ndoro ordered sentries at the wood's boundary, rotating the guards throughout the night. He fell into a heavy, dreamless sleep, totally exhausted from the victorious day.

He awoke to the light of dawn as it weaved its way into the forest. The sentries had kept their watch during the night, reporting no movements within the walls of Nala. The men were awake and eating when they heard the approaching rumble of Otuhu and his noble cavalry. The sanafaran wasted no time, galloping through the bush to Ndoro's tent. He leapt off his horse and marched to Ndoro, who sat before his fire roasting a freshly killed rabbit.

"You were told to hold the bridge!" Otuhu shouted.

"I did," Ndoro replied.

Otuhu glared at Ndoro. "You disobeyed orders and moved forward without the support of the rest of the army!"

"The Bordubu fell apart," Ndoro repeated. "We had to pursue them to prevent them from regrouping."

Otuhu trembled as he spoke, his hand seeking the hilt of his sword. "You have no respect for my authority. When this campaign is over, you and I will deal with this, cow stealer." Ndoro stood, looking directly into the sanafaran's eyes.

"We stand before the ramparts of Nala, a goal that was unattainable until this day. Only a wall stands between you and Jafaru, and you complain about respect? If you wish my respect, earn it."

Ndoro glanced down at Otuhu's hand. "The next time you touch your sword hilt before me, be prepared to draw your blade."

"Will we fight the Bordubu or each other?"

Biton made his way through the bush accompanied by his bodyguards, stepping between Ndoro and Otuhu.

"Ndoro is correct about one thing, Otuhu. You should be thankful we are here. Though I must say his tactics concern me, especially the lack of respect. But what matters is what has been accomplished."

Biton gripped Ndoro's shoulder and smiled.

"Well done."

Biton turned to Otuhu and the nobleman looked at the ground.

"It was a good decision," Otuhu admitted. "Now that we have him confined, we must lay siege to the city."

Biton wave his hand. "I have no time for a siege. Once the elders make their pronouncement, Songhai support may sway in Jabaru's favor. We must return to Jehnay with his head now."

"Now is the time to honor tradition," Otuhu urged. "If I challenge Jafaru to duel he must accept. It would be a great dishonor to refuse me. His griot would sing his shame the rest of his life."

"Be careful, Otuhu," Biton warned. "Jafaru is a skilled warrior. He's slain many nobles to reach the position he holds among the elders."

Otuhu mounted his horse. "If he kills me, he deserves to be Askia. My death will be honorable and the praise-songs will record my valor."

Biton's expression showed unhappiness with Otuhu's decision.

"Losing you is not a situation I look forward to, honor or not."

"You have the cattle thief," Otuhu replied. "Maybe he and his slaves will find a way to fly over the walls of Nala and bring Jafaru to you."

Ndoro gained a grudging respect for Otuhu despite the insult. A challenge between two formidable warriors was well known among the Sesu. It was the future he envisioned for himself once he returned to Selike to confront his father.

"I wish you well," Ndoro said.

Otuhu scowled. "Wishes have no place on the battlefield."

"You will need the parley sword," Biton suggested. The fari sent his servants to fetch the ceremonial blade.

Otuhu summoned his squires. "Bring me my father's sword."

The squires hurried to Otuhu's packhorses and returned with an ebonywood box decorated with intricate carvings and cowry shells. They placed the box down at the sanafaran's feet, and then backed away. No sooner had they retreated did Otuhu's griot appear. He knelt before the case and sang as he passed his hands from end to end. Finishing his song, the griot stepped away and Otuhu took his place. He opened the box and revealed the most magnificent sword Ndoro had ever seen. The metal shone like light and reflected like the clearest water, the blade long and sharp. The hilt was carved from ivory, with gold inlaid throughout. Otuhu took the sword from the box, handling it like a precious lover. His servants hung the elaborate leather baldric from his shoulder. Though Dingane was a great chief and possessed untold wealth in cattle, Ndoro was sure the sword at Otuhu's side was worth more than all the treasures of Sesuland. The world outside his homeland contained wonders he was just beginning to experience.

Biton interrupted his thoughts.

"Pick your best men. You will accompany Otuhu." The fari leaned close to Ndoro's ear. "Otuhu seeks honor in death, for you have shamed him by accomplishing what he could not. He is no value to me dead. Don't let him throw his life away because the ancestors granted you luck."

Ndoro nodded. He called the Diatanee to him. They were his best, selected before leaving the village from among the hundreds of Diaka. These were the men Ndoro felt possessed the true spirit of the Sesu. Their ranks included Jawanza, Kamau, the indunas and other select warriors. The Diatanee formed ranks behind Ndoro, who led them to stand behind Otuhu and the Songhai cavalry. The sanafaran led the group from his horse, the parley sword held high.

They were half way to the city walls when the gates opened and the Nala cavalry charged toward them at full gallop.

"Kimbia, Diaka!" Ndoro shouted. The Diatanee surged past the trotting horses and locked shields before Otuhu.

"Get out of the way fools," Otuhu bellowed. He turned to Ndoro. "This charge is only a show. They will back down as soon as they recognize the parley sword."

Ndoro wasn't convinced. He wasn't sure about Nala tactics, but deception was the root of Sesu warfare.

"Hold your positions," he ordered.

Otuhu glared at Ndoro before turning his head toward the approaching Nalans. He raised the parley sword higher, stabbing it into the sky for emphasis. The Nalans continued to charge.

"Lances ready," Ndoro commanded. He glanced at Otuhu as the Diatanee braced their horse slayers into the earth, their broad spearheads at a horse's breast height.

"What kind of treachery is this?" Otuhu said. "Warriors, swords ready!"

Otuhu flung the parley sword to the ground and freed his magnificent sword from its jeweled scabbard. Waving it over his head, he charged forward to meet the Nalan cavalry, disrupting the Diaka formation.

The cavalry charged by Ndoro in full gallop. He turned his head toward the remaining army, waving his shield and sword. The Diaka responded immediately, running to him from the bush. The conscripts followed in ragged formation, urged by Biton to go forward.

The horsemen crashed into each other with a thunderous roar. Ndoro signaled the Diatanee to spread out as they attacked the Nala cavalrymen with their lances. As the other Diaka arrived, they fell into battle, instinctively surrounding the Nalans. The fighting was fierce, the desperate Nalans trying to break the spear-tipped ring imprisoning them while dueling with Otuhu and his cohorts. They fell one by one; soon only one remained. The man sat upon a magnificent horse that moved defiantly, snorting and pounding its metal-shod hooves against the ground. The rider held a sword just as dazzling as Otuhu's, swinging the blade with deadly precision as he drove his attackers back. His intense face revealed no fear, only anger.

Ndoro called the Diaka away. The cavalry fell back, forming ranks behind Otuhu. The sanafaran advanced, stopping at sword length before the lone man.

"Jafaru, your time to join the ancestors has come," Otuhu announced.

"You cannot deny me my right!" Jafaru retorted. "The elders chose me!"

Otuhu smiled. "But fate has not," he said.

Jafaru attacked Otuhu in a furious assault. Otuhu parried desperately, but it was obvious he was no equal to Jafaru. The other cavalrymen saw this as well, but they did not interfere. Ndoro remembered Biton's words and snatched a javelin from a nearby Diaka. Hefting the javelin to his shoulder he ran headlong toward the dueling nobles. Jafaru slammed his horse into Otuhu's, knocking the sanafaran from his saddle. Otuhu struck the ground hard, his sword flying from his hand. Jafaru pulled back on the reins of his stallion, and the animal rose onto its hind legs.

"If Sudetu wishes me dead, he will have to kill me himself!" Jafaru declared.

Ndoro threw the javelin with all his strength. The missile streaked through the air and into the head of Jafaru, the impact knocking him from his horse to the ground before Otuhu. The stallion tumbled onto its back, righted itself, and fled toward the walls of Nala. Ndoro had no time to dwell on his action. As the cavalry rushed to Otuhu and the body of Jafaru, Ndoro summoned the Diaka and they fell into defensive formation, anticipating a second assault from the Bordubu. As he surmised, the gates of the city swung open. Instead of disgorging a mass of warriors, one man emerged mounted on a donkey. His head was half shaven and he was naked except for a simple loincloth. He carried a ceremonial sword similar to the one Otuhu discarded.

"A royal messenger," one of the conscripts said.

"Maybe they will truly talk this time and we can go home," another said.

"Don't hope too soon," Ndoro replied. "The Nalans don't seem to respect this custom of parley unless it suits them. Maintain formation until we know their true intentions."

Ndoro knew the conscripts were under the command of the cavalry, but their masters were occupied with the spoils of Jafaru and his doomed cohorts. A few of them glared at him. Ndoro ignored them, his attention on the approaching messenger.

The rider halted before Ndoro. He dismounted and immediately touched his head to the ground.

"Honorable High Chief Mamadou Sekou sends these words for all to hear. Jafaru you came for and Jafaru you have. This matter between Nala and Jehnay is settled. Leave now and we offer safe passage. Stay any longer and the ground will shake with the horses of Nala as they trample the bones of the Soninke and Diaka."

Ndoro stepped forward. "Tell your chief we will leave immediately."

The messenger knelt again, mounted the donkey and rode away. He was a small image in the distance by the time Otuhu and Biton found their way to Ndoro.

"What did the messenger say, and why did he say it to you?" Otuhu demanded.

"The chief of Nala will not attack us if we leave now," Ndoro answered. "His loyalty to Jafaru ended with his life."

"It was not your place to accept his message," Biton added. "You are not the leader of this expedition!"

"I apologize for my error," Ndoro replied. Whatever he had done seemed to set both men against him. His concern was to get the Diaka back to their village.

"Gather your warriors, Sesu," Biton ordered. "You will form the rear guard. Otuhu, secure the head of Jafaru. Sudetu will be pleased with our proof of his death. The elders will have no choice but to name him Askia now."

Otuhu marched away, calling his cavalry and conscripts to order. The horsemen responded but the conscripts remained with the Diaka. One of them, a tall man with small features approached Ndoro. He wore a red band of cloth on his upper arm, a sign of rank.

"What do you want us to do, Koi Ndoro?"

"Go back to the Soninke," Ndoro replied. "I am not your master."

The conscript officer smiled. "But you are, Koi Ndoro. You are the master of this field." Before he could stop him the conscript knelt and touched his forehead to the ground, sprinkling his head with dirt. He backed away a few feet, stood and returned to his men. He barked at the others in a language Ndoro didn't recognize and the conscripts returned to their position with the Soninke.

Ndoro watched Biton and Otuhu as they made final preparations for the return. He was disappointed with his first taste of organized war. Gone was the celebration of victory, the looting of the vanquished. There were no cattle to take home, no loot to fill his knapsack, and no woman waiting to soothe his psyche and help clear his mind. Although he understood Biton's eagerness to return to Jehnay, he was disturbed by the sour mood of the fari. He called his officers to him.

"Let the Soninke and their men get far ahead. Keep your units in battle formation."

"Do you think the Nalans will attack?" Jawanza asked.

"I don't fear the Nalans. I'm concerned about the wolves before us."

They looked at Ndoro and he saw the uncertainty in their eyes.

"We will march to the bridge. Kamau, if the canoes are still there you will take them back to the village with as many of the wounded you can carry. Take the archers with you as well. When you get back to the village tell everyone to stay in their compounds until we arrive."

Kamau's face betrayed his fear. "Why would they attack us? Aren't we allies?"

"It is my fault," Ndoro replied. "The fari asked me to make you warriors. He didn't expect me to succeed."

The Diaka went silently to their units. Ndoro walked ahead of his unit, his shoulders drooping with the mental burden riding them. In order to save the Diaka, he may have doomed them.

The Diaka slowed their pace until the Soninke disappeared. They marched silently, eyes shifting back and forth. Ndoro felt the uneasiness biting the back of his neck, so he straightened himself and picked up the pace. The road became hazy the closer they came to the bridge; Ndoro smelled smoke and his hands tensed around his assegai.

The Soninke conscript ranks rustled at the far end of the bridge, obscured by smoke rising from the river below. Kamau's canoes burned, blocking a Diaka escape by the river. The cavalry loomed behind the conscripts, Otuhu in the center, the sword of Jafaru in his grasp. Biton sat upon his stallion beside him.

"Archers forward!" Ndoro commanded. The archers rushed to their position, forming a line just before the entrance of the bridge. Ndoro didn't have to call for the indunas. They appeared at his side immediately. The mounting smoke from the burning canoes masked the far side of the bridge, reducing the vision of the archers.

"Otuhu thinks he's taken away our advantage with the archers. At this distance we will get one volley at the most. We'll position the spearmen directly behind the archers. Make sure to leave gaps to allow the archers room to pull back. Have them regroup on both sides of the bridge. They can fire at will once they are in position. If Otuhu sends the conscripts, we will signal the lancers to switch to swords and orinkas."

The indunas returned to their units to pass on his orders. No sooner had they done so did the smoke begin to rumble like thunderclouds.

"Swords!" Ndoro shouted. In practiced unison the Diaka dropped the spears; swords sang as they were freed from their scabbards. The Diaka archers loaded their bows and waited for the first sign of the charge. Midway on the bridge, the Soninke emerged like ghosts from the smoke. It was a mixed charge; two columns of warriors followed by a company of horsemen.

"Archers, fire on the foot soldiers only!" Ndoro shouted. He raised and dropped his orinka and the arrows flew, bringing down the conscripts with lethal alacrity. The archers fell back to the banks, as the cavalry became tangled among the sudden mass of dead and wounded warriors.

Ndoro watched the cavalrymen shouting at the conscripts, trying to restore order. The faces of the conscripts told him what he needed to know. He ran to the lances, grabbing a lance from the ground.

"Follow me!" he yelled and ran to the bridge. The spearmen quickly caught him, forming a shield line. Ndoro sensed fear among the conscripts and pressed the attack. By the time the Soninke realized what was happening, the Diaka were only strides away, the closest conscripts already falling to the bold attack.

The conscripts ran. Otuhu and his cohorts struck at them with their swords, but the exodus continued. Some slipped past the cavalrymen while others jumped over the sides of the bridge, disappearing into the rising black smoke of the burning canoes. The Diaka pressed forward, Ndoro at the lead. His target was Otuhu. The Songhai nobleman had betrayed him; he was not fit to live. Ndoro jumped over a falling conscript and struck at Otuhu with his assegai. Otuhu, still carrying the gilded sword, sliced the spear in half. Ndoro ducked a vicious swing at his head then leaped onto the horse with Otuhu. They struggled, hands locked as they wrestled for the advantage. A passing Diaka drove his lance into Otuhu's horse and the animal jumped to its hind legs, throwing both men. Ndoro landed on his back, the impact knocking him into darkness. He opened his eyes to see Otuhu looming over him.

"Did you think you could dishonor me and live?" He raised his sword. "It ends today, thief."

Ndoro rolled as the sword came down, sparks flying from the blade as it bounced off stone. He grabbed a broken lance from the ground and plunged it into Otuhu's gut. The noble dropped his sword as he fell backward. Ndoro stood with the bloodied lance in his hand.

"No one betrays me and lives," he said. He stabbed Otuhu again, this time driving the lance point where he knew the heart should be. Yanking the weapon free, he ran toward the growing horde of Diaka. He took Otuhu's life; now he had to save Biton's.

The fari was surrounded by angry Diaka. He swung his sword frantically as his bodyguards tried to drive back the attacking horde.

"Diaka back!" Ndoro yelled, but not one man heeded his order. A few Diaka running to the fray gave him a menacing look. This was revenge, no less than his own against Otuhu, but more justified.

The last bodyguard went down under flailing swords. No sooner did he disappear did Biton's horse toppled. The fari fell into the midst of his former slaves, his body beaten and hacked without remorse. The Diaka backed away, revealing his mutilated form to Ndoro's angry eyes.

Smoke swirled around Ndoro as he approached Biton's body. The ground was littered with the dead and dying, Diaka and Soninke. Warriors walked among the carnage, finishing off the wounded Soninke with orinka blows. Ndoro was disturbed by their efficiency; the former farmers were now ruthless warriors. He didn't know whether he should be proud or ashamed.

The Diatanee approached him, their faces solemn yet unremorseful. In their eyes they had done what had to be done, but they had also opened a door of unknown consequences. Otuhu's death could be explained; the death of Biton was another matter.

"What do you wish, Koi Ndoro?" Jawanza asked, looking away from Ndoro's eyes.

"Now you ask what to do," Ndoro replied. "Maybe I should be the one asking the question."

The indunas remained quiet, all looking at the ground like sheepish boys.

"Gather the wounded that can travel," Ndoro finally said. "Use the horses to carry them if you can. We must return to the village as soon as possible."

The Diaka limped back to the village, arriving by dusk on the fifth day. A runner had been sent ahead and they were met by family and friends. Mothers, sisters, fathers and brothers found their warriors, welcoming them with hugs and tears of joy. Others relieved the warriors of the injured, rushing them back to family compounds to be cared for. Then there were the most unfortunate, wandering the fields searching the faces of those returning, slowly realizing their men were not coming home. Their painful sobs mixed with cries of relief as more Diaka warriors streamed into the village.

Ndoro, Jawanza and Kamau were among the last to arrive. They were swarmed by sisters and brothers. Ndoro saw Sarama running to him, tears staining her face. The wall he'd erected in his mind came down; he dropped his weapons and met her, arms open wide. Their embrace was full and deep.

"My shumba slayer has returned," Sarama whispered.

Ndoro didn't reply, his joy all too brief. There were other matters to deal with.

"I need to talk to Jabulani," he said.

"Now?" Sarama looked puzzled.

"Yes, now."

"Come, I know where to find him."

Sarama took his hand and he followed her to the village pasture. Jabulani sat on the hill watching his prized goats graze on the verdant grass. Sarama was about to take him closer but Ndoro stopped her.

"I need to speak to him alone."

Sarama eyes became suspicious. "What is wrong, Ndoro?"

He didn't answer. Ndoro walked calmly despite the anger boiling inside him. Jabulani sat cross-legged, his eyes closed.

"Baba," Ndoro said.

Jabulani opened his eyes. "You return victorious?"

"Yes."

Jabulani looked at Ndoro, fatherly admiration in his eyes. "You wish to talk to the elders. You wish an explanation."

"I deserve one," Ndoro replied, his anger evident in his voice.

Jabulani stood. "Come."

They met the elders under the great tree. The village seemed deserted, everyone cloistered in family compounds celebrating or mourning. Ndoro sat with his back to the tree, the position of leadership among the Diaka. The elders formed a crescent around him. Jabulani leaned on his staff, his place halfway between the elders and Ndoro.

Shaihi spoke first. "I know you are angry, Koi Ndoro, but there is a reason we did not tell you everything."

"You were younger than we expected," Jabulani said. "We believed if we revealed too much you would leave us to our fate."

"You knew your sons would kill Biton. You counted on it," Ndoro said.

"It is as it should be," Jabulani replied. "Since you are our koi you should know the full story of the people that chose to follow you."

"This land is not our home. We Diaka come from the south, from a land of forests and valleys. We came to Galadima as refugees from war, a war we instigated but lost. Our enemies, the Tacuma, possessed the land of gold dust that we coveted. So we attacked them, not knowing they were under the protection of the river spirit. Every river we crossed on our way to battle struck out with fast currents, hungry crocodiles and protective hippopotami that crushed our canoes. When we finally reached Tacuma, we were no match for their well-rested and well-armed warriors. We were driven from our homeland. Those who fell behind were taken as slaves.

"When our ancestors came here, they discovered they had fled one war for another. Jehnay and Nala were at war then as they are now. Tired and desperate, our ancestors accepted the yoke of slavery in return for protection by the Soninke. That yoke has chaffed our shoulders for three hundred years."

Shaihi leaned toward Ndoro. "It was foretold by the Oracle that a shumba slayer would come, that he would make us warriors again and free us from the Soninke. Our medicine priests prayed to the ancestors and the spirit of the lake, offering our precious goats as sacrifice. Jabulani is the blood of our priest, the most talented of our healers. It was his prayers that were finally answered."

Ndoro looked at each of the elders, their eyes reflecting their belief. Though he knew the circumstance of his arrival, nothing he said would change their minds. He killed the shumba, he made them warriors again, and he led them from slavery to freedom, if only for a moment.

How could he judge them when he had been dishonest as well? The Diaka were an answer to his vow of revenge against his own. They were a seed, a beginning that if nurtured properly could bring him everything he desired.

"We cannot stay here," Ndoro finally said. "As soon as the word of Jafaru's death reached Jehnay, Sudetu will claim the title of Askia, and then he will send the bulk of his army to find the slayers of Biton."

"We considered this, Koi Ndoro," Shaihi replied. "It is time we returned home."

"We have prepared canoes for the journey," Jabulani said. "The people are ready."

Ndoro nodded his approval. "We need a few days' rest," Ndoro said.

"Then it is settled," Shaihi announced, relief evident on his face.

"Ndoro," Jabulani said. "Are you still our koi?"

Ndoro smiled. "If you will have me."

Jabulani smiled back. "You were given to us by the ancestors. It is not our choice to make."

Ndoro left the elders to make plans for the exodus. The days were catching up to him, his wounds aching and his body tired beyond anything he'd experienced. The family greeted him quietly as he entered the compound, their emotions subdued until he smiled. They joyfully assaulted him, pulling and hugging and kissing him the entire walk back to his home.

As he went to the door, Talana emerged.

"You don't live here anymore," she scolded. Sarama emerged behind her, a sly smile on her face.

Talana turned to Sarama. "Take this boy home."

Sarama sauntered to Ndoro and took his hand, sparking a roar of laughter. She led him out of the family compound down the narrow alleyways to his completed home. He'd been so distracted by his revelations he didn't notice the structure was complete.

"We only have a few days to enjoy it," Sarama whispered. "Make them count, Askia of the Diaka."

"The free Diaka," Ndoro replied.

* * *

Ndoro helped load the canoes for the journey south. Sarama worked by his side, assisting him with the provisions. Jabulani leaned on his staff as he watched the Diaka prepare for the journey home. They had no idea where they were going, only the sketchy details of a legend. Ndoro selected fifty of his best warriors to man the lead canoes. They would leave three days ahead, guided by Jabulani's directions.

His canoe was finally ready. He looked at Sarama, her constant smile tainted with a hint of worry.

"You're risking your life for a story," she said. "You don't even know if it's true."

"Your father believes it," Ndoro replied. "That is good enough for me. Besides, the Diaka must leave this land regardless. There is no turning back now."

Sarama placed her head on his chest. "Be careful, Ndoro. Come back to me."

Jabulani interrupted them with a growl. "There will be enough time for that nonsense once we find Diakaland. Sarama, go help your mother."

Sarama departed, glancing back at Ndoro.

"Are we ready?" Jabulani asked.

Ndoro looked down at this adopted father and smiled. "Yes, baba, we're ready."

"Then let's go!" Jabulani shouted.

Ndoro laughed. "You've waited three hundred years. You can wait a little longer."

Ndoro signaled the drummers and they pounded out the cadence to assemble. He helped Jabulani into the lead canoe and then boarded. There were five canoes, ten men per boat with provisions. A small group gathered about the shore, waving a brief farewell.

They were ready. Ndoro gave the signal and they launched the canoes into the Kojo, placing themselves at the mercy of Jabulani's memory and the river's secrets. As Ndoro looked out on the expanse of water before him, he realized he was again embarking on a journey into the unknown, his vow of revenge his only guide. But at least this time, he was not alone.

12

The city was named Alamako, which in the tongue of its inhabitants meant 'God bless'. To Obaseki's eyes, its name was ill-suited. As he led Eshe, Pajonga, and Olushola down the wide dilapidated avenue separating the family compounds, he was struck by the fear in the eyes of the people watching them from behind the decrepit walls. At first he thought it was because of Pajonga, whose towering height and fierce expression always brought stares. But he soon realized he was the one who caused the stares. It was as if they saw his gift and feared it.

Their journey began months ago during the dry season. Though Obaseki chose to leave Abo, Noncemba refused to let his grandson depart in shame. He held a celebration, inviting all those that did not agree with the elders' decision. There was another reason for the celebration; Obaseki and Eshe were to be married. Noncemba presented Eshe's family with a thousand head of Zebu cattle, a treasure of ivory, cowry shells, gold dust and salt. The grounds of his umuzi came alive with celebrants honoring the young apprentice and his beautiful wife throughout the day and most of the night. On the morning of their departure, the mood was more subdued. Their families cried and hugged them goodbye. In a final gesture, Noncemba presented Pajonga and Olushola to the couple. Pajonga had served Noncemba as a faithful bodyguard and was eager to accompany Obaseki on his journey. Olushola, a short, slight woman with a round face and shy smile, was a treasure in disguise. Her purpose was to help Eshe with cooking and other chores, but Olushola was Malinke. She knew the way to Alamako.

The final words he heard spoken in Abo came from Fuluke.

"This is an important journey," he said. "Ndoki is a powerful medicine-priest, more powerful than I could ever be. It is said he also controls a mayembe possessing a fallen spirit. He can teach you how to control Moyo and how to tap into its power. But be careful, for Ndoki can only be trusted so much. He may see you as a rival, and he is a very jealous man. It will be up to you to choose your time to leave."

The words rang in his ears as they made their way to the marketplace on the far end of Alamako.

"These people are afraid." Olushola whispered. "See the walls? Those talismans and gris-gris are to ward off evil spirits."

"The city is cursed," Pajonga said. "We should leave. I'd rather camp in the forest."

"We'll stay one night," Obaseki replied. "We need to rest, our donkey needs good feed, and we need to find someone to lead us to Infana."

The avenue opened into a wide circular plaza. High mud walls, similar to those in Mawenaland, enclosed the area. But the plaza was void of life. The millet fields grew untended, weeds and other invaders strangling out the remaining crop needed in times of siege. Piles of spoiled bananas lay below their former perches, rotting in the intermittent sunlight. Above them, the oba's compound loomed over the mud walls surrounding its hilltop perch. The building appeared abandoned as well; thick vines surrounded the terra cotta figurines decorating the pillars accenting the corners of the wall.

"You don't want to go there," a child-like voice warned.

They turned to see a small boy standing behind them. His head seemed too large for his small neck, and he wore only a soiled loincloth and a golden necklace much too valuable for his appearance.

Pajonga stepped forward, his hand on his sword hilt.

"Leave us, thief, before I cut off your head and return that necklace to its true owner."

"No, wait," Obaseki interjected. There was something about the boy's eyes that told Obaseki what he needed to know.

"Are you a guide?"

The boy smiled. "It depends on where you wish to go."

"We wish to go to Infana."

"I am not your guide there, not today," the boy replied. "Today I will take you to the inn. Tomorrow I will take you to Infana."

"Did you hear my master?" Pajonga demanded. "He wishes to go today!"

The boy glared at the bodyguard. "As I said, you will rest today, for the journey to Infana is arduous."

Pajonga was flustered by the boy's arrogance. "Why you . . .!"

Obaseki grabbed Pajonga's sword arm before he drew the blade. "You'd be wasting your time striking him, my friend. He is already dead. Save your zeal to protect us when it matters."

Pajonga's eyes widened as he looked at the smirking boy. "I am sorry, master."

Obaseki turned his attention back to the boy. "Thank you for your help."

The boy bowed slightly and trotted from the plaza, gesturing for them to follow. They retraced their steps for a moment, and then plunged into a confusing maze of alleys and passageways, emerging suddenly before a large plain rectangular building at the edge of the city. Smoke floated from the mudbrick chimney; like the other buildings of Alamako its walls were plastered with talismans.

"Rest well," the boy said. "I will meet you tomorrow morning. There is food, water, and bedding inside."

"Won't you come inside and show us where to find these things?" Obaseki asked.

The boy flashed his sly grin and ran away, disappearing into the alleyways.

Pajonga ran after him for a moment. "Insolent monkey!" he growled.

Obaseki laughed. "Let him go, Pajonga. He couldn't enter the building if he wanted. The gris-gris was placed here to keep him and his kind out."

"He is a demon!" Olushola said. "We should not go into this place."

"She's right," Pajonga agreed. "This could be a trap."

"No, the inn is fine," Obaseki decided. "He was probably sent by Ndoki to welcome us."

Eshe, who had been silent since they entered Alamako, walked into the building without hesitation. Despite his assuring words, Obaseki rushed after her, his chest tight with dread.

The inn was in perfect order, a stark contrast to the outside. Low chairs sat neatly around worn mahogany tables. Red and yellow calabashes filled with water rested on each table surrounded by ceramic cups. The smell of cooked meat drifted from the open kitchen, reminding Obaseki how hungry he was. On the opposite side of the room were sleeping quarters, five in all. The largest had been prepared for the donkeys, fresh straw covering the stone floor.

Eshe grabbed a calabash and went to one of the rooms. Inside were a low table and two beds, complete with blankets and headrests.

Obaseki cursed. “I should have seen it sooner. You are sick.”

Eshe smiled as she sat the calabash down on the table. “You were leading us here, Seki. You can’t be aware of everything.”

“When it comes to you, I should,” he replied. He eased her down onto the bed and examined her.

“You have a fever, but I don’t feel the presence of any spirits.” He reached into his herb pouch, selecting a special blend of leaves and bark. “Chew this with your water. It will break your fever and ease your aches until I can discover the reason for your sickness.”

Eshe obeyed and in moments was fast asleep. Obaseki stepped back into the main room. Pajonga and Olushola were unpacking the donkey, whispering to each other as they looked about furtively.

“Is there something wrong?” he asked.

“No, master,” Pajonga replied. “We are grateful for the rest and the food.”

“You are worried about Eshe?”

The duo looked at each other, giving him his answer.

“She will be fine,” Obaseki assured them. “Now is not the time to worry. It is time to rest.”

Obaseki joined them in a meal of cooked chicken and yams. They ate voraciously, remembering only at the last minute to save a meal for Eshe. Afterward, Pajonga and Olushola slept, preferring blankets and the dirt floor to the bedchambers.

Obaseki paced the floor, unable to sleep. Fuluke warned him of the power of Ndoki, but he didn’t expect what they encountered today. The sight of the dead boy disturbed him; maybe this was wrong. How could he protect Moyo from a medicine-priest that raised the dead and knew he was coming before he arrived?

"Fuluke thinks too much of me," he whispered.

"Fuluke believes in you as I do." Eshe was awake, her smile bright but her eyes groggy. She stood and walked to the dining hall, kissing him on the cheek as she passed. She sat at the table with the rest of the food, Obaseki joining her.

"I have no idea what I am to do," he said. "I sense strangeness about this place. Not just among the living, but among the spirits as well."

"Maybe that is your purpose," Eshe replied. "You must bring balance here."

"I don't have the power to do so."

Eshe looked up from her meal. "You don't know."

Obaseki smiled. She was weak with sickness and still encouraging him on his unclear quest.

After she finished her meal, Obaseki helped Eshe back to bed. He lay down and fell quickly to sleep. Instantly he found himself standing before Fuluke, although he knew his mentor was hundreds of miles away. The ground was cold beneath his feet, the wind teasing the white robes gathered about his cold body. They stood on a high precipice with the entire world below them, people and spirits living their lives unaware of the silent observers above them.

He saw himself sleeping beside Eshe, Pajonga, and Olushola resting in the lobby. He pulled away, seeing the ring of fear surrounding them like a sinister moat, kept at bay by some unknown glow. Whatever it was, Obaseki was certain it was no spirit.

"Where are the souls?" he asked.

"Stolen," Fuluke replied, though his voice seemed unfamiliar. "They were taken to serve the babalawo of Ifana. Such is his power."

"Will he see me as an enemy or a friend?"

"Neither if you are lucky. It is best he thinks of you as someone of no consequence."

Fuluke turned his head to Obaseki. As he looked into his mentor's eyes, he realized it was not Fuluke to whom he spoke.

"But then, you are no mere priest."

Obaseki sprang erect from his bed. He was cold, just like the image in his dream. Warmth came with the early morning light, creeping into the inn through the uncovered windows as the light cast long shadows across the wooden floors.

The morning quiet was shattered by thunderous drumming. The rhythm reeled about the walls, driving Obaseki to his feet. He stormed to the entrance of the building and saw the boy prancing about as he struck the drum.

"Wake up, my friends!" he sang. "We have a long journey and a short day!"

Obaseki returned to the inn and woke everyone. Pajonga and Olushola grumbled as they packed. Eshe stirred and smiled as Obaseki placed his hand on her forehead. The heat was gone and the color of her eyes was brighter.

"We must travel far today," Obaseki warned. "Are you up to it?"

"I am ready," she replied. "Don't worry about me, Seki. I'll be fine."

Obaseki looked skeptical, aware how Eshe never wished to be a burden.

"Still, you will ride the donkey until we need to walk."

"We need the donkey to carry our supplies."

"We will split the load among ourselves."

Eshe smiled. "Pajonga and Olushola will not be pleased."

Obaseki laughed. "They are never happy. Come, let's go."

They set out a few hours after daylight, following their guide through the city and outside into the surrounding forest. The heat increased with the rising sun, summoning steam from the foliage. They followed the strange boy in silence, the sounds of the forest their only distraction. The road became steep, snaking upward through a ridge of hills blanketed by forests and mists. Climbing into the hills was more difficult than Obaseki expected. The road was muddy and narrow, his feet sinking into the mud with each step, sapping his energy. The donkey had no better time of it, braying and grunting in protest, moving forward only because of the pulling and cursing of Pajonga.

"Hurry up!" the boy admonished. "We must reach the top of the ridge by nightfall."

Obaseki stopped. "Those of us that still breathe are tired. We have no talisman to give us strength."

The boy smiled. "If you don't make the top of the ridge by sundown, even my master's powers will not protect you. There are many dangers in this forest beyond his control."

The words spurred the travelers. They struggled with the steep hill all day, reaching the crest as the sun receded below the hills along the western horizon. A house stood in a small clearing before them. A circle of staffs protected the house, each one crowned by animal figures carved from ivory. As with the inn, the boy did not step within the staffed perimeter.

"Now you will rest," the boy sang. "Tomorrow we go down the hill. It will be much easier."

Flashing his grin, the boy disappeared into the bush. The quartet trudged into the house after securing the donkey. The house seemed larger inside, though still modest in comparison to the inn. Olushola quickly set about starting a fire while Obaseki and Pajonga unpacked provisions. Eshe sat down hard by Olushola, attempting to help with the fire.

"Mistress, please," Olushola said. "I will tend to the fire. You should rest."

"I'm fine," Eshe replied.

Olushola edged closer, lowering her voice as she spoke. "I am an old woman, despite the youth of my skin. I know a pregnant woman when I see one."

Eshe's eyes widened. "You know?"

Olushola looked away smiling. "Your secret is safe with me."

Pajonga unpacked his weapons and hurried outside. Obaseki was concerned and followed him. He came up to the bodyguard staring into the forest.

"What is it?" he finally asked.

"The donkey is gone," Pajonga replied. "I think the boy stole it." He looked about, his hands tight on the sword.

"Listen," he said.

"To what?"

Pajonga looked into the trees. "Something is coming."

The quiet was shattered by the wail of the donkey. Branches before them exploded and the donkey sailed through the air, crashing at their feet. The animal lived despite its broken body.

A low, ominous moan wafted from the dark. A sinister chorus answered, the entire forest reverberating with the foreboding sound emanating from unknown throats.

Olushola stuck her head from the house.

"Come in now!" she urged. "They are coming!"

Obaseki grasped his mayembe beneath his robe. It was hot to the touch; a sure sign that whatever came was more than normal.

They ran for the house as the source of the sound emerged from the damp leaves. Obaseki glanced back to see the hulking figures, human-like in their gait but much larger and wider. Their bodies were covered with black coarse hair; their chest, face, and hands were swathed in leathery black skin. One of the creatures opened its mouth and moaned, exposing a ragged row of sharp teeth and elongated fangs.

Obaseki looked away, daring not to look again until he was in the safety of the house. He rummaged through his belongings and found his sword.

"What are those things?" he asked Olushola as he armed himself.

"Ghoulas," she replied, her voice trembling. "They look like mountain apes, but they are not. They hold the souls of evil men, witch doctors who gave up their human bodies for the powerful bodies of the apes. It is said they go mad when they transform, hunting in the high mountains for human flesh."

Pajonga went to the door and stood with his sword ready.

"They will come to eat us," he said.

"They cannot pass the staffs," Obaseki reminded them. "They will come no closer than the ring. Their magic is too powerful. It will keep the ghoulas out."

"And the ghoulas will keep us in," Olushola said.

Obaseki watched the ghoulas encircle the house, their human-like expressions showing they were not happy with the staffs. They looked at the mangled body of the donkey and became more agitated, grunting loud and pounding the ground with their massive fists. More ghoulas emerged from the woods, summoned by the howling of their brethren.

"What is happening?" Eshe asked, eyes wide with fear.

"They want the donkey," Obaseki replied.

"Then we must give it to them," Olushola urged. "They tasted its blood and won't be satisfied until they have it... or us."

Obaseki looked at Pajonga. "We must give them their kill."

Resignation conquered Pajonga's face briefly, replaced by his stern frown. He secured his armor, picked up his lance and shield, and then stepped into the doorway. Obaseki followed with his sword in his left hand, Moyo in his right. The mayembe glowed green, passing the aura of confidence into Obaseki as it did during the battle of Abo. Together they stepped through the door and the ghoulas fell silent. As soon as they neared the donkey carcass, the ghoulas went into frenzy, pounding their chests and the ground, hitting each other violently as they glared at the duo approaching their kill.

"Let's do this quickly," Obaseki said. They lifted the donkey, Obaseki grasping the front legs as Pajonga lifted with the rear legs. They swung the body back and forth, gaining momentum, as the ghoula protest grew heated. On the third swing they let go, the corpse passing through the barrier. As it passed through the invisible shield, two nearby ghoulas fell through.

Obaseki wasted no time. "Moyo zuka!" he shouted, uttering the words that unleashed the essence of Moyo. The painful blinding light consumed him, blurring his sight of the ape-men and Pajonga.

"Pajonga, get behind me!" Obaseki managed to say before the deadly tendrils flew out in all directions. Pajonga dived for the safety of the house; the ghoulas were much less fortunate. Jagged streams of power pierced their chests, dragging out the souls of the witch doctors that corrupted the animals' bodies. Screams filled his head as the bolts breached the barrier, spearing the ghoulas that tore at the donkey. The other ghoulas fled into the bush.

Obaseki slowly exerted his will on Moyo, forcing the malevolent force back into the mayembe. The smell of burned flesh and hair invaded his nostrils, the bodies of the ghoulas at his feet, the others strewn about beyond the staff barrier like broken dolls. Fatigue consumed him and he fell into darkness.

* * *

Obaseki awoke inside the house, his head resting on Eshe's lap. His forehead felt damp, so he tried to touch it. Pain jolted him and he quickly put his hand down, fighting the urge to pass out again.

"Relax, Seki," Eshe whispered.

"What day is it?" he asked.

"It is still night," Eshe replied as she changed the cloth on his forehead. "You slew the ghoulas a few hours ago."

"So it was as bad as the last time."

Eshe was quiet for a moment. "In a way, no."

Pajonga rose from his cot and came close to the couple.

"How is he?"

"Awake," Obaseki replied.

Pajonga fell to his knees immediately, pressing his head against the ground.

"Again I am privileged to witness your power!"

Obaseki closed his eyes with the next wave of pain. "Get off your knees, Pajonga, and get some sleep. We should be safe now."

Olushola cowered on the opposite side of the house. She stared at Obaseki, eyes wide with fright. He struggled to sit.

"What is wrong, Olushola?"

She did not reply. Olushola closed her eyes and hid her face behind her hands, a muffled whimper escaping between her fingers.

"She's been like this since you drove the ghoulas away," Eshe said.

Obaseki struggled to his feet and approached the woman. "Olushola, it's alright. The ghoulas are gone."

Olushola flinched when he reached toward her.

"This place is cursed. We will die here," she whispered.

Obaseki felt what Olushola feared. He wondered if the babalawo sent the ghoulas to kill him. He regretted bringing Eshe and the others along, though he would have never made it as far without them. It was not his place to put the lives of others in danger, ancestors or not.

Obaseki went to his medicine bag and removed a soothing herb blend. He shared it with Pajonga and Olushola, who both fell asleep. When he offered a portion to Eshe, she refused.

"I am fine," she said. "I am just tired."

Obaseki sat near his wife. "Tomorrow I want you and the others to return to Alamako"

Eshe's eyes widened. "Why?"

"Olushola has a right to be afraid. If this medicine-priest is responsible for the ghoula attack, I fear what he might do to you in order to control me."

Eshe sighed. "We may be in just as much danger in the village."

"You'll be welcomed without me. Olushola will help convince them that you were my servants and I forced you to come with me."

"You will face this man alone?"

Obaseki nodded.

Eshe grasped his hand. “At least take Pajonga with you. You might need his strength.”

“I dare not leave you and Olushola unprotected.”

“Pajonga will come with us to the village,” Eshe decided. “If the villagers accept us, we will send him to you.”

Obasekik nodded in agreement.

“If I do not return in a month, go back to Abo,” he said.

“I don’t want to think that way,” Eshe said.

“Promise me you will go back,” Obaseki insisted.

Eshe hesitated. “I promise, but not before I try to find you first.”

“I can’t convince you otherwise, can I?”

Eshe smiled. “No.”

“Then I will have to accept as much. Now get some sleep, sweet flower.”

They did nothing of the sort, making love throughout the night, both aware it might be their last moment together. As the sun forced its way through the dense foliage, they lay side by side, pleasant weariness settling in.

Obaseki sat up and dressed slowly. He crawled to his herb bag and made a quick blend of ginseng root, coffee beans and other herbs, a concoction sure to sustain them both through the day.

“A clever blend, but the local taba root is more effective.”

Obaseki looked up to see the door blocked by a huge man, the sun reflecting off his gold-capped head. He was bare-chested, a jewel-encrusted mayembe hanging from his neck. The talisman pulsed with the familiar green glow, the sign of an active spirit inside. The intruder’s small eyes, black skin and broad nose resembled those of the ghoulas. A brightly colored sash held the tunic around his waist and the dagger at his side.

Pajonga sprang to his feet, sword in hand. As the intruder slowly turned toward the bodyguard, Obaseki hastily stood between them.

“Thank you for your advice,” he said. “May I ask your name?”

“Ndoki,” the man answered, revealing a mouthful of filed gold teeth. “Welcome to Ifana, Obaseki of the Mawena.”

Ndoki sat cross-legged on the ground. “I take it your journey was pleasant?”

Obaseki glanced at Pajonga, signaling him to put away his sword. He sat before Ndoki. “Except for last night, it has been uneventful.”

“Oh yes, the ghoulas. I have no control over them, although they can be useful without knowing.”

“Such as keeping a person in one place?” Obaseki asked.

Ndoki let loose a deep rumbling laugh that shook his necklaces. “I didn’t expect them to attack you, but I protected the house just in case. You were perfectly safe.”

“Tell that to our donkey,” Pajonga said. “They killed it and came through your barrier.”

Ndoki’s eyes narrowed as he looked toward Pajonga.

“Pajonga is my companion,” Obaseki said. “I would appreciate it if you would refrain from casting spells his way.”

Ndoki jerked his head to Obaseki. “He doesn’t deserve our attention, let alone our friendship.”

“I am no different from him,” Obaseki said.

“Oh, you are, young Mawena. Your place is not among these pets, I assure you. You have much to learn about who you are.”

Ndoki sprang to his feet with surprising agility for a man of his girth. “We’re wasting time. Your companions are welcomed to stay here until you return. I do think, however, you would find Alamako more to your liking.”

“Will the ghoulas return?” Pajonga asked.

Ndoki smiled. “One never knows about ghoulas. It’s possible they were satisfied by your donkey, but they might seek revenge for their unfortunate brothers. Either way, you are safe here as long as you stay within the staffs.”

“We will only be here one more day,” Eshe said. “We have decided to return to Alamako. But we will need a donkey.”

“The boy will bring you another,” Ndoki promised.

“No, not him,” Eshe said. “Send a real boy.”

Ndoki looked at Obaseki and smiled. “She must be good, for she steals secrets from your lips.”

“There are no secrets between us,” Obaseki replied.

Ndoki frowned. “So be it. You will have your donkey. Come, Obaseki, I have no more desire to be on the trail at night than you.”

There was nothing else left to say to Eshe. Obaseki packed quickly, hugged and kissed his sweet flower, then followed Ndoki down the narrow path leading away from the house and into the woods. The dense foliage made quick work of his view; in moments, it was if the house never existed. The forest spoke around them, monkey calls and birds competing for their place in the chorus. Ndoro found himself almost running to keep up with Ndoki.

"Ifana is not far," Ndoki said. "You will love it. It is the perfect city for ones such as us."

"And why are we so alike?" Obaseki asked.

Ndoki stopped suddenly and Obaseki almost ran into him. Ndoki lifted the mayembe about his neck.

"My mayembe contains the soul of a fallen spirit as well, though she was not as powerful as Moyo. She is Delu and this land was once her realm. I discovered her mayembe in Ifana, so I have made it my home."

Obaseki saw an image in the distance. As they drew closer, he recognized it as a spirit, sauntering down the trail as if carrying a basket on its head. It stopped upon seeing them, turned and ran into the bush. Ndoki sprang forward, chasing the spirit into the bush. The pursuit was brief. The sorcerer emerged from the brush smiling, the mayembe glowing brighter.

"The first fact you must accept is that Moyo must be fed," Ndoki stated. "He is starving; that is why you fight to control him when he is released."

"But he consumes spirits," Obaseki said.

Ndoki's face became solemn. "I sense your talent. You have affinity with souls and you wish not to harm them. Your destiny, however, depends on the mastery of Moyo. Moyo must be controlled. You must feed him to control him."

Obaseki closed his eyes, the image of consumed souls flashing in his head.

"Can you hear it?" Ndoki asked

"What?"

"The sea! We are almost home!" Ndoki exclaimed.

Ndoki ran ahead of Obaseki, disappearing around a bend in the path. Obaseki sighed, too tired to chase his strange companion. He trudged around the bend then rolled his eyes at the sight of the steep hill before him. Ndoki stood on the crest, waving his hands like an excited child.

"Come, come! Ifana waits!"

Obaseki's thighs burned as he climbed the hill. A roaring sound came to his ears and the smell of seawater, fish, and salt filled his nose as he struggled to the top of the hill. At the crest he was struck by the view below him. Ifana, the city of Ndoki, sprawled among broken cliffs that plunged into the churning waters below. Towering waves crashed against the base of the cliffs, tossing sea spray high over the cliff edge. The water stretched as far as he could see and Obaseki was amazed. The stories he heard as a boy had not prepared him for the reality of the ocean's vastness.

He broke his attention from the sea long enough to look down into Ifana. There was movement below in the streets, but it was not human movement. The city was filled with spirits, more that he could count. There had to be thousands of them, he thought.

"It is beautiful, isn't it," Ndoki said, startling Obaseki.

"Yes, yes it is." Obaseki looked at Ndoki, the questions in his mind making him wary of his companion. "There are spirits but no people."

"Only some of the spirits are of those who lived in Ifana. The rest are from everywhere; Kossa, Sesuland, the Sahel, even as far as the Talsa Mountains. I brought them all here from around the world to serve me."

"I guess there are many spirits from Alamako as well."

Ndoki ignored his comment. "Come. We will go to my home and rest."

They descended into the city together. Obaseki observed spirits tending invisible millet fields, cooking over empty fires and herding long dead cattle. The Zamani was powerful among the cliffs; the spirits appeared as clear as the living despite their translucence. Above all, he saw the terror in their eyes as they looked at Ndoki. They looked back at him in curiosity and fear, a few faces drawn in despair. Obaseki took their looks as warnings. He would have to be careful with Ndoki so as not to end up among them.

Ndoki's house was modest for one who claimed to be the master of the Ifana's spirits. The rectangular structure rested on a low rise outside the city walls, surrounded by its own brightly colored wall. There was no physical gate, only the familiar totems placed on either side. As they neared, they were greeted by two boys, each wearing necklaces similar to that worn by the boy sent to lead them to the house camp. To Obaseki's surprise, they came directly to him and took his belongings.

"They can touch?"

Ndoki chuckled. "Ifana is a special place. The physical and spirit world are one here, if you choose to experience it. Ifana was the home of the old gods in the days when the gods lived among men. Moyo lived here, as did Delu. The buildings stand the same as they did thousands of years ago. Even the plants and animals of the forest dare not intrude upon this sacred ground."

"But you live outside its walls," Obaseki commented.

"The city is for the spirits and gods," Ndoki replied. "I am not ready yet, but I am close, as you will be."

"I'm not sure that is my fate," Obaseki replied. "I came here to learn to control Moyo, not to become a god."

Ndoki turned, his face angry. "You do not control a god spirit! It is not your place to choose your fate."

Obaseki studied Ndoki with both forms of sight. Though the man stood before him, the spirit was something again.

"You are correct," Obaseki replied. "I am tired and not thinking clearly."

Ndoki smiled. "It's been a long journey. Rest here and I will have the servants bring you food. You will find it very satisfying."

Ndoki left the house grinning broadly. Obaseki sat on a gilded stool before a low stone table. He was in danger, no doubt. Ndoki's soul was being slowly consumed by the spirit within his mayembe. He had to leave this place.

Two boys entered the room with trays of food and placed them before him on the table. Despite the delicious smells and sights before him, Obaseki noticed the warning in their expressions. There was something in the food other than spices, but Obaseki was too hungry and tired to care. He ate until his stomach hurt, and then he lay on the plush pillows and slept.

Ndoki jostled him awake. Darkness filled the room, his host's golden smiled illuminated by the torch he carried.

"Are you rested?" he asked.

Obaseki nodded.

"Good. Come with me."

Obaseki stood, startled by the strength in his limbs. He grasped Moyo and felt the heat rising inside. He tensed, expecting the uncontrollable surge of power. Instead, the flow remained gentle and constant.

He stared at Ndoki.

"What did you do to me?"

"It is a potion," Ndoki said. "It links you with Moyo, but it is only temporary. That is why we must go now. You will need Moyo's strength for this task."

Ndoki handed Obaseki a torch and lit another for himself. Together they walked the undulating roads of Ifana, the sound of the ocean louder with each step. A full moon emerged from the horizon, the city walls incandescent from its light.

The road became rocky as they neared the cliffs. The smell was overwhelming, but Obaseki managed to calm his stomach and continue forward. The full moon rested directly above them, the ocean's surface shimmering under its pale blue radiance. Waves thundered against the broken rocks as sea spray drizzled down on them.

"This trail leads to a cave below the cliffs," Ndoki shouted. "On a night like this, moonlight reflects into the cave, lighting it like the sun.

"On the far end of the cave grows seaweed that is necessary for you to gain the power of Moyo. Pick as much as you can and bring it back."

Obaseki started and Ndoki halted him.

"You will need this," he said.

He handed Obaseki a gilded double-pointed spear. Obaseki felt the weapon's weight and could tell it would have been too heavy to lift without Moyo's energy. He waved to Ndoki and descended the trail, torch in one hand and spear in the other. The rocks rose on either side of him, the trail narrowing as he progressed. Darkness engulfed him save the light of the torch. The sound of the ocean was deafening in the corridor as Obaseki inched forward, sucking in his breath to pass. Just when he thought he could go no further, the path widened. Light crept in from ahead, gradually overpowering the flickering torchlight. Obaseki stumbled into the cave. It was enormous, with long stalactites extending from the ceiling toward the swaying sea. Directly across from him the mysterious weeds thrived, broad-leafed plants emitting an eerie light. He searched the edges of the cave for a path to the weeds; he was a poor swimmer and had no intentions of entering the water unless he had no other choice.

He tipped between the broken stalagmites, keeping his balance with the spear. The waves roared inside the cavern, so much so that he didn't hear the explosion of water behind him. A column of water slammed into his back, knocking him forward into the rocks. He threw his hands out, losing the spear but sparing himself serious injury among the jagged stones. Before he could turn he was struck again and crashed against the cave floor. Moyo's contact dulled the pain, but he knew he was injured. As his eyes cleared, he saw the source of his pummeling. The creature towered above him like the branches of a baobab, its serpent-like head glistening in the moonlight as it swayed back and forth with the rhythm of the sea. Its jaws swelled and then tightened as the creature spat a wide stream of water toward Obaseki. He rolled away, the water slamming into the stone beside him. The serpent dove into the sea and Obaseki clambered to his feet before scrambling to the cavern entrance. He was only a few steps away from safety when the serpent emerged from the water again. He fell to the ground and took the brunt of the water against his back. His cry was drowned by the voice of the sea reverberating throughout the cavern. He lay stunned, gasping for breath as the serpent plunged back into the water. Obaseki groped for and found the spear, turned about, and then sat up. He had one chance to kill the serpent and he had to take it. Obaseki struggled to his feet, wishing he'd paid more attention to his weapon-training as he braced himself for the next emergence of the serpent.

The creature rose again. Obaseki brought the spear to his shoulder as the serpent came to its full height. The moment it hesitated, its mouth full of seawater, Obaseki hurled the spear with all his strength. The projectile flew from his hand with a speed that startled him, striking the serpent below the jaw and bursting out the top of its head, ending its flight lodged into the cave ceiling. The serpent's mouth sagged open, releasing a waterfall of bloody liquid.

Obaseki sprinted to the narrow pass as the serpent fell forward, the ground trembling as its bulk struck the rocks. The force threw him into the gap, his head bashing against the wall. Blinding pain sent him into unconsciousness.

The light of the rising sun filled the cavern and Obaseki opened his eyes. His head ached; he licked his dry lips and tasted blood. A wave of nausea enveloped him, and he almost passed out again. He coughed and vomited instead. He was weak; whatever Ndoki gave him to tap into Moyo's strength had dissipated. The mayembe lay stagnant against his chest.

Obaseki sat up against the rocks, giving his eyes time to adjust to the light. As they focused, he realized the brightness did not come from the outside of the cave. It emanated from a mysterious orb hovering before him. The orb took a featureless human form. It was some sort of spirit, one like he'd never seen. Instinct told him he should fear it, but he was too tired and hurt to care.

"You are well," it said in a deep, soothing tone.

"No," Obaseki replied.

"If you fought a saba and lived, you are well. Can you heal yourself with the mayembe?"

"I don't know," Obaseki answered. "I have not yet mastered it."

The spirit reached out with a line of light and touched the mayembe. It responded by glowing with a red, angry light.

"Moyo," it said with disgust. *"His essence cannot heal you. He was a destroyer."*

The light expanded, swallowing him in brightness. He felt himself mending, his strength increasing. The light contracted back to a thin line and pulled back into the spirit.

"What are you?" Obaseki asked.

"You have forgotten me," it replied. Obaseki detected sadness in its voice.

He focused his eyes on the shimmering image as it took form. His eyes went wide as he recognized who hovered before him, his heart leaping with joy.

"Lewa!"

Lewa drifted down before Obaseki. *"Hello, Seki."*

Obaseki reached out to his friend. They touched and he felt her love flow into him, healing his wounds.

"You moved on to the Zamani?"

Lewa nodded. *"It was the only way I could watch you and keep you safe."*

"I thank you." Obaseki's mood changed suddenly as he remembered his situation.

"Fuluke said I would find my destiny here."

"Fuluke thought Ndoki would help you, but Ndoki no longer exists as your mentor knew him," Lewa explained. *"Celu used him to hide from us. Ndoki revived her and has paid with his soul."*

"Where is Celu?"

"Waiting for you. She was Moyo's lover once and wishes to be so again. We cannot take her from this world, so you must send her to us."

Obaseki's heart raced as he realized what he must do. "I can't destroy Celu! I am too weak to battle an orisha!"

"You have no choice." Lewa's image flickered with the sea breeze. *"You must use what she desires to defeat her."*

Obaseki looked at the mayembe as he came to his feet.

"Why must I do this? What purpose does it serve?"

"The path is not always clear when the destination is true. Celu will tell you where your purpose lies."

Lewa faded, taking the light away.

"Lewa, wait!" Obaseki shouted. The cave fell back into its unusual radiance and Obaseki was alone again. He heard his name echo down the passage, bringing him back to his dilemma. He couldn't go back on the path knowing Celu waited to destroy him. The only other way out was the cave, although he did not know where the currents would take him. He decided uncertainty was safer. He crept to the water's edge and lowered himself in. The warm buoyant liquid soothed him as he made his way toward the cave's mouth. The cave floor gradually descended beyond his reach, forcing him to swim. He stayed as close to the jagged rocks as possible despite the dangerous swells and eddies.

The waves grew stronger near the mouth of the cave, forcing him to strike out for deeper water to avoid the rocks. He was not a strong swimmer. The distance was short, but to Obaseki it seemed like miles. The waves hammered the rocks ahead, swallowing them in foam. Obaseki took a deep breath and swam.

A wave surge lifted him, pushing back into the cave. Obaseki thrashed toward open water to avoid being thrown against jagged stones behind him. As the waves retreated he followed them, his crawl becoming a sprint to the sea. Obaseki fought the water and himself, his breath threatening to burst out, his arms and legs burning as he struggled to the opening.

Blinding light signaled his escape into open water. Obaseki stopped swimming and waited for the waves to carry him to shore. The water lifted him, and he rode the, bracing himself for the impact sure to come. He hit the rocks hard, letting out a gasp. The roaring water masked his panting as he flailed about to anchor himself among the stones so not to be dragged back out to sea by the receding waves. His breath came back to him as the water disappeared, and he dragged himself away from the sea edge. When he finally reached higher ground, he felt as if he had been beaten like a drum. He ached everywhere.

"Obaseki! Obaseki!"

Ndoki's urgent call reminded him his plight was not yet over. He peeked over the rocks and spied the rotund witch-doctor pacing about, wringing his hands as he peered down the narrow trail into the cave.

"He must be dead," he whispered. "He has to be dead by now."

Ndoki jerked, the desperate look on his face transformed into an angry glare.

"I did not want him dead! I cannot revive Moyo with him dead!"

Obaseki watched in fascination. Ndoki argued with the spirit possessing him, Celu. He was trying to break free. Obaseki wished he could help him, but he did not know how.

Fear took hold of Ndoki's face again. "I would rather see him dead than suffer as I have."

Ndoki's face changed again to anger. "I have no use for you. It is time you join your brother. Moyo and I will be together again. He will take me to his city in the Mahgreb, where we'll rule our lands together."

Ndoki's face returned to fear, then pain. His skin glowed red, smoking rising from his head and limbs as he fell to the ground. His skin boiled as his clothes burst into flames. Ndoki opened his mouth to scream and light emerged, spilling down his chin then flowing over him until it covered his entire body. Obaseki watched Ndoki's body burn and shrink, taking the dimensions of a woman. Celu emerged from her human cocoon, her face featureless except for amber-colored eyes that blazed like fire.

Obaseki wanted to stay hidden among the rocks, waiting for Celu to disappear into the city. But she would not go to the city. She would follow the path into the cave and discover he escaped. She would hunt him down, forcing him to summon Moyo from the spirit world, condemning him to the same fate as Ndoki. Then she would destroy all those he loved and the ancestors would not stop her.

Obaseki remembered Lewa's words.

"You must use what she loves the most."

His fingers tightened around Moyo. More and more he found himself depending on its power, realizing he had to find a way to truly control it. But it was not to be that day, nor was Alamako the place. Before he came to his feet to confront Celu, Lewa's words emerged in his head again.

"Celu will tell you where you need to be."

He gathered his remaining strength and stood. Celu turned toward him, her eyes expanding.

"You live?"

Obaseki smiled. "Your attempt to kill me failed."

Celu floated toward him. "You don't have to end as Ndoki did. Moyo is weaker than I imagined. In order to revive him, the two of you must merge into one."

Obaseki tightened his grip on Moyo. "And what becomes of my body, of my spirit? Does my flesh burn away to reveal your lover? Is my soul consumed by Moyo's hunger?"

"You are a foolish man, Obaseki," Celu replied harshly. "I offer you immortality and power, and you whine about your frail flesh. You are no better than Ndoki."

Obaseki unleashed Moyo just as Celu sent a ball of flame at him. The fireball collided with the light tendrils and Obaseki felt the heat as the projectile soared over his head and exploded into fire and steam as it hit the ocean surface, throwing a plume of steam into the air. Unlike his other releases, Obaseki fought Moyo to exert control over the random violence. Celu sent another fireball at him and Obaseki concentrated, bending a tendril to meet it. Instead of deflecting it, the tendril absorbed the ball, knocking Obaseki back onto the rocks.

"Don't make me kill you!" Celu shouted.

Obaseki pushed the pain aside, continuing to concentrate. But suddenly he realized his error. He was fighting Moyo and it fought back, refusing to be controlled. So he stopped, wiping his mind blank with thoughts of dark solitude. The tendrils emanating from him ceased thrashing. They pulsing with the rhythm of his heart.

"Moyo?" Celu said.

Obaseki was oblivious to Celu's words. The tendrils retracted into him, forming about him and outlining him as Celu's essence had done Ndoki. Opening his eyes, he observed Celu approaching him warily. He tensed, not knowing if what he was about to do would work. It was his only chance. He had to throw full concentration on Celu, sending all of Moyo's energy at her.

Celu edged closer. "Moyo?"

Obaseki attacked. The energy rushed from him in one solid stream, striking Celu in the head and lifting her into the air. Obaseki screamed, his body being ripped apart, every particle separating from another. Celu struggled against the onslaught, the stream of light lifting her higher, pulling rocks and water with it, sucking the life from every living creature surrounding it. Through his pain, Obaseki heard the howls of spirits as they were dragged upward into the vortex of his attack.

Then suddenly there was silence, followed by a sound like the origin of all thunder. Obaseki became whole again, falling against the rocks. He would die soon, he thought. This was his task then, to destroy Celu before she revived Moyo to fight the ancestors again. He used the god-spirit against her and prevailed; now his time was over. He closed his eyes, waiting for eternal peace. Instead he heard the familiar voice from the cave.

"You did well," Lewa said.

Obaseki lay still, waiting.

"Your journey is not over," she continued. *"We are not ready for you yet. There is yet one more task for you to perform."*

"I must go to the Mahgreb?" Obaseki managed to say.

"Yes."

"I will not go." Obaseki whispered. "I wish to die."

"Those who love you will come soon. You will live for them."

Obaseki was done talking to spirits. He closed his eyes and wished for death, falling into peaceful oblivion until another familiar voice caught him.

"Seki?"

Eshe's warm, soft lips touched his forehead, lifting away his death wish. Pain rushed back into his body and he screamed.

"Hold him tight!" an unfamiliar voice ordered.

Unseen hands locked him down, his body struggling on its own. He felt a liquid pass his lips and through his teeth, making a warm stream down his throat. The pain followed the liquid downward, congregating in his abdomen and dissipating. He dared to open his eyes and was rewarded with Eshe's lovely face.

"Sweet Flower," he whispered.

Eshe lifted his head gently and kissed him.

"Thank you, Lumumba."

The masked man behind her nodded. "It is the least I can do. We have our ancestors back because of him. We can live in peace again."

"I thank you as well, Lumumba," Obaseki said.

Lumumba fell to his knees and touched his forehead on the floor. "Your words honor me, master of Moyo."

Pajonga and Olushola entered the room. They knelt as well, a gesture Obaseki found embarrassing.

"Please, everyone rise. This isn't necessary."

"Pajonga found you," Eshe said. "He insisted on searching for you after a week passed and we did not hear from you."

"You are a true friend," Obaseki said. "A friend should not be a slave. Before these witnesses, I grant you your freedom."

Pajonga jumped to his feet, his eyes glistening. "What did you say, master?"

"I am no longer your master," Obaseki replied. "I was never comfortable with it, and after this journey, you deserve to be free."

Obaseki looked into Olushola's expectant eyes. "This is your home, isn't it?"

"Yes, master, yes it is."

"Then stay. I grant your freedom as well."

"Thank you, Obaseki," she stammered.

The two embraced and hurried from the room. Obaseki looked into Eshe's eyes and met her approval.

"You are a good, brave man, my husband," she said. "Will Alamako be our home as well?"

Eshe's question triggered the last words of the messenger in his head. His face turned somber.

"My path does not end here, sweet flower."

Eshe's face remained peaceful, though Obaseki sensed her disappointment.

"Where do the ancestors send us?" she asked.

"North," Obaseki replied, "to the Mahgreb."

13

The Diaka stood on the cliffs where the Nyoka River plunged into the misty gorge below. The descent was dizzying, the deafening voice of the river rising from the base of the falls as tons of water smashed into massive rock. The powerful waterway emerged from the spray into an expansive valley, its wide banks crowded with towering trees. Ndoro was in awe; surely no other Sesu had stood where he stood, witnessing the artistry and power of Unkulunkulu.

He turned to Jawanza. "It is beautiful," he said. Jawanza stood behind him, his assegai at his side.

"This land is truly a gift from the ancestors," Jawanza replied.

"It is home," Jabulani declared, "just as the legends describe it."

Ndoro scratched his chin. "Now how do we get down there?"

Jabulani extracted the weathered map from his pouch and sat on the ground, spreading it out before him.

"We will have to go further east. The cliffs are not so high there. I estimate two or three days."

Ndoro and Jawanza squatted beside him. "Good. We will camp here and continue on in the morning."

They made camp, building a large fire to keep away the chill of the approaching darkness. Ndoro did not worry about the fire being spotted; from what he could see the land was empty and probably had been so since the Diaka fled. There were thirty of them total, the group a week away from the temporary village established further down the river. For three months the Diaka traveled the river, facing the dangers of the waters, cataracts and animals as they followed the map to their former homeland. Some were lost along the way, never to reach their destination. Now they were only a few days away from the prize, and a feeling of anticipation swept through the weary tribe. If old Diakaland was anything near what the legends described, the arduous journey was well worth the cost.

Ndoro, Jawanza, Kamau and Jabulani sat before the fire, eating dried buffalo and yams. The trees bustled with sound as night creatures became active, continuing the struggle to survive in the shadows. Ndoro watched Jabulani and was concerned. He was sullen, which did not bode well.

"What is wrong, baba?"

Jabulani chewed his food slowly. "I thank the ancestors for guiding us so far. Despite those who have died, this has been an easy journey."

He looked into Ndoro's eyes, his expression turning grim. "But our ancestors fled this land for a reason. I wonder if that reason waits to drive us away again."

"That will not happen," Jawanza said. "We are strong now, and we have Shumba."

Ndoro smiled when Jawanza spoke the name the Diaka had given to them.

"Jabulani is right," he agreed. "From now on we must be on our guard. We will post sentries tonight."

Everyone nodded. Ndoro stood, stretching as the rigors of the day caught up with him.

"We are tired," he said. "We should rest to prepare for tomorrow's surprises."

Ndoro and the others dispersed, finding a place to rest among the trees.

* * *

Morning brought muted sunlight to the sleeping warriors. The calling of a troupe of passing vervets woke them. They broke camp, with Jabulani leading the way into the valley. The path sloped downward, taking them deeper into the dense forest. Everyone became wary, remembering the conversation from the night before. Ndoro walked with confidence as an example, fully in tune with what was happening around him.

The path narrowed and they were forced to leave the donkeys behind. They unpacked what they could carry; while Ndoro checked to make sure they had all their weapons, including the poison-tipped arrows. They clambered down the steep slope, Jawanza leading the way. Moisture from the vegetation covered them every time they brushed it; by the time they reached the valley floor, they were drenched. The view ahead was in great contrast from where they stood hours ago. A green wall of trees, vines, and bushes loomed before them, allowing only a few feet of viewing ahead. Ndoro clutched the amulet around his neck, the one given to him by Sarama. He whispered a prayer before plunging into the thicket. He did not know the gods of this land, nor the countless spirits that obviously dwelled in such a place. He only hoped that Ukulunkulu's strong hands would extend its protection there.

A few miles into the bush, they came upon what looked like an elephant trail. Jabulani halted.

"Something's wrong. We should be there by now."

Ndoro moved beside him. "Maybe the map is wrong. It's been hundreds of seasons."

Jawanza walked pass them. "We must keep going."

He pushed through the thicket before them and disappeared. No sooner had the leaves enveloped him did they hear him yell.

Ndoro charged through the bushes, his assegai held high. Blinding light struck him and he stopped in his tracks.

"Jawanza!" he shouted.

"Ndoro!" his brother replied. "Come, come see!"

He found Jawanza, a broad smile on his adopted brother's face. Before him, about one thousand feet down, was the valley of the Diaka. The Kojo River snaked between high mountain ridges, a wide and gently sloping plain on either side that ran to the base of the tree-covered peaks. There were no signs of any other humans. The banks teemed with animals of all kinds; antelopes, buffalo, elephants and others could be seen from the heights.

Jabulani bumped into Ndoro, closely followed by the others. He saw the vision before him and fell to his knees.

"We are home," Jabulani whispered.

"Jawanza, go back to the village and spread the news," Ndoro said. "Have everyone prepare for journey tomorrow. I will take Jabulani and the others down into the valley. We will set up camp and wait for you."

Jawanza looked disappointed. Ndoro smiled and place a hand on his shoulder.

"Just one more day, my brother," he said. "Now go; the longer you wait, the longer it will take you to return."

Jawanza selected his party and left quickly, all of them with dejected looks on their face. Ndoro turned to Jabulani, but the old man was gone. He was far away, sprinting down the trail to the valley.

"Jabulani, wait!" Ndoro called out.

He and the other warriors laughed as they ran to catch up with Jabulani. Their laughter turned into effort when they realized the elder was faster than they thought. By the time they caught up to him, he was at the base of the hill, standing motionless.

"Baba!" Ndoro said. "You've been saving your energy."

Ndoro fell silent when he saw what held Jabulani's attention. A stone pillar the height of a man blocked the path. It was triangular, crowned with the carving of a crocodile. Writing ran down the length of the pillar. Jabulani shook as he read.

"What does it say?" Ndoro asked.

"Those that once lived here are cursed by the river god," Jabulani read. "Those who follow will suffer the same fate."

Ndoro pushed Jabulani aside. Bracing his shoulder against the stone, he dug in and pushed. The other saw him and came to his aid. They strained against the stone as if opening a heavy door that hid a long-sought treasure. Slowly the the obelisk tilted, leaned, and then crashed to the ground.

Ndoro looked at his adopted father and smiled. "Let us tempt fate."

He stepped over the obelisk and entered the Diaka homeland.

The remaining Diaka arrived the following day. They set about their task quickly, building a makeshift village on the edge of the river. As the women and children built homes and cleared fields, the men hunted the woods for the abundant game. Ndoro called the first elders meeting after two weeks, greeting the learned men and women under a modest ironwood tree near the new village.

Joy radiated from the old ones sitting in the semi-circle about Ndoro. They jostled about like children, smiling and joking while Jabulani tried to call them to order. They finally calmed down when Ndoro stood.

"Welcome home," Ndoro said. The elders clapped and touched their heads to the ground before him.

"We have come far for this day. Homes have been built and fields are planted. Our hunters bring in game and our fishermen fill their nets daily. But there is much more for us to do."

"Tell us what you wish, Shumba," Shaihi asked. "You have led us to freedom and to our homeland. It is obvious the ancestors have chosen you."

Ndoro was still not used to the admiration of the Diaka, especially these elders who held more wisdom among them that he could ever wish to have. He hesitated before revealing his plan because he knew it was selfish. But if he were to one day return home, he would need these brave people to help him.

"I wish to make the Diaka strong. I wish for all the tribes between our valley and Songhai to fear the warriors of this land."

The mood change was sudden, like a rainy season storm. The elders looked among themselves with knowing expressions before Shaihi spoke.

"You are a young man, Shumba," he said. "The path before you seems new, but to us it is old and worn. It is good enough for us to sit here and see our people free. But fire burns inside you. We saw it the day you first came into our village. We used your fire to free us. Do not use it to destroy us."

"I am only asking you to be what you can be," Ndoro replied.

"Your dream is a Sesu dream, not Diaka," Shaihi replied.

"The Diaka are warriors," Ndoro replied. "Do you think the Songhai lick their wounds and forget the Diaka? Do you think the Tacuma will welcome us back when they discover we have returned?"

Ndoro regretted instigating the worry he saw in the elders' faces, but it was necessary. He had no idea what the Songhai planned; he did not even know if the Tacuma still existed. He did know that by bringing up these hated and feared enemies, his argument would be heard.

"You are Ndoro, the Diaka-koi, our Shumba," Shaihi said. "If you share your dream with our warriors, they will follow you. But we ask that you wait. We have much work to do here. We have no wealth but the land we farm and the food we raise. We have no cattle, no items to trade, and no iron to make weapons. We need time, Shumba."

"Patience is the key to all good things," Jabulani added.

The elders' point was well made, Ndoro admitted to himself.

"Your council comes with wisdom," he said. "We will concentrate on what we have. But we must be mindful of our defense. The Songhai is a distant enemy but the Tacuma are a present worry."

"We agree as much," Shaihi said.

"I think we should build a stone city closer to the mountains," Ndoro said. "The river village is vulnerable to attack. A walled city against the mountains would provide a sound defense."

"The river is also the home of the Tacuma's totem, the ngwena," Jabulani added. "The further away we are from this bad omen the better."

"Again you show your wisdom," Shaihi said. "We will gather our stone-smiths and find a quarry. We will begin work immediately."

The gathering broke up with everyone in better spirits. Ndoro retired to his home where Sarama waited, stirring the pot of stew as she hummed.

"So, my warrior returns triumphant?"

Ndoro came up behind her and wrapped his arms around her waist. She was plump with child, her fullness a welcomed sight to everyone in the family. Ndoro was now a true Diaka.

"No one triumphs over the elders," he corrected. "We agreed."

"But you got your way."

"Of course."

"It won't be so easy when this little one comes," Sarama said as she rubbed her stomach with his hand.

"He will be a fine warrior," he said.

"She will be a proud Diaka maiden," Sarama retorted.

Ndoro eyes went wide. "You know this?"

"Mama told me. She is never wrong."

Ndoro went to the stool and sat hard. "So I must wait for a son."

Sarama hit him on the head with her spoon. "And be happy for your daughter."

Ndoro reached out, grabbing her around the waist and pulling her onto his lap. They laughed and kissed and forgot about the stew until much later in the evening.

The following weeks hummed by to the rhythm of a busy multitude. Fields were planted and the farmers waited while the hunters continued to harvest the bounty of the valley. Unlike the lands to the north, the rain seemed to spread itself evenly throughout the seasons, allowing for longer growing seasons and bigger harvests. The stonecutters found their quarry and began the arduous task of cutting stone for the new city. The mysterious brotherhood of blacksmiths located a source of the rock from which they summoned the metal essential for tools and weapons. Though it seemed a time for peace, Ndoro, Jawanza and Kamau kept the Diaka men sharp with drills and mock battles. Patrols were organized to keep constant vigil, sometimes staying out for weeks as they surveyed the valley and the surrounding hills. A new generation of boys was coming of age and Ndoro organized them into the peer groups he remembered as a child. Sesu stick fighting was taught to develop their martial skills, and competitions were arranged to foster unity among the peer groups and the boys as a whole.

It was during the first full moon of the sixth month when the Diaka discovered they were not alone. Night came early to the valley as it always did, the sun disappearing behind the verdant peaks. Ndoro and Sarama enjoyed each other's company in the compound, chatting over an intense game of oware, when they were interrupted by an urgent rapping on their door. Ndoro opened it to reveal the worried face of Jawanza.

"Shumba, you must come quickly."

"What is it?"

"The night patrol captured someone breaking into the granary."

"Who is it? What family does he belong to?"

Jawanza hesitated. "He is not Diaka."

The two men ran through the streets to the granary at the center of the city. A crowd gathered, people pushing to get closer to the warriors before the granary door.

"Move aside!" Jawanza shouted. "Make way for the Diaka-koi!"

The crowd parted immediately, revealing the intruder. He sat cross-legged on the ground, his hands tied behind his back. His head shaven, the man looked about angrily at his captors. He was thin, his ribs showing through his scarred skin. His chest was covered by a large ngwena brand, a ragged loincloth his only clothing.

Ndoro walked to the man and squatted before him.

"Who are you?"

"I am a beast," the man replied. "Kill me and be done with it."

Ndoro tried again. "What is your name?"

"I have no name," the captive replied. "I am a beast, and my masters will come for me soon."

"Who are your masters?

"The people who will soon be yours; the Tacuma."

Ndoro kept his face stern despite the worry in his chest.

"The Tacuma know we are here?"

The captive smiled. "They suspected, but now they know. They will come to kill your men and take your women and children. This land has been cursed since the Diaka were driven away. You have condemned yourselves by coming here."

Ndoro smiled back. "I see you didn't mind stealing a little condemned food."

He stood erect. "This land is not cursed to us. It was ours before; it is ours again."

The man's smile melted away. "Diaka? No!"

"Diaka, yes," Ndoro replied. "Take this man and hold him in the empty storehouse," he said to the patrollers. "Make sure he is fed."

He faced the terrified man again. "Sleep well, beast. We have much to discuss in the morning."

Ndoro spent a restless night wondering about the captive's words. If the Tacuma knew they were in the valley, how long would they wait before attacking? Did they know they were the Diaka, or did they think they were a wandering tribe that knew nothing of the curse? The questions spun about in his head as he fell in and out of sleep the entire night, the last awakening made final by the emerging daylight. Ndoro was the first to the stockade. The sentries greeted him with a sharp bow. They opened the door to the empty granary and he entered.

The air burned with the smell of decaying grain and rodent droppings. The captive sat upright on the opposite wall, his face passive.

"Do we have a name today?" Ndoro asked.

"I am a slave. Tacuma slaves have no names, as you will discover soon."

Ndoro did not like the arrogant words of this man. He would have killed him by now if not for the information he sought.

"You speak of the Tacuma as if they are gods, but gods need no slaves."

"The gods have men to serve them in respect and fear," the captive replied. "The Tacuma have men to serve them as slaves."

"If you praise them so much, why did you run away?"

The captive smiled. "I did not run away. I was sent to find you."

Ndoro's eyes narrowed, focusing on the ngwena brand on the captive's chest. There was something about the eye that bothered him.

"Yes, the eye of the crocodile sees," the captive said. "It sees what I see. My masters know where I have been and where I am. What I see, my masters see."

Ndoro stood upright, the captive laughing. "Yes, yes, you know now, don't you? You will meet the Tacuma very soon."

Ndoro snatched his sword and stabbed the man in the chest where the eye of the ngwena stared. He ran from the granary to his compound.

"Sound the attack drums!" he shouted. "The Tacuma are coming!"

No sooner had the words escaped his lips did screams rise from the river's edge. Ndoro and the guards ran to the river as the attack drums rumbled through the village. Warriors streamed out of their family compounds, falling into formation behind Ndoro. The army was full force as they reached the river

They met a crowd of women running for their lives. They had been washing along the river when the canoes appeared. There were bodies on the ground, arrows protruding from their backs. Ndoro was hit by a wave of terror; Sarama had left earlier to wash with the other women.

Tacuma warriors rowed to the banks, driving Ndoro and Diatanee back with a shower of arrows. They poured out of their canoes armed with short broad swords and wooden shields, their heads covered by wooden masks carved in the shape of the ngwena, the long snouts brandishing jagged white teeth. Ngwena hide protected their torsos and legs.

The Diaka locked their shields, covering the fleeing women and themselves as their archers fired back. Ndoro charged forward, followed by the other Diaka. He threw his orinka high with his men and the Tacuma raised their shield in response, falling for the diversion. The Diaka hurled their assegais at the unprotected midsections, cutting down scores of Tacuma. Ndoro led the charge as they crashed into the warriors.

It was a vicious battle. Ndoro was blind in his rage, swinging and hacking with unbridled fury. The Diaka swarmed over the Tacuma, killing those on the banks and driving the others back to the canoes.

"Don't let them escape!" Ndoro shouted. "Kill them all!"

The Diaka ran into the river, tackling the fleeing Tacuma and stabbing them in the water. Those that reached the canoes found only a brief respite as the Diaka archers joined the fight again with their deadly volleys. The distracted Tacuma did not notice the Diaka swimmers. They capsized the war canoes, spilling the warriors into the river and the waiting blades of the Diaka.

The battle ended as quickly as it began. The Tacuma were wiped out to a man, but the Diaka suffered as well. Women and children ran to the river, searching for their loved ones. The wailing echoed from the riverbank as families found their dead sons, fathers and brothers. The wounded were taken to the village center to be tended.

Ndoro heard a familiar voice cry out. He stood motionless, daring not to move until he heard the cry again He trudged to the riverside and to the circle of his family on their knees. The crying sunk into his chest as he neared. Everyone saw him approaching and parted, revealing the sight he dreaded. Strength left his legs and he fell to his knees, dropping his weapons then reaching out to the body of Sarama. Talana held her daughter in her arms, cradling her as well as she could. Ndoro looked into Talana's eyes and saw the pain.

Something inside him disappeared and he stopped crying. The pain found a place to hide, escaping the rage that coursed through him like a flooding river. He picked up his weapons and stood.

"Take care of her, mama," he said. "I have something I must do."

The family warriors came to their feet, the meaning of Ndoro's words clear. They followed him back to the main village where Jabulani, despite his loss, performed the necessary ritual to appease the souls of the slain Tacuma. The sight of Sarama's father chanting among her killers drove his rage to a higher level.

"Stop!" Ndoro shouted. Jabulani glared at him.

"You know what must be done," Jabulani said. "Their souls must be honored to rest in peace."

"Let their ngwena spirit give them peace," Ndoro replied. He turned to his warriors. "Throw them into the river!"

The Diaka swarmed past Jabulani and set about the task. They dragged the Tacuma corpses to the river's edge then flung them into the river.

Ndoro grinned. "Now their totem can decide whether to save their spirits or eat them."

Ndoro turned his back to the river and strode away, his warriors following. He had only taken a few steps when a strange sound arose from the river. The waters churned like a tempest, the bodies of the Tacuma warriors breaking surface and transforming. Arms and legs shrank as the torsos extended. Their heads elongated, their mouths filling with pyramid shaped teeth. Leathery scales encased the skin as tails emerged from their backs.

Jabulani appeared at his side, tugging his arm. "We must flee, Ndoro! The Ngwena spirit comes!"

Ndoro snatched his arm away. "Let it come."

Jabulani let go of Ndoro then fled into the woods with the other villagers. The warriors remained, though their shifting eyes betrayed them. Their fears were answered as the Tacuma warriors attacked again, this time in flesh of ngwenas. They drove back the Diaka, pushing them away from Ndoro but not attacking. Ndoro seemed oblivious to the reptiles as they swarmed around him, growling and snapping. He glowered at them, a cruel smile creasing his face. Sarama and his unborn child were with the spirits. He wished to be with them.

A dark shadow appeared under the roiling surface, weaving its way to the shore, its large eyes focused on Ndoro. It reached the bank then climbed from the water. Even in his sorrow and rage Ndoro was moved by the size of the beast. The perimeter of the reptilian circle opened and the bull ngwena entered. Ndoro's hands clenched about his assegai and shield, anticipation coursing through him. The ngwena let out a long bellow as it morphed, rising on its hind legs as its body took shape. Its hind legs extended as its forelimbs took the shape of massive human arms. The crocodile man's eyes sparked as it looked down on Ndoro.

Ndoro charged the beast and was knocked aside by the sweep of its tail. He struck the ground and almost rolled into one of the ngwena, blocking its snapping jaws with his shield. He was coming to his feet when the beast struck at him with his claws. Ndoro ducked as he swung his sword. The blow glanced off its scales. It swung its tail again but Ndoro jumped over it, slipping behind his attacker. He threw his assegai and watched it bounce off the thick back scales.

The beast spun about.

"What are you?" it hissed.

Ndoro extracted his sword again as his answer. The beast moved toward him then stopped, turning its head from side to side.

"You are no man," it said. "A man would be dead by now."

The ngwenas surrounding Ndoro rustled, edging closer to him. The beast was summoning them to attack, Ndoro thought. It could not defeat him alone. Ndoro smirked. This river spirit was not much to fight, let alone fear.

He charged the crocodile-spirit and it lunged at him, mouth wide and teeth glistening. Ndoro stepped aside and stabbed low, striking the beast in its underbelly. It howled and its servants fell still. The beast grabbed the blade before Ndoro could pull it out and dragged him toward its gaping jaws. He brought his shield about and jammed it between its teeth. The beast bit down, tearing through leather and wood. Its grip loosened on the sword and Ndoro snatched it free. As the beast reached for the shield in its mouth, Ndoro brought the sword down on the beast's wrist. The blade hesitated then sliced through the joint, the paw falling to the ground. A cry came from the beast that tore at his ears. The ngwenas spun on the ground as they did when tearing a victim apart, but this time in pain. They fled to the river, transforming back into the still bodies of the slain Tacuma. The river-spirit held its damaged arm against its body with its good paw and ran for the safety of the water, but Ndoro was not about to be denied his kill. He chased after the beast and grabbed its massive tail, lifting its hind legs from the ground. The Ngwena-beast fell to its front legs, tearing at the mud with its good paw and stub in a vain attempt to reach the murky river.

"Ndoro! Hold him," Jabulani shouted. Ndoro twisted his head about to see his foster father pick up the severed paw and drop it into a gourd. He placed the gourd on the ground and drew a series of patterns on it. The beast attempted to twist free but Ndoro's grip was unyielding. Jabulani ended his chanting then clapped his hands.

The beast ceased struggling, breathing heavily. Ndoro let the tail go and picked up his sword

"Thank you, baba," he said as he raised his sword over the beast's head.

Jabulani scampered forward and stepped in between Ndoro and the beast.

"No, Ndoro, you don't have to kill him."

"Of course I do," Ndoro replied.

"You don't understand," the medicine priest replied. "His paw and his soul are trapped in the gourd. As long as you possess a part of a spirit it must obey you. It cannot return to the spirit realm without it. You are its master now."

"I have no faith in magic, Baba," Ndoro replied. "This beast is better off dead."

"You can kill him, but by doing so you destroy your revenge," Jabulani said. "If you control the beast, you control the Tacuma."

Ndoro looked at the beast. "Is this true?"

The beast did not answer.

"Answer me!" Ndoro shouted. He saw the beast struggle against opening its jaws.

"Yes. It is true," it said.

A grin came to Ndoro's face. "Baba, can we build some type of cage to hold him?"

This is the only cage you need," Jabulani replied. He handed Ndoro the gourd holding the paw with a leather string. Ndoro tied it around his waist.

"He is yours now," Jabulani said. "You are his master."

Ndoro frowned at his captive river-spirit. "Stay here until I return." A moan seeped from the beast's jaws.

"Come, baba," Ndoro said as his rage ebbed. "We must mourn."

They walked together in silence, the cries from their compound growing louder with each step. As they entered the group of homes, the tears came from their eyes as well. The women gathered outside Ndoro's home, their mourning ritual loud and aching. They came to him, wrapping their arms about his neck and crying into his chest, their words incoherent in their sorrow. Ndoro pushed them aside as politely as possible. The doorway was clear; he opened it and went inside.

Sarama lay on the floor as if asleep, her body covered with a white cotton sheet. Talana knelt beside her, rocking back and forth, singing softly. Ndoro dropped to his knees and laid beside his wife, wrapping his arms around her coldness and burying his head into her arm. Sobs shook him and he did not fight to keep them inside. Together he and Talana cried for Sarama, pleading for her spirit to stay close to them and accept this new land as her home. They cried for the unborn child, the daughter that was never named, one of the first victims of the war that was about to begin.

Ndoro lifted himself from the floor. He had allowed himself the luxury of mourning; he would never do so again. He stepped away from Talana and nodded, making way for her to perform a last task for her daughter. Ndoro left the house amid the constant wailing of not only his compound, but also that of the entire city. The sounds became too much for him so he walked away, ignoring the urgent words of other villagers asking for a council. He followed the main road out of the village, the road that led to the stone mines in the eastern mountains. He walked through the sunlight and the night sky, oblivious to the animals scampering in the canopy of the high forests and totally ignoring those that threatened him on the ground. Two days after he began his trek, he passed the camp of the stonecutters. The men recognized him, but Ndoro ignored them, stepping into the woods at the end of the path. Ndoro began to climb the ridge. Digging his feet into the soil with each step, he fought his way upward, using the hanging vines to pull himself up the steep slope. The dense foliage engulfed him; darkness prevailing where light had no right to be. He continued climbing, lungs burning with each step, until he reached a granite outcrop. A path worn by the gait of men snaked its way ahead of him and he followed it. By dusk he was at the top of the highest peak on the ridge. Ndoro stopped and spread his blankets on the stone. He removed his weapons one by one, laying them next to his blanket. As he began to lie down he heard human sounds and he grabbed his assegai. The crocodile-spirit appeared and sat opposite him.

"I wish to be alone," Ndoro said. "Leave me."

The ngwena spirit stood. "As you wish. I would not want to see you mourn like a woman."

Ndoro came to his feet. "Your mouth will get you killed."

"Better death than be a servant to a weak fool," the beast replied.

Ndoro smiled. The beast goaded him, preferring death to slavery. "Why should I kill you and make your life easy?"

"If you won't kill me, at least make my service worth the humiliation."

"What can you do for me?" Ndoro asked.

"You come here to understand your place," the beast replied. "Your wife is dead. There is nothing you can do about it. You can run as far as you like and she will still be dead."

"What do you know of humans?" Ndoro shouted.

"You can't imagine how long I've lived," the beast replied. "I've been hunted and worshipped by your kind for thousands of years. I've come to know you very well."

"I'm tired of talking and I am disgusted looking at you," Ndoro replied. "I need to think."

"Then think of this," the beast replied. "You defeated a spirit, something a man should not be able to do. The ancestors have a plan for you whether you believe so or not."

The beast closed his eyes, transforming into a human form more disturbing because of its perfection. He smiled and sauntered away, disappearing into the foliage. Ndoro lay back down, but he did not sleep. He thought of his journey since fleeing Selike, of his adoption by the Diaka, his training them and making them warriors, of their trek to the new homeland and his defeat of the river-spirit. Buried under it all remained the promise he made to himself, the promise to return to Selike and claim the Royal Stool as his own. The river beast said the ancestors had a plan for him. As far as he was concerned, the ancestors did not figure in his life. Each of his triumphs he'd accomplished alone. Life with the Diaka had distracted him from his purpose. If he were to see Selike again, he would have to take control of his life.

As the morning sun peered over the eastern peaks, Ndoro stared down on the valley. In the distance, smoke of the morning fires rose from the Diaka villages. He heard the clattering of the stonecutters at the quarry below him. Somewhere to the north, the Tacuma waited in vain for the return of their warriors while their priests called on a god that would not appear. He heard the rustling of branches and the river beast appeared.

"Do you have a name?" Ndoro inquired

"Nakisisa," the beast replied.

"You know where the Tacuma live?"

The beast nodded.

"You will lead us to them, Nakisisa."

Nakisisa smiled. "The night's rest has done you well. Maybe you will serve the ancestors purpose."

"I could care less about the ancestors," Ndoro replied. "I have my own reasons."

"As you say, master."

They returned to the village after the mourning ceremonies were complete. A pall hung over the village, the people lethargic in performing their daily chores. Ndoro went to Jabulani's compound and found the same mood. His adopted family barely noticed his return as he walked through the compound to his home. Ndoro stopped and opened the door. The house was empty. He closed his eyes and imagined Sarama squatting before the fire, stirring her delicious stew, the smile that pushed away his worries on her beautiful face. The shadows of grief reentered his mind, swallowing Sarama's memory and he closed the door. Ndoro stepped away and went to the house of Jabulani. The old man sat before the door, slowly chewing on a kola nut. He smiled at Ndoro.

"You have returned," he said. "Many thought you went back to your people."

Ndoro sat beside his foster father.

"We would have understood if you did," Jabulani continued. "Sarama was special. It is difficult to lose someone you love."

Ndoro refused to contemplate Jabulani's words.

"Baba, I require council with the elders."

Jabulani's smile disappeared. "Why?"

"We need to discuss war against the Tacuma."

Jabulani nodded slowly. "I will send Jawanza."

The council meeting was short. Ndoro made his intentions clear and the council did not stand in his way. The stonecutters were summoned back to the village to help build war canoes. The ironsmiths went to work creating spear tips, wrist knives, swords and other weapons of war. Life flowed back into the veins of the Diaka in a grim form. The Diaka were no longer fishermen and farmers; they were warriors again.

Three weeks after Ndoro's return the village rang with the sounds of celebration. Women and children danced to the drummers who stood on rooftops beating out praises as the army ran through the streets. Ndoro, Jawanza, and Kamau, dressed in full Diaka battle dress, waited at the docks with the elders. Nakisisa languished in the water in his reptilian form, his eyes just visible over the rippling surface.

Ndoro raised his assegai and the drummers changed the rhythm, summoning the warriors to the canoes. The army marched into the shallow mooring and climbed aboard. Kamau led the archers into the lead boats; Jawanza loaded his warriors into the boats to the rear. The largest boat floated before the others, an enormous canoe with metal plating on the bow, a platform rising over the edge. Fifty Diatanee boarded the massive craft in single file, chanting as they took their places. When the last had entered, Ndoro boarded, taking his place on the platform. Nakisisa remained in the water, awaiting Ndoro's signal.

One hundred canoes filled with warriors undulated upon the river. Diaka lined the banks of the Kojo, an entire nation present to witness its new beginning. Pride resonated in their voices as they sang; their arms raised high as they danced. Ndoro scanned the war fleet and smiled. This was his monument to Sarama. He promised to make her a wife and he did, but he was never able to make her a queen. Ndoro circled his assegai over his head, the same assegai that slew Old Simba. In unison the rowers pushed off and the crowd cheered. Nakisisa swam before Ndoro's canoe as ordered, leading the Diaka army to Tacumaland.

According to Nakisisa, Tacumaland lay two weeks north. Once they arrived at the borderlands, it could be another two days before they reached the capital city. The river spirit warned Ndoro of the size of Tacumaland, convincing him the Diaka could not defeat them in a long war. Ndoro decided to make a decisive strike at the center of the kingdom itself, the city of Jinja. He hoped the show of force would keep the Tacuma at bay long enough for the Diaka to build their strength and complete construction of the stone city. There was also Nakisisa. The Tacuma's reaction to their fallen god was critical to the success of the attack. If it did not go as he anticipated, the Diaka would have returned to their homeland only to be destroyed by the same people that drove them away.

The days were spent rowing, the nights resting along the banks. The river held few cataracts to slow their progress; their biggest obstacles were the groups of hippopotami scattered along the river. The fearless beasts blocked their progress numerous times, ignoring the threats of the warriors. Nakisisa was no help; being part crocodile, he held a great respect and fear of the animals. Only the constant beating of the water with the oars forced the beast to move, more in annoyance than fear.

With only a half day's rowing from the borders of Tacuma, the Diaka settled into their last camp before making the run for the city. There would be no rest the next day. Ndoro's orders were clear. The canoes would not stop until they reached Jinja.

Ndoro sat by a small fire with his brothers. They ate silently, each deep within his thoughts. Ndoro hated idle moments such as this, for it gave his mind a chance to wander back to memories of Sarama. Nakisisa sat just beyond the light of the fire, his eyes glowing. Ndoro rose and walked away, headed for the war canoes. Nakisisa followed him. As Ndoro inspected the canoes, the crocodile-spirit slid into the black waters. He listened to the beastman splash about as it found and devoured its prey, hoping a man was not the victim. The beast returned in human form, his face bright red with blood.

He looked at Ndoro and smiled. "It humors me when humans look at me that way. You act as if you've never seen blood, yet tomorrow you will spill much of it yourselves."

"We are not much different from you," Ndoro said.

"You are the first to admit it," Nakisisa replied.

"I have no reason to lie," Ndoro replied. "I know the only way to survive is to be stronger than those that oppose you. My father was weak and allowed me to be driven away. If he were stronger, he would have defied the elders and stopped the smelling out that condemned me."

"Tradition is a powerful force," Nakisisa replied. "The Diaka follow you only because of tradition. Power alone is nothing; power within tradition is everything."

"You are a wise slave," Ndoro replied.

"And you are a fast learner," Nakisisa said. "It will be an honor to kill you one day."

* * *

The Diaka rose before first light and boarded their war canoes. They abandoned their supplies at the campsites, making for faster travel. Ndoro arranged the boats in attack formation, the archer boats near the river edge protecting the warrior boats in the center. At the front of the formation was Ndoro's armored canoe flanked by two smaller canoes manned with fire archers. They penetrated the borders of Tacuma before dawn, pushing forward as fast they could row. They passed scores of fishing villages, their inhabitants harvesting the river's bounty along the banks. Some waved at them, apparently thinking they were returning Tacuma. It was well into the day before their approach upon the tiny villages transformed from friendly waves to angry glares and shouts. Ndoro knew runners were trying to outpace them to warn the villages upriver.

Ndoro scanned forward and saw the villagers of the upcoming town pushing their boats into the river.

"Increase the pace!" he ordered.

The drummer beat faster and the rowers responded. The lead boat archers loaded their bows. Up ahead the Tacuma fishermen lashed labored. Some tied the boats together while others ran from the banks to the boats with armloads of sticks.

"They are building a firewall," Nakisisa said. "Look behind us."

Ndoro strained his eyes and saw a large number of canoes filled with Tacuma warriors rapidly approaching their rear.

The boat barricade came into bow range. Diaka arrows jumped from the bows in a chorus of twanging bowstrings, the iron-tipped missiles falling upon the blockade workers with devastating accuracy. Another volley cut down the torchbearers attempting to light the straw-filled canoes. Though the canoes did not burn, they were still tied together. The Diaka would have to cut the boats free in order to pass. Three Diatanee jumped into the water without urging, swimming for the boats. Arrows flew toward them from the banks and the Diaka responded, driving the Tacuma back behind the trees for protection. The warriors reached the canoes and cut them free with their wrist daggers, clearing the way to move on.

The pace drummer renewed his rhythm and the fleet surged ahead, pulling away from the pursuing Tacuma canoes. The water-bound Diatanee clambered onto Ndoro's canoe as it sped by, and they took their place among the others. They raced upriver through a gauntlet of arrows and spears as the Tacuma responded to this bold attack. Warriors ran along the riverbanks trying to anticipate where the Diaka would make landfall, none suspecting the objective of the attack until the granite walls of Jinja rose over the horizon.

The Tacuma unleashed a torrent of arrows at the Diaka canoes. The deluge was too much for the Diaka to return; they raised their shields and hid under the protection of wood and leather. But still they rowed, headed for the island. Tacuma warriors jumped into the river, swimming for the canoes under the cover of the arrows. Nakisisa attacked them, blood swirling in the currents as he struck them one by one. The Tacuma on the banks looked on in terror as their river-god betrayed his worshippers. They fell away from river's edge, many of them dropping their weapons and falling to their knees.

The canoes approached the banks of Jinja unopposed. They ran aground and the Diaka poured out, the Diatanee first to set foot on the sandy banks. A massive spiked iron gate sealed the towering walls, a formidable barrier between the Diaka and their prize. Tacuma warriors stood along the ramparts like statues, their faces locked in disbelief as they watched Ndoro march toward them, Nakisisa trailing behind him in obvious servitude. Ndoro continued forward until he was within shouting distance of the walls, ignoring the fact that he was also in arrow range.

"Tacuma! I have come for what is mine!" Ndoro shouted. "Your god stands beside me, master to my will. We stand before your walls because your ancestors have forsaken you. Your warriors flee like children upon the sight of true men. Open your gates and live; raise your spears against us and die!"

Ndoro watched the ramparts of the city walls for signs the Tacuma might fight. He dared not look behind; he knew the Tacuma warriors pursuing him upriver now stood behind him. He was surrounded. They all waited for a signal from the city, Diaka and Tacuma alike. A lone figure appeared on the ramparts. The man stood for a moment, and then disappeared. Soon afterward, the gates of the city swung open.

Ndoro and Nakisisa walked through the metal portal into Jinja. A broad avenue extended before them, bordered by squat reed homes with high pointed roofs surrounded by shrub fences. Jinjawa peered from windows and doorways, their eyes transfixed on Nakisisa in his ngwena shape. The duo was deep into the city before the warning horns sounded, sending the Jinjawa scrambling into their homes and emptying the streets with amazing speed. The primal fear they held for the river-beast spread like fire on dry grass. Those that did not flee stood paralyzed, their eyes following Ndoro and Nakisisa as they made their way up the main avenue toward the gates of the inner city. Ndoro spotted armed men peering at them from behind buildings but none made a move to block their path. He knew eventually someone would marshal his fear and challenge them; he hoped their procession would be over by then.

Ndoro and the ngwena approached the heart of Jinja. He held his shield and assegai at the ready, constantly scanning for anyone brave enough to try to stop their advance. He searched for a building of significance, a place where he and his companion could confront the inkosi of the Tacuma. Ahead of them lay the central city surrounded by a bleached white stone wall painted with geometric shapes and patterns unfamiliar to Ndoro. The iron and wood wall gate was open.

What Ndoro had seen of the outer city did not compare to what he gazed upon as he stood amid the royal compound. The city brimmed with spacious gray stone dwellings crowned with ochre tiles. Each home was encircled by a wooden fence and possessed a stone tower attached to the house. The home towers grew in height as they came closer to the city center. Ndoro guessed that the height of the tower might signify the status of a family. If the inkosi's palace resided in the city center, then those closest to the palace would be the homes of the chosen clans, hence the higher towers. Over the door of each home rested a gilded staff carved with totems unique to each home. At the right end of the staff, an ivory carving of an animal's head was attached. Ndoro noticed that groups of homes contained the same animal head, be it elephant, gorilla, or monkey. Apparently, the animal totem designated the family clan to which the house members belonged. The doors were richly carved, scenes of heroic feats and religious faith depicted in ebony. Despite the opulence, there was still no sign of life. The ngwena's presence was working too well. Ndoro realized if he did not find anyone to deal with, he could not complete his plan.

He finally focused on the building in the center. A wide pyramid formed the core, bisected by a stone stairway ascending to a square chamber at the pinnacle. Two rectangular buildings with tiled dome roofs flanked the pyramid, each one punctuated with a thin minaret equal in height to the pyramid. Ndoro surmised this structure was either the palace of their inkosi or some type of temple; either way, it was a building that would probably be protected.

"We will go there," he ordered the ngwena.

No sooner did he point at the building was his assumption proven true. Scores of warriors emerged from the chamber and charged down the steep stairs, forming a spear-tipped barrier at the base. Behind them came three elderly men dressed in red robes, each holding golden staffs similar to the ones before the homes just passed. They stood stoically, their eyes void of emotion. Ndoro sensed he was in a situation that hinged on his next words.

One priest stepped forward. His wrinkled faced edged with a white beard marked him as the oldest of the three, but he moved with the confidence of one much younger. The warriors made way as he came forward; the man halted well within the protection of the Tacuma spears.

"Why have you come here, Nakisisa?" he asked with a deep, resonant voice, his eyes locked intensely on the river-beast. There was no fear in his voice, only curiosity and annoyance.

The priest continued to speak. "When my father's father first confronted you, it was agreed that you would spare his life if he made sacrifices to you. We have not broken our promise; why have you broken yours?"

"He is not here of his own free will," Ndoro replied. "He is here because I command his presence."

The elder raised an eyebrow. "Nakisisa, is this true?"

"Do not talk to him!" Ndoro roared. "Look at his right paw."

The elder looked and his eyes widened. He stumbled away, falling as he scampered up the stairs. The warriors, seeing the fear on the priest's face, broke their positions and began to scatter.

"Stop, all of you!" Ndoro commanded. The Tacuma halted, their backs turned and shoulders hunched as if expecting some final blow.

"No longer will you fear Nakisisa," he announced. "From now on, you will fear me!"

Ndoro turned his attention to the eldest councilor. "Step forward," he said.

The elder turned slowly toward Ndoro, tears running down his cheeks.

Ndoro almost felt sympathy for the man, but reality would allow him few luxuries.

"Do not fear, old one. You will not die this day." Ndoro spoke loud so those around him could here. "Your inkosi is weak like a sick child. Despite the gris-gris he has gathered about him, he could not stop me from marching before the steps of his palace. I am Ndoro of the Sesu, son of inkosi Dingane, Koi of the Diaka. Ask your ancestors who would better lead the Tacuma; a warrior who has conquered that which you fear, or an inkosi that hides behind priests and women to spare his own life?"

A roar rose from the top of the temple. More Tacuma warriors spilled out, running down the stairs like an angry flood. Ndoro smiled as he and Nakisisa prepared for the onslaught. At the head of the Tacuma warriors was the inkosi himself, his gilded shield held before him, his sword raised high. It was his last chance to keep his bloodline in control of his people. Killing Ndoro would surely restore his right and erase the shame of their city's violation. If he failed, he would die by the hands of his people. No strong people would allow an inkosi defeated in battle to rule them. It was a sure sign that the gods did not favor him, that his place among men was now low.

Ndoro felt something brush his shoulder, turning him sideways. He turned back in time to see the ngwena in mid-air, its claws and fangs bared, suspended over the inkosi. The man had only a moment to see the creature before it fell upon him, the two of them crashing to the stone steps. The Tacuma warriors froze, backing away from the horrible scene as the river-beast tore at their leader, the inkosi screaming as he struggled against the beast. The priests fell to their knees, crying out to their ancestors to stop the bad fortune that was destroying them.

The river-beast stopped and stood, its muzzle drenched with blood. The inkosi lay still at his feet, his eyes locked in a lifeless stare into the cloudless sky. Everyone watched as the creature loped back to Ndoro's side, licking at the blood on its claws. It turned toward Ndoro.

"They will listen to you now," he said.

Ndoro looked away from the river-beast to the people surrounding him. They all gazed at him, faces contorted by fear and uncertainty. The old priest came to him, his eyes mournful and desperate.

"What must we do to rid ourselves of the fate that is upon us?" he asked.

"Accept me as your inkosi," Ndoro replied, "so that the gods see you are led by one of strength. Deliver those of noble blood to me, so that their weaknesses will never shame you again."

"And what of the Tacuma?" the priest asked. "What will happen to us?"

"Take your place below the Diaka," Ndoro replied. "Your time as masters has ended. Resist and you will perish. Serve me well and the Tacuma will live to see the Diaka take their place as the true masters of this valley."

The priest nodded thoughtfully. "We cannot deny what we have seen. Duma has shown us your strength; by mastering the river-beast, you have proven your favor among the ancestors." The priest rose to his feet. "What shall we call you?"

"Shumba," Ndoro replied.

14

A bonfire built from the limbs of the Sesu meeting tree blazed in the center of the royal umuzi. A mournful sound rose over the crackling flames, the sound of female voices lamenting a loss so deep the consequences couldn't be imagined. Below the royal umuzi the drums spoke in a steady sonorous rhythm, echoing the sorrow filling the breast of every Sesu man, woman and child. Dingane, the Bull of the Sesu, was dead.

Inaamdura cried into the hem of her long skirt, thankful for the concoction Cacunja gave her to stimulate tears. A portion of the Great Wife's mourning was sincere; there was a time that she loved Dingane fiercely. She had defied her obligations as a Bongo wife and given up her Shamfa heritage for him, immersing herself into her new tribe. It was for those memories she cried, those times when her future for the Sesu was clear. Her feelings changed when Ligongo was born. A mother's love dampened the flame for her inkosi, and his indifference to their son doused it. Though outwardly Dingane followed the restrictions set upon Ndoro, inwardly she knew he admired the abomination. She'd hoped Ndoro's murder of Mulugo and flight from Selike would disgrace him, but the opposite was the case. Weeks after his disappearance, the rumors began. Ndoro the disgraced transformed into Ndoro the perfect warrior, a man sent by the ancestors to judge the Sesu. She found it easy to ignore the stories among the common folks; it was the rumors of the Royal Umuzi she could not tolerate. The other wives whispered of impis sent to find Ndoro and bring him home, of Dingane growing tired of his foreign wife and longing for the embrace of Shani. But the lies against Ligongo stung the most. He'd grown into a fine man in her eyes, but in the eyes of the Sesu he was just as foreign as his mother. He was tall and lean where the Sesu were thick; his narrow nose and thin lips looked anemic compared to the proud Sesu noses and lips. Where the Sesu men were often challenging and sparring in the stick fights, Ligongo preferred less martial pursuits. Dingane never asked him to accompany him on his hunts and he barely took him along on the mandatory royal raids. Ligongo was just as brave in battle as the best Sesu, but respect for his skills came grudgingly. To the Sesu he would never be one of them.

It was the frustration of rejection that drove her to Cacunja once again. The poison was subtle, requiring months of ingestion to do its work. To the victim, the gradual weakening would be taken as the natural decline with age. A man like Dingane would never admit his failing skills. On that fateful day, he went into the bush with his most trusted indunas, intent on bringing back the pelt of a simba. Instead, he and three of his companions fell victim to the pride, slain in proud Sesu fashion.

She waited until the Royal Stool Room was empty before hurrying to her study. The crucial time was rapidly approaching. Once the mourning days passed, the Sesu kingdom would be without an inkosi, which meant it would be without laws. The empire she worked so hard to build would briefly fall into chaos, remaining so until the elders selected a new inkosi. Inaamdura labored over the years to insure that the anarchy would not last long. She had deliberately dispersed her bribes unevenly among the elders, hoping to cause discord. A unanimous decision would be too suspicious, and the disunity among the families would work to Ligongo's favor while he consolidated control.

She sat at her desk, extracting the scrolls from her drawer and began writing. Her first messages would go to the elders, confirming and denying her support as she planned. The next messages would go to her allies beyond Selike, those whose loyalties were bought with gold and cowries. The final message would go to Bikita. Her sister was now ruler of Shamfa, her mother and father shells of formality. Under Inaamdura's secret supervision her younger sister rebuilt the Shamfa army, leading it over the mountains into the Barrens and ending Amadika and Twaambo's ambitions once and for all. Inaamdura's help was in the end selfish; she needed an army she could count on just in case the Sesu rejected Ligongo's right to rule and revolted. Her mercenaries would be effective only if she had an army. That army waited at the foothills of Shamfa.

A servant entered the room, a thin girl covered in a leather tunic; her hair braided and beaded Shamfa style.

Inaamdura rose from her desk, the scrolls tucked in an elaborate leather pouch.

"What is it, Thembeka?"

Thembeka fell to her knees, touching her head on the floor. "Great Wife, the elders wait for you by the bonfire to lead the general mourning."

Inaamdura walked past the girl, handing her the bag.

"Take these to the Shamfa messengers," she commanded.

"Yes, Great Mother."

Inaamdura was leaving the palace when she met Ligongo. His face was long with grief, his red eyes despondent. He was dressed in formal Sesu warrior garb, covered in magnificent cow tails; a leopard headband sporting two stork feathers adorned his head.

"Momma," he pleaded. "Let me go with you."

"It's not safe, my son," she replied. "This is a delicate time, especially for you. There are many who don't wish to see you become inkosi."

"And how will hiding in the palace during my father's mourning strengthen my support? They will say I hide like a bush mouse from my enemies while my mother faces them."

She couldn't deny the truth in his words.

"Come then, show your father the respect he never showed you."

Ligongo ignored the barb and accompanied her outside. The household waited for them, every servant, wife and child present, everyone except Jelani and Shani. Inaamdura covered her mouth, hiding her smile. It was no matter. Once the mourning bonfire took its last breath, Shani's time among the Sesu would be done.

On other side of the Royal Umuzi Shani knelt before her small fireplace, her tears genuine. Dingane's death was an aching blow. Only recently had he begun to visit her again, coming to the hut usually during the evening. They would sit outside and talk of old days, the days before the twins were born. Their relationship had never been easy, roiling like a rock filled river. They eventually grew accustomed to each other, and they were becoming close again. She could tell something was wrong, but she attributed it to the stresses of rule and the ravages of age. She never suspected he was dying.

A light touch interrupted her mourning. Jelani looked down at her awkwardly, not knowing whether to feel sympathy or anger.

"We must go, inkosa," he urged. "Inaamdura will come for you as soon as the bonfire dies."

"I know, Jelani," she replied. "Where is Thembile?"

Jelani looked disappointed. "She refuses to go. She says we will be caught and killed."

Shani smiled. "She has lost the bravery of youth. Does she think she has a better chance here?"

"She may be smarter than the both of us," Jelani said.

"No. Inaamdura has no use for me. She hates me more than Ndoro because I created him. Dingane's recent attention didn't help, either."

Jelani laid out a wide wool cloth and filled it with her meager belongings. As a Great Wife, she would have needed a wagon to hold her possessions. Though Dingane showed her favor shortly before he died, she still held the lowest-wife status. She filled the cloth with a few items, treasured objects she brought from Mawenaland.

Shani pulled the corners of the cloth together then secured it. Jelani stood before her, his travel pack thrown over his shoulder, his black skin flickering before the firelight.

His shield rested against his back, as did his spear and quiver of fletchless arrows. A broad Mawena sword rode his hip. He watched Shani as she tied the blanket. She looked at him when she was done.

"Come, we must hurry," he said.

Jelani exited the house first, his keen eyes scanning the darkness for interlopers. He opened the door wider and Shani emerged, her eyes darting furtively from side to side.

"It's too dark," she whispered. "We cannot leave now. We should wait until dawn."

"Dawn will be too late," Jelani replied. "Follow me."

They skirted north of the city, avoiding the light of the bonfire and the knots of mourners surrounding the enclosure. The route took them away from Mawenaland, but it was necessary. Jelani's night vision was like the hyena; they barely stumbled as they ran away from Selike. They continued north for half the night, resting briefly whenever they found a small rise. By dawn they were heading east. Jelani wished to make sure they were far from Sesu borders before heading south toward Mawenaland. They ran the risk of encountering enemies of the Sesu, but it was worth the risk to escape Inaamdura's wrath.

The sun was high overhead before Jelani allowed them an extended break. Again he chose a small hill as refuge, a high point that allowed him to see any approaching animals or Sesu well before either were close enough to threaten them. Shani opened her blanket, removing two loaves of bread. They sat before the blanket and ate.

"How are you?" Jelani asked.

"I am good."

"The pace is not too swift?"

Shani looked up from her bread. "The pace is fine."

"I can slow down if you wish."

"No, you cannot slow down. If we do, we'll be caught."

Silence settled between them again as they finished their bread, a tension building for more reasons that the threat of death.

Shani folded her blanket. "Thembile was right not to come. She would not have been able to keep up."

Jelani nodded. "What puzzles me is how you have been able to."

Shani wrapped the blanket with the leather strip and hung the bundle from her shoulder.

"My son and my husband are dead. All the family I have left is in Mawenaland. I will not let the Sesu deny me my father and my living son."

Jelani scanned the landscape. Wildebeests languished in the distance, huge herds gathering for the migration signaling the beginning of the dry season. Simbas lurked in the shadows, constantly looking for the weakness that spelled opportunity to a hungry pride.

"We have another hard day ahead before we can relax," he said.

"Will we be far enough away?"

"No. You have impressed me with your endurance, inkosa, but a determined impi would catch us. We have the advantage of a head start, but that is not enough. I'm counting on Inaamdura's joy when she discovered we've fled. If we are lucky she will be happy to be rid of us, or she may decide testing Noncemba's wrath not worth the possible consequences."

"I don't care what she decides, as long as she doesn't send an impi after us," Shani concluded.

They ran until nightfall. Jelani made camp under an acacia and they slept soundly until a group of foraging giraffes woke them.

Jelani gathered his items and went to gather Shani's. She pushed him away.

"You don't have to serve me, Jelani. I am no longer the wife of an inkosi."

"You are still Noncemba's daughter," he replied.

"Not out here," she announced. "Here I am just a woman, and you are just a man. We will both do what we need to do to survive until we reach Mawenaland."

"So I am 'just' a man?" Jelani folded his arms across his chest in mock anger.

Shani smiled. "You are just a brave, handsome, and good man."

Jelani nodded. "And you are just a beautiful, strong, caring woman."

They shared a brief smile. Jelani gazed across the landscape, the serious look returning to his face.

"We will walk today. The sun will be hot and we need to conserve our strength. There are few waterholes here, so we must watch our water supply."

Their walk was leisurely but wary as they kept a close eye on the wildlife filling the grasslands. The simbas of this region learned the lesson of the Sesu long ago and avoided the duo, even though the prides contained enough females to quickly overwhelm them. The elephants proved more difficult. Twice they found themselves charged by a large female protecting her herd. Luckily the matriarchs were satisfied by bluff; neither of them could have outrun a female in full fury.

For the first time in all the years as Dingane's wife, Shani took a long look at the land that had become her home years ago. She spent those years adjusting to the Sesu way of life, never taking the time to really see the domain her husband ruled. It was truly a beautiful place, rolling hills speckled with cloud-top acacias and fat baobabs, undulating grasslands vibrant with massive animal herds of all types. Its gentle appearance hid the harshness of its core, a quality that created men like the Sesu.

She realized, despite her miserable last years, she would miss this land. It had been her home; it was the place where her sons were born.

The thought of the twins sent sadness racing through her. Ndoro was lost, probably dead, his body rotted away in the swaying grass, his bones bleached by rain and sunlight. Tears filled her eyes and she forced them away. She had mourned longer for Ndoro than she had for Dingane, for Dingane's weakness was the reason Ndoro had to flee. He had driven their son into the bush to die.

Then she looked at Jelani, his gait still easy despite the miles they had traveled. He had come to Sesuland a young warrior, but now he walked with the confidence time bestows on those who survive its ravages and uncertainties. He performed Ndoro's initiation rites and taught him how to fight the Mawena way. He taught her son the secrets of men and women and finally risked his life to insure Ndoro's escape. Shani realized then that she was looking at Ndoro's true father, not by blood but by deed. He had performed everything Dingane had not. Every quality Ndoro exhibited as a man, he learned from Jelani. Ndoro had been so focused on proving himself to Dingane and the Sesu that he never realized who truly made him the man he was. In truth, she had been just as blind as her son. Dingane's presence had overshadowed Jelani's work. The Mawena never complained once. He did his duty for her and for her son.

She remembered the day Jelani shared his feelings for her. Her cheeks warmed as she recalled his words. "I wish I could do more," he said. He didn't realize he had done far beyond anything she expected. Ndoro's father had not died days ago; he walked before her, leading the way home.

Shani hurried forward to walk beside him, brushing her hip against his hand. He jerked his hand away instinctively.

"I am sorry, inkosa," he said automatically.

"I told you, Jelani, out here I am neither inkosa nor princess. I am just a woman and you are just a man, a man that deserves the woman he desires."

Jelani dared to look in Shani's eyes. She saw the want clouded by confusion, so she decided to clear the matter for him. She reached up, placing her hand behind his neck and pulling his lips down to hers. After a brief kiss Jelani pulled away, his eyes clear, his smile joyful.

"Shani," he said.

"Jelani," she answered.

They walked side by side for the rest of the day. By nightfall Jelani had found another tree to rest under for the night, situated by a clear lake. No sooner had they finished their meal did they unleash the feelings that had been denied for so long. They fell asleep in each other's arms.

Jelani awoke in a dream. He gazed into Shani's sleeping face wondering why the ancestors brought this unbelievable moment upon him. So many obstacles stood in the way between what occurred that night, insurmountable barriers of caste and customs. He held no false hopes. They were in between worlds in the bush; once they arrived in Mawenaland, life would once again place its rules upon them. She would be princess and he would be servant.

Shani opened her eyes and saw the questions in her new lover's face.

"It will be different," she said.

"How can it be?" Jelani asked. "Your father will never agree to it. The elders will never allow it."

"They cannot deny what has happened between us."

Jelani sat up, surprised. "You would tell them what we did? You'll be dishonored!"

"I don't care about honor anymore, Jelani. I married a man I didn't love for honor. I gave up my child for honor."

Jelani stood. "We shouldn't talk about this now. We must eat and move on. The day is passing us by."

Shani nodded. She wanted to talk, but she knew Jelani was confused. There would be plenty of time before they reached Mawenaland.

Shani walked in front of him, her hips swaying hypnotically. Jelani's mind was filling with amorous intentions when a stern voice interrupted his thoughts.

"They are coming."

Jelani stopped, shaking his head. Shani turned to look at him, her face puzzled.

"Jelani, what's wrong?"

He held up his hand to silence her, his head tilted awkwardly.

"They are coming. They are close."

Jelani recognized the voice reverberating in his head. A sad smile formed on his face.

"Shani, keep walking forward." Shani obeyed, her hands trembling.

"Jelani, tell me what's going on."

"The Sesu have found us," he answered.

Shani stumbled as she heard his words but she continued to walk.

"How do you know? I haven't seen anyone."

Jelani shifted uncomfortably. "I was told."

"What are you talking about? We are the only ones here. Who could tell you?"

"Husani," Jelani said.

Shani stopped and spun to face him. "Husani? Don't play with me this way!"

Jelani grasped her shoulders and turned her back around. "Husani has warned me of the Sesu, as he should. He is my older brother; it is his duty."

"I don't understand," Shani confessed. "How could Husani...?"

"There is no time to explain, Shani. You have to listen to me very carefully. The Sesu haven't seen you yet. When I tell you to stop walking, you must lay down in the grass. I will cover you with my shield. Do not stand until you hear me yell, then run as fast as you can. Don't look back."

"Jelani, don't do this. We can outrun them."

Jelani hesitated. "No, Shani. We can't. Please, lay down now."

Shani descended to her knees then lay in the prickly grass. Jelani knelt behind her, placing his shield and assegai by her side.

"Take them with you," Shani said. "I don't need them."

Jelani chuckled. "These are Sesu tools. I will meet them as I am; a Mawena."

Jelani stood and spun around. He walked away from Shani and any chance of them having a future together. His brother had come from the Zamani to remind him of his duty. He drew his sword, swinging it back and forth to test his grip. The blade was sharp, the point keen. He extracted his dagger in his left hand, holding the hilt so the blade rested against his protected forearm. He was ready to fight.

The impi bobbed over the horizon as his brother foretold, ten Sesu warriors with bare head rings. They were young ones, probably running ahead of the older warriors to claim their first kill. They would be eager, reckless and tired; all qualities that would be in Jelani's favor. But they were still Sesu; he would have to be very precise in his attack.

They spotted him and let out a triumphant yell. Their pace quickened and they glided across the grass toward Jelani. The wise Mawena kept walking, studying the charge and calculating his plan. He watched them shift their assegais to their left hands with their leaf shields then reach across their shoulders to extract throwing spears from the quivers across their backs. At least they had the patience to wait until they were in range before throwing in unison. Jelani trotted forward and the spears fell harmlessly behind him. The Sesu line was ragged; some of the warriors seemed to be breathing hard. This was good. He waited until he could see their eyes before he attacked.

"Mawena!" he yelled, hoping Shani recognized the signal. He rushed the warrior in the center of the line, deliberately exposing his chest. As the young Sesu raised his assegai in triumph Jelani spun away and struck the man beside him with his dagger, burying the blade in his throat. He kept spinning through the line and ended behind the warriors. His sword was in and out the back of the first warrior in an instant. The warrior before him managed to raise his shield and block Jelani's dagger. The Mawena let the man's assegai graze his torso while he hooked his sword behind the shield and stabbed the Sesu in the head. He turned in time to deflect another assegai, striking it so hard the Sesu lost his grip, the spear flying from his hand. He reached for his orinka, exposing enough of himself for Jelani to run his sword into the man's shoulder. He wanted to finish the man, but the other Sesu were attempting to respond to his swift assault by forming a line behind their shields. He jumped between two of them, stabbing the men simultaneously with sword and dagger. The remaining three managed to lock their shields, their assegais protruding between the gaps as they advanced toward him. Jelani dropped to the ground and swung wide, cutting each man across the shins. They fell in unison, their shields and spears tangled. He killed them before they could rise.

Jelani looked at his grim work with no emotion. They were brave men, but they were inexperienced. He went to each one, cutting the head ring from their scalps and sticking them in his waist belt. He was about to turn to find Shani when he heard the war chant of another impi.

"We are coming; we are coming for you."

Ten more warriors approached him in a uniform line, shields locked and assegais raised. Each man wore adornments with their head rings; stork feathers, leopard headbands and eagle plumes. They were seasoned warriors, veterans of cattle raids and military campaigns. They would not succumb so easily to his swift, deceptive skills. Jelani wiped his sweaty hands on his kilt and walked toward the impi, singing a Mawena song of valor and death.

The second impi slowed as it spotted the bodies of their comrades strewn around the arrogant Mawena. They advanced in unison, careful not to make the mistake their younger comrades committed. Still the Mawena's furious assault took them by surprise. Two of them were dead before they regained composure and attacked.

Jelani knew he was trapped, but he fought despite no chance of surviving. There was no pattern to his assault; he fought on instinct, moving, striking and blocking with the desperation of a cornered simba. He felt pain, wounds that would take their toll, but he battled with the energy of a fresh man. He struck until there was no one to strike; he stopped, surprised by the bodies of ten more warriors lying at his feet. But this victory came with a price. Blood flowed over his body like little rivers; an assegai protruded from his thigh like an odd branch. These were wounds he would soon heal from if it weren't for the deep pain in his abdomen, a wound that sapped his strength like poison.

He heard the chant rising from the distance. Another impi was approaching, another group of Sesu determined to fulfill Inaamdura's sentence. He could not stop them. He would be dead before they reached him.

"You have done well, brother," Husani said.

"They will find her and kill her," Jelani gasped.

"They will not," Husani replied. "Others are coming."

Jelani turned to look behind him. Warriors approached, running with shields and assegais, their faces grim and determined. He read the shield pattern and managed a smile. A promise made long ago was being fulfilled.

The kaShange sprinted pass Jelani and attacked the impi. The Sesu fought honorably but were no match for the numerous kaShange. Jelani watched on his knees insuring that no one survived to threaten Shani. As the kaShange approached him, Jelani let go, collapsing into the grass. He rolled onto his back; his eyes wide open to the sun and sky.

Shani swayed nervously as she waited for the return of the kaShange impi. Mayinga stood beside her, his personal warriors a few steps behind. They watched the remaining kaShange warriors return with Jelani. He was lying on his shield, his arms hanging over the edges. She ran to the warriors carrying the shield, tears running down her dirty face.

"Jelani! Jelani!"

The inyanga came to her, placing a hand on her shoulder. "I've done all I can do. He is not dead, but he should be."

Shani's eyes widened with relief. "We must get him to Mawenaland. The healer there can save him."

The inyanga looked skeptical. "The wound to his stomach is a fatal one. There is too much damage."

"He will not die!" Shani shouted.

Mayinga came forward. "We will take him to Mawenaland."

"He is not dead now, but he soon will be," the inyanga insisted.

"Ndoro brought my father home to die among us," Mayinga answered. "I have not forgotten."

He looked at Shani with sympathy. "We are not far from the borderlands. Can you run?"

Shani looked back at Mayinga, her face resolved. "I will run."

They reached the borderlands by dusk, approaching the trees with caution. The kaShange warriors placed Jelani down as close to the forest as they dared and stepped away. Shani knelt beside him as Mayinga approached her.

"This is as far as we go," he said. "We have no quarrel with the Mawena, but we are kaShange. If we cross into Mawenaland our actions might be seen as hostile."

Shani looked concerned. "How will they know we are here?"

Mayinga grinned. "Believe me, inkosa, they know. The Kosobu are very diligent."

The kaShange warriors sat water and food beside Shani and Jelani. Mayinga raised his assegai and the kaShange trotted back to their umuzi. The inkosi hesitated, bowing to Shani one last time.

"When you see Ndoro again, tell him Mayinga of the kaShange still considers him a friend."

Shani looked away. "Ndoro is dead."

Mayinga smiled. "I do not think so." He turned and ran away to catch up with his men.

The Kosobu appeared in force soon afterward. They gathered about the two, covering Shani in blankets and picking Jelani up from the ground. A wagon appeared soon afterward and both were placed inside for the ride back to Koso. Jelani was taken to the medicine priest's home while Shani was led to the house of the chief. His wives dressed her in Mawena finery, transforming her in moments from the wife of a Sesu inkosi to the daughter of Oba Noncemba. The difference was jarring to Shani; only moments ago she was running for her life; now she was surrounded by strangers treating her like the princess she had been many years ago. Her mind was still reeling when the Kosobu chief, Olatunde, entered the main room with the village elders. They bowed and sat on their stools before her.

"Thank you for saving us," Shani said.

Olatunde nodded again. "You are Mawena. We would have come for you even if the kaShange had not brought you to the border."

"You knew we were being hunted?"

"Only recently," the chief admitted. "Our spies could not get close to the Sesu compounds in Selike due to the restrictions imposed during the mourning period. Things became easier after the bonfire died. The interregnum worked to our advantage and we heard of your escape. You made good time."

"Jelani would have it no other way," Shani said. "How is he?"

"He is not dead," the chief said. "Our medicine priest says he may recover, but he won't be the same. Too many spirits are involved."

"Spirits?"

"The souls of the Sesu he killed wish to drag his soul with them into the Zamani, but Husani fights to keep him alive."

Shani stood. "I wish to see him."

Olatunde's eyes reflected sympathy. "We have prepared a boat and an escort for your return to Abo. It is not safe for you so close to the borderlands. The Sesu may attack if they know you are here, but they will not if they hear you are in Abo."

"I will not leave until I know Jelani is fine," she said.

"There is nothing you can do, princess. I promise I will send word on his condition."

Shani stood in defiant silence. Olatunde sighed and stood.

"I will take you to him. I hope you realize you are putting us at a great risk."

The medicine priest's home was next to the chief's. Olatunde knocked on the door and the medicine priest appeared. He was younger than Shani expected, his body more suited for a warrior than a healer, his tunic festooned with the customary talismans and gris-gris. He bowed, and then stepped aside.

"Welcome, princess. I've been expecting you."

"Where is he?" Shani asked.

"Straight ahead in the back room."

Shani hurried to the room. Jelani occupied a small bed, his head propped up on a worn headrest. Healing candles burned in low iron lamps in each corner. A small table heaped with jars sat next to the table, accompanied by a stool. Shani sat in the stool and grasped Jelani's hand.

"The princess wishes to stay with him until he is better," Olatunde said.

"Good. It will help his spirit fight to stay among us," the medicine priest answered. "I am Jumoke. I will provide whatever you need."

"Thank you, Jumoke." Shani dismissed Olatunde with a nod. The chief frowned and left the house.

"Olatunde is not happy," Jumoke commented.

"Neither am I," Shani replied. "Olatunde is a chief and my father is Oba. I suggest you concentrate on Jelani's needs and mine."

"Yes, my princess, of course," Jumoke stammered.

Shani spent the next three weeks at Jelani's side, administering his medicines while Jumoke performed the rituals to aid his healing. Olatunde grew more impatient with each passing day, sending his servants to ask Shani daily when she would leave. She ignored them, concentrating only on Jelani. When the warrior finally opened his eyes, it was as much a relief to the Kosobu as it was for Shani.

"Hello, man," Shani whispered.

Jelani managed a smile. "Hello, woman."

Shani bent over him and kissed his cheek. "I knew you wouldn't leave me."

Jelani reached up and touched her cheek. "But you must leave me."

Shani straightened. "I told you I don't care."

"You should," Jelani replied. "You are home now, and you know what that means. You must be a princess and I must be a warrior. It is our way. It is what makes us strong."

Shani wanted to defy his words, but she knew in the end she would be overwhelmed. She kissed him one more time.

"Jumoke!" she shouted. The medicine priest came quickly.

"What is it, my . . . By the ancestors!" Jumoke folded his hands and bowed.

"Tell Olatunde I am ready to depart," Shani said. "Today."

"Of course, princess. I will tell him."

Shani stood. "Thank you, Jelani. Thank you for saving me. Thank you for raising Ndoro. Thank you for loving us both."

She turned and walked out the house, fighting to maintain her dignity before the Kosobu. Jelani's words were painful but true. They were in the world again and protocol must be followed. She was the oba's daughter; he was her servant. She would wear the mask, but inside she would hold on to their love. It was all she had that truly belonged to her.

15

Zimfara awoke as the rising sun chased away the previous night's chill. Perched on the northernmost edge of the Mpanda savannah, the city served as a rest stop for weary caravans completing the journey across the vast and terrible Mahgreb desert. A towering stone wall enclosed clusters of mud-brick buildings lining narrow roads that meandered to the sprawling marketplace at the city's core. Unlike the homogeneous villages of the interior, Zimfara consisted of many tribes with no one group holding dominance over the other. The Grand Merchant held sway, a man whose skill, reputation and wealth gave him the right to control the vast and diverse city. It was a metropolis filled with dreamers and wanderers, the wrong and the righteous. It was also the home of a young man seeking answers to unknown questions.

Obaseki awoke and had no idea where he was. The bed in which he lay was simple yet comfortable, the headrest padded with expensive silk. A large storage chest loitered against the wall opposite him; its surface covered with jewelry and etched brass clasps. An intricately woven carpet decorated the wall above the chest, its abstract calligraphy unfamiliar to his eyes. Along the other walls were shelves filled with gourds of various colors, shapes and sizes. He slowly realized they belonged to him, containing the herbs that were the tools of his profession. Despite the clarity of the previous night's dream, he was still in Zimfara.

He donned his turban and robes, then went into the next room. Eshe knelt before the cooking pots; her loveliness covered by a white Zimfaran dress, her hair hidden by her elaborate blue headscarf. The Zimfarans wore too much clothing for his taste, even though the garments were essential to protect the body from the harsh sun. Eshe fell into the traditional dress quickly, but Obaseki drew the line when she talked of wearing the veil that would hide her face. He did not like the ways of the Zimfarans and would be happy the sooner they were on their way. But Eshe resisted, insisting they stay a few months more to make sure they had enough provisions for their journey. Obaseki acquiesced, but he knew Eshe had other reasons for wanting to stay.

She looked up when he entered the room, her smile as effervescent as ever.

"You did not sleep well, Seki," she said. "Was it the dream?"

"Yes." He went to her side and sat. "It is getting stronger. I think it is time for us to leave."

Eshe's warm smile waned as she served Obaseki his food. They ate in silence, the tension present as always. He knew what the problems were; with Moyo her feelings and thoughts were no secret to him, though he would never let her know. It was time he spoke up.

"You do not wish to leave, do you Eshe?"

"No." She continued to look at her plate. She'd become quite the merchant of late, selling and exchanging fabrics and decorated leather for clothing and other goods. It was one of the reasons she did not want to leave Zimfara. The old Eshe would have stared him in the face, arrogant in her response. Instead she continued to stare at her food as she replied.

"Maybe this is the destiny planned for you, Seki. You are well respected here. People come from many towns and cities just to receive your healings. We can become wealthy here."

"I did not agree to banishment just to become wealthy," Obaseki said harshly. "There is something beyond this, Eshe, something far greater than being a healer."

"What else can there be?" Eshe looked him in the eye then, her face a mixture of anxiety and confusion. "You dream of a place that might not exist, a land that buries the bones of gods. Maybe your dreams are only dreams."

Obaseki flinched as if struck. Eshe, the one person who had long known of his inner self seemed to have finally lost her faith. The reasons were clear. The loss of their child during the journey from Alamako had been difficult for them both. Though his pain was dulled by his knowledge of the beyond, Eshe had no such solace. And then there was Zimfara, its citizens constantly scrambling to accumulate wealth with no sense of tribal honor. The two were a sickness that fouled her mind and spirit.

"You above all else should know better," he said. "You know the power I possess. The ancestors have not led me this far just to become a healer."

Eshe said nothing as she wiped her plate with her bread.

"You no longer believe, do you Eshe," he asked.

"I do, yes, I do Seki, but..."

They heard the chimes in the shop, indicating a customer. Eshe rose abruptly and ran down to the shop below their room.

"We will discuss it later," Obaseki called out. He sulked back to his meal though his mind was miles away. He had to go. Every day in Zimfara took him farther away from where he should be. He would ask Eshe one more time, and if she refused, he would go alone.

Eshe reappeared, a concerned look on her face.

"Seki, there is someone here to see you."

She was shoved aside and a man entered the room, filling the doorway. He was covered completely in dark blue robes that draped to his scuffed brown boots, and a veil that hid every facial feature but his eyes. A large *sheska* wrapped around his head. A sword hung from his shoulder in a leather baldric, his ring-encrusted hand resting on the hilt. The stranger stared at Obaseki in a way that made the young medicine-priest feel inferior in his presence.

"You are the healer?" the man asked, his voice forceful despite his covered mouth.

"Yes I am," Obaseki replied.

"You will come with me," the man ordered. "My master is sick and needs your help."

"Who sends you?" Obaseki asked.

"The Grand Merchant," the man replied.

Obaseki frowned while Eshe grinned. He had no respect for the nobles of this city, people gaining status not by ancestral right but by wealth. It was the reason Obaseki never saw spirits here; the dead were treated like so much trash and never honored. No spirit would linger in a place so foul. But disobeying the Grand Merchant was a death sentence. He had to go.

"What is his ailment?" he inquired.

The man's eyes narrowed. "How should I know? You are the healer; you must come see for yourself."

Obaseki went to his gourds, selecting a wide range of remedies since he was not completely familiar with the ailments of this land. He packed them in his saddlebag and threw it over his shoulder.

"I am ready."

The man turned and walked out. Obaseki followed, pausing briefly to look at Eshe.

"We will finish our conversation when I return, sweet flower," he said smiling. Eshe smiled back nervously.

Obaseki followed the envoy into the busy streets and to another shrouded warrior standing with three camels. The excess of wealth, Obaseki thought to himself. The Grand Merchant's villa was not far, surely not far enough to warrant the use of camels. They mounted, the envoy taking the reins of Obaseki's camel before setting off. But they were not heading in the direction of the villa; they were heading for the city gate.

Obaseki stuck his hand into his robes and found Moyo, the horn's warmth clearing his head. Those that passed them looked at the warriors with anger in their eyes. An old woman shuffled up to the warrior leading him and spat, barking at him a language Obaseki did not understand. Something was wrong; whoever these men were, they were not envoys of the Merchant.

"Who are you?" he finally asked, tensing for their response. The false envoy jerked his head to face Obaseki, gripping his sword hilt in response.

"Do not say a word," he warned. "There is a man watching your home. If you attempt to escape, your wife will die. Do you understand?"

"Yes," Obaseki managed to say. He was stunned, his mouth suddenly dry and his hands sweating. He was being kidnapped, but he did not know why or by whom. If they meant to rob him, they could have done so at his home. He never denied anyone assistance and often went to the surrounding villages to administer medicines and healing to those lesser folks that served the nobles. The only people he could not reach were the mysterious Tuaregs, known for their fierceness and their habit of raiding the countryside.

Obaseki stiffened when he realized who his kidnappers were. Zimfarans were constantly on its guard against Tuareg raids, maintaining a crack mercenary guard to protect the city and patrol the major highways leading into and out of the city. There had been no attacks since he and Eshe had been in the city, but the fear was real and constant.

They rode through the gates without notice, the Tuaregs keeping a close eye on Obaseki as they passed the sentries. He thought of yelling, but the Tuaregs were too close and could take his life before the guards responded. So he remained silent, his hopes dwindling as they traveled farther and farther away from Zimfara along the road leading into the desert.

Once they were out of view of the city, his captors left the trail and headed into scrub brush and sand, the loping camels settling into a steady rhythm. After only a few moments Obaseki was totally lost; every direction seemed the same to him. He was in Fate's hand now; no one could insure his return but the Tuaregs.

They spent the bulk of the day climbing a dune that seemed as high as a mountain. The crest of the dune revealed the Tuareg settlement; scores of domed camel-hide tents dotting a basin adjoining a sparse oasis. The settlement came to life as the riders approached, a crowd forming about the oasis. Obaseki found them to be a handsome, regal looking people. The men looked at him with fierce, intelligent eyes, the women, unveiled, stared with equal intensity but with more subtle grace. They spoke in their own language, leaving Obaseki totally unaware of his situation. The two riders dismounted before a man dressed similar to them, but with a turban of purple and gold threads indicating his status. One of the riders approached Obaseki.

"Come with me," he ordered. Obaseki clamored down from the camel and descended into a crowd of children that gathered around him and made a cautious procession through the settlement. They were neither malicious nor friendly, just trailing him silently, their eyes the most inquiring aspect about them.

He was led to an enormous tent located in the middle of the oasis beside the well. Two guards blocked the entrance. They were dressed similar to his captors, each holding ayar shields and iron lances. The man motioned and the guards stepped aside. As Obaseki entered he was forced to the ground, his face pushed into the sand. He struggled for a moment, but realized he was in the presence of a chieftain. He relented, remaining in his position until allowed to raise his head.

The chieftain lay in a bed of lamb's wool, his head propped by an ivory headrest. A woman sat beside him, her brown oval face a striking complement to the handsome face of the chieftain. An amber necklace encircled her elegant neck and her earlobes drooped with large crescents of gold. The tent was filled with the trappings of hundreds of tribes, the fruits of the Tuareg caravan raids. If Obaseki had any doubts he was in the presence of a chieftain, they were quickly dispelled by the opulence surrounding him.

He was also surprised to see the white glow of possession outlining the chieftain's body. At least there were some people of this land that still honored their ancestors.

The man in the rich turban came to Obaseki's side. "He was wounded in a raid. We did what we could, but he is still dying."

"There is a spirit in him," Obaseki replied. The woman jerked her head toward him, terror in her eyes.

"His body heals, but his soul is still sick," Obaseki continued. He walked to the chieftain and was about to touch him when the man grabbed his hand.

"You cannot touch him!" he shouted.

"Then he will die," Obaseki warned. "You kidnapped me to save your chieftain, so let me. It is the only way it can be done."

The man gave Obaseki a suspicious look, then let go of his hand. Obaseki pulled away the robes, revealing a wicked gash along the chieftain's right side. The wound was treated with a useless mixture of animal-derived medicines. Obaseki wiped the concoction away and replaced it with the healing herbs in his bag. The poultice would speed the healing of the wound; the spirit was another matter. Going back into his bag he extracted the herbs essential for spirit-raising. He carefully outlined the chieftain's body with the plants, invoking a silent prayer with each herb. Once he'd surrounded the chieftain, Obaseki turned back to his wealthy guardian.

"I must use my mayembe," he said. "It is not a weapon, only an object I use to heal others." Obaseki extracted Moyo from his robes and the Tuareg seemed astounded. He looked at Obaseki respectfully, stepping away with a slight bow.

"Do what you must," the man said.

Obaseki stood beside the bed, holding the gilded horn over the chieftain. He chanted, his rhythmic voice setting a compelling tone. He swayed with the rhythm of the chant, feeling a part of his spirit extend into the mayembe and descend into the blackness of the world between worlds, the abyss that years ago threatened to consume him whenever he dared use Moyo. Obaseki no longer felt fear in this void; the duel with Celu had taught him the patience and skill essential to raise spirits. Fuluke would be proud to see how his young apprentice had evolved. He was right to leave Abo, for as Fuluke foretold, his talents would have never reached the level he now possessed.

The world took shape around him and he was immediately beset by the sounds of struggle. Obaseki rushed to the scene, seeing what he suspected. The chieftain fought the spirit of the man he had slain in battle, a wild-eyed Bedouin who obviously was more than just a warrior. What this mystical assassin had not conquered in life, he was trying to accomplish in death. The chieftain, weakened by the spiritual extraction, struggled against the killer, but it was obvious that he would succumb. Obaseki had no choice; he would destroy the opponent.

Obaseki raised his hand and opened it. Resting in his palm was the essence of Moyo, the lost ka of a fallen god, the consumer of souls. Obaseki pushed Moyo away, the spirit growing as it moved toward the struggle. By the time the assassin realized something was wrong, Moyo had grown into a ball of searing light. The spirit screamed as it was sucked into the consuming fire. The chieftain's spirit dissipated, released from the Zamani to return to its body. Obaseki followed, traveling through the mayembe and back into the familiar form of his body. The chieftain lay before him, his face filled with the color of life. Moyo had taken the soul of the attacker. The healing was complete.

Obaseki collapsed onto his pillow. His clothes were drenched, but he felt a sensation of serenity that often accompanied the use of Moyo. The elder was still in the room, so was the chieftain's wife.

"I've done my task," Obaseki stated. "Your chieftain will live. Now please take me back to Zimfara."

"You will be returned when El-Fatih regains consciousness," his captor replied.

Obaseki studied the man before him, tapping into the powers of Moyo to search his feelings. The man cared little for this El-Fatih; in fact he seemed disappointed. Obaseki was not surprised. The wickedness of Zimfara seemed to have reached into the desert as well.

"If I must stay, I will stay with your chieftain," Obaseki said. "If he must survive for me to leave, then I will make sure he does."

The nobleman raised an eyebrow at Obaseki's statement then turned to the woman. She nodded her head in approval.

"So be it," the nobleman replied. He disappeared from the tent with a swirl of his robes.

Obaseki moved his pillow closer to El-Fatih. He was tired and famished, his stomach protesting loudly with growls like a desert wolf. It didn't help that beside the chieftain's wife sat three plates filled with foods that would be a feast anywhere Obaseki had traveled before. He dared not asked for anything, for he was unsure of what the results might be. It was always good to show strength, his grandfather had taught him long ago. Any weakness may make the difference between life and death.

The chieftain's wife rose from the foot of the bed and picked up the plate of fruit. She strolled to Obaseki and sat down before him. She looked up into his eyes and smiled.

"Thank you," he said.

"You saved my husband," she replied.

"We won't know for sure until he revives."

"With Moyo there is no doubt," she answered. "Every Tuareg knows this, even Jussein."

Obaseki almost choked on the date he was chewing. "You know of Moyo?"

"Yes," she replied. "Your mayembe is the soul of the fallen god, the orisha of the Tuaregs. Every Tuareg has heard the story of his fall from grace as a child, although it has been so long since anyone has seen the mayembe or been to Yakubu."

"Yakubu?"

"It is the place where Moyo fell from heaven and where the first medicine-priest fought for the possession. It was once a holy place for us until gold became our god."

Excitement squelched any hunger Obaseki once had.

"What does Yakubu look like?" he asked.

"It sits atop a plateau, an oasis crowning a dry mountain. I remember visiting with my clan, when a terrible sickness spread through our camp. We went to Moyo with sacrifices of goats and bread, hoping he would be generous and stop the sickness. But we did not know he was gone. Our priests cursed him and we continued to die. Many lost their faith, but I believe because my family was spared." The woman smiled at the remembrance, her eyes far away.

The chieftain stirred. His wife ran to his side, whispering to him. Obaseki turned away, giving the couple a private moment, his mind filled with what the woman has just told him. The image that had haunted his dreams since he left Ifana was real. Not only that, it was close. Moyo had led him to this place, and a crisis among the Tuaregs brought him closer. But he was uncertain of his fate among them. He was promised his life if the chieftain lived. Since that seemed certain, he waited to see if the Tuaregs were true to their word.

A commotion broke his musing. The chieftain was trying to sit up against his wife's will. She tried to hold him down; he pushed her away. His light brown eyes widened when he finally noticed Obaseki.

"You are the man from my dream," he said. Obaseki nodded.

"I am El-Fatih Habre. You saved my life."

"I am only a healer," Obaseki replied.

"Come closer," El-Fatih commanded. "I wish to see Moyo."

Obaseki was concerned, but the chieftain's smile conveyed his honesty.

"Only a healer possessing the fallen one could do what you did," El-Fatih said. Obaseki took the horn from his robe. El-Fatih nodded.

"So my near-death has borne good fruit," he said, smiling. "How long has Moyo possessed you?"

Obaseki smiled at the accuracy of El-Fatih's words. "Five years, but we hold to common ground."

"We shall see," El-Fatih smirked. "Thuria, summon my warriors."

"You are still weak," she admonished. "It is better you rest until you are strong enough to deal with Jussien."

"If I wait too long, he will be lost in the desert."

Thuria wrinkled her brow, her thick eyebrows almost meeting. "I will have the warriors search the camp. If they do not find him, they will go after him and bring him back. Meanwhile, you will rest."

"Not until I deal with the healer," El-Fatih replied. "You saved my life, so what do I owe you?"

"I wish to go back to my wife," Obaseki said quickly.

"So be it," El-Fatih declared.

"I would also like to go to Yakubu," Obaseki finished.

El-Fatih's generous smiled transformed into a look of concern. "Do you know what you ask?"

"Yes, I think so," Obaseki replied.

"Do not think, healer," El-Fatih replied. "Yakubu is the only place in Sudan where Moyo can take his true form. If you cannot control him you will die."

"Moyo is a part of me," Obaseki replied. "It is why I am here. I don't know what will happen at Yakubu; I only know it must be."

El-Fatih eyed Obaseki. "A man seeking certain death is either foolish or brave. I think you are a little of both."

El-Fatih swayed as the effects of his wound re-surfaced. He lay back down.

"I will have a tent prepared for you. We will return you to Zimfara in the morning."

The tent was a welcomed sight. The interior was almost as lavish as El-Fatih's, worthy of a diplomat's room in the palace of the Grand Merchant. Obaseki welcomed the sight of the bed most of all, exhausted as he was from his ordeal. He stripped off his garments, collapsed into the soft cushions and fell immediately to sleep.

But it was not a restful sleep. The dream of Yakubu was gone; in its place was something horrifying. A city burned, black smoke billowing into a sharp blue sky. Bodies were strewn about, some mutilated beyond recognition. The smell of death was overpowering. Outside on the blood-covered streets, a huge army marched, one larger than any Obaseki had ever witnessed. A man strode at the head of this army, a war club in one hand and a short spear in the other. The sea of warriors surrounding him chanted with the rhythm of unseen war drums, one word bursting from their lips; Shumba. Obaseki realized this was his twin, the part of him that surfaced in his dreams in the past. This time he knew this was not just a hint of his evil spirit. This other side of him existed; the suffering and death he caused was real. Staring into his soulless black eyes Obaseki saw his destiny. He awoke, the night still ruling the desert sky. He felt a familiar touch on his cheek and turned to see the face of Eshe. He immediately grabbed her, squeezing her in joy and relief.

He felt himself enfolded by her strong, supple. He savored their embrace a moment longer and then pushed her arm's length.

"What are you doing here?"

"The Tuaregs brought me here." Her voice was bitter.

"I don't understand," Obaseki said. "El-Fatih promised he would take me back to Zimfara."

"There is no Zimfara!" Eshe blurted. Her head fell against his shoulders as she cried.

"What are you talking about?" he asked.

"The Tuaregs sacked it, Seki. They burned it to the ground. I was on my way to market when someone grabbed me from behind and pushed me into an alley. Before I could struggle they put a bag over my head and pushed me into a cart. I was so afraid, Seki! I started to struggle, and then someone told me I was being taken to you, that I would be safe. Then they said I should be grateful I was the wife of Moyo."

She stopped for a moment, raising her head from Obaseki's shoulder. He looked into her eyes and was angered by the shock and pain he saw.

"The cart stopped and the bag was taken away," she continued. "That's when I saw what they did." She trembled in his arms as she spoke.

"They killed everyone, Seki. Men, women, children; they spared no one."

Obaseki pulled Eshe close, stroking her hair. She had been happy with life in Zimfara. She had worked hard to establish a living for them while he struggled to find his destiny. Now it was gone, burned to the ground by the Tuaregs.

"Come, Eshe," he said. "Let us speak to El-Fatih."

"Who is El-Fatih," Eshe asked. "What can he do?"

"He is the leader of the Tuaregs, and I saved his life. He owes me an explanation."

Obaseki led Eshe across the encampment to El-Fatih's tent. He half-expected to be stopped by the guards, but they let him pass, one guard actually holding the tent flap open for him. When they entered, they were stopped immediately by a well-armed warrior, apparently one of El-Fatih's bodyguards.

"I ask your pardon, Moyo, but El-Fatih has business he must complete," the warrior said. Obaseki nodded; puzzled by the deference he was suddenly receiving. He held Eshe's hand and turned his attention to the center of the tent. El-Fatih sat on a gilded stool, his chin resting on his fist. He was surrounded by his bodyguards and others of his entourage, every person wearing a hard expression. At El-Fatih's feet three men knelt, shackles around their wrists and ankles. Two of the men Obaseki recognized immediately.

The portly, bearded man prostrated at El-Fatih's feet was the Grand Merchant of Zimfara. He sweated profusely, his once elegant silk shirt drenched and torn. The other man was Jussien, Obaseki's gilded captor, dignified even in chains. His face was battered, but he showed no signs of pain. The third man Obaseki did not know. He wore the uniform of the Zimfara garrison, but his facial features betrayed him as an outlander, most likely an ally of Zimfara or a mercenary. He attempted to imitate Jussien's stolid pose but his trembling hands gave away his true emotions.

El-Fatih glanced at Obaseki and acknowledged his presence with a slight nod of his head. He then turned his attention back to his captors, coming to his feet to deliver their sentences.

"You have conspired to bring down the noble clans of the Tuareg and have been found guilty by the tribal councils. As the Jackal clan claims highest status, I have been given the privilege to choose your punishment."

El-Fatih dealt with the mercenary first. "The mercenary will be released. Give him a day's worth of water then drive him into the desert. Let us see how his warrior's luck holds out." Two warriors stepped from the entourage and dragged the man out of the tent, striking him along the way.

El-Fatih turned to the Grand Merchant. "If we learned from our ancestors, we could save ourselves so much pain," he said. He strode back to his stool and sat, never taking his eyes off the unfortunate man.

"Every Grand Merchant thinks he is greater than the one before him. Sooner or later he thinks he will be the one to rid the world of Tuaregs. So the lesson must be taught over and over again, as it will be today."

The Grand Merchant sprang to his feet, his face desperate. "Fatih, I beg you to spare my life! I have much more than you can possibly imagine; wealth ten times the worth of the entire Uhuru. Spare me and I'll take you to it."

"Your gold means nothing to me," El-Fatih said. "It is as worthless as your loyalty. But you will not die, fat man. You belong to me."

The Grand Merchant lost all semblance of nobility when he heard El-Fatih's words. He prostrated himself before the chieftain, his huge bulk trembling. "Thank you, great Fatih, thank you for your mercy!"

El-Fatih turned to one of his warriors, a menacing man with a uniform of black from his riding boots to his turban. "Take this fool away and castrate him. He will make a fine eunuch."

The Grand Merchant scrambled to his knees. "No! I cannot..." The warrior struck the Merchant on the head with his sword hilt and the Merchant crashed into the dirt unconscious. With the help of two other warriors, they dragged the limp body from the tent.

Only Jussien remained. El-Fatih's face took on a shadow as if the sun had fled his soul and left darkness behind. He trudged back to his cushions and sat hard. They stared at each other, Jussien's expression as emotionless as before, El-Fatih clearly upset. The chieftain seemed to be waiting for his betrayer to say something, but if he was, he was sorely disappointed. With exaggerated effort El-Fatih rose and walked to Jussien, kneeling close to whisper to his old friend.

"Why, Jussien?"

"You have no vision, Fatih," Jussien answered. "We live in the Mahgreb, our children starving, our mouths filled with sand while the Zimfarans grow fat from trade. We raid their caravans for only a fraction of their wealth when we could control the entire region. But we do not, because you hang on to old ways and old values."

"You could not have brought this up before council?" El-Fatih asked. "You had to conspire with Zimfarans and order my death?"

"The council would not listen to me and you know this," Jussien retorted. "They are not as rigid as you, but they would never go against you because they fear you. And what is your death compared to the lives of our people?"

El-Fatih shook his head slowly. "What did they offer you?"

"Half the tariffs collected on caravans and one thousand pieces of gold."

El-Fatih sighed. "That is a handsome price, my brother. And you would build a city as fine as Zimfara, no longer living in tents, using our camels for food instead of war, becoming as fat and as lazy and as godless as the Zimfarans. We would die as a people, but we would be rich and our children would not starve." He spat into the sand. "Better we all perish than to suffer such a fate."

Jussien closed his eyes and lowered his head by bending at his waist. He looked up at El-Fatih, his eyes fearless. "You will be the ruin of us all."

El-Fatih stood and drew his sword. With both hands gripping the ivory hilt, he brought the blade down on Jussien's neck. Jussien's head rolled free, the body tumbling into the carpets.

Obaseki watched in horror as two more warriors wrapped the soiled carpet around Jussien's remains and carried them from the tent. He and Eshe quickly opened a way for them to pass and found themselves holding the tarp for the rest of the witnesses of Tuareg justice. This was obviously not the time to discuss Zimfara with the chieftain. Obaseki grasped Eshe's hand; they proceeded to leave with the rest of the people.

"Medicine-priest!" El-Fatih called out. Obaseki grimaced at the call of the title; he turned and immediately bowed. Eshe did also, though her response was slow and defiant. Obaseki hoped she would be more cautious until they learned everything about the attack on the city.

"I see you have found your wife," the chieftain commented with a grin on his face. It was as if nothing had happened. He strode over to the duo, stopping before Eshe.

"Stand up, woman," El-Fatih ordered. Eshe glared at him as she stood.

El-Fatih laughed. "You have a fine wife, medicine-priest. Full of fire and strength."

El-Fatih bowed to Eshe, which seemed to catch her off guard. Her eyes widened; she looked at Obaseki for an explanation. Obaseki could do nothing but shrug.

"You are angry with me," El-Fatih stated. "That is your right. What happened this day began long before either of you came to Zimfara. The scourge of the city always reaches out to our young ones, drawing them into a life of decadence and despair. I will not allow this to happen to the Tuaregs. I would burn a thousand Zimfaras first."

Fatih's tone let them both know the discussion was over. He turned his eyes to Obaseki.

"You are well?"

"Yes," Obaseki answered. "I thank you for your attention."

"Good, for tomorrow we break camp." El-Fatih strode to his stool and sat. "We will go to Yakubu to see if you are truly favored by Moyo."

Obaseki was struck silent by El-Fatih's words. Eshe looked at him, the pain gone from her eyes, replaced by a wife's fearful worry.

Obaseki took Eshe's hand in his. "We will be ready," he answered.

* * *

They were deep into the desert, a land of endless sand and terrible heat. The Tuaregs made camp at the edge of the harsh land, a place whose name meant hopeless in their native tongue. El-Fatih, Obaseki, and Eshe were the only ones to continue on, heading for the place that the Tuaregs knew as the cradle of their god, the land of Yakubu.

Obaseki felt this was surely the place. Moyo burned so hot he had to place it in a leather pouch and drag it behind his camel. He felt the power of this land emanating from the sand, the sky and the constant, abrasive wind. It was a land gripped in chaos, and Obaseki knew why. Moyo was lord of this land; his power set the balance of the spirits that called it home. Without him, there was no order. Without him, there was chaos.

The further they advanced, the stronger the maelstrom became. Obaseki could barely see either of his companions; his eyes straining against the sand blanket surrounding him. Sand scraped his exposed skin, pushing into his mouth despite the scarf protecting it. Eshe rode beside him, but it was clear the journey was wearing them both down.

Obaseki's camel collapsed. He tumbled into the sand and was immediately enveloped by the churning winds.

"Eshe! Fatih!" Howling wind swallowed his voice and enveloped him in blinding sand. He jerked his head about desperate for any signs of his companions. A glow caught his eye; it was the horn, sitting alone in the sand, pulsing with white light. Obaseki made his way to the mayembe, kneeling down to retrieve it. The horn shifted and Obaseki jerked his hand away.

"The sand," he said. "It must be the sand."

He reached for the mayembe again and this time he knew it was not the sand. The mayembe expanded, losing its shape and flowing over the sand like water. He stepped away from the flow as it widened, afraid of what might happen. Was Moyo returning? Was the closeness of Yakubu causing his resurrection? He did not know, but he was sure this would not bode him well.

The glowing pool of light grew to the size of a man, and then began to move away. Its passage calmed the air in its path, the abrasive winds dying down as it progressed. Obaseki followed the apparition, uncertain of what to do. The pool glided for a long time then abruptly rose from the ground into the sky. As the shimmering shape moved away, it lost its grip on the world below and the winds swelled in size and fury. Obaseki was again beset by a twisting torrent of wind and sand. He fell to his knees and groped forward, trying to find some protection. He traveled up a slope that quickly became a steep incline, forcing him to climb. Above him the light that was once Moyo hovered. His dark hands dug into the jagged rock, his feet feeling for a foothold while the circle of light moved before him. The light seemed to be leading him so Obaseki followed, deciding that wherever he went would be better than the torment he was experiencing. He climbed for hours, following the light to an unknown end but feeling a compulsion to go on. His future was with the light. No doubt entered his mind on this one thing.

He reached out his right arm and touched a level surface. He pulled himself up and rolled onto a bed of grass. After a brief rest Obaseki struggled to his feet, searching for the golden glow. The light hovered before him, shifting and expanding into the shape of a man. It darkened as features appeared; Obaseki found himself staring into the face of his nightmares. The altered image of himself crouched low like a lion, his eyes blank with hatred. In his right hand he held the white cowhide shield; his left hand grasped the short spear. The pelt of a simba rested on his head and shoulders, the empty skin of the head and mane shrouding his face, the arms tied before his chest. Obaseki wanted to speak, but before he could open his mouth his twin attacked.

Obaseki dodged a spear thrust but was caught by the shield. He rolled with the blow, coming to his feet when he was well away. The image of him spun and charged again. Obaseki ran toward it, ramming himself against the shield and grabbing the spear hand. He was immediately engulfed in pain like no other, a searing that razed every particle of his body. Obaseki grabbed his nemesis with his right arm, his mind lost in a struggle of his emotions. The image spirit passed into him as he tightened his grip around it, the pain replaced by a level of contentment Obaseki had never known. It was within him; Moyo had given his soul up to Obaseki in order to survive and, through the horn, led the medicine-priest to the only ground where the transformation could occur. His mind raced as it assimilated the knowledge of centuries. The onslaught made him dizzy; he staggered, and then fell. He lay on his back, the land around him suddenly familiar. Every rock, crevice, tree, and grain of sand was known to him as it had been known to Moyo. His memory raced back to images of men and women similar to the Tuaregs living peacefully upon the raised plain, tending fields and pastures rich with cattle and crops. Above it all Moyo reigned until that fateful moment when he defied the gods, when Moyo tried to be more than those who created him. Obaseki saw chaos grip the land; the terrible winds, the rainless skies. Cattle wilted and died like grass as waterholes dried into nothing. The grasslands became brown patches of dust. The Tuaregs prayed to a god that no longer existed, hoping for salvation that never came. So they left, migrating into the surrounding desert in hopes that they would find another fertile land. Instead only desert awaited them, the land which they now held sway.

Obaseki stood in the center of a tempest. He closed his eyes, extending his arms like the wings of an eagle. He thought of calm and the wind responded. Silence surrounded him and Obaseki was pleased. He extended his hands skyward, the image of storm clouds in his mind. The sky darkened with blue-gray clouds that hung low with their cargo of water. With a wave of his hand the sky split with the lightening and the rain fell in torrents.

Obaseki felt a hand on his shoulder and turned to see Eshe and El-Fatih. Eshe froze when their eyes met. El-Fatih walked toward him, a solemn look on his weathered face. The ground turning to mud under his feet, El-Fatih stopped before Obaseki and prostrated himself.

"Moyo," he said. "You have returned to us."

Obaseki reached down and pulled El-Fatih to his feet. "I am not your god. I am the same man as before, but Moyo's spirit has left the mayembe to bond with me."

"He sits on your head?" El-Fatih asked.

"Yes," Obaseki replied. "Listen to me, Fatih. Bring your people back to Yakubu. Your ancestors are here; this is your home. The land is still fertile and the rain will bring it back to life. You can build a city here."

"You sound like Jussien," El-Fatih said suspiciously.

"Jussien wanted the Tuareg to emulate others, to become something they are not. But this is your home. You know this."

"The desert made us strong," El-Fatih countered.

"The desert will always be a part of you," Obaseki answered. "Moyo drew me here to say these words to you. Moyo has returned to the land. It is time for his children to return as well."

El-Fatih regained his regal composure. "I shall go to my people and send out the word. It is time for Tuaregs to come home."

Eshe approached Obaseki timidly, touching his hand.

"Are you still my husband?" she asked.

"I am, sweet flower," Obaseki replied.

She embraced him and Obaseki smiled.

"You have changed, Seki. What does this mean?"

Obaseki smiled.

"It means we are finally home."

16

Sesuland languished under a moonless night sky, the air still warm from the day's heat. In the villages surrounding the grand city of Selike, the people settled in for the night, gathering about the scattered fires to talk of the day and hear stories passed down from elders to children for generations. Behind the city walls, the time for rest came much later. Sesuland had prospered much over the last twenty years. It was still not the great city its founder Dingane had envisioned, but it was the largest city in the grasslands and the center of one of the most powerful kingdoms of Uhuru.

Three men made their way to the outskirts of Selike that night. They moved cautiously, traveling through the grass instead of the roads. They carried no shields or assegais, but the slap of leather scabbards against their thighs warned of their intent. They advanced quickly, covering the miles in short time, moving between farms and villages unnoticed, continuing until they could see the outline of the watchtowers of the city, their perpetual lights burning like ever-observant eyes. The men finally rested, two squatting in the high grass, one standing to full height as he stared at his former home.

If Ndoro had been alone he would have wept. The emotions in him were stronger than he expected. The memories of his life in the city flooded his mind; the years living as a royal outcast, the tainted son of Dingane. Images of his mother resurfaced and he felt shame for not returning sooner. She would have enjoyed the status of Shumba's mother, not the humiliation of being Dingane's lesser wife. The thought brought back the anger that fueled his every step since the night he was driven from Selike twenty years ago.

Jawanza stood beside him. “It is a beautiful city.”

“Yes, it is,” Ndoro replied.

Nakisisa joined them in his human form. “Do you have many enemies there, Shumba?”

Ndoro turned to the river spirit, reading his grim intent. “Yes, I do.”

Nakisisa grinned.

Ndoro knelt and opened the traveling pouch strapped to his side, extracting the red warrior robes of Sesuland. He discarded his Diaka garments and donned the robes of his former home.

“If I have not returned by morning, do not hesitate to attack, Jawanza. Selike must burn.”

Jawanza scowled. “I still advise against this, Shumba. If you are discovered and killed, all that you built will shatter like shells against stone.”

“All we have achieved has been for this moment,” Ndoro replied. “I am back to claim what is mine, what my father meant for me to have. I will not be denied!”

Ndoro cursed himself for the anger. He managed to smile, placing his hand on Jawanza’s shoulders.

“I must do this, my brother. It is what I’ve lived for.”

Ndoro trotted to the main road, leaving his companions in their hiding place as he set of at a warrior’s pace. After a half an hour, he stood before the gates of the outer wall. He hesitated, realizing that once he stepped into Selike, he would be stepping into his past.

If Ndoro was prepared for old memories, he was not prepared for what he saw when he entered the city. Nothing was familiar to him; the broad avenue leading to the city’s center had degenerated into a narrow maze of cluttered huts and stands. If not for the palace light towers, he would have had no idea how to find the royal umuzi. Fortunately the streets were almost empty and he moved quickly through the winding streets, eventually discovering the main road leading to the umuzi. He hadn’t decided how he would breach the wall surrounding the umuzi; he’d handle that obstacle when he came to it.

Few guards patrolled the streets, and those Ndoro passed seemed to care less about any strangers wandering the city. But then Ndoro was no stranger. He was more Sesu than these people living in his father’s city. Many of those he encountered were not Sesu. Some tribes he recognized; other he didn't. He wondered for a moment what could have happened to his father that would let his city sink to such a state. Whatever the answer, Ndoro would find out from his father himself before killing him.

He finally reached the royal umuzi. It was the one place that remained intact, the only structure where his memory did not fail him. The white royal herd had been replenished, grazing in darkness by the umuzi wall. Dingane's palace crowned the summit of the hill; still as foreboding as it was the first time Ndoro laid eyes upon it. The homes of the wives ringed the umuzi wall; Inaamdura's the first to the right of the umuzi gate, the others farther away. Ndoro knew which hut held his mother, the last hut of the umuzi ring. No one was present as he crept to the hut, moving in close to listen. He had not seen his mother for twenty years; she probably would not recognize him. He suddenly remembered Jelani, the brave bodyguard who risked his life so Ndoro could escape. There was so much he'd left behind, good and bad. But he had returned and it was time to end this episode in his life. He took a deep breath and entered the hut.

The woman inside leapt from the table where she sat and scrambled into the dark end of the hut.

"Wait, mama!" Ndoro called out.

"You could never be my son, warrior, unless you rested in my womb when I was born." The woman eased out of the shadows. It was not Shani.

Though Ndoro was distraught by the sight of this woman in his mother's hut, he could not help but stare at her. She was the most beautiful woman he'd ever seen, even more lovely than Sarama. She wore the full simple dress of a married woman in a way that heightened instead of deterring his attention. Her beauty deadened the shock he felt finding his mother gone.

"Who are you?" he demanded.

"I am Kenyetta Matiku," she replied with a voice as regal as her face. "You are obviously a stranger, for any Sesu of Selike would know all of Inkosi Ligongo's wives."

"Inkosi who?" Ndoro mind spun. "What happened to my...Inkosi Dingane?"

Kenyetta was not intimidated by Ndoro's threatening manner. She emerged into the light, her full beauty revealed to him. Surely this inkosi Ligongo was foolish to keep Kenyetta as such a lowly wife, Ndoro thought.

"Dingane died ten seasons ago," she replied. "He was killed during a simba hunt, if you believe some."

Disappointment and shock struck him like an orinka. He struggled to keep his stoic façade.

"What do others say?" he managed to ask.

"They say his death began after Ligongo was born, every time he ate supper with Inaamdura. Some believe she gave him a mild poison knowing it would weaken him, enough to make him easy prey for the simba."

Ndoro's blood burned with anger. "What would she gain from Dingane's death?"

"Ligongo became inkosi and she his advisor. It was a plan she began many years ago when she conspired with Cacunja to drive Dingane's favorite son from Selike."

Ndoro staggered back from the force of Kenyetta's words. He always suspected Mulugo's intentions to be rid of him, but he never suspected Inaamdura. Cacanja was a mystery to him. The woman had destroyed his family to lay claim to the power of Sesuland for her and her son.

He composed himself before asking his next question.

"What happened to Shani?"

Kenyetta's face changed from casual to curious, her questioning eyes making Ndoro cautious.

"She fled in the night when she heard of Dingane's death. The inkosi protected Shani from the full fury of Inaamdura's hatred while he was alive but, with his death, she was sure to suffer under Ligongo. So she and Jelani fled back to Mawenaland."

Ndoro looked away from Kenyetta, his eyes glistening in the pale light of the hut. Sadness sat heavy on his shoulders. If he'd returned sooner, he could have rescued his mother from Dingane's and Inaamdura's cruelty and showed his father the true meaning of power. But the chance was lost to time; there would be no such satisfaction. There was still the matter of Inaamdura and Ligongo.

Ndoro moved to leave the hut but Kenyetta stopped him.

"Were you sent by Hondo?"

Ndoro was irritated by her question. "Who is Hondo?"

Kenyetta expression returned to its original nonchalance. "He is the conqueror of Uhuru, a warrior from the forests.

They say he leads an army of slaves and his general is the ghost of a river spirit. They say the noblest of Hondo's enemies get the privilege of being eaten by the river creature."

Ndoro smiled; his spies had done well spreading the rumors of his advance. His time in Kenyetta's hut was finished; his mother was gone. It was time for him to leave as well.

"Wait! Take me with you!"

"No," Ndoro replied. "I must move quickly."

"Take me or I will scream," Kenyetta threatened. "Take me to Hondo and let him decide what to do with me."

"And why should I? If you scream I will kill you and any guard that answers."

"I'll make a good wife for Hondo," she said, a desperate look on her face. "I am a beautiful woman, the daughter of a powerful chieftain."

"You would be his slave, his concubine."

"I'd rather be a slave than spend another night under that fool Ligongo!"

"I will not slow down for you."

"You won't have to," Kenyetta replied. She ran to a wooden chest by her bed and removed a long cloak that she threw over herself. The duo stole into the night, hurrying through the winding city streets. Once they exited the main gate, Ndoro started a warrior's pace, Kenyetta close behind. The sun's rays reached for the horizon, orange-red light creeping westward across the plain. They met Jawanza and Nakisisa where Ndoro had left them, both men well rested and ready to move on.

"Who is this?" Jawanza asked.

"This is Kenyetta, wife of Inkosi Ligongo," Ndoro replied. "She is to be a prize for Oba Hondo, leader of the slave army."

Jawanza looked puzzled. "What are you talking about, Koi Shumba? You are Hondo."

Kenyetta jerked her head toward Ndoro, who smiled back.

"I am your Hondo. My warriors named me Shumba. But to the Sesu, to Inaamdura, Shani and Dingane, I was Ndoro."

Kenyetta's eyes went wide, and then closed as she slumped to the ground.

"Nakisisa, can you carry her?"

"Yes."

"Good. Let us go. Tomorrow will be a very busy day."

... *

Inaamdura awoke to the natural melodies of her aviary as she had done every day since Dingane's death. The room was built immediately afterward and filled with imported trees and plants from Shamfa. Songbirds from all the lands within her tradesmen's reach flittered about between the exotic branches and vines. The garden was maintained by five slaves hand-picked for their special talents. It was her throne, a subtle symbol of her power among the Sesu.

Inaamdura always knew the Sesu would never allow a foreign queen to rule them, so she groomed Ligongo from the time he could walk to sit upon the golden stool of Sesuland. He had grown into a handsome and charismatic man but lacked the focus needed to rule a people. Ligongo spent too much time with his wives and concubines, a habit frowned upon by the elders. The old men were the least of her worries; they knew where the real power lay and were careful not to cross her. The surrounding kingdoms were less respectful. A major merchant route was developing through the grasslands, a thread of bare land that meant wealth and power to the city that controlled it. Sesuland straddled this route, but other kingdoms, such as Kesh and Bugodaland, were becoming belligerent with their claims to parts of the route that bordered their territory. And then there was Hondo and his slave horde, whose activities in the south at the forest's edge were becoming more than a nuisance. Refugees poured into Sesuland daily, taxing the burden of the cities and fueling crime in their desperation to survive.

Inaamdura contemplated these matters as a servant boy dressed in a white robe and glittering sandals appeared at the entrance of the aviary.

"Great Mother, Inkosi Ligongo wishes to see you."

Inaamdura nodded for the boy to leave. Though many seasons had passed since her arrival in Sesuland, her body appeared as if it knew nothing of the passage of time. Her beauty waxed as strong as it had the day she and Dingane were wed. She took no suitor after his death, nor did she heed Sesu tradition by becoming the wife of Dingane's brother Mpanda. With her son in power she did as she pleased, and it pleased her to stay alone. An occasional dalliance with a passing dignitary was the only pleasure she allowed herself.

She found Ligongo in his stool room, sitting proudly between two of his wives. Around him his children played, their games causing an incessant clatter throughout the stool room. Inaamdura entered and all motion ceased. A dignified calm fell over the room as Ligongo's wives took their place behind their husband, their children following behind them like little warriors. Everyone was well aware of Inaamdura's insistence on formality and it was always exercised in her presence.

Ligongo rose from his stool to greet her.

"Mama, you look beautiful as always."

Inaamdura smiled despite herself. Ligongo had a way with her, but she only let it go so far.

"What do you want of me, Gongo?" she asked, using her pet name for him to signal informality.

"Kenyetta has disappeared. No one has seen her for two days."

Inaamdura cursed under her breath. "She has been trouble from the very beginning. She was not a good choice."

"Her other sisters were ugly," Ligongo retorted.

"An ugly girl bears children just as well as a pretty one," Inaamdura snapped. "Children form alliances and alliances mean power. Kenyetta has denied this of you." Inaamdura clicked her teeth. "Better she stays lost."

"Kenyetta will be found!" Ligongo shouted.

Inaamdura was surprised by his outburst. Kenyetta was more special to him than she imagined which was not good. A chill ran through her chest. This reminded her too much of Dingane and Shani. She would have to put an end to this situation immediately.

"I will send my personal guard to search the city for her," Inaamdura offered.

"My warriors are already doing so," Ligongo replied. "I think she may have left the city."

"Have you questioned your other wives?"

Ligongo laughed. "They would not tell me even if they knew. Kenyetta has many enemies among her sisters. They are glad to see her gone."

Inaamdura frowned. She knew well the politics among wives and was disappointed none of Ligongo's wives had taken the control of the household. Even Mudiwa, his Great Wife, remained docile, preferring to be Ligongo's plaything than a true wife.

The doors to the stool room flew open, banging against the stone portal. A warrior stumbled through and fell to his knees, his body glistening with sweat. He lifted his head, exhaustion on his face, his chest heaving as he spoke.

"Inkosi, you must come quickly!"

Inaamdura was furious. "Who do you think you're talking to, dog?"

The warrior gave Inaamdura a glare that brought her to silence. "You must come, inkosi. Hondo is approaching!"

It cannot be!, Inaamdura said to herself. He wouldn't dare attack Selike, not with the allies she'd gained or the army she trained. She approached the warrior.

"How do you know it's Hondo? How do you know that this is not just a raiding party?"

The warrior came to his feet, somewhat rested and clearly irritated with Inaamdura's questioning.

"A raiding party does not cover the ground of the Simba Plains." He turned to Ligongo. "Inkosi, you must come!"

Ligongo rose from his throne, striding across the room to the warrior. He was about to leave when Inaamdura grabbed his arm.

"You are inkosi. You cannot face this renegade. Let Zuberi earn his pay."

Ligongo pulled away from his mother, catching her off guard. He charged out to the stool room, heading for the council room where Zuberi and his officers waited. His bukra servant waited patiently by the royal stool with his armor. Ligongo sat as the servant dressed him.

"What is the situation, Zuberi?" he asked.

Zuberi stood. He was Suburu, an extremely tall man with charcoal skin and piercing brown eyes. He wore the robes of his people but displayed the head ring of a Sesu warrior.

"Our sentries awoke this morning to screams. Hondo's army crossed the grasslands during the night and burned the farms along the border. They sacked Isala and killed everyone inside the outpost. By the time word reached us, they were only miles away. They marched within sight of Selike before halting."

"How many are there?" Ligongo asked.

"Eight, maybe nine thousand warriors. No sign of cavalry, but they may be holding them back as reserves."

"They have no cavalry," Inaamdura said. "Horses and camels cannot survive in the forest. If this is truly Hondo, he would have no knowledge of cavalry."

Ligongo seemed contemplative. "Can we get word out to our allies?"

"We sent messengers to Abo and Shamfa," Zuberi replied.

"Good. What is our current strength?"

"Three thousand warriors, including the royal guard. With conscripts we can raise another twelve thousand; if we include the mercenaries, sixteen thousand."

"So, my general, what is your plan?"

"It is best we wait them out. We have more than enough supplies in the city to withstand a siege. That will give Abo and Shamfa enough time to send reinforcements."

"Hondo will realize the odds are against him," Inaamdura finished. A great smile graced her face. This was the reason for alliances; this was the power she'd been bred to build. Zuberi's plan was the strategy she envisioned many seasons ago when the rumors of Hondo first reached her ears. She would not be outsmarted by some bush chief with grand ideas. The southern tribes had been easy conquests for him; their leadership was weak and their armies small. But Sesuland was a kingdom with a long tradition of war. Hondo and his dreams would die beneath the feet of Sesu warriors.

"Let us see this Hondo," Ligongo said. "Zuberi, prepare the warriors. I will meet you soon."

The warriors left the council room, making their way through the palace and out into the courtyard. Royal attendants waited with their mounts, and they galloped through the barren city streets to the outer wall. The ramparts were manned by Kusa archers; their keen eyes scanning the grasslands, their quivers bulging with arrows.

The royal entourage galloped to the central observation tower on the outer wall. They dismounted and clamored the spiraling stairs to the deck. Zuberi and Ligongo leaned out over the railing, Inaamdura standing behind.

For as far as the eye could see, the grass plains were filled with Hondo's warriors. They sat cross-legged before the walls of Selike, their backs turned. It was a classic Sesu insult.

"This dog will die for sure," Ligongo said. "I will put the blade in his heart myself!"

"Calm down, my son," Inaamdura advised. "War is not ruled by emotion. Our adversary plays games to taunt. Zuberi will..."

A voice rose in the distance, and the invaders stood in unison with a thump of their shields. The voice called out again and they turned, facing the city walls.

"Signal the archers," Zuberi commanded.

Ligongo placed his hand on Zuberi's shoulder. "Look."

A group of Hondo's warriors ran down the main road outside the city walls, chanting as they trotted. They were dressed differently than the other warriors, their heads covered by lion manes, their shields raised before them. The other warriors took up the chant, a chant familiar to every Sesu warrior since the day they were first blooded.

Many men, many spears,
Many spears, many raids,
Many raids, many cows.

Inaamdura was struck with foreboding. There was something escaping her here, a wild thing that lurked in the shadows of her well-thought-out plans. As she watched the strange formation advance, that thing took shape, emerging from the recesses of her memory and becoming a clear, coherent thought. It was what Dingane possessed, what Ndoro thrived on, what every warrior within and without the walls of Selike was infected with. Within them all burned a sense of pride so strong it overcame common sense. That was why Hondo came despite her plans, why this war would take place despite making no logical sense. But it was Hondo's doom, not hers. When he died, he and the ancestors would have much to talk about, she mused.

The warriors halted just outside bow range. The chant ended abruptly, the warriors falling still. From within their ranks a voice called out, a sound that struck Inaamdura like an assegai in her chest.

With sudden precision the warriors snapped their shields down. They stepped away, revealing a solitary warrior. His head was down, a body of a young male simba draped across his shoulders. Terror made Inaamdura speechless; the name she could not utter escaping in a whisper from Ligongo's lips.

"Ndoro!"

Inaamdura watched the man she schemed to eliminate walk slowly to the outer wall, a nightmare image of that same scene twenty seasons ago on Dingane's birthday. He was half-way to the gate when Inaamdura regain her senses. He was within bow range.

"Shoot him, shoot him!" she shouted, but no one responded. Even Ligongo was caught in a silent trance, his angry eyes never wavering from his half-brother.

Ndoro stopped before the gates, lifting the lion over his head, and dropped it in the dirt.

"Here me, Sesu! The son of Dingane has returned! The golden stool on which Ligongo sits belongs to me. Many seasons ago you were deceived. You were told I was possessed and drove me away. Some of you thought I was dead. But look what I have done, Sesu!"

A deafening roar burst from Ndoro's army, a war chant accompanied by the beating of shields and stamping feet. Ndoro stood perfectly still, a broad smile on his face. He waited until the chant died down before he spoke again.

"In the deep forest they call me Shumba for the fierceness it possesses. I built a kingdom that reaches from the bowels of Tacuma to the edges of Sesuland. My warriors were once slaves but now hold their head high as conquerors."

Ndoro raised his spear, pointing at mother and son. "You belong to me, Selike, you and all you possess. It is my right by my blood, by my ancestors, and by my hand. I will not be denied my right!"

Inaamdura looked into Ndoro's eyes and saw her death. He returned her stare, a cold grin slowly coming to his face. He was Dingane reborn, but without his father's weakness, nor Ligongo's excesses. She realized she made a grave mistake those many seasons ago. If Ndoro had stayed in Selike, time would have worn him down, rejection forcing him to accept his status. The man she looked down upon knew no such thing. No man could stop him. No army could stop him.

Ndoro called out in an unknown tongue and his warriors formed around him. They turned away from the city and set off at a warrior's pace, a cadence chant strong in their throats. As they passed the other warriors they too followed, forming two columns behind Ndoro and his guard. The entire city watched them as they trotted away, eventually disappearing into dust and horizon.

Ligongo left the ramparts without a word. He scampered down the steps, mounted his horse and galloped away. Inaamdura and Zuberi followed him back to the palace.

"Zuberi, gather your officers," Inaamdura said. "I will tend to Ligongo."

Zuberi's stern face became even colder. "Begging your pardon, Queen Mother, but I think Ligongo needs the company of his warriors."

"You forget who holds the power here," Inaamdura replied. "Now go!"

Zuberi gave Inaamdura his detached stare, turned and walked away. Inaamdura rushed to the stool room. She found Ligongo sitting alone, holding the royal orinka in his hand. He looked up at Inaamdura as she entered.

"So this is how you handle war, my son? Run away and hide like a boy?"

Ligongo looked at her clearly angry. "What did he mean?"

Inaamdura replied carefully. "What are you talking about?"

Ligongo sprang to his feet. "What did he mean about being deceived?"

"So you listen to the words of a demon? A man possessed?"

"Is he really?" Ligongo sat back in his stool. "I am no fool, mama. I know how baba died, and I know of others that suspect. I know how easily your enemies disappear. Tell me the truth."

"It doesn't matter now," Inaamdura replied. "You must hold onto what I've accomplished."

"What you've accomplished?" Ligongo laughed. "Yes, mama, this is all yours. This palace, our allies, my wives, they are all yours. But I am left to answer Ndoro's challenge; I must fight your war."

"If I could be beside you with a shield and assegai, I would," Inaamdura intensely.

"Please, mama. Allow me one last chance at manhood." Ligongo sat back on the stool. "Now go. I must meet with Zuberi. We have a war to wage."

Inaamdura turned on her heels and stormed out of the throne room. How dare he speak to her that way? How dare he question her judgment? She stomped into her private chambers, slamming the door behind her. Ndoro had returned to destroy her just as his mother's presence had threatened to do before. But she would handle him this time. In seconds she was out of her regal garb and into the clothes of a common Sesu woman. In her garden she found the secret tunnel and descended in haste, for every moment counted. She ignored the smells and sounds of the narrow passage, thankful that the dim light of her torch could not reveal the tunnel's inhabitants. The passage ended abruptly, a stone door carved with hieroglyphics before her. She pushed it open, revealing a deserted alleyway in the merchant sector. Inaamdura made her way through the alley and emerged onto the main road. The streets were still relatively quiet; apparently everyone was discussing Ndoro's return. She hurried down the road until she reached a narrow street packed with carts, boxes and debris. Inaamdura picked her way through the dilapidated maze until she reached her destination, a stone house bleached white with the symbol of the spider painted over the entrance. Inaamdura looked about quickly, and then entered, knocking as she swung open the door.

The smell of incense and cow dung was overpowering. A thick haze hovered over her head, a smoke that burned her eyes and caused her to cough. Through the grayness she could see the figure of the man she sought, his tall frame hunched over the fire producing the pungent smoke, his hands tracing invisible writing in the air.

"Cacunja," she called out.

"Queen Mother," he responded, his blank eyes never leaving the fire. "A cloud of doom hovers over your clan, a cloud that thunders the name Ndoro."

Inaamdura shook with the mention of Ndoro's name. "Then you know why I am here."

"To give yourself to me?" Cacunja threw his head back with hysterical laughter.

Inaamdura ignored his comment. "I need to know the future."

The strange man's jocularity disappeared. He turned and looked at Inaamdura, his blind eyes focusing on her stronger than those of any sighted man.

"You know the price. Be sure what you seek is worth it."

"Do as I ask, Cacunja," she replied. "I need to know tomorrow."

Cacunja ambled into the haze. There was a commotion in the smoke, the rattling of gourds, the rustling of baskets, and the screeching of an animal followed by a wet thud. Inaamdura stepped back as Cacunja returned, carrying a bloody mass of herbs and animal entrails in his right hand, a freshly used knife in his left. He held the entrails over the fire, chanting in a language Inaamdura did not recognize. Cacunja dropped the entrails into the fire, and it flared with a white-hot glow. The medicine priest nodded with approval, and then turned toward Inaamdura. She approached him slowly, extending her hand. In a sudden motion Cacunja grabbed her hand, jerked it over the fire and slit her wrist with the blade. Inaamdura screamed as he twisted her hand, letting the blood run into the fire. A thick black smoke rose from the flame. Inaamdura grew weak and dizzy, months of her life spilling from her veins and into the flames. She felt herself giving way when a searing pain enveloped her, emanating from the wrist. She managed to jerk away, stumbling and falling onto her bottom while she looked at her wrist. The cut had been cauterized by Cacunja's blade, a charred band of flesh replacing the open wound.

The dark smoke ceased billowing from the fire. It hung before her, a dense blackness that pulled her toward it.

"Look into the smoke and see your future," Cacunja said.

Inaamdura saw nothing at first, wondering if she gave up her lifeblood for nothing. But then images appeared in the center of the cloud, darting colors that seemed more stable with every passing moment. A vision emerged from the dancing lights, the revelation that Inaamdura paid the ultimate price to see. Selike burned, flames churning in a storm of destruction, ebony smoke climbing into the sky. Bodies were strewn through the devastation, broken figures of Sesu warriors. On the hill of the royal umuzi victorious Diaka rallied, their shields and assegais pumping with the victory dance of their war drums. Ndoro stood on the roof of the royal palace, flanked by two men she did not recognize. Behind them, impaled on a sharpened wooden stake, was Ligongo.

Inaamdura fell to her knees, her face falling into her hands.

"He must die," she said aloud. "Ndoro must die tonight!" She looked at Cacunja, desperation full in her eyes. "Can you kill him?"

"I can," Cacunja replied. "For a price."

Inaamdura stood, a seductive look coming to her face. "Anything you wish."

Cacunja broke into laughter. "Your body does not interest me. I demand a higher price."

Cacunja lifted his closed hand, opening it to reveal a small pile of white dust. "What I want is a piece of your soul."

Inaamdura gazed into the white eyes of Cacunja, not knowing what he meant by a piece of her soul. Would his spell claim her life as well? No, the witch-doctor would be too smart to attempt such a thing. His life would be worthless once Ligongo discovered her death. If this was the only way to stop Ndoro then she must do it. She had no other choice.

"So be it," she said.

Cacunja's grin evaporated with her words. He whispered over the powder in his hand and with a sudden breath, blew it into Inaamdura's face. Again Inaamdura's body was torn with pain. The powder plunged into her like a thousand jagged knives, tearing at her from the inside. She tried to scream but no sound came from her throat, her contorted face the only sign of the pain she experienced. A part of her was being ripped away, something so deep no human hand could have reached it. She collapsed to the floor in a final rush of fire. She lay still as the pain subsided, leaving a burning sensation throughout. Finally she was able to sit up. Her eyes cleared and she saw Cacunja standing over her, his face obscured in the smoky haze. There was something else though, a sense that they were not alone. Looking about the hut, she saw movement near the opposite wall. Inaamdura rose to her feet; Cacunja grabbed her wrist and jerked her to his side.

"Look into the mirror of spirits," he said. "See yourself as you truly are."

A creature stepped forward through the smoke and Inaamdura screamed. The creature screamed with her, their voices an unnatural chorus of fear. It was a hideous distortion of her, talons where manicured nails should be, fangs protruding from where normal perfect teeth should rest, the hair matted about its malformed head. The creature stared into her eyes, its chest heaving, and its putrid breath visible as puffs of vile steam.

"Send it away!" she pleaded.

"That is your task," Cacunja replied. "You asked for a way to rid yourself of Ndoro, and I have given it to you. I have made your hate real. It is yours to command. No man can stand against it and no one else can control it. But be careful, my inkosa, for you will suffer whatever your hate suffers."

"What happens once its task is complete?"

"It returns to you," Cacunja answered. "Do not worry. The entry will not be quite as painful as the exit."

Inaamdura stepped closer to the monstrosity. The creature stood still, its heaving chest the only movement.

"Do you hear me?" she asked. The creature nodded its head.

"Will you do as I say?" Again, the creature nodded its head.

A smile formed on Inaamdura's face. "You are a part of me. My mind is your mind. You know the face of Ndoro. Outside our walls he sleeps with his warriors, hoping to dance his victory on our bones. But you will find him, and when you find him, you will kill him."

The creature nodded its head again.

"Go," Inaamdura ordered. "Rid us of this fool!"

The creature reared back its head and let out a piercing scream. It charged off into the darkness with amazing speed despite its bulk. Inaamdura turned her attention to the still smiling Cacunja.

"You've done well, very well. Once Ndoro is dead, you will be rewarded as always. Until then, this will have to do." Inaamdura clasped the witch doctor's cheeks between her hands and kissed him. Cacunja wiped his mouth and spat.

"I'd rather have gold."

Inaamdura smiled as she left his hut. "You will have that, too. Soon."

* * *

Ndoro sat at the war council with his indunas, his face stern. Inside he was a mix of nervousness and excitement. Twenty years of war had brought him before the walls of Selike, ready to take his place on the royal stool of the Sesu. But his mood was not shared by his officers. He looked at the men beside him, all with serious expressions. By indulging himself, he had broken a trust that every man with him depended on for survival. He waited for the arguments to begin.

Jawanza spoke first. "Shumba, I know today gave you great pride. But we have put our army in jeopardy. We have lost the element of surprise, and we will pay for it with warrior blood."

Many heads nodded in agreement. Ndoro stood, sweeping his eyes across the circle before him.

"For twenty seasons we have marched across Uhuru, singing the warrior's song and filling our umuzis with cattle. You have stood beside me and placed your lives in my hands. Now we stand before the gates of Selike, our final goal. Those of you who know me understand the importance of this day, so you must also understand why we did what we did today. I hoped by showing the Sesu their true inkosi, they would take matters into their own hands and rid themselves of Ligongo. The Sesu are my people. I do not wish to shed their blood if it is avoidable."

He paused to let them consider his words.

"Tomorrow I will send an envoy to the Sesu to ask them their decision. If they refuse, we will attack. The Diaka I know need not have surprise on their side."

It was a challenge to their bravery, one he knew they would accept.

Jawanza spoke for the group again. "You know us better than we know ourselves; we are your creation. We do as you wish, Shumba."

Ndoro smiled. "Rest well, warriors. Tomorrow may call on your full fury." The indunas stood as he left the council, flanked by his bodyguards. Making his way through the camp quickly, he entered his tent to find Kenyetta waiting for him.

"What are you doing here?" he demanded.

"I was waiting for you," she replied, a smile on her face.

Ndoro was unsettled by her appearance. She was a beautiful woman, and her intent was clear. He had not allowed himself the touch of a woman since Sarama, not willing to lessen her memory. But it had been so long, and Kenyetta was so close.

She sauntered toward him. "If you are the true inkosi of Sesuland, then I must truly be your wife."

"Ligongo is your husband," Ndoro answered, angry at the weakness in his voice.

"I no longer wish to be his wife. I wish to be yours."

Kenyetta wrapped her arms around his neck and kissed him. Ndoro's hands went to her waist and he pulled her close, savoring her sweet smell. He found himself removing the wrap around her waist when he heard the violent tearing of his tent flap. He spun to see Nakisisa standing before him, a wild look in his feral eyes.

"What is going on?" he demanded.

The river-beast's head jerked about. "My hand, where is my hand?"

It had been so long ago since Ndoro took his companion's hand that he did not understand what he was asking. Before he could answer the river-beast transformed and Kenyetta screamed.

"Give me the hand!" There was another scream, but this did not emit from Kenyetta. It came from a distance, sounding like the cry of an angry beast, but not one Ndoro could place. He heard the scream again; it was closer. It was coming toward them.

Ndoro ran to his chest, rummaging through it for the gilded box that contained the river-beast's hand. The encampment exploded in shouts and yells that rolled toward his tent like a swelling storm.

"Hurry!" Nakisisa urged. "She is almost..."

Claws ripped into Ndoro's tent and tore the side away. Ndoro abandoned his search, grabbing his assegai and orinka. He turned to the river-beast and saw the creature standing before him. It was Inaamdura, a terrible deformation of her. Its claws dripped blood as saliva ran down its fangs. Before it could move, the river-beast attacked. It dove into the beast, burying its teeth into its throat and wrapping its arms around the creature's torso. The creature roared and fell away, startled by the sudden attack. The camp was frantic, some warriors fleeing, others running to the battle, their shields and assegais ready. Ndoro felt a tug on his shoulder and turned to see Kenyetta's fearful face. Jawanza stood beside her.

"Come, Shumba!" he urged. "We must flee. This creature comes for you."

"No," Ndoro replied. "Form the men. Nakisisa will not fight this battle alone."

Jawanza called out to his warriors, and in moments the bravest gathered around them. The beast had forced Nakisisa onto his back, biting at him with bloody fangs and swinging its claws. The river-beast held onto his grip, his rear legs drawn up to protect its torso, raking his foot claws at the demon's chest.

Ndoro raised his assegai and the warriors readied themselves. He dropped his arm sharply and hundreds of assegais sped toward the beast. Only inches away they shattered, the splinters returning like lethal rain. Many warriors went down, wounded or killed by the shards of wood.

"This is sorcery at work," Jawanza yelled. "There is nothing we can do. This is Nakisisa's fight."

Jawanza's words reminded Ndoro of the hand. He ran back to the chest and found the gilded box. He opened the box and took out the gourd containing the hand. With a yell he ran toward the struggle.

A roar rose from his warriors, a sound that was drowned by the growls and groans of the struggle before him. While the beast was distracted by its struggle with Nakisisa, Ndoro made his move. Like lightening he drove his assegai into the beast's side. The creature raised its head and Ndoro brought his orinka down, smashing the creature's face and knocking it back stunned. Nakisisa shoved the creature away, struggling to his feet.

"Here!" Ndoro shouted, tossing the river-beast his hand. "I will hold this thing off as long as I can."

"No! It has come for you!"

Ndoro grinned. "Then let it come. I have a score to settle with its master."

The beast turned to look at Ndoro. An expression came to its face, its teeth bared.

"Time for you to die, abomination!" it roared in a voice that resembled Inaamdura's.

Ndoro braced himself for the creature's charge. With a shriek the creature pounced. Ndoro fell to his knees, raising his assegai above his head. The beast landed on him as his assegai shattered against its breasts. Ndoro felt the weight of the beast, his body wracked with pain. Suddenly the pressure was gone. Ndoro managed to roll on his side, the pain almost causing him to black out. He looked up and saw the beast rolling away with Nakisisa upon it, slashing with both hands. The river-beast locked onto the creature, his fangs firmly embedded in the creature's throat. Despite the ngwena's weight, the creature stood and the surrounding warriors ran in fear. Locking its eyes on Ndoro, the queen-beast staggered toward him, a low growl emanating from its damaged throat. Its legs buckled and it collapsed, falling on Nakisisa.

Nakisisa threw the dead beast aside and struggled to his feet, changing form as he approached Ndoro. His human form displayed terrible wounds, but it walked as if nothing had happened. He halted before Ndoro and struggled to smile.

"It is good to be whole again," he spoke, holding up his hand.

"I should have given it back sooner," Ndoro replied. "You stopped being my captive long ago."

Nakisisa swayed and Ndoro caught him.

"The beast is dead, and so is Inaamdura," Nakisisa said. "It was a creature made from her spirit, and she suffered what it suffered. Ligongo weeps for a death he cannot explain. The city is yours if you attack now."

Nakisisa coughed, blood seeping from his nose and mouth. He looked at Ndoro and managed a smile. "It is time for me to return to the river. Live long, Great Shumba."

Nakisisa went limp in Ndoro's arms. He held the river-beast for a moment, unsure how to feel about the creature that had tried to take his life but had become a loyal companion. Nakisisa died a warrior's death, giving his life for Shumba. Ndoro eased the river-beast to the ground then watched in amazement as its body shimmered and became a pool of water. The liquid lingered for moment and then dissipated into the dry earth. Warriors gathered about Ndoro, gazing at the place where Nakisisa's body once occupied. He felt Kenyetta's hand against his back but ignored her comforting touch.

Ndoro grasped his assegai, picked up his orinka and ran. His warriors parted before him like grass before the wind. Nakisisa told him Inaamdura was dead and Selike was his for the taking; if so he would take it this night. Behind him he heard the shouts of his indunas as warriors formed ranks and fell into place. By the time he reached the crest of the hill hiding the encampment, the Diaka war chant shattered the silence of the moonless night. As he reached the base of the hill his army was with him, running the warrior's pace to the city.

Selike slept as the Diaka approached. Sesu custom forbade battle at night lest the spirits of the darkness be disturbed. As Ndoro learned among the Songhai, customs can lead to disaster. A few strides before the city walls skirmishers broke free, running ahead of the main army with ladders. Behind them rushed the archers, their bows at the ready, their quivers filled with poison-tipped arrows. They were deathly efficient; the archers fell any guard appearing on the ramparts while the skirmishers put their ladders in place. They clambered up the ladders, spilling onto the ramparts. Silent clashes broke out as the Diaka fought the Sesu sentries for control of the outer wall.

Once the ramparts were secure, Ndoro called a halt. The archers reloaded, this time with arrows tipped with oil-soaked rags. Torchbearers ran down the single file line, lighting the arrows as they went to the center. Ndoro, standing before the archers, raised his orinka and the missiles flew like shooting stars, arching through the sky and falling down into the city darkness. The archers reloaded as the first volley ignited the homes below them. The second volley went, and then the third before screams rose from the city.

"Diaka, Kimbia!" Ndoro shouted from below, leading the charge to the drawbridge as Sesu warriors attacked the Diaka on the ramparts. The Diaka struggled to hold them back, surprised by their fury. These were not the lazy warriors and conscripts that made up the complacent kingdoms of the interior. The Sesu were well accustomed to war; they were a people forged by metal and fire.

The Diaka neared the gate, but it was still closed. Ndoro's men attacked the barrier with axes, protected by the shields of their companions. While Ndoro and his men hacked the gate, the Sesu reclaimed the ramparts. The Sesu archers were not numerous enough to form organized volleys but good enough to slow the advance. They shot poisoned arrows from their small bows, Diaka warriors falling into convulsions as the lethal concoctions took quick effect. A few ladders were destroyed and the others were being threatened. Kamau directed the Diaka archer fire to the ramparts and the Sesu fell back, allowing more Diaka skirmishers to climb the ramparts.

As the Diaka fought to regain the ramparts, their comrades below broke through the gates, revealing the inferno inside. Ndoro charged through the opening and into chaos, his destination the royal umuzi. His bodyguards broke rank to follow him, forming a shell of shields about him. More and more Diaka poured into the city. The Diaka archers commanded the ramparts, shooting down into the fiery confusion. Small groups of Sesu warriors appeared to meet the onslaught, but without organization they were overwhelmed by the charging Diaka.

Ndoro kept running, weaving through rows of burning homes and barricades. He and his guard met little opposition;

the few warriors brave enough to challenge them were quickly dispatched by his guards. Ndoro's running had begun as a rage; it was now for a purpose. Having been taken by surprise, the Sesu would sacrifice the outer city. They would organize at the city center, surrounding the royal umuzi and the elders' huts. The Diaka had to reach the inner city before the Sesu organized and retreated to the second wall.

As they swarmed the second wall protecting the inner city, the Diaka finally met the full fury of Sesu resistance. Warriors flooded the streets, throwing their light spears at Ndoro and his cohorts. The guard locked shields and deflected the deadly downpour, then quickly formed ranks to meet the coming onslaught. Ndoro knocked away a Sesu's shield with his orinka and slashed his abdomen with his assegai, jumping over the body as he continued to run to the palace. Together he and his guard cut a terrible path, battling their way through the inner city to the jewel of the center, the royal umuzi.

By the time they reached the third wall, the rest of the Diaka army had joined them. But what Ndoro feared loomed before him. The walls of the royal umuzi were covered with Sesu archers, their bows drawn and ready. Ndoro imagined what waited behind them; thousands of Sesu warriors, their bare chests painted with the blood of a bull from the royal herd, a sign that this would be a battle to the death. The Diaka could not defeat such a determined foe, Ndoro was sure. For the first time since laying Nakisisa to rest, Ndoro ceased running. Raising his orinka, the Diaka halted, just outside bow range.

In moments Jawanza was at his side. "What do you wish, Shumba?"

"Bring the archers and skirmishers forward," he replied. "I want constant probes under cover of the archers. We might find a weak point in their defense."

Jawanza nodded and set off to his orders.

"Jawanza, wait!" Ndoro called out. His second quickly returned to his side.

"Shumba?"

"Did Kenyetta come with us?" he asked.

Jawanza's expression went from calm to anger. "Yes, Shumba. She refused to stay at the encampment."

Ndoro smiled. She was the only person that wanted to see the end of Selike more than himself.

"Where is she?"

"At the rear with the reserve column," Jawanza replied reluctantly. "I insisted she stay with them. I assigned two Diaka to guard her."

Ndoro dismissed Jawanza and made his way to the reserve column. Kenyetta's bodyguard had constructed a tent for her. As if by instinct the flap flew open as Ndoro neared the tent and Kenyetta ran to him. "Shumba!"

Ndoro pushed her at arm's length. This was no time for amorous emotions.

"Kenyetta, does the Great Wife house still contain the bedchamber passage?"

Kenyetta closed her eyes in thought. "Yes, yes it does. Why?"

Ndoro was striding away before Kenyetta had time to finish her question. He signaled for two more squads of warriors to follow, and they set a warrior's pace, running past the ranks of Diaka warriors until they reached the section of wall where the homes of Ligongo's wives were located. Ndoro summoned the induna in charge of the warriors.

"Direct the archers to fire on my signal. Your skirmishers will advance with us."

The induna did as ordered. When Ndoro dropped his orinka, the archers fired and the Sesu answered. Soon after Ndoro's group and the skirmishers advanced. Halfway across the gap Ndoro's group broke away, running to the great wife's home. Breaking down the door, Ndoro went to where Kenyetta told him the bedchamber would be. A huge chest rested there, causing Ndoro to smile. Apparently Ligongo was not a welcomed visitor to Kenyetta's bed. They shoved the chest aside and lifted the wooden door. Lighting small torches, Ndoro led his men into the bedchamber pass.

Time was of the essence. It would not take long for someone to figure out what was truly happening. Ndoro and his party had to be out of the narrow tunnel before the Sesu could capture them there.

The Diaka ran up the incline leading to the royal palace. Ndoro stepped aside and his men rammed the entrance door, bringing it down with a thunderous crash. Ndoro followed them into Ligongo's bedchamber. There, lying on his bed was the mutilated body of Inaamdura. Though she was dressed in regal mourning garments, the wounds showed clearly on her face. Apparently the wounds inflicted on the spirit-beast scarred her as well. Ndoro was disappointed. He wanted the satisfaction of killing his father's murderer himself.

They left the royal bedroom, headed for Ligongo's stool room. The palace was empty, which made the infiltrators more wary. They were easy prey for an ambush; Ndoro hoped he could find Ligongo before they were discovered.

They descended a stairwell that emptied into a long broad corridor lined with soapstone sculptures, woven tapestries and animal hides. A commotion could be heard coming from a doorway at the end of the hall. Ndoro ran forward and his men followed.

They charged into Ligongo's stool room. Ligongo was seated, flanked by his personal guard and his wives. His officers were before him, all on their knees before a leather map in deep in discussion with their leader. It was one of the inkosi's children that spotted them first, a young boy who smiled and tapped his mother on the shoulder. She looked up at Ndoro and screamed.

Ligongo leapt from his stool, grabbing the royal sword from his servant. His personal guards charged toward Ndoro and his men, but Ligongo raised his hand for them to halt.

"So we meet, my brother," Ligongo said. Ndoro advanced also, his men close behind.

"If you had not been banished, this would be your throne," Ligongo said. "Mama told me baba Dingane favored you, despite what he led people to believe. He would have eventually made you inkosi despite what anyone thought."

Ligongo slowed his advance, taking a defensive stance. "I did not want to be inkosi, my brother. I had no such ambitions. But my mother wished it to be, so it was."

Both brothers stood before each other, weapons at the ready, Ligongo with his shield and gilded sword, Ndoro with his assegai and orinka.

"I would give the stool to you gladly, but I've grown fond of it. I do owe you the chance, though. We are blood, aren't we?"

Ligongo was much better than Ndoro expected. His sudden attack drove Ndoro back, knocking his assegai from his hand and leaving him with his orinka as his only defense. His warriors surged forward to protect him, but Ndoro held up his hand, stopping them.

They circled, each brother wary of the other's skill. Ndoro charged, catching Ligongo by surprise. As Ligongo swung his sword to decapitate him, Ndoro rolled under and came to his knees, striking Ligongo in the back with his orinka. He stood and was struck by Ligongo's shield, knocking him off balance. Ndoro felt a line of pain race across his chest, the tip of Ligongo's sword slicing a bloody crease. Ignoring his wound, Ndoro took advantage of the opening, jumping past Ligongo's swinging arm and hitting his brother in the head with his orinka.

Ligongo's bodyguards attacked. They were met head on by the Diaka and a melee broke out around the two. Ndoro hit Ligongo again and again until his brother no longer moved. Ligongo's bodyguard, seeing their inkosi defeated, broke off their attack and ran. The Diaka ran them down, killing every man before they could leave the stool room. The sound of battle was replaced by the wails of Ligongo's wives and children, terror in their eyes as they looked at Ligongo's body and the warriors before them.

Ndoro approached them. "You will not die," he said. "You are my daughters now, and you will attend the new Great Wife when she is selected. But I warn you not to cross me. Your children are mine; if any harm comes to me or my own, your children will suffer. Do you understand?"

The women went silent. There was no use resisting; only the lives of the children mattered to them now. It was a cruel threat to make, but Ndoro knew it was necessary for him to control his palace first before he could control the city.

Ndoro rallied his men, leaving a few Diaka to guard his new family. They scoured the palace, searching for any hidden warriors among the rooms. Finding none, Ndoro lead his warriors out to the royal pasture.

The Diaka were attacking the walls on all sides, but the Sesu held firm. Ndoro scanned the perimeter and found what he looked for. To his west the Sesu line was sparse, held only by archers on the ramparts. The other Sesu were massing near the main gate, preparing a counterattack.

Ndoro led his men down the hill. They were on the ramparts before the archers knew what was happening. After clearing the path, Ndoro signaled his warriors. The Diaka charged the breach. They were within the walls and flanking the Sesu in minutes. The Sesu indunas yelled desperately, pulling their warriors back from the wall to meet the attack on their rear. As they pulled away, other Diaka poured over the unprotected sections of the wall, surrounding the remaining Sesu. Though hopeless, they continued to fight. Ndoro led his group, battling with spear and club until the rumble of the royal drums reverberated over the carnage. Everyone looked toward the source of the sound to the royal palace. Ligongo's wives marched in a procession, bearing the body of their slain husband. The Sesu warriors lowered their weapons, the fight leaving their limbs at the sight of the dead inkosi. They prostrated themselves before Ndoro, sprinkling dirt on their heads in the Sesu sign of submission. Ndoro felt a hand on his shoulder and turned to see Jawanza standing by his side.

"It seems, son of Dingane, that you have won," he said.

A smile came to Ndoro's face.

"Sesuland is mine."

17

The sun rose over the Mahgreb as it had for millennia, its light shimmering over the fine, pale sand. On the crest of a certain plateau, the sand gave way to the lush growth of the high oasis. Life had returned to Yakubu and with it the Tuaregs. From the ends of the Mahgreb they came, bringing whatever they could carry on their donkeys and camels. Wrapped in their blue robes and turbans they returned; the proud and brave Ihaggaren, who remained in the desert rather than leave their homeland; the Imrad, who prospered in the caravan towns with their trading and farming skills; and even the subservient Iklan, who despite having escaped their lowly status at the fall of Yakubu could not resist the call of home.

But all would not be as it was. Others came as well, people drawn not by the wealth of the oasis, but by the man who resurrected it.

Obaseki rose from his bed as he did every morning and gazed upon the city from his tower window. He went to his shrine, pouring libations to his ancestors and to those that inhabited Yakubu. He saw the spirits as always, mingling with the lives of the living, but they did not approach him as they once did. He was among them now, a noble spirit in their world and the world of the living. This saddened him, for he had always found companionship among the spirits. Now, sitting alone in the tower, he felt the loss of their nearness like the death of a family member.

He returned to his room and donned the blue robes of the Tuaregs without the turban. The headdress protected the wearer from the evil eye and the evil mouth, a protection Obaseki did not need.

He descended into the dining area for his meal. As always his table was prepared and, as always, Eshe was not there. She was probably inspecting the marketplace, making sure the day's business was honest and fair. Tuareg life suited her well; women were well respected and her status as his wife gave her the power to choose her position, which she did with relish. Many of the Ihaggaren were concerned about her decision to rule over an occupation dominated by the Imrad, but they said nothing, respecting her choice and fearing Obaseki's anger.

Once his meal was done he would proceed to the Grand Hall. There he would sit on his blankets, listening to the happenings of the day, settling disputes and healing those too sick to respond to the herbalist's cures. Afterward he would ride through the city, touching those who pushed through the crowd to be near him in hopes he could heal them. It was a routine obligatory of a chief and a life he was ordained to live. Obaseki despised it.

This was not his destiny. The restless urge that filled him every day was worse than in his days in Abo, Ifana and Zimfara. There was still a task for him, some duty that had yet been revealed. The gods did things in their own time. He would have to wait.

Obaseki was finishing his breakfast when Eshe burst into the room; her beautiful smile was brighter than the sun.

"My husband, you are awake!" Her voice sounded more shocked than pleased. El-Fatih came in behind her, his eyes wide through the slit of his turban. He removed his veil, having no need to protect himself from Obaseki.

"Thank you for escorting me," Eshe said to El-Fatih.

"The city has become dangerous since the arrival of the refugees," El-Fatih replied. "Be sure to summon the city guard from now on."

"I will, Fatih."

El-Fatih bowed to Obaseki. "My lord."

Obaseki nodded his head and El-Fatih exited.

Eshe sat beside him. "The market is well, Seki. You should come and walk with me sometimes."

Obaseki looked into his wife's eyes and saw the truth despite her happy mood. He'd known for some time about her feelings for El-Fatih, but it had only been recently the leader of the Tuaregs harbored the same feelings for her. Obaseki felt no anger or jealousy, only sadness.

"I know you love El-Fatih," he said. "I know he has feelings for you."

Tears welled in Eshe's eyes and she threw her head down on her folded arms. Obaseki watched her sob, feeling sorry that he had not found a better way to tell her. He reached to her, caressing her neck. Eshe looked up at him with wide fearful eyes.

"What will you do to us?"

Obaseki smiled. "Nothing." He leaned forward and kissed her on the forehead. "You are my sweet flower."

"You are not angry?"

Obaseki rose and walked to the tower window. "There are powers I wish I did not possess, Eshe. The spirits read the hearts of men and tell all. You no longer see me as a man to love. I cannot blame you. I am no longer a man, but I am not a god."

"What are you then, my husband?"

Obaseki turned to her. "I do not know. I only know the ancestors are not done with me yet."

A servant entered the room.

"My oba, the crowds are gathering in the healing room."

Obaseki nodded, dismissing the servant. "We will talk later," he said. He touched her soft cheek and for a brief moment felt the warmth he'd felt when they first touched many seasons ago. Then he was gone, walking briskly through the corridor to the Grand Hall. As he entered, the throng that had waited since daybreak fell to its knees in unison, their heads touching the dirt. Obaseki took his place on his stool, a modest wooden seat given to him by a merchant from the northern lands beyond the Mahgreb. Tuareg warriors formed a path to him, keeping the people orderly as they approached.

The haggard conditions of the disciples worried him.

"These people are not from the city," he whispered to El-Fatih, who stood beside him.

"No. They are refugees from the south."

"Refugees from what?"

"Not what, who. Hondo's armies are on the march."

Obaseki tensed at the mention of his brother's alias. Now he occupied his waking hours as well as his sleep.

"I have a feeling that we will have our chance at this Hondo soon," El-Fatih said. "We shall see how he likes Tuareg steel."

Obaseki said nothing. The first refugee came to him, an emaciated woman holding an equally thin child.

"My oba, please heal my daughter."

Obaseki placed his hands on the child. She was cold; there was no telling how long she'd been dead. He looked among the spirits mingling with the people in the chamber, asking a silent question.

"Does anyone know this child?"

A male spirit came forward and sat on the head of the child's mother.

"I know her," he said. "She is Kesse, and her spirit hides in the forests with her ancestors."

"Her mother wishes her to come back," Obaseki replied.

"She will come if you summon her, but she will not be the same."

Obaseki looked at the mother with sadness. "Is she close to the Zamani?"

"Yes." The spirit relinquished his hold on the woman, who almost stumbled.

"What happened?" she asked, her voice weak.

"A spirit from your village," Obaseki replied. "Your daughter dwells among your family and is content. She does not wish to live away from her home."

Tears came to the woman's eyes. "I was selfish to bring her here. I carried her body when I should have buried her with our family. But Hondo came so fast! If I could be with them..."

Obaseki placed his hand on her head, letting her grief flow into him. A mother's pain was always difficult for him, but this feeling went much deeper than before. Tears came to his eyes and with them a deep ache within his chest.

"Moyo?" El-Fatih asked. "Are you well?"

"Call off the session," Obaseki said. "Send everyone away. I must rest. I must..."

The pain consumed his senses, blinding him to everyone and everything. He tumbled in its wake, tossed like grass in a monsoon wind, rising upward while hands grabbed at him like a human rope in a cosmic tug-of-war. He hurdled into the heavens, his body crushed by the terrible pressure. He screamed, a cry that ripped into the force surrounding him. His horrid ascent ceased, the feeling of foundation forming under his back. Faces stared down on him, perfect masks carved from the finest ebony wood. These were the ancestors; their countless names ringing through his head in a litany of tongues alien yet familiar to his tortured mind. The voices increased in cadence, a blur of sound which at first was unintelligible, but ultimately coalesced into words he understood.

"Two must become one," the chanters demanded. With these words the restlessness that filled Obaseki throughout his life was swept away, replaced by a burning fire of purpose. He fell from his spiritual perch as rapidly as he had climbed, finding himself back on his stool, El-Fatih shaking him and calling his name. He grasped his friend's wrist tight.

"I am fine, Fatih. I won't be able to continue the healing. Please disperse the crowd."

El-Fatih looked at him puzzled, and then did as he was told. The people were disappointed but orderly, following the Tuareg warriors out of the chamber.

Obaseki left the chamber and went back to his quarters. Eshe was waiting for him.

"My husband," she said cautiously. "What have you said to El-Fatih?"

Obaseki did not respond. He went to the ivory chest that rested by his bed and opened it, revealing the mayembe. The horn glowed with spiritual fire, confirming what he suspected. The spirits were freeing him. He no longer needed Moyo with him to use its power. With the spirit force of Moyo in both the mayembe and himself, there was no reason for him to stay in Yakubu.

El-Fatih came into his room, Eshe following close behind. "Moyoseki, I am worried about you."

"Don't be," Obaseki replied. He handed the chest to El-Fatih.

"This box contains the mayembe that holds Moyo's soul. Keep it safe and Yakubu will prosper forever."

El-Fatih took the chest, his expression one of distress. "Moyo, are you...are you leaving?"

Obaseki looked at El-Fatih and Eshe and was pleased at what he saw. The city would prosper in their capable hands, even without his healings. He was content, even though he knew the outcome of his journey.

"I must go," he finally said. "There is something I must do, something I was born to do."

El-Fatih set the chest down. "You saved me, and I pledged to protect and serve you. If your journey is dangerous, then I must go with you."

Eshe came and stood by his side. "No matter what you think, I am still your wife. I watched you grow from the unsure medicine-priest that healed my mother to the Healer you are now. It is my duty to be with you."

Obaseki smiled at their loyalty. "I must do this alone."

He placed his hand on El-Fatih's shoulder. "Find me a good camel and provisions, for I have a long journey ahead." El-Fatih bowed and left as commanded.

Obaseki turned to his wife. Tears ran down her cheeks, a pleading expression on her face. He gently placed his hands on her cheeks.

"My sweet flower, do not cry. You know my heart is with you and yours with me. What I must do is the final road in my journey, I am sure. When I am done, I will return as your husband, nothing more, and nothing less."

Eshe sprang to him, locking her arms tight around his neck and kissing him.

"Be safe, my husband. Come back to me. Come back to me."

Obaseki saw El-Fatih enter the room. He kissed Eshe once again then pulled away. Without a word he walked past them both to the courtyard where the camel awaited. It was a fine beast; surely one of El-Fatih's best, if not his best.

"He is a good one, and easy to handle," El-Fatih said from behind him. Obaseki turned to see his friend approaching him, his arms carrying a bundle of blue cloth.

"You came to us as a stranger," he said. "We will not have you leave as one."

Like a proud father, El-Fatih dressed him in proper Tuareg fashion, carefully wrapping his head with the blue turban with the face shroud. He stood back, admiring his work.

"One more thing," he said. He clapped his hands and a young servant appeared, carrying another bundle of cloth that he handed to his master. El-Fatih opened the bundle carefully, revealing a Tuareg takouba in a finely decorated leather scabbard. He draped the strap of the scabbard over Obaseki's shoulders.

"Now you are a true Ihaggaren," he said.

"Thank you, my friend," Obaseki said. "Take care of Yakubu, and take care of Eshe."

"I will," the Tuareg chieftain replied.

Obaseki mounted the camel and it rose to its full height. Looking down on El-Fatih, he began his journey. Yakubu and Eshe were in good hands. He made his wife a promise to be careful and he would. One promise, however, he would not be able to keep. As he passed through the streets of his adopted city each step enhanced the feeling of purpose in his heart. His destination was Selike, the city of his brother. He did not expect to return.

* * *

A battle of words raged among the Sesu. The man that now claimed the stool of Sesuland was of royal blood, the destined leader of their people. But another dilemma presented itself that could not be ignored. Ndoro, son of Dingane, was one of twins, an abomination in the eyes of Sesu tradition, and the murderer of the medicine-priest Mulugo. In a way, their arguments seemed a waste of time since the warriors of Ndoro patrolled the streets of Selike, his conquest firmly established. Many Sesu welcomed the change, especially the young men. Ligongo was content entertaining himself with his wives, leaving the expansion of power in the hands of Inaamdura. The Queen Mother preferred political intrigue to warfare, reducing the opportunity for a warrior to gain honor and cattle. Ndoro was a leader more suited for the fortunes of a Sesu warrior, and many were ready to serve him. The will of the young warriors would have to wait on the ruling of the elders. If it was determined the ancestors did not approve of Ndoro, the Sesu would not support him. They would serve him, but they would not claim him as inkosi.

Ndoro knew the conversations whispered among the Sesu but had little patience or time for them. The endorsement of the elders was not his concern. Sesuland was his; if the elders caused trouble he would have them killed. His immediate concern was the indunas sitting cross-legged before him at his war council, serious looks on their faces. The conquest of Sesuland did not result in the spoils of war normally allowed to the warriors by Ndoro. The men were not happy.

"We understand your feelings, great Shumba," Jawanza said. He was the only commander brave enough to speak to Ndoro in such a way and the only person other than Kamau to have earned the right. "No one is closer to your dreams than I. But it is not good for the men to risk their lives with no reward. It will be difficult to lead them on our next march."

Ndoro felt the anger rising in him. "The Diaka fight for the honor of Diakaland and for me. Reward is secondary to their valor."

Kamau cleared his throat. Though he had grown much in courage since the confrontation with Mulugo years ago, Kamau was not known for speaking in a council. He shifted back and forth before speaking.

"What you say is true for our warriors, but not our allies. It is loot they seek. We might find ourselves fighting our own if something is not done soon."

Ndoro had heard enough. He stood before his indunas to deliver his final words on the subject.

"You are all correct. The conquest of Sesuland was my dream, not yours. It is wrong for me to think f you believe as I do. Go to your men and tell them this; once I have become the true inkosi of Sesuland, I will open the royal umuzi to them. Each clan is granted one bull and one cow to add to their herds. This is my word before all of you."

The indunas stared at Ndoro, eyes wide and mouths agape. The proclamation had the desired effect. This was far beyond anything they expected. Ndoro thought this gesture would end the council, but he was wrong.

"There is another matter we must discuss," Jawanza said, breaking the spell.

Ndoro was irritated with his old friend. "What is it?"

"Sesuland has fallen, but Abo still stands," he answered. "A lion with one tooth can still kill."

Ndoro wished Jawanza wasn't so thorough. "We will deal with Abo when the time comes."

"Great Shumba, although we are Diaka, we are still recovering," Jawanza replied. "Abo is a strong ally of the Sesu and will not take our conquest lightly."

"Don't presume to tell me of Abo," Ndoro snapped. "I'm well aware of Abo's relationship to Selike; I grew up under its shadow. I also know that Abo will listen to diplomacy before declaring war. We are a mystery to them, so they will be cautious. Besides, the oba of Mawenaland is of my clan."

"But he does not know this," Jawanza replied.

Jawanza's persistence was angering him although he knew his old friend meant well. His mood reflected that of the men, an overall feeling of restlessness that hung heavy in the Diaka camp. Fear crept among the warriors; fear that with the fall of Sesuland Ndoro's days of conquest were done. Shumba would lay down his assegai and shield and take the path of peace. It was a future for which the Diaka were not prepared.

"Send ambassadors to Abo carrying diplomacy swords," Ndoro decided. "Tell them that Hondo wishes to visit their great city to pay honor to their illustrious oba. You will keep your units in training during the rainy season. Replace the fallen with Sesu conscripts if necessary. The Diaka will march next dry season."

Jawanza smiled. "It is a good plan, Shumba. Meeting with the Mawena will give us time to strengthen our forces. I will arrange for the messengers to leave immediately."

"Good. Now go and enjoy your victory."

The indunas touched their heads on the ground, sprinkling dirt on their heads as custom. Ndoro waited for them to leave before rising. He turned to see Kenyetta standing before him, her face disapproving.

"Why did you lie to Jawanza?" she asked. Although they'd been together for weeks, Ndoro was still not used to Kenyetta's insight.

"I did not lie to him."

"You care for Abo like I care for a rock," she said. "I am your wife, Ndoro, and though you try to keep your feelings closed, I know when you are troubled."

Ndoro gazed into the night, the smoke-like haze a sign of the approaching wet season. Kenyetta's words hung before his eyes, the truth in them clear. These feelings Kenyetta mentioned so easily were new to him. All his life he had known nothing but the anger that coursed through his veins cold and hard. It drove him to build the empire he now ruled. But with the conquest of his former home, his enemies vanquished, he saw no future before him, just like the warriors that followed him.

Ndoro sat cross-legged on the blankets of the council room, Kenyetta sitting beside him, placing a comforting hand on his back.

"The night I fled my village, Jelani told me to go to Abo and seek the protection of my grandfather," Ndoro said. "But I was so afraid that I didn't listen to him. I ran into the darkness, not knowing where I would find myself.

"Sometimes, when I was alone, I would dream of Abo. I would imagine my grandfather rescuing me from the wilderness and teaching me the secrets of the Mawena warrior. I would become oba and lead a great army against my baba. But there would be no battle, for Dingane would be so frightened he would give up his stool and flee."

Ndoro hung his head laughing. "A boy's wishful dreams. I realized when I found myself among the Songhai conscripts that no one would save me but me. I had to exact my own revenge. But in my heart I still saw Abo as my sanctuary. For many years it was my solace."

"You will never march on Abo," Kenyetta stated.

"No I won't. I will make peace with Abo and my grandfather. Hopefully I will finally see my mother again."

Kenyetta snuggled against him and he welcomed her warmth. "The dreams of a boy do not die in the man. Abo will be your sanctuary. Your dream will be fulfilled."

The Diaka war drums raised the new day's sun, rumbling across the outskirts of Selike. Jawanza wasted no time acting on Ndoro's commands; the messengers had been sent the day before and the Diaka were training for the march once again. Despite Ndoro's generous gift, the young warriors were eager for the chance to earn more wealth and honor while the older men relished the chance to lead warriors into battle. The Sesu warriors did not share the Diaka's excitement. Although they accepted Ndoro's right to rule they resented the preference showed to the Diaka. They were the true people of Ndoro and expected to be treated as such. Many had not forgotten the murderous purges following the conquering of the city. Whatever soldiers coming to the Diaka armies from the Sesu were mostly former slaves seeking the freedom and wealth Jawanza offered.

Despite the resistance, Sesuland was soon swept in the excitement of a new campaign. Young boys fought mock battles with sticks and shields while the warriors prepared themselves throughout the rainy season for whatever fortunes the march would bring. Ndoro again sat with his indunas, this time pleased with their appearance. Intense training worked them into fighting shape, the fat of easy life burned away. Still, Jawanza stood out among them all, his seriousness making Ndoro proud.

He addressed his adopted brother. "Is Shumba ready to roar?"

"He is," Jawanza replied.

"Good. I wish you well on your campaign."

The statement caught Jawanza off guard. "Shumba, I thought you would..."

Ndoro stood. "It was you who brought back the spirit to us, who realized we had strayed from our purpose. You trained these warriors, so it is only right that you lead them."

Jawanza bowed his head to hide his smile. "Shumba, I am but a shadow of you. The warriors expect to see you before them, not a mere servant."

Ndoro placed his hand on Jawanza's shoulder. "You are my brother and your people have risen to greatness. I have achieved all that I wish on the battlefield. The fire you saw in my eyes was a reflection of yours."

Ndoro removed the simba pelt that graced his shoulders since his first battle. He placed the robe upon Jawanza.

"As of this day, I proclaim a new rank, the rank of Shumba. The wearer of this robe shall claim the privilege of command of the Diaka and be answerable only to the ancestors and myself."

Ndoro knelt behind Jawanza, who trembled.

"You are the closest friend I have," Ndoro whispered. "Make sure you come back from this campaign alive."

"Yes, Shumba. Yes, I will."

"No, my friend. From this day on you must call me Ndoro."

Jawanza looked directly into Ndoro's eyes. "As you wish, Ndoro."

Ndoro nodded his approval and came to his feet, turning his attention to the others. "You are witness to this day. Spread the word among the people. My word is law."

The indunas excused themselves. Jawanza remained, his eyes filled with confusion.

"I do not understand what has happened, but I promise I will not fail you."

"You have nothing to prove," Ndoro replied. "Now go and gather the Diaka. I wish to see the army you will lead."

Jawanza rushed from the palace. No sooner had he left did Kenyetta appeared.

"Do you think that was wise?" she asked.

"Jawanza is a good man. He will administer well until we return. Have you finished the arrangements?"

"Yes."

"Good. Let us join in Jawanza's celebration."

The procession was glorious. Ndoro looked upon Jawanza as a father would on his own son. The army did not stop to join the revelers; they continued their march out of the city and into the grasslands, where they took up the warrior pace. They headed east, toward the boundary between Sesu territory and Ndogoland. Ndogo settlers had crossed into Sesuland, building villages and raiding Sesu livestock. Instead of raiding in return, Jawanza was marching to strike at Abija, the main trading city in Ndogoland. It would be a stern warning, one the Ndogo oba would do well to heed.

No sooner had the warriors disappeared into the distance did the celebrations begin. Dancers filled the royal courtyard as beer flowed throughout the streets like a river. Ndoro and Kenyetta slipped away from the revelry, making their way quickly to the awaiting escort at the outskirts of the city. There was a litter for Kenyetta and himself; the others would have to walk the distance as warriors. The royal duo mounted and the group set off for Mawenaland and the city of Abo.

* * *

Obaseki tethered his camel on the tree that had been just a bush the last time he saw it. Though his final destination was Selike, he could not resist the urge to see his homeland for one last time. The hut looked the same as always, smothered with the various vines and plants that supplied Fuluke with his precious herbs. He had trouble finding the trail that led to it; the forest reclaimed what once belonged to it. He felt comfortable, yet sad. Fuluke was obviously dead, passed away so long ago that Obaseki could not sense his ka. With no children to remember and honor him, his spirit probably did not linger long in the world. He was among the ancestors, as he should be. A medicine priest's soul as powerful as his mentor would rest no other place.

The door of the dilapidated hut had long since fallen away. Obaseki stepped inside and was shocked to find a nude man sitting on the dirt floor before a libation altar. The man moved his head slightly enough to let Obaseki know he was aware of his intrusion.

"I am sorry," Obaseki said. "I didn't mean to intrude upon your home."

"This has always been your home too, Seki," the man replied. "No need to apologize." The man stood and turned, revealing himself to Obaseki.

"Fuluke?" Obaseki was startled. "But..."

"Yes, I am gone, yet I am here." Fuluke smiled and gestured for Obaseki to sit.

"I did not sense your ka," Obaseki said, obviously confused.

"I did not wish it."

Obaseki was again confused. "You can do such a thing?"

Fuluke smiled. "It is a strange thing to be in between worlds. Not among men, yet not among gods. I could be closer to the spirits, but I am selfish. I enjoy this gift."

"It is good to see you," Obaseki admitted. "I have thought of you often. There were many times I wished for your counsel."

"If you had my counsel, you would not be the man you are now. I was the forge that shaped you; it took life to temper you."

"And made me into what?" The confusion leading him back to Mawenaland rose close to the surface, cooling his mood. "I serve a people, yet I am not their oba nor do I wish to be. Now the ancestors send me to fulfill a prophecy of which I do not know the outcome."

"Who said the tempering is complete?" Fuluke asked.

"What do you mean?"

The medicine priest grinned then vanished. Obaseki stared at the space, frustration tight in his throat. This quest did not fill his heart like the others. The purpose was like a fog that blurred his mind. Were the ancestors playing tricks on him? Was their jealousy of his powers causing them to show him their true strength?

He shook his head as he stood to leave the house. He was becoming selfish. No matter whom he was or what he possessed, it was vain of him to think Olodumare would take him personally. Jealousy is an emotion of men. His purpose had been given to him; the uncertainty came from his reluctance to follow it through. He left, but not before pouring libations to Fuluke. Once done, he mounted his camel and continued his journey to Abo.

Nightfall found him at the outskirts of the city. It was dry season, the night air cool and soothing. Though he was close enough to enter the city before darkness, Obaseki chose to spend the night alone in the woods. Setting up camp quickly, he made a small offering to the wood spirits. Everywhere he traveled, the knowledge of his journey preceded him, and the spirits gave him a wide berth. Obaseki had never felt so alone. As he rested his head on his bundle, a haze appeared before him, transforming into the form of Fuluke.

"Tired so soon, Seki?" the spirit asked.

"It has been a long journey," Obaseki replied. He sat up before Fuluke.

"What awaits me in Abo?" He was not afraid to let Fuluke hear the fear in his voice. "Do the memories of my past run deep?"

"Most who remember you are too old to care, but others have lived only to see this day."

"What about my grandfather?" Obaseki asked.

Fuluke smiled. "Your grandfather is like the coconut; hard on the outside but inside, soft. He has never forgiven himself for banishing you. But he is not the one."

"Then who?"

Fuluke grinned. "You will know when you know." With that, Fuluke slowly faded away.

Obaseki shook his fist. "Why do you tease me this way? What is the purpose?"

He was answered by the murmur of the forest. His anger wasted, he dropped his head on his bundle and let sleep find its way into his eyes.

Obaseki awoke the next morning thankful the spirits allowed him a restful slumber. He ate and broke camp, wishing to be in the city before noon, before his grandfather made his processional. The farmland and forest gave way to the clutter of homes and huts that sprawled beyond the city walls. Soon he walked among others making their way to the city. As he drew nearer to Abo, he noticed this was no ordinary trek. Whole families were traveling together, baskets of food in their arms and balanced on their heads. A certain excitement flowed among the throng. This must be a special day, Obaseki thought. He searched his memory but could remember nothing significant for this day. But he'd been gone many years; some special event could have occurred on this day during those years. The excitement infected him as well. He found himself as anxious as the others, though his emotions were dulled by the reality of his purpose.

The dense crowd became sluggish as it neared the city. Obaseki noticed the guards upon the walls, a sign that did not bode well for him. If Abo was in a state of war, strangers such as himself would not be allowed beyond the first wall. At worst he might be questioned and his identity revealed. He slowed, contemplating his decision. There was no real need to go to Abo, business lay further south in Selike.

"You must go inside," Fuluke said, interrupting his thoughts. "What you seek is here."

"Have the ancestors made you their spokesman?" Obaseki whispered, knowing his teacher was invisible to those around him.

"You have," Fuluke replied. "The word of the spirits come in a way that receiver will accept."

"So you are not the spirit of my teacher," Obaseki said.

"I am Fuluke," his teacher replied. "I speak for those whom I serve."

"So my brother is coming to Abo?"

Fuluke smiled. "Your brother is here."

* * *

Ndoro and his party made good time, traversing the barren roads as fast as the night's light allowed. During the day they slept, hiding in the safety of the tents that obscured their identity. This was to be a secret meeting; Ndoro did not want his enemies to suspect an alliance between Selike and Abo. Such a threat would spur some type of pre-emptive action, and the Diaka were not ready to deal with such a situation so soon. Overall the trip was going well. The warriors were in good spirits and even Kenyetta seem to enjoy the rigors of the road.

Ndoro did not fare as well as the others. Since they set out for Abo, his sleep had been interrupted by strange dreams. In the beginning, they were incoherent visions dominated by a sense of foreboding. As the group came closer to Abo, the dreams took form, revealing images alien to him. He saw deserts, ruined cities and terrified faces, the carnage of war. He saw a magnificent city in the midst of sand, inhabited by an endless collage of people. One man hovered in the sky over them all, one man whose face he could not make out but whose image struck him with fear. He woke suddenly, his body wet with sweat, Kenyetta clinging onto his shoulder.

"My husband, was it the dream?" she asked.

He came to his feet and walked away with a flush of anger. Kenyetta followed.

"I have traveled many lands, fought many battles and conquered many people," he finally said. "But never have I felt the fear that I have during this journey."

Ndoro turned to his wife. "I have never cared much for the spirits. Those I knew who possessed such power abused it for their own purposes. But could it be the spirits are trying to send me a message?"

"Don't waste your time with the spirits," Kenyetta replied. "Many nights I poured libations to my ancestors, hoping they would deliver me from my tortured life. But I found freedom on my own, not through some medicine-priest's bones."

She took Ndoro's hand and pulled him to her. "Come, Shumba. I will drive away your dreams."

Ndoro was tempted, but not even Kenyetta's seductions could push away the feeling that rested in his heart.

"I must walk," he said, and left the tent.

The open air eased his mind. It felt good to move about in daylight. Small trees and shrubs intruded on the grasslands where they camped, a sign they were nearing the forest kingdom of Abo. Mixed herds of springbok, zebras and wildebeests grazed on the short grass while keeping their distance. Even the great simbas were careful not to get too close. They knew well the difference between ordinary men and Sesu, giving the latter much respect and a wide berth.

Ndoro climbed a small hill that hid a river on its western side. He clamored down the steep slope to the river's edge, startling a flock of ostriches that fled on his arrival. Looking about warily for predators, he knelt for a drink.

"Your life has always seen change in rivers," a familiar voice spoke.

Ndoro snatched his head about and was shocked by who stood in the river before him.

"Nakisisa?"

"I have returned, my friend and master," the river-beast said with a grin. He was in human form, nude but for a small loincloth around his waist. He showed no scars from that terrible night, a true sign Ndoro was speaking to a spirit. Suspicion put Ndoro on edge. Although the river-beast saved his life, he was still vengeful.

"The spirits have kept you well," Ndoro said.

"And the ancestors have smiled on you, Shumba." The river-beast stepped from the river. "And to think you were to be my meal."

Ndoro tensed. "Why have you returned?"

"The ancestors wish it so."

"Since when do they intrude on my life?" Ndoro replied. "I have no need for spirits, ancestors or otherwise. My destiny has been shaped by my shield and spear, not by some old ngoma throwing bones."

"But what of your dreams?" the river-beast asked.

"What do you know of my dreams?"

"Your dreams are clues to your destiny, hints of what the spirits wish you to become."

Nakisisa's eyes strayed from Ndoro. "Remember your destiny. The Diaka will march again soon, for the last time." He extended his hand, giving Ndoro a worn leather pouch. Ndoro took it warily then undid the straps. Inside was an emaciated ngwena paw.

"Do you remember?" Nakisisa asked.

"Of course I do," Ndoro replied as he closed the pouch.

"I belong to you once again," Nakisisa said. "If you summon me, I will come."

The river-beast disappeared into the rushing waters. Ndoro's bodyguards appeared soon afterward and found their leader in stunned silence.

The next morning the Sesu set out again. Ndoro rode quietly in his litter, his thoughts focused on Nakisisa's parting words. The Diaka would march one last time? The uneasiness he felt concerning the journey returned in full force.

The weak trees and sparse shrubs became more numerous as they traversed the savannah. Soon the forest towered before them, a green wall full of secrets. As they neared, Ndoro heard urgent voices. His warriors were immediately on guard. Raising their shields and assegais, they formed a sharp wall around Ndoro and Kenyetta. The voices died and their source emerged from the foliage. A man walked toward them wearing a white waist robe, his chest bare. Around his neck a rectangular gold bar hung, engraved with the symbols of his rank. In his right hand he carried a ceremonial sword, signifying him as an official messenger of the Oba of Mawenaland. He was flanked by four horsemen, two on each side. Men and horses were covered in kapok-quilted armor.

The two groups approached each other slowly, finally stopping a javelin's throw apart. The messenger continued to approach the Sesu. Ndoro motioned one of his warriors forward. The men met, exchanged words then the warrior returned.

"Great Shumba, these warriors were sent to escort you to Abo. They have extra beasts for you and the Great Wife."

"We will not ride," Ndoro replied. "I walk with my warriors."

Kenyetta whispered in her husband's ear. "Among the Mawena, the nobles always ride to show their status. Don't insult them with your arrogance."

Ndoro bristled at Kenyetta's words but yielded to her truth.

"Bring the animals. We shall ride into Abo as your custom, so long as they honor our customs when we arrive."

The warrior conveyed the message and the horses were brought forward. Kenyetta mounted easily, coming from a people who used animals frequently. Ndoro had some trouble but managed to retain his dignity by not falling completely off the beast.

On the messenger's signal the entourage proceeded into the thick forests, the path to Ndoro's dark future.

* * *

Obaseki found shelter in the Kossi section of Abo. He was surprised to see it still existed despite their treacherous attack. There was still nervousness in their manner; they seemed even more nervous around him.

He'd just finished his libations when he heard a shuffle behind him. He turned to see a Kossi, his eyes darting to him and then away.

"May I help you?" Obaseki inquired.

"Pardon my intrusion," the man replied. "I am Kanata, the keeper of the Kossi house. My brothers and I were curious to what a Tuareg was doing so far from the desert."

"The stories of the greatness of Abo have spread far," Obaseki replied. "I was curious, so I came to see for myself."

"Tuaregs don't just come to see," Kanata said. "They come to scout."

"As do the Kossi," Obaseki countered.

Kanata flashed a smile. "The Kossi have always recognized Abo for the jewel it is. Long ago we tried to make it ours."

The Kossi's words sat heavy on Obaseki's chest. Images of that terrible day emerged in his head, the lives lost because of his ignorant decision.

"I am here for my own reasons," Obaseki finally said. "Good day, Kanata."

The innkeeper left quickly. Obaseki followed close behind, eager to be away from his former enemies. The sights and smells of Abo awakened old memories and he fought the urge to weep. He had no idea how much he missed the city until that moment. He moved with the flow of the people, working his way to the market.

He had reason for visiting the marketplace. He knew sometimes his grandfather would visit it disguised as a common villager to spy on the mood of his people. Obaseki looked into the faces surrounding him, searching for a familiar smile or gesture. As he scanned the morass, he realized it was a foolish search. His grandfather was much older and probably left such things to his warriors. Still he found himself searching until a familiar voice caught his attention.

"Is it as you remembered?" Fuluke asked.

"It is," Obaseki replied. "It is beautiful."

"So it is fitting that your destiny is revealed here."

Obaseki wished to stop and confront the spirit of his master, but the gesture would draw attention. He continued to walk.

"What is my destiny?" he asked.

"You heard the words yourself," Fuluke replied. "With Moyo, two shall become one."

Obaseki stopped. "What do you mean?"

"With Moyo, you have the power to become what you were meant to be."

"Moyo is not here," Obaseki said.

Fuluke looked stunned. "You did not bring it?"

"Moyo serves its purpose in Yakubu," Obaseki replied. "It has brought only death to Abo."

Fuluke's face became solemn. "Then you will fail." He disappeared into the crowd.

He would not fail, Obaseki thought. The ancestors would not have sent him here to do so. Besides, Fuluke was not aware of his newfound abilities. He was a spirit, but he was not close to the ancestors.

His thoughts were pushed aside by the roar of drums. The throng at the market turned toward the sound and surged in its direction. Obaseki saw oba's warriors moving through the crowd in their red and yellow quilted uniforms, riding horses covered in matching quilted armor. Behind them his grandfather followed, surrounded by the elders. Obaseki pushed his way through, the hordes of Mawena giving way easily to the Tuareg stranger among them. The procession stopped at the center of the market. Obaseki still could not see but he knew by memory what was happening. His grandfather's retainers set his stool in place. He sat, flanked by ceremonial guards holding golden swords. Those with disputes would be brought before him one by one to have their disagreements settled. But as Obaseki neared the edge of the crowd, he saw this meeting was different. The entourage was larger; the guards more alert. He emerged from the crowd and was hit by a wave of emotions that nearly toppled him.

His grandfather sat in his stool, gray haired but regal. Standing behind him was a woman he did not recognize, but who apparently was important enough to hold such a place with his grandfather. The woman bent close to his grandfather to whisper and Obaseki immediately saw the resemblance. He was looking at his mother for the first time in his life, the woman he never knew. This was the secret Fuluke hinted at earlier. Only his grandfather would speak of her and then only briefly. Whatever she'd done to deserve such treatment had obviously been forgiven, for now she stood beside her father in the position as his advisor.

His grandfather rose from his stool and the multitude fell silent.

"Mawena, hear what is to be said. For many years I have been honored to be your oba, and I have done my best to rule in a way to bring prosperity to our lands. Today I have the privilege to bring you news of great importance. The Mawena have been offered the brotherhood of a neighboring people, a tribe whose blood once mixed with ours. Today, that bond is renewed. Today, the Sesu and Mawena are united again!"

The Mawena warriors parted, revealing a small group of Sesu warriors that came forward. Behind them walked the man Obaseki had seen only in his dreams. Ndoro strode to his grandfather, his simba headdress regal on his shoulders. Behind him followed his second, a man who though he wore the warrior's garb of the Sesu was surely not of the same blood. Ndoro addressed the crowd.

"I stand before you not as the inkosi of the Sesu, but as the grandson of Oba Noncemba, the son of your sister Shani. Within my veins the Sesu and the Mawena are one!"

Ndoro faced Noncemba. A retainer stepped forward to present the ceremonial unity sword to the most senior of the elders. The elder took the sword, walked to the pair and presented the hilt to them. Grasping the hilt together, Ndoro and Noncemba raised the blade over their heads. The market erupted with the roar of drums and shouts of approval as ceremonial dancers filled the streets to celebrate the reunion of the two powerful nations. As the crowd danced Obaseki saw his chance. He joined in, working his way slowly toward the royal entourage. The revelers were amused at the awkward Tuareg and made room, speeding his approach. Soon there was only a weak barrier of distracted bodyguards between him and his brother. He saw the woman who was his mother embrace Ndoro, a look of pride in her eyes. He had the privilege of her love, a realization that sparked unexpected anger in Obaseki. He summoned the power of Moyo and shoved the Sesu warriors away to either side, clearing a path to Ndoro. In an instant he lunged past the guards and sprang face to face with his brother. Pushing his mother aside, he reached into his robes and revealed the dagger. Ndoro looked puzzled, and then his eyes went to the knife. Obaseki lunged, the knife barely piercing Ndoro's skin before Ndoro grabbed his wrist. The touch struck both men like a blow. Obaseki fell back, the knife flying from his hand. Ndoro tumbled away, his flailing hands grasping Obaseki's face veil and pulling it free.

Obaseki struck the ground. He lay stunned, the faces above him looming like dark clouds, the bewildered look of his mother and grandfather mixed with the angry glares of the elders. They were suddenly pushed aside, replaced by the terrifying countenance of the man who stood by Ndoro. Obaseki saw a flash of metal and his abdomen burned. He yelled and struck out with his right hand, the force lifting the man into the air and flinging him into the crowd. Obaseki fell into darkness as he was dragged away, the silence replaced by the clanging of metal and angry shouts. He was lifted, dropped and lifted again. Anxious hands carried him swiftly then placed him on what seemed to be a camel. He jolted as the beast ran, his consciousness spinning down into a vortex of blackness. Before the darkness swallowed him, he heard a familiar voice.

"I have you, Moyo," El-Fatih said. "I will take you home."

18

Abo's marketplace spun in chaos. The crowd was in full panic, fearing the Tuaregs had used their time of celebration to invade the city. People fled to their homes while angry Sesu and Mawena warriors darted among the throng looking for any remaining camel men. The oba's guards formed a solid wall of kapok, shields and swords around the royal entourage as the war drums summoned the army.

The turmoil that prevailed outside the ring of warriors flourished inside as well. Ndoro was surrounded by faces and hands, his ears clogged by desperate questions and the wailing of women. His wound was painful but he'd suffered much worse in battle. What gripped him was the sensation when his hand grasped his brother's. For an instant it seemed he was stabbing himself, as if he held the knife meant to bring him death. He shut his eyes, shaking his head violently to rid himself of the image.

Three healers managed to work their way to him, covering his wounds with herbs and mouthing chants to soothe any angry spirits wishing to see him dead. Ndoro shoved them away and struggled to his feet.

Noncemba sat on his stool, his head cradled in his hands. Beside him Shani knelt weeping. The elders surrounded them, their voices forming an incessant chatter.

"Leave us," he ordered.

"This is the second time your brother has brought evil to this city," one of the elders said.

"He is determined to see Abo destroyed," another said.

"My son is not evil!" Shani shouted at them all. "No child from my womb could be so vile."

"Maybe the Sesu were right," a third elder commented. "Maybe the twins should have been..." The priest stopped, realizing who stood among them. Ndoro felt the rage of his past swelling in his chest.

"Leave us now or forfeit your lives, old men," he growled. The elders scattered into the crowd. Ndoro watched them disappear, and then stood before his grandfather.

"Why does my brother want me dead?" he asked.

"Who knows what is in his mind?" Noncemba replied. "His thoughts don't belong to him."

"What are you talking about?" Ndoro asked.

Noncemba raised his head, his face stained with tears. "Obaseki was trained to be a medicine-priest. His teacher Fuluke claimed he was special since he was born a twin. Reluctantly I allowed this, for it seemed to be his calling."

Noncemba straightened, regaining his regal stance. "Then the Kossi attacked. We charged out to drive them back and were surrounded. Obaseki pulled out the mayembe and unleashed a terrible spirit he could not control. It killed anyone in its path, Mawena and Kossi alike. After the Kossi were driven away, the elders met to decide Obaseki's fate. Many of them lost family to the spirit and wanted it destroyed and Obaseki banished. The decision was made; Obaseki could remain in Abo if he gave up the mayembe Moyo. If not, he was banished."

"And he left," Ndoro finished.

"I did not think he would. But I'm sure the spirit of the mayembe possessed him by then. He went to Ifana, the city of spirits. It was too late to save him."

"When a man is possessed there is only one way to drive out the evil," Ndoro said.

"Why must death always follow my sons?" Shani said. "How can you stand before me and talk of Sesu ways, Ndoro? Sesu ways condemned you to death as well! You forget so easily, my son."

Ndoro became angry despite the recent reunion with his mother. "He tried to kill me! He brought death to your city and disgraced your traditions and you ask me why I mention Sesu ways? The demon can only be driven out by death."

"As it was to be driven out of you?" Shani retorted. "Do I speak to Ndoro, or the demon that wishes to kill its own brother? Maybe you both are lost to evil!" Shani fell to her knees, letting out a moan that seemed to come from the inside of her bones.

The despair of that sound drained Ndoro's anger and he knelt beside his mother, embracing her with his massive arms.

"Mama, during my childhood you and Jelani were the only people to show me love. When I thought I was a man, I ignored you to gain the attention of my father. But during my life your love has kept me alive."

"I don't want to see you suffer again, but know this. You do not speak to a demon; you speak to your son. I believe though, Obaseki is no longer your son. He has lost his spirit to Moyo. We must stop him."

"Yes, we must," Noncemba agreed. "We must destroy this spirit inside him and hope we can rescue Obaseki's soul. Abo and Selike are not safe until we do."

Shani glared at Ndoro and Noncemba.

"I saved my son's life so he could be killed by his brother," she said.

Noncemba let out a breath. "Didn't you hear me? A demon's soul possesses Obaseki!"

Shani looked past Noncemba to Ndoro. "Remember your past, son. You are not so mighty to change that."

She came to her feet then staggered away. Her words were meant to hurt, and they did. Ndoro pushed the pain aside, making room for a feeling he thought he'd never experience again. The spark of hatred he thought disappeared with the fall of Selike flared, kindled by the face of his twin, Obaseki.

"Grandfather, this is the time for the Mawena, the Sesu and the Diaka to come together as one. The evil that once was my brother must be destroyed!"

* * *

The Tuaregs rode throughout the day and night, stopping long enough to rest their animals and tend their wounds. They hoped to take advantage of the chaos in Abo to put a safe distance between themselves and the city. They were well into the desert before they stopped for a full rest.

El-Fatih knelt before the pool at the oasis, removed his veil and splashed his face with the warm water. They were home now, safe in the domain they mastered. After cleansing himself, he went to the tent of the medicine-priest. Obaseki lay before the old man, his eyes closed and skin ashen. Only the slight heaving of his chest gave any indication that he was still alive. El-Fatih despaired as he looked upon the savior of his people. Obaseki never liked being thought of as a god, but the fact was most of the people of Yakubu considered him so. They came to the city for his healing and protection, but they and all their ancestors could not protect him.

"How is he?" El-Fatih asked.

"Not good," the medicine-priest replied. "He is very close to the Zamani. The spirits are gathering to celebrate his arrival."

El-Fatih looked about the tent although he did not have the eyes of a medicine priest.

"I don't understand his condition. His wound is not so terrible."

The priest stood, wringing his hands. "I cannot save him. He must save himself."

"We must get him back to the city," El-Fatih announced. "Moyo can heal him."

From that day on, El-Fatih allowed little rest on their journey to Yakubu. The Tuaregs recalled their nomadic ways, jumping from oasis to oasis, avoiding those claimed by their enemies, the Bedouins. Still, despite their carefulness, there were clashes with roving bands of nomads. The Tuaregs finished them mercilessly despite their fatigue.

After three weeks the fertile plateau of Yakubu loomed before them. The Tuaregs picked up the pace, energized by the sight of their homeland. El-Fatih was particularly uplifted. The sooner they returned Obaseki to Moyo, the sooner his strange sickness would be broken. Outriders met them at the outskirts of the Low Town. Bringing their camels together at El-Fatih's instructions, they hid Obaseki from the crowds that packed the narrow streets, the dust stirred like a sandstorm by countless feet. They were soon met by El-Fatih's second, Hussein, and the city guard.

"Did you find him?" Hussein asked anxiously.

"Yes, I found him, but I cannot save him," El-Fatih replied. He gestured to the litter holding Obaseki between two camels.

"Then it will be worse," Hussein prophesized.

"What do you mean?"

"The people suspect Moyoseki is gone. They ask for his presence and his healing. Many are threatening to leave."

"Let them," El-Fatih growled. "Yakubu is a Tuareg city. Moyo is our protector, not theirs. Besides, if they can survive the desert crossing to Zimfara, they will not survive Shumba."

The two men looked as the crowd came closer, almost too close.

"Hussein, clear a path to the palace," El-Fatih ordered. "We must get him to Moyo as soon as possible."

Hussein spun his camel about with a jerk of the reins. He took out his horsetail swatter and struck at the throng, his men repeating his actions.

"Hai! Hai! Make way!" he shouted. The human flow separated and El-Fatih's party rambled through the gauntlet of onlookers, up the narrow climb to the summit of the plateau. As the walls of the palace came into view El-Fatih raised his banner and the gates swung open. When they reached the second wall its gate was open as well, their arrival signaled ahead. Eshe appeared from the palace, running as fast as her garments would allow, her attendants struggling to keep pace.

"Did you find him?" Eshe's voice was strained and almost unfamiliar to El-Fatih. He nodded his head and the camel bearing Obaseki came forward. Eshe's servants quickly surrounded the camel, taking great care as they removed Obaseki. They rushed him to the palace temple where a bed had been hastily prepared. El-Fatih and Eshe followed, the queen clinging to El-Fatih's arm.

"What happened? Why is he like this?" she demanded.

"We followed him to Abo," El-Fatih replied.

Eshe's eyes widened. "Abo?"

El-Fatih nodded. "He went to kill a man who looked just like him."

"Oya protect us!" Eshe exclaimed. "I didn't know he was hurting so much. He knew his grandfather had no choice but to banish him."

"This was no old man," El-Fatih corrected. "This man was a warrior, an oba in his own right."

"The evil one in his dreams," Eshe whispered.

"Moyoseki tried to stab him, but one of his warriors stepped in the way and struck Moyoseki with his assegai." El-Fatih's head sagged as he hid his eyes from Eshe.

"I was not swift enough to prevent the first blow. We rescued him and fled the city. He is not dead, but he is not alive."

They entered the temple. The room was brightly lit with torches and candles; the smell of incense and offerings heavy in the air. The servant placed Obaseki on the bed and stepped away. Eshe approached, touching his face lightly as tears ran down her face.

"Seki, please don't leave me," she pleaded. "I am not ready to respect your memory." She kissed his cheek, and then laid her head on his chest, her arms embracing his still form.

* * *

Obaseki sensed Eshe's warmth and reached out for her with arms that would not move. He was a prisoner in his own body. He suffered every jostle and bump during the hard ride back to Yakubu, heard the whispers of the men speculating on his death, the questions to El-Fatih of why he was being so foolish bringing a corpse back to the city, god or not. Obaseki expected such doubts, learning early in his life not to trust the faith of men. But his heart ached, for the ancestors had abandoned him, even after he had attempted to do what was asked of him.

"You did not do what was asked of you," Fuluke answered, his spirit standing behind Eshe.

"You can hear me?" he asked.

"You are among us now. Of course I can hear you."

"So I am dead," Obaseki stated.

"No," Fuluke replied. "Your destiny has not been fulfilled. You will have another chance."

"How?"

Fuluke gave Obaseki his familiar knowing smile. "You will see your brother again. Of this, I am sure."

* * *

The rainy season came early to the borderlands of the Sahel, announcing its arrival with thin gray clouds and gentle rains. The Mawena army, farmers as well as soldiers, left the ranks of the oba to plant their fields. It was because of this that

Ndoro could expect support from his new ally for his latest campaign. It was of little consequence; the Diaka had always marched alone. They would, however, have the added manpower of the Sesu. Their warriors were full of themselves of late, the celebration drums still playing for the victory against the Ndogo. What had begun as a swift strike to establish the boundaries between the two tribes became a rout. The neophyte warriors returned to Selike not only with victory, but also with the promise of tribute from Ndogoland. The Sesu had proven themselves as equals to the Diaka, and Jawanza proved himself worthy of Ndoro's appointment as Shumba.

The Simba of Diakaland stepped out of his royal palace and gazed upon his umuzi. The massive enclosure spanned from the edge of the thorn fence cattle enclosure to the stone wall surrounding the base of hill. Below him rested thousands of Diaka warriors camped outside the stone enclosure wall prepared to march. His indunas gathered before the gate, their leopard skins and headdress distinguishing them from the others. In the lead stood Jawanza, proudly wearing the simba mane given to him by Ndoro. Ndoro felt the burning in his chest, the fire that had fueled him all his life. His hand reached down to rub the scar inflicted by his brother, another notch on his assegai of revenge.

He sauntered to where the throng could see him. Immediately the air shook with the chant of his name.

"Shumba! Shumba! Shumba!"

Ndoro raised his assegai and stabbed at the air with the rhythm of the chant, the volume rising with each jab. Drummers joined in, and the warriors danced, falling into song they knew well.

Ndoro danced with them, his body surging with his newfound spirit. The purpose that had been missing since he gained the Stool of Sesu returned, rekindled by the demon that possessed his brother. The fire was back in his eyes, Jawanza said, and he was right.

As the warriors danced, the people of Selike joined in, the women's high-pitched voices ringing joyously with the deep serious tone of the men'. Children ran among the celebrants, singing exuberantly with the others.

Ndoro planned his last campaign during the previous rainy season. Mawena and Sesu merchant spies had fanned out across the forestlands, the Sahel and the Mahgreb, asking questions among various cities about the man Obaseki and his city of Tuaregs. The answers led them north across Mahgreb to Zimfara. From there the interlopers plunged into the desert in search of Yakubu, the home of Obaseki and his demon mayembe.

Ndoro danced vigorously as he contemplated what he had to do. The image of his brother tormented his nights, waking him with sweaty chills. It was unnatural to have to kill a brother, despite the possession. Kenyetta suggested he send Jawanza to lead the campaign and spare himself the conflict. But this was something he had to do. There must be no doubt of Obaseki's death. The only way to insure it was to do it himself.

What if he was wrong? Shani's words cut deep, the doubts she planted growing like weeds in his mind. If there was any chance of him being wrong about his brother, he would not carry out his obligation. Inside he hoped time would prove him wrong.

Shani was unaware of the conflict in Ndoro's mind. Soon after her son selected the merchants to seek out Obaseki, Shani met with each one, offering a small fortune to insure that she would hear any word of her son before it was given to Noncemba and Ndoro. She cried with joy when the existence of Zimfara and Yakubu was confirmed; her dances were for her own reasons. The day after the news she prepared for her departure from Selike. Thembile still attended her, though at her age there was little she could do but be good company. But she was loyal, so when Shani revealed her intention to see the son she never knew, Thembile set about making the desire a reality.

The rainy season unleashed its downpours while Shani was still traveling. She rode in a covered cart, a ragged thing that smelled of goat and amplified each bump of the battered road with bone-jarring efficiency. Her traveling companions, Kossi merchants headed for Zimfara, walked beside the cart. They seemed impervious to the constant drizzle, their heads protected by their white turbans. Mingled with them were the bodyguards Thembile hired to protect her on the long journey. Shani was skeptical at first, unwilling to put her life in the hands of people not bound to her by loyalty and servitude. Thembile assured her the Blood Men were people of their word, known throughout Uhuru for their honesty and fighting skills. Using members of the royal guard would have revealed her intentions to others, for everyone knew there were no secrets in a royal household.

The group finally came across a modest trade village. The Kossi took refuge from the rain with their livestock in the stables; Shani and her entourage went to the hostel, the largest building in the village. The proprietor was happy for their visit, for travelers were rare during the rains. Pleased to be out of the rain, Shani fell onto the straw cot in her room as if it was the finest bed in Uhuru. She changed into dry clothes and lay on her back, refusing to rise. The knock on her door startled her; she quickly finished dressing and found the knife concealed in her bags before answering.

"Who is it?" she asked.

"Dike of the Blood Men."

Shani cracked open the door, revealing the hard face of Dike. Thembile introduced him as the leader of the bodyguards, the one to speak to when necessary. The others were not to be addressed directly. Though his face was always set in a frown, his eyes conveyed a gentleness that brought trust. Shani agreed to hire them for that reason.

"Queen Mother, may I enter?"

Shani opened the door and stepped away. Dike entered, ducking under the doorframe and sitting on the floor cross-legged before her. He placed his sword across his exposed legs, and then gave Shani a curious look.

"Is this man you seek worth your life?" he asked.

Dike's question made Shani nervous. She gripped the hilt of her knife tighter.

"He is my son," she replied. "He is worth everything."

Dike smiled with his eyes. "Then the priestess was true to give us to you."

Shani was confused. "What priestess?"

Dike's eyes shifted to puzzlement. "Thembile did not tell you? Forgive me, Queen Mother, I thought you were aware. The Blood Men do not accept employment from just anyone, not even nobles such as you. Money is accepted only to hear a petition for our protection. The plea is heard by our priestess, who consults the spirits for her decision. If she decides the person needs our protection, then we accept the task."

Shani relaxed and sat on her cot. "I am grateful your priestess thought me worthy."

"Do not feel this way," Dike replied. "If our priestess granted our help, it is because your life is in great danger."

Shani's breath became short. "In danger from what?"

Dike eyes smiled again. "I do not know, but don't worry, Queen Mother. The Blood Men are sworn to protect you to death, and we do not die easily." He nodded his head. "Sleep now, Queen Mother. You need your rest for tomorrow's journey."

Dike turned around in his sitting position, his face toward the door. He meant to stay in the room with Shani, with his men outside her door. Thembile made the right choice, she realized. She lay down on her cot and quickly fell to sleep, feeling the safety of a child.

She awoke to chaos. Dike held her shoulders with his hard scarred hands, shaking her as gently as he could.

"Queen Mother! Queen Mother! We must leave!"

Shani cleared her head and became aware of the danger. "What is happening?"

"Slavers are raiding the inn. They have not reached this floor yet, but there is only one way out." Dike removed the leather strips from the blades of his wrist knives and unsheathed his sword.

"Come. My men are waiting." Dike opened the door to the confusion outside. The other bodyguards stood blocking the door, dead Kossi at their feet. Dike took his place before his men and they proceeded down the stairs. They made it to the main floor before the slavers saw them. Shani tensed, expecting a charge, but the slavers moved away. Their scowls did not hide the truth in their eyes. They knew the Blood Men and were afraid.

Outside the hostel, the city burned. Black smoke billowed from burning huts and filled the streets, stinging Shani's eyes. Dike led them through the melee, crouching low to see through the smoke. He raised his hands and they stopped.

"Queen Mother, stay behind my men. Grab onto the arm of the man closest to you and do not let go."

Shani locked her hands about the stout arm of the nearest Blood Man. She stumbled as they ran, the confusion accented with the ringing of clashing steel and the grunts of struggling men. All around her people fled, fought and died. She stumbled again, almost falling; the Blood Man jerked her over the body of a dead child. Behind her she heard urgent shouts. The Kossi gained nerve in numbers, approaching the Blood Man, their eyes fixed on Shani. The Blood Man halted and turned in the direction of the voices.

"Queen Mother, there are too many. You must flee, while we fight to keep you safe. There is no one between you and the forest. You must hide."

Shani was terrified. "How will you find me?"

The Blood Man looked at her intensely. "I will find you, Queen Mother. Now please, go."

Shani let go of the arm and ran to the forest. The other Blood Men rushed past her and joined their brother. She turned her head to see the Blood Men charging a horde of slavers, swinging their swords over their heads. The odds were impossible, she thought. They should have run with her. Suddenly feeling exposed, she jumped into the cover of the forest. All around her people fled the village. Men, women and children scattered among the trees, desperate to escape the slavers. Shani ran and then stopped. She was exhausted and she needed to rest, if just for a moment. She found a tangle of brush and thorn and forced her way into it, ignoring the scratches and pricks. She closed her eyes, wishing away the pain in her body and the fear in her heart, concentrating on Obaseki. She held in her mind the glimpse of his face the day he attacked Ndoro. They were true twins, identical in almost every way. She wondered had he suffered after being banished from Abo, if he and the woman he fled with had children. The thought of being a grandmother brought a smile to her face despite the imminent danger about her.

"Queen Mother?"

Shani recognized the voice of Dike and emerged from her hiding place. Ten Blood Men had come with her from Abo; seven stood with her in the bush. Those remaining showed wounds that bloodied their garments, their chests heaving.

"We must travel through the bush for a few days," he said.

"The slavers will be looking for us," she replied.

For the first time since their journey, Dike smiled. "There are no more slavers here but there may be others on the road. We will move through the trees until it is safe."

They set out again. Shani didn't ask Dike how they would know which direction to follow in the thick brush. The Blood Men possessed skills she'd hardly imagined. She promised she would reward Thembile generously when she returned to Abo. As the sun faded into the shadows of the forest, Dike and his men set up camp, building a small hut for Shani to spend the night. It was well constructed; the thatch roof blocked the rain and the walls were embedded deep enough into the ground to prevent the seepage of water. Such a structure had taken time, too much for the Blood Men to build protection for themselves. As Shani watched them prepare for a night in the forest, she realized they had no intentions in building another shelter. Those not chosen for the first watch piled thick stacks of brush and leaves to lie on, then covered their bodies with their shields. The others positioned themselves about the camp, disappearing into the forest as they took watch, motionless in the rainy, moonless night.

The morning brought no end to the rain. Despite their best efforts, the water eventually seeped into Shani's hut; she awoke in wet clothes and with a deep cough. She covered herself as best she could before entering the downpour. The Blood Men were awake, sitting about the camp apparently waiting for her to emerge from her shelter. Dike saw her and nodded his approval. He came to her and offered her a yam with a strip of dried meat. She accepted eagerly, realizing at that moment how hungry she was.

She was almost done with the yam when she began to cough again, this time a grating cough that hurt her chest. Dike was at her side immediately, his hand to her forehead.

"You are burning," he said, his voice grave. "We must get you to a healer."

"I am fine," she answered, then coughed so violently she dropped the yam.

Dike gathered the men about him with a jerk of his hand. "The Queen Mother is sick. We must get her to the nearest town quickly. We will have to take the road."

A serious look passed among them. Taking the road meant exposing themselves to the Kossi.

"We must be diligent," Dike warned. "Do not be unaware. You will kill us all."

Shani swayed then fell. She stared upward, her head spinning, the image of Dike above her. Her stomach churned and she convulsed, spewing the food she'd just eaten onto herself.

Dike's voice penetrated her weakness and found her ears. "Queen Mother, please be still. You are very sick. We are . . ."

Another voice came to her, the voice of Cheelo, the man who led her from the city.

"Dike, look!"

She felt a tug on her leg and heard Dike curse. His face reappeared, distorted by her pain. He grabbed her chin and forced her mouth open. His hand appeared, holding a small brown pouch. He tilted the pouch and a white liquid poured into her mouth. It went too deeply and choked her, but Dike clamped his hands around her mouth and would not let her spit it out. The vile liquid burned its way through her body, her screams muffled by Dike's strong hands.

"Cheelo!" she heard him call out. "Take two men into the village and bring back a cart and a donkey if you can find one." His eyes came back to Shani.

"You were wounded by a poison arrow that struck your ankle. I can't stop the poison; I can only slow it down."

He smiled as best he could. "There is another village ahead. Maybe there will be a healer that can help you."

Shani's ears exploded with sound. She turned her head toward the source and saw Cheelo with the cart and a donkey. She rose like a petal in the wind as the Blood Men placed her carefully into the cart, her body cushioned by dry straw and blankets.

"Do not die, Queen Mother," Dike urged. "You have yet to see your son."

But Shani was already drifting away, the dim light of the cloudy sky fading into a dense and empty darkness. She felt isolated, like a leaf floating still on a lake. Silence surrounded her; she could hear her breathing and feel her chest moving, but as hard as she tried she could not stand. Then she felt something else, a twinge of familiarity that blossomed into rush of joy.

"Obaseki!" she exclaimed.

"Mama!" he replied.

A faint light appeared in the distance. She began to rise, but felt an unseen force holding her down.

"Please stay where you are, mama," Obaseki said. "I must come to you."

The light grew brighter as it neared. Shani found the strength to stand, squinting to see her son come into view, a smile gracing his face.

"My son, my son," she cried. "I should have never sent you away!"

Obaseki embraced her. She felt his warm tears on her unseen shoulders.

"You saved my life," Obaseki said. "Now I must save yours."

Shani stepped back from her son. "You are too late. I know where I am. Are you dead as well?"

"No. We are both still alive."

"So where are we?"

"We are between worlds. You are very sick. The poison was discovered late, but I will not let you die."

"Do you possess such power?"

Obaseki smiled. "I am no demon, mama. I am only a son that loves the mother he never knew. I will not let you be taken away from me."

Shani fell to her knees, her shoulders shaking with silent sobs. "I should not have sent you away. I could have protected you."

"Dingane would not allow it. Mulugo had spoken; if I had not stayed with Grandfather, Ndoro and I would both be dead."

Hearing her former husband's name stilled her tears. "Is he here?"

"Of course he is," Obaseki replied. "But some spirits do not linger near the living. When their time among the living is done, they move quickly to the Zamani. Even the memories of their loved ones cannot hold them. Baba was such a spirit."

"Even in death he is never satisfied," Shani commented. "I am content here. I don't wish to go back"

Obaseki looked at his mother with pleading eyes. "You must go back. Your journey is not complete. You must be present when the time comes."

Shani looked at her son, a glimmer of understanding in her eyes. "The ancestors have a purpose for you both. I can see that now. You are true meji, and you are my sons."

She stood in the darkness and placed her hand on Obaseki's face. "I will go back. I'll return to Abo and wait for you to call me."

"I love you, mama," Obaseki whispered. He kissed her on her cheek and Shani opened her eyes to bright light.

"She comes back to us!" Dike exclaimed. He hovered over her as before, but now there were others smiling around her. A woman with a calming expression placed a hand on her head.

"I wish I could say this was my doing," she said to Dike. "She was too close to death for anything I could have done." She grasped Shani's hand and squeezed. "Thank your ancestors for your life."

"No, I thank my son." Shani sat up in the bed and looked about. The Blood Men gathered about her in a splendid room, furnished with items alien to her, yet beautiful. The cloths decorating the wall spoke of travels to different lands, places far beyond Uhuru.

"Our guest awakens," someone said. A tall woman appeared before them, dressed in fabrics that shone like water covering her from her shoulders to the floor. Her face bore no tribal scars, her hair braided and bound. Her features were sharp and severe like the buckra folk she'd seen on occasion, but her skin spoke Uhuru.

"I am Tadalesh Badebo. Welcome to my home."

"Thank you for your kindness," Shani replied.

"Your protectors say you seek your son. If your son is truly Obaseki of Yakubu, then it is I who should be thanking you."

"Your son is Moyoseki?" the healer exclaimed, her eyes wide. She fell to her knees before Shani. "Then it was he who saved you."

"Then you know where he is," Dike said.

"Of course." Tadalesh gave Dike a sly smile then sat beside Shani. "The presence of Obaseki's mother in my house can be nothing but good for my family. I could not let this opportunity pass."

Dike's face contorted into a snarl. "You risked the life of the Queen Mother for your blessing?" His hand went to his sword.

"Dike, no," Shani said. "This woman, for whatever her intentions, took us in. I don't think my son would want to see her killed."

Shani stood, her balance unsure. "Dike, we leave tomorrow. We will return to Abo."

Dike looked at Shani oddly but said nothing.

Tadalesh's face took on a look of dread. "You are leaving? What of your journey? You wish to see Obaseki. He is across the desert in the Tuareg city of Yakubu. I could raise a caravan to take you to him. Of course, I would accompany you to guarantee your safe passage to his city."

"I have seen my son. Now is not the time for us to meet. That day will come."

Shani walked toward the door. Tadalesh stood in her way, and Dike's hand again went to his sword.

"Please, Queen Mother," she said desperately. "There is no reason for you to leave today. The Kossi may be still about. Stay here in my house and rest before your long journey home. You are a noble guest and will receive noble treatment."

Shani thought on Tadalesh's offer. She did not want to go back to Abo, not as it was before her journey. Ndoro was there, planning his campaign, and the helplessness she felt in preventing him from attacking Obaseki was what drove her away. Nor could she travel to Yakubu. Obaseki warned her it was not the time.

"We will accept your offer, Tadalesh. I will stay until the dry season begins."

Tadalesh smiled and tears came to her eyes. "Thank you, Queen Mother!"

Shani turned her attention to Dike and his men. "You have performed your duty well, Blood Men. Dike, please bring me my saddle bag."

Shani reached into the leather bag and pulled out a smaller leather pouch. "Here is the remaining payment."

Dike shook his head. "The Queen Mother has not returned to Abo. Our duty does not end until you arrive there."

Shani smiled with relief. She hoped Dike would answer so. She was tired, too tired to travel soon, but she was wary of Tadalesh.

"Can you provide care for my bodyguards?" she asked the matron.

"Of course, you are all welcomed." Tadalesh turned to the door and called out in a language unknown to Shani, and immediately servants appeared. They picked up the possessions of the Blood Men and hurried away. All the guards left except Dike.

"I stay with you, Queen Mother."

"Of course," Shani replied.

"Is this fine with you, Tadalesh?"

"It is your will, Queen Mother," Tadalesh replied, her head bowed.

"Good. Now, if you don't mind, I would like some time alone."

Tadalesh smiled, bowed, and then left the room, a skip in her step.

"I don't trust her," Dike said.

"She is a strange one," Shani agreed. "But I think her heart is good."

Dike nodded his head, a faraway look in his eyes. "You wish to stay until the dry season."

"Yes."

"You are waiting for Ndoro."

Shani looked away from Dike. "Yes. I could not stop him in Abo. Maybe I can stop him here. The Obaseki I saw was no demon. He was no more possessed than Ndoro was when he escaped Selike."

Dike sat cross-legged on the floor before Shani. "Our priestess tells us that your sons are involved in a great struggle, one that will change Uhuru. The spirits tell her this."

Shani was surprised. This was something new, a fact Dike had hidden from her until now. She felt cold inside as she looked at the leader of her bodyguards, a realization slowly forming in her mind.

"Why did you decide to protect me?" she asked.

"To keep you from harm, Queen Mother."

"Harm from whom?"

Dike let out a sigh, his shoulders heaving with some invisible burden. "Our priestess says what will happen between your sons must happen. They were born meji for a reason. No one must block the path before them. Even Obaseki knows this."

Shani sprang from her bed. "So what am I, your prisoner?"

Dike stood before her. For the first time since leaving Abo she feared this man.

"No harm will come to you, Queen Mother, but it is essential that you do not interfere. We will stay with Tadalesh until events take their course."

Shani managed a desperate smile. She had one chance left.

"And what will you do when Ndoro comes? What will you tell him?"

"I will tell him that I have done as he asked."

Shani felt the energy drain from her body. She sat hard on the bed, grasping her head. The ancestors were still punishing her for some unknown sin, some error she'd committed to bring their wrath. Her sons would die knowing each other as enemies. With nothing left inside her, she fell into the cushions of the bed and cried.

19

The rainy season finally ended in Sesuland, the constant drizzles and downpours diminishing into hazy sunshine. Throughout the city, people darted about with anxious energy. The dry season was the time of war and the Sesu were ready to march. Under the leadership of Ligongo, Sesuland suffered too many years of peace for a people whose boys graduated into manhood through battle. So many had already passed their prime; their sulking faces visible in the throng lining the wide avenues on that hot day. But those who could march knew of no prouder moment. Not only were they going to war, but they would carry the banner of Shumba Ndoro, their true inkosi.

Ndoro's mind was on other concerns. He sat before his grandfather, watching him as he paced the floor and occasionally cast an angry glance at his grandson. Ndoro shrugged inwardly; apparently his secret was exposed. No doubt it was Thembile who told; she was the only one outside his circle aware of his plan, but she did not have all the details. Shani's handmaiden agreed to help him because she feared Obaseki more than she feared Ndoro. The Mawena entourage arrived during the night, Noncemba accompanied by his bodyguards and a host of noble cavalry. It was a show of force, an example of his anger. With twenty thousand warriors camped about the city ready for the march, the Mawena force was a weak show at best.

Noncemba stopped pacing and sat hard. He glared at Ndoro and motioned as if he was going to rise again.

"You are truly Dingane's son," he said, the tone in his voice making it plain his statement was not a compliment.

"Your own mother!" he exclaimed. "You made your mother a prisoner!"

"She is not being held prisoner," Ndoro replied calmly despite being irritated by Noncemba's words. "She is being detained until I have a chance to deal with Obaseki."

"Don't play with words before me," Noncemba roared. "Whatever you may think, Shani is your mother and my daughter. If she took it upon herself to warn Obaseki of your coming then so be it. Nothing you have planned is worth the humiliation you've caused."

Though Ndoro respected his grandfather, he was not about to be handled like a child.

"You forget yourself, grandfather," he replied. "Outside this city are twenty thousand Diaka and Sesu warriors. That is an example of the respect you should give me."

Noncemba eyes widened. "You wouldn't dare!"

"Would I?" Ndoro rose to his feet. "I have spent my entire life fighting to be where I am today. No one—not you, not mama—has shared my burden. I've earned every ounce of respect due to my own decisions, and I will not let anyone block my way."

Noncemba's anger drained from his face. He looked solemnly at the floor, his words low and melancholy.

"I do not know what stands before me. Since the day you both were born, the world has seemed askew, as if your lives have disturbed some type of balance. Everyone around you has tried to understand this."

Noncemba stood to leave. "Do what you wish. I have not the strength or the will to stop you. Whatever I believe about Obaseki, I don't approve of what you did to my daughter. The Mawena will not march with you. This revenge you must accomplish on your own."

Ndoro burned inside with Noncemba's refusal. "On my own as always. But understand me, grandfather. I once asked my indunas which kingdom posed the biggest threat to Sesuland, and the answer was Mawenaland. I have not forgotten their advice."

Ndoro watched Noncemba storm away. He waited until the Mawena were well on their way to Abo before hurrying through the palace and out of the city to his encampment beside the shaded banks of the Kojo River. Hundreds of grass huts were scattered among the acacias, Diaka and Sesu warriors moving restlessly among them. As Ndoro passed, the warriors fell to their knees, sprinkling their heads with dirt. Ndoro ignored their supplication, his eyes focused on his council tent. He burst into it, finding Jawanza and his generals sitting in a circle around a large leather map.

"Jawanza, break camp," he ordered. "We march today."

"What of the Mawena?"

Ndoro closed his eyes as his anger surged to his head, threatening to boil over.

"The Mawena choose not to join us."

Jawanza smiled. "We cannot leave an enemy behind us."

"Mawenaland is still our ally," Ndoro conceded. "They will not interfere with our march. Prepare the men. We leave at nightfall."

Jawanza issued the order to mobilize. The combined army was an impressive sight, the martial amalgamation of different cultures joined for the purpose of conquest. Each unit maintained the uniform of its people but they all wore the head ring of the Diaka, the symbol of their loyalty to Ndoro. The tents were taken down and stored on the support wagons with the provisions. There would be intervals where the army could live off the land, but the provisions provided an assurance of uninterrupted marching. Merchants had been sent ahead during the rainy season, loaded down with gold and other rare items found in the forests of Tacumaland, their task to set up outposts in strategic sites along the route that would serve as bivouac areas when the army needed rest. It was a well-thought-out plan that would succeed with or without the help of the Mawena.

Sesubu lined the avenues of Selike awaiting the departure of the army. Excitement pulsed through everyone, resulting in the constant singing of the women in the throng and the incessant beating of drums. Ndoro watched from his palace as his army formed ranks; Tacuma archers and skirmishers at the front, neophyte Sesu warriors at the center, and the seasoned Diaka at the rear. The ranks stood five wide and stretched beyond the city limits.

Jawanza appeared at his side. "We are ready, Shumba."

"Then let us end this," Ndoro replied. With Jawanza's assistance he donned his simba headdress, strapped on his body armor and wrist knife, and then took up his shield and assegai. Ndoro strode from his room and his indunas fell in step behind him, making their way through the palace and onto the grounds. He exited the palace and saw Kenyetta, surrounded by his servants and his adopted wives. She flashed him a wicked smile, and then with a soulful cry began the traditional wailing. The other wives joined her, striking themselves and pulling at their hair, the expression of losing their husband to war. Ndoro responded in stoic ignorance, walking past them to the mud brick path leading to the royal avenue. His wives followed, making sure the rest of the city knew of his coming. Upon seeing their inkosi descending the path, the Sesubu responded the opposite of the wives. The city exploded with drumming and joyous voices. Everyone danced; women, children, men, the young and the old rejoicing the return of Sesu glory. The army took up the chant, swaying side to side with the rhythm of the drummers, beating their weapons against their shields and the ground. Ndoro felt the rhythm of his people in his heart and knew that this was his destiny. He halted before his army, observing the entire city in synchronized motion, and wished that he could die that day. An arduous path lay before him; the outcome uncertain. He knew this was the true path he was meant to take. Every moment of his life had prepared him for this day. He forgave his father, fari Biton, and all those who caused suffering in his life. They were teachers, their hard lessons essential for the role he now stood to play. He raised his assegai, turning slowly as he spread his gaze over the city. He turned and took up the warrior's trot. A thunder of padded feet erupted behind him as twenty thousand warriors took up the pace. They were heading south to the desert, and eventually to Yakubu.

* * *

Shani paced the floor of her bedroom, running scenarios through her mind to escape her soft prison. She cursed Ndoro every day, disgusted that he could do such a thing to her. The Blood Men were holding her until he arrived, which meant she would never see Obaseki again unless he killed Ndoro. She had to escape, but how could she? Although Tadalesh did not prevent her from leaving the house, she was constantly under watch by Dike and his Blood Men. Her tirades kept them at a distance but did not make them disappear. Besides, Zimfara was an alien city to her. Its narrow, crowded streets seemed designed by madmen. Some roads led nowhere, while others seemed to run endlessly. The language was totally different from the tongues spoken near Mawena and Sesuland. Sometimes after another frustrating stroll through the city, she would sit in her room and gaze toward the north, hoping to see a contingent of Mawena cavalry led by her father coming to rescue her. It was a child's fantasy in a woman's mind and she admonished herself for such thoughts. If she were to escape, she would have to do it herself.

Shani was summoned as always by Dike. The voice that once made her safe now reminded her of her confinement, and her hate showed on her face.

"Breakfast is ready, Queen Mother," he announced, his tone still respectful despite the reversal of their roles.

Shani said nothing, rising from her bed and heading to the dining room. Tadalesh was there, her ever-present smile growing more annoying each day.

"Queen Mother, it is good to see you as always," she beamed. She presented a basket filled with exotic fruit. "These came yesterday with a caravan from Jadina. It is said they grow on trees fed with the blood of bulls!"

With a smooth motion Tadalesh picked up knife and sliced open the fruit, revealing the pulpy innards that ran with a juice the color of blood.

Shani stood. "I will walk in the market," she announced. She'd lost her appetite with Tadalesh's disgusting display and desperately yearned for the crowded streets. Despite being watched, at least there she could feel alone and free.

Shani dressed quickly and left the house. The Blood Men followed, spreading out once they exited the house but staying close enough to keep an eye on her. Shani had learned to ignore them, losing herself in the confusion of Zimfara. She headed to the market, strolling slowly through the cramped alleyways, her senses assaulted by the sights, sounds, and smells that were still alien to her. She wondered how her sons had adapted to these different cultures, each going so far as to become leaders in their own rights among foreigners.

A hand touched her shoulder and she turned angrily, expecting to see the face of a Blood Man. Instead, she looked up into the intense eyes of a tall, lean man with dark skin and sharp features. A ragged robe covered his tall frame. A sword hung from his shoulder. He seemed disturbed by her direct stare and looked away.

"Queen Mother," he said respectfully. "You must come with me. Your son demands your presence."

Shani jerked away from the man. "Hasn't my son sent enough people to hold me hostage?"

The man smiled. "I do not speak of Ndoro. I serve only Moyo, the man you know as Obaseki."

Shani's hand went to her mouth in surprise. She could see it now in his eyes; he resembled the men that rescued Obaseki from Abo. Without the turban, face veil and flowing robes she'd missed the obvious. Her heart surged with joy. Obaseki was going to rescue her.

That joy suddenly transformed to dread when she thought of the Blood Men. She looked about frantically.

"You look for the men that followed you," the man said.

"Yes."

The man smiled again. "They were dealt with. Please, Queen Mother, we must go before others realize you are not returning."

Shani followed the man through the maze of the market place to a small wagon hitched to a donkey. The wagon contained various plants and fruits, typical needs of the nomads of desert. Two other men stood by the wagon, nodding as they recognized the man leading Shani. They cleared a spot in the wagon for her and she climbed in among the produce.

Shani and her saviors made slow progress through the crowded city, fighting off vendors and beggars as they approached the city gate. The guard waved them past without much notice, not wanting to be bothered with what he saw as desert rabble. They continued their silent trek into the desert until dusk. They were well out of sight of the city, climbing a low dune before the man who approached her spoke.

"We will rest when we reach the other side."

The summit of the hill revealed a large encampment bustling with activity. Her protector called out in his native tongue and the entire encampment looked to them. She caught the word Moyo and they all fell to their knees, sprinkling sand onto their heads.

"You are among friends, Queen Mother. You are home."

* * *

Sharif Citadel loomed over Zimfara like a jealous lover, its minarets peering down in constant scrutiny. Beyond the steep hills that constituted its perch, the desert stretched out beyond the horizon. Ndoro gazed out onto the endless sands knowing that beyond his sight was a city he must conquer and a brother he must destroy.

He turned his attention back to his war room. The dining room of the citadel was normally filled with dazzling items from every region of Uhuru; exquisite vases from Ptush, colorful gourds from the southern rainforests and numerous terra cotta figurines from the Sudan. All these items had been gathered and dumped in the wide hallway outside. The only item allowed to remain was the massive mahogany dining table, an obvious symbol of the wealth of its former owners. Surrounding the table, however, were not the merchants and noblemen who had feasted on its smooth surface many times. Draping its surface was a large canvas map, hastily but accurately drawn by the local merchants. Peering down on the map were his indunas. Jawanza stood prominent among them, his bearded face contorted in a frown. He rubbed his chin as Ibrahim talked, pleas falling on obviously deaf ears.

"It is impossible!" Ibrahim stuttered.

Ndoro strode to the table. "Nothing is impossible. This land is waterless and treeless and yet your people survive. We do what we wish."

"No army has ever crossed the Mahgreb, not even an army as magnificent as yours, Shumba. There are too many of you, too many!"

"Yakubu is said to be larger than Zimfara; some say it is larger than Selike. You don't think that is impossible?"

Ibrahim closed his eyes, his fingers pressing tight on his temples. "Yakubu lies on an oasis plateau, and Moyoseki is..." His voice trailed off as he stared in fear of Ndoro.

"A god?" Ndoro finished. He felt the heat of anger behind his eyes. Everyone in this cursed place thought his brother was some sort of deity. If they did not worship him, they either respected him or feared him.

Ndoro charged Ibrahim and grabbed his neck, pulling him close.

"He is a demon, Bedouin. He fools your people with false miracles and feeds their thirst with blood!"

Ndoro shoved the man to the floor, clearly disgusted.

"Jawanza," he barked. "How does a caravan cross the Mahgreb?"

Jawanza answered without taking his eyes from the map. "A caravan carries provisions to reach half the way to its destination. A rider is sent out to bring supplies for the rest of the journey."

"We won't have that option," Ndoro commented. He joined his men at the table. Yakubu stood out like a green jewel surrounded by a ring of sand. Scattered about the map were drawings of date trees, the artist's sign for an oasis. Dispersed here and there were small water droplets, the artist's symbol for waterholes. Above each waterhole was a symbol signifying the tribe that claimed it.

"How complete is this map?" Ndoro asked. This time the question was aimed at Ibrahim.

"It is as much as I know," Ibrahim replied.

"Is it everything?" Ndoro asked.

Ibrahim looked nervous. "No. Many tribes keep secret waterholes known only to their people."

"Can we persuade them?" Ndoro asked.

"They would die first," Ibrahim said defiantly.

Ndoro walked slowly back to the window, worrying his chin with his right hand.

"Leave me, everyone," he said.

The indunas exited the room, dragging Ibrahim with them. Ndoro waited until he was sure everyone was gone, before rubbing the medicine bag strapped to his waist. Nakisisa materialized before him, his arms folded across his chest. He bowed slightly.

"My friend," he said. "You have use of me?"

Ndoro stared at the spirit of his old friend. It was difficult for him to get used to the transformation and his growing dependence on Nakisisa's guidance. Magic had brought him much pain in his life; this new use still did not have his full trust. Faced with this current challenge, he had no choice.

"Do you know where all the waterholes of the Mahgreb are found?" Ndoro asked.

Nakisisa grinned. "I was once a river spirit, but no more. This water is protected by local spirits."

"Can you discover where they are?"

"Will it aid your march to Yakubu?"

Ndoro folded his hands behind his back. "I need to march three hundred strides across the desert. What do you think?"

"Shumba's bell is full of thorns!" Nakisisa laughed. "You have no reason for impatience. Your path has been woven."

Ndoro sat on a stool near the table. "This is taking too long! Yakubu should be ours by now, desert or no."

"I will do what I can," Nakisisa replied.

Nakisisa vanished with a rush of wind. Ndoro looked where the spirit had stood and massaged his forehead. For the first time in his life he was uncertain of his next move. No clear path beckoned. This business about his brother, of marching on Yakubu to take the life of one demon made him uneasy. Nakisisa told him it was something he must do to fulfill his destiny; Ndoro had no idea of what destiny he spoke. All he wished for since the day he fled Selike was to become inkosi of Sesuland. That dream fulfilled, he desired nothing more until Obaseki intruded on his life. Destiny was for those foolish enough to believe the words of the ancestors. Ndoro lived in the world of men.

He left the dining hall for his umuzi. Although he understood the advantage of stone buildings, Ndoro's heart was in the grasslands, preferring the open space of a umuzi. The grounds surrounding the castle bustled with activity as thousands of Diaka warriors settled into their temporary homes. They parted as they recognized Ndoro, some forming a wall around him as he made his way to the umuzi. He smelled meat roasting and realized he was famished.

"Inkosi, you have returned!" Kenyetta stood before him, smiling.

Ndoro feigned anger. "What are you doing here?"

"Nakisisa visited me and told me I was needed." She smiled and tilted her head, a gesture that Ndoro well recognized.

He looked about at the servants preparing the meal.

"Leave us," he ordered. No sooner had they exited the tent Kenyetta ran to him, throwing her arms around his shoulders and kissing him fiercely.

"The Royal Umuzi has been cold since you left Selike," she whispered. "And very quiet."

"Then we must make sure the Royal Tent is not the same," Ndoro replied. He swept Kenyetta into his arms and took her to the sheepskins.

A week passed before Nakisisa returned. A dust storm raged, blotting out the sun and covering the citadel in a sandy darkness. Ndoro and his indunas took refuge inside, covering the windows with heavy camel blankets to block the sand. Ndoro found himself back before the map with Jawanza. They were plotting a route to Yakubu when a familiar voice entered his head.

"I have returned," Nakisisa said.

"Jawanza, take the indunas and inspect the men. I will be along soon," Ndoro ordered. Jawanza gave him a suspicious look but obeyed.

Moments later Nakisisa appeared at the window. Ndoro was stunned at what he saw. The river-beast bled almost everywhere. He smiled, revealing missing teeth, his left arm hanging useless at his side. The sight reminded Ndoro of the night the river-beast killed Inaamdura.

"My friend, what happened? Can a spirit be damaged so by men?"

"Not by men, but by jinn," Nakisisa replied weakly. "The water spirits of the Mahgreb do not give up their secrets easily." He sat on the window ledge, oblivious to the sandstorm pummeling the curtain behind him.

"I have a present for you, inkosi of the Sesu," Nakisisa announced. Despite his haggard look, the river-beast strode to the table. Waving his good hand across the canvas, the number of water signs doubled. Ndoro's smile showed his satisfaction.

"Well done, my friend," he said.

"Wait, Great Inkosi," Nakisisa interrupted. "You haven't received my entire gift."

With another wave of his hand, a thin blue line appeared at the base of the drawing of Yakubu. The line took on a life of its own, snaking its way across the canvas, linking the waterholes and oases before ending at the foothills of Zimfara.

"What is this?" Ndoro asked.

"A river," Nakisisa replied. "An underground river created by the rains of Yakubu. It flows from the plateau to the foothills of where we stand."

Nakisisa pointed to three points on the river. "The river can be reached at these points through caverns. All you need to do now is to find enough food to feed 20,000 warriors and Yakubu is yours."

"That will be easy," Ndoro replied. "You have put Yakubu in our hands."

The river-beast smiled weakly. "Then my task is done."

There was finality in the river-beast's voice that alarmed Ndoro.

"Nakisisa, what is wrong?"

Nakisisa rose above Ndoro, his wounds healing as he spoke. "Your destiny lies across the Mahgreb, in Yakubu. It was my duty to guide you through the last leg of your journey. I have done so; now I must go."

"You say I have a destiny," Ndoro answered. "But I say this is not it. I seek my brother only to revenge his attempt on my life and to drive the demon from his body."

"Your reason is your own, but your purpose belongs to all."

"What does that mean?" Ndoro asked.

"From the day I emerged from the river to kill you, I sensed a difference in you. After you defeated me and took my hand, that feeling grew every day until I fought the witch. As I passed into this life, the truth became clear. I offered myself to the ancestors to act as your guide. I knew you would not trust this path."

"Sorcerers have their own agendas," Ndoro retorted. "I know this better than most."

"Believe me, my friend. No sorcerer guides your path. Your blessings come from the ancestors. It is their strength that flows through you and that will guide you across the desert."

"And when I reach this goal?" Ndoro asked.

"Then you will see me again," Nakisisa answered. He showed Ndoro his perfect smile, then faded quickly into the storm.

Ndoro gazed where the river-beast had been. What did he mean by seeing him again? The unfamiliar feeling of fear crept back into his mind. Was he to see his friend again in victory, or was he to join him in the spirit world in defeat, a wandering spirit far from home?

He shook his head violently. He was Ndoro, inkosi of the Sesu, Shumba of the Diaka, ruler of every land which he'd set foot, and, according to Nakisisa, chosen for greatness by the ancestors. He would not die by any man's hand or any demon. Ndoro threw back the simba's robe draping his shoulders and strode from the safety of citadel into the howling winds of the sandstorm.

* * *

For generations to come, griots would sing of the events in Zimfara those fateful weeks of the dry season. Ndoro's Diaka legions swept through the city, overwhelming what little resistance its militia could muster. The Sesu warriors followed, bringing with provisions for the journey across the desert. The city was surrounded by camps; the sound of war chants constant like the desert heat. The people of Zimfara witnessed this occupation with mixed feelings; those who were forced to provide lodging for indunas and nobles found their anger soothed by the seemly endless supply of gold and cowries paid for their services. So much gold flowed through the city that it bought less than before, though no one complained of the surplus. Ndoro was careful to make sure the Bedouins understood the Sesu were not there as conquerors, for their help was vital for his plan to succeed.

The city was a human termite mound of activity, every smith's anvil ringing with the making of knives, swords and assegais, the clacking of looms as weavers busied themselves making robes and desert garb for the unprepared Sesu. The camel merchants' corrals bulged as the beasts were gathered to provide transport for the supplies needed for the coming trek. Tons of forage rolled into the city daily, supplying food for thousands of cattle held in huge umuzis surrounding the Sesu camp. Cattle were brought in to supply food for the warriors, but also as a special delicacy for a population used to sheep and goat as a mainstay.

Such a build-up of forces could not go unnoticed. Word spread throughout the Mahgreb, reaching Yakubu first as rumors and whispers, then later as facts and details. The time had come for action. Ndoro could not afford to wait any longer.

Night came early to the desert. The sun escaped behind the lofty mountains, conceding the day to darkness. The mild warmth of the day submitted to the cool night, the stars bright in the dark sky. Ndoro stood on the city walls wrapped in a thick wool blanket. Beyond the fortifications to the west the horizon glittered with campfires of Sesu warriors awaiting his orders to march. To the east lay the desert and beyond his sight, Yakubu. Ndoro pulled the blanket tighter, realizing the coldness he felt was not from the night air, but from within. He would lead thousands of warriors across the sands, many of them to their deaths, and for what? He'd almost forgotten the shock he felt when his brother attempted to kill him. But was it worth a war? Maybe this was wisdom, he thought with a smile. Or maybe it was fear. He quickly shook that thought from his mind. They would march tomorrow, Yakubu would fall, and he would be victorious again. But what did this mean? Ndoro turned slowly, descending the tower stairs with a heavy gait.

The morning sun had barely struggled over the steep walls when thirteen men jumped to their feet and charged from their camps, each headed for the same destination. Each man wore the armband of his unit, his drum gripped closely to his side. They met at the main road of Zimfara. The city guards swung the doors wide and the drummers ran in, climbing the stairs to the parapets. Once in place they began to play, their sound like thunder rolling from the cloudless sky. With voices as loud and urgent as their drums they sang;

On guard! The battle is coming!
Whoever runs away will get the whip!
Diaka! Rise with your spears!
Sesu! Stand and march across the sand!
Follow Shumba to Yakubu!
When a scorpion stings without mercy,
You kill it without mercy!
Come, my brothers, the scorpion must die!

The Diaka broke camp with amazing precision. In minutes the warriors were stepping in time with the drummers, chanting the words the drummers played. The Bedouin camel herders ran about confused as they hurried to follow the Diaka out of the city and into the desert. They scurried about yelling and waving their hands, miraculously organizing themselves quickly enough to follow the warriors through the gate. Throughout the city, people came out of their homes to witness the spectacle. Men, women, and children clamored atop houses and each other to get a glimpse of this vast army beginning its march of conquest and vengeance. Some found themselves caught up in the excitement and danced with the marching rhythms while adding their own shouts of encouragement to the black-skinned warriors.

A whisper swept the masses as the army trotted through the gates. Though his warriors were everywhere their leader was absent. For a people with no love for their occupiers, they were eager to see this mysterious conqueror march off to what he called his final campaign. The whisper became a murmur, the murmur talk, and soon the crowd chanted his name with the rhythm of the drums. But Ndoro was nowhere to be seen. His army marched out of the city, oblivious to the absence of their inkosi. As the last warrior exited the gate the inhabitants ran behind them, clamoring to the ramparts to watch the army march into the desert.

As the first Bedouins appeared atop the ramparts, they were stunned at what they saw. The Diaka shifted from a double file to a single line that stretched the length of the city walls. Before them Ndoro stood upon the dune in the distance, magnificent in his warrior regalia, his cowhide shield on his left arm, his gilded assegai stabbing the sky.

"Come, my shumbas!" he shouted. "Let us run to the walls of Yakubu and tear them down!"

The Diaka raised their assegais in unison, roaring with pride to their leader. They marched again, Ndoro waving them forward. As his army made its way effortlessly up the dune, Ndoro felt the fire rising in him, displacing the fear and uncertainty that poisoned him the past days. The march was on. The final war had begun.

The mild heat of the Mahgreb winter allowed Ndoro's warriors to cover much ground during the day. Jawanza had drilled the men for months in the sand, strengthening the already chiseled bodies for the arduous march. The Bedouins were amazed by their stamina, continuously falling behind despite their camels and horses. In three days they reached the first outcrops of stone, the home of the caves that led to the underground river. Warriors descended into the darkness, emerging with fresh, cold water, much to the delight of the others. The Bedouins made mental notes, sure to mark the spot for a future dispute among the nomad tribes.

Ndoro spent his days focused on the march and his nights on the coming battle. He walked among his warriors, personally checking their energy so he would make thoughtful decisions on the rest stops and camps. Each warrior was put on strict rations to ensure supplies would carry them to their destination. The nomads were well aware of the advancing army and abandoned their oasis camps for the safety of open sand. These abandoned islands of life kept the Diaka spirits high as they supplied shade and date fruit.

In ten days of marching, the Diaka had covered half the distance to Yakubu. They reached the second landmark on the map, a small collection of rocky hills, surrounded by brush and camels. The camp surrounded the hills as far as the eye could see, even on the low horizon of the desert. Ndoro walked among his warriors and was concerned by what he saw. Though they smiled proudly as he spoke to them, he saw the fatigue in their eyes and the thinness of their arms and legs. Back at his tent, he summoned Jawanza. The Diaka leader came immediately.

"What is it, Shumba?"

Ndoro looked at his companion and saw the same worn look. "How are the men?"

"They are good," Jawanza lied.

"I don't think so," Ndoro countered. "Tell me the truth, Jawanza."

"The march has been harder than we thought," Jawanza admitted. "The men are not used to the heat and the rations are low, especially meat. The Bedouins are stealing food and sending it back to their tribes, the lamb in particular. It is hard to control."

"I cannot have a weak army when we reach Yakubu," Ndoro said. "We will rest here for five days. Send riders, Diaka riders, back to Zimfara to secure more supplies. Once you have done so, gather the Bedouin leaders and bring them to me."

Jawanza bowed and left. Ndoro summoned his servants and put them to work. They took down his tent, clearing away everything except the royal stool. He donned his full inkosi trappings, including the lion pelt he claimed so long ago.

When Jawanza arrived with the Bedouins, Ndoro was seated on his stool, an intimidating image flanked by the Diatanee. Warriors gathered about in curiosity as the Bedouins were brought before him. Some of the nomads were clearly nervous as the crowd grew; others seemed annoyed that they had been taken away from their duties.

The men stood before Ndoro, making no attempt to show respect by kneeling before him.

"Who speaks for you?" Ndoro demanded. One of the Bedouins, a tall, bearded man with skin almost as dark as Ndoro's stepped forward. His eyes locked in a permanent squint; he spoke with a deep, clear voice.

"I do, inkosi," the man replied. Though he chose a respectful response, the tone of his voice said otherwise. "I am Hassim."

"I am told Bedouins are not subject to the rules of the march," Ndoro said.

"What do you mean inkosi?"

"Bedouins are receiving more rations than my warriors," Ndoro replied. "Are you planning to lead us into battle, Hassim?"

A low laugh passed through the crowd. Ndoro, however, did not smile.

Hassim shifted, seeming to be uncomfortable. "We have taken no more than we have been given."

"Yet our supplies run low ahead of schedule," Ndoro mused.

"Maybe the inkosi's warriors are not as disciplined as he thinks," Hassim answered. "Those not of the desert tend to be wasteful in its midst."

Ndoro stood and walked toward Hassim. "The Diaka are not conscripts and they are not liars, Bedouin. They would march until they died if I asked them. They do not disobey orders. If any rations are missing it is your doing. You will not jeopardize this operation, and you will not insult my men!"

Hassim was opening his mouth to speak when Ndoro slammed his gilded orinka against the man's head. Hassim fell to one knee; his hand reaching out for support as Ndoro struck him again, knocking him into the sand. Ndoro bent over the Bedouin and struck him a third time. Hassim lay motionless, the life gone from his eyes. Ndoro looked at the man for a moment and glared at the other Bedouins.

"I have treated you with respect and you return my kindness with lies, insults and deception. From this day on, all Bedouins are considered my property. Any Bedouin found stealing rations will be executed and his family driven into the desert. I will not tolerate any resistance."

Ndoro walked slowly to his stool and sat. "Leave my sight. Take your leader with you."

The camel drivers scrambled to claim Hassim's body. Fear flooded their eyes, their heads darting about as if they expected another sudden attack. No such thing would happen. The Diaka would not attack them unless Ndoro gave the signal. He watched the Bedouins, angry that they forced him to make such a decision. There would surely be resistance among them now that their status had changed. He would have to move quickly before any organized opposition could be mounted. Any large-scale conflict with the Bedouins would delay his march on Yakubu.

As if he was reading his mind, Jawanza appeared before him.

"Our situation changes," he said.

"You are right, brother," Ndoro replied. "Take five thousand warriors and return to Zimfara, but you will take a different route."

Ndoro had the desk map brought to him.

"These oases are camps of major Bedouin clans. You must destroy these clans on your way back to Zimfara. Leave no one alive."

Jawanza looked up from the map. "I will follow your command as always, Shumba. But these are hard orders. The men have no fear of warriors, but to kill everyone? It will be difficult for them to do."

Ndoro sat hard on his stool, rubbing his head. "I cannot risk fighting a two headed serpent. A message must be sent to keep the Bedouins quiet."

Jawanza's eyes brightened. "We will march to the oases as you order, Shumba. But we will take the elders with us to Zimfara as our 'guests' until you return victorious from Yakubu. The clans will find it difficult to organize without their headmen to move against us. If they do, we will hold out in Zimfara and await your return."

Ndoro was impressed. Jawanza had become a leader in his own right. If the battle went badly in Yakubu, the Sesu and Diaka would find an excellent inkosi in Jawanza.

"An excellent plan," Ndoro replied. "We must act on it immediately."

"I leave today," Jawanza answered.

Jawanza and his contingent of warriors were gone before nightfall. Ndoro stood on the dune looking toward Zimfara. A sliver of moon crept over the horizon, the warmth of the day fleeing quickly to leave a void for the cool night air to fill. This was a setback. The Diaka that marched away with Jawanza lacked the zeal that normally accompanied them, which did not bode well. Angry warriors responded cruelly, which could stir the anger of the Bedouins even higher. He would have to bring this business to an end quickly before they found themselves mired in this desolate land.

Something flashed in the moonlight, catching his eye. He strained to get a better look, realizing that whatever it was, it was moving toward him. He stood and looked about, realizing he wandered too far away from camp. On his own insistence, the Diatanee had remained behind in camp. Ndoro felt his hand tighten around his assegai as the image became clear. They were Bedouins, six in all, trudging wearily up the dune. Instinct made him brace for an attack, but a strange premonition kept him calm. These men did not move like normal men. They seemed to glide above the sand, showing no sign of the laborious steps deep soft sand requires.

Ndoro stepped back as he realized what he saw. This was a procession of the dead; he was being approached by spirits. He froze, not knowing what to do. He wore no charm bag to protect him. A smile came to him; the Bedouins sent an adversary he knew not how to fight.

The ghostly desert men approached him and stopped. Their expressions changed from blankness to recognition.

"Moyoseki," they said in hollow unison as they prostrated on the sand. They stood, smiled and walked through him over the dune, disappearing into the dark.

Hearing the name of his brother spill from the mouths of spirits chilled his blood. A true demon he must be to command the respect of the dead! The resemblance between him and Obaseki was such that the spirits could not tell them apart. But then another question struck him cold. Why could he see them? Had they made themselves visible to him because of whom they thought he was, or was he becoming what his brother had become?

Ndoro broke his stance and ran for the camp. The Diatanee was apparently watching him from distance, for they sprinted with equal vigor toward him, weapons at the ready.

The first to reach him ran past him and halted, scanning the darkness for potential pursuers. Other bodyguards fell in beside the inkosi, running with him to camp. Ndoro saw the worry in their eyes, but this was no time to console. He needed answers and he needed them soon.

Ndoro halted at the edge of the camp. He turned to his guard, his eyes intense.

"Find me a medicine-priest, now!" he commanded.

The Diatanee faded into the camp, eager for the purpose. They returned as quickly as they left; dragging a tall, thin man with large fearful eyes behind them. He was a straggler, one of those that followed large marches, profiting off the warriors by selling exotic foods, women and charms. The man's protests fell away as he recognized who he was about to see. He dropped to the ground, prostrating himself.

"Bring him," Ndoro commanded. He spun and strode to his tent. His bodyguards lifted the medicine-priest and dragged him along. Ndoro was sitting as the guards tossed the man before him.

"Leave us," Ndoro said. The Diatanee left the tent. Ndoro leaned toward the man, studying his face.

"You are not Sesu or Diaka," Ndoro stated.

The man dared to look up. "No, inkosi. I am Giguyu. I am from the east."

Ndoro nodded. Since his flight from Selike he trusted no sorcerers, especially those from Sesuland. But he had no choice. Without Nakisisa at his side, he was blind to the spirits.

"What is your name, sorcerer?"

"Faraji," the man answered nervously.

"Tell me, Faraji, do you talk to the spirits?"

Faraji smiled. "Yes, inkosi. I see the spirits and I talk to them. But as with any such gift, the use of this talent comes with a price."

Ndoro's right hand flashed from his side, his palm striking Faraji's face. Before the man could cry out the same hand gripped his neck.

"The price is your life, sorcerer! Now I will ask you again. Do you see spirits?"

"No," the medicine-priest answered.

Ndoro tighten his grip on the man's neck.

"Wait, wait!" Faraji managed to say. "I have a way."

Ndoro pushed the man away. Faraji fell to the ground onto his side, gagging. He crawled back to a kneeling position.

"Inkosi, I am no great sorcerer," he admitted. "My sight is weak, which is why I follow the trail of soldiers to tell them what they wish to hear."

Ndoro said nothing, letting his glare answer for him. Faraji's eyes darted about, and then settled on Ndoro again. He rubbed his temples tortuously then stopped, an immense smile on his face.

"I remember a spell from my apprenticeship long ago," Faraji said. He rummaged through his medicine bag and extracted a collection of stones, shells and small bones. Faraji studied them as he shifted them about with his index finger.

"Yes, yes, I have them." He looked at Ndoro triumphantly. "These are the ones."

Faraji selected a few bones from his hand then spread them on the ground before Ndoro. He chanted, swaying his body with the rhythm of his voice. Ndoro watched him cynically. He should feel something, he thought, some type of sensation to let him know the spell worked. He felt nothing.

He raised his hand to strike Faraji when the priest jerked still, his eyes jolted open. He stared past Ndoro, focusing on something beyond Ndoro's sight.

"Hello, my friend," Faraji said. Ndoro was startled as a familiar voice emerged from Faraji's lips. His thoughts were confirmed when Faraji's face contorted the best it could to resemble the familiar smile of Nakisisa.

"No matter where I go, you manage to find me," he said to Ndoro.

"I need a spirit to deal with spirits," Ndoro replied. "I saw spirits tonight."

"As it should be," Nakisisa stated. "As your time draws near, you and your brother become more alike. He moves among the spirits and you are gaining the same ability."

Ndoro felt a chill of fear. "Am I becoming a demon?"

"I don't know," Nakisisa replied.

There was a moment of uneasy silence before Ndoro spoke again.

"How much time do I have?"

Faraji's face looked solemn. "The time draws near; two must become one."

Faraji's eyes rolled and he collapsed. Ndoro stood quickly, donning his armor. The message was sent; there was no more time. The fear and uncertainty that plagued him since the beginning of the campaign were engulfed in a firestorm of urgency. His life was at stake, simply enough. If it was Ukulunkulu's wish for him to die, it would not be at the hands of a demon.

The truth teller rose groggily to his feet. "What happened? What did I say?"

"Enough," Ndoro replied. The Diatanee snapped to their feet when Ndoro emerged from the tent.

"Rouse the camp. We march tonight."

The Diatanee took quickly to their task. In moments the muster drums erupted and the Diaka swarmed from their tents, breaking down their tents in minutes. But Ndoro could not wait. He marched out of the camp alone, his eyes focused on the darkness ahead. His bodyguards were the first to catch up with him, falling into step beside him. The clatter of a marching army filled the night soon afterward. Ndoro heard nothing but Nakisisa's last words. It was time for two to become one. He would not stop marching until he reached Yakubu.

20

Obaseki sat among friends, some from his childhood, some he'd met on his journeys. They were all dead, passed from the world of the living to the Zamani, the land of ancestor spirits. Fuluke sat beside him, gazing admirably at his former student.

"Fuluke, I have never felt this good in my entire life," Obaseki confessed. "It's as if my life among the living has been a prison sentence."

Fuluke smiled. "This is where you belong. We will all be here eventually. But you cannot stay."

Obaseki looked at his teacher in shock. "Why? Am I not dead? Did I not die from my brother's wound?

"No, Seki, you did not die," Fuluke answered. "Your brother opened a door for you, one you could not have opened yourself."

Fuluke swept his arm around. "This is your kingdom, Seki. You have seen the spirits since you were a boy. They've always been close to show the way. But your brother gave you the key."

"So what must I do?" Obaseki asked.

"You must go back," Fuluke said. "Two must become one."

Fuluke stood and met Obaseki's eyes. "Remember what you see here. Men forget their ancestors and lose their mouth to the gods. Your purpose is to restore their faith, to lead them back to the ancestors and back to the gods. Just as men need the gods, the gods need men. Neither can survive without the other."

Obaseki was stunned by Fuluke's revelation. The gods need men? Surely Fuluke was wrong.

"There is no reason for me to lie to you," Fuluke said, answering Obaseki's thoughts. "Remember my words."

"What does Ndoro have to do with all this?" Obaseki asked.

"He approaches," Fuluke answered, his image becoming blurry. "The closer he comes, the more your grip on the Zamani slips away."

Obaseki reached for the others but they drew away, their images less distinct. Obaseki tried running to them but instead he drifted like a feather trapped in a dark wind.

"Fuluke! Help me!

But Fuluke did not help him. Obaseki fell from the Zamani, away from the world in which he felt most at home, his spirit crashing into his body. Someone was shaking him and yelling his name.

"Seki, Seki!" Eshe screamed.

El-Fatih rushed into the room, his guards close behind.

"My queen, what is wrong?"

Eshe looked at El-Fatih, her eyes filled with water. "He spoke, Fatih, he spoke to me!"

Obaseki heard their voices, but he was very weak. The fatigue pressed down on him like a thousand stones.

"My sweet flower," he whispered.

El-Fatih rushed to his side. "Moyoseki, can you see me?"

"I see you, Fatih," Obaseki replied. "And I hear you very well."

Obaseki tried to move his head and almost blacked out. He was close to death and he felt so.

"Fatih, have Jamela make a healing broth," Eshe commanded. El-Fatih was out of the room before Eshe finished, shouting orders at the top of his lungs. She turned back to Obaseki, placing her hand gently on his chest. She smiled and Obaseki felt the chill of his body subside. It was a smile from long ago, when they cherished each other like young lovers. Was she falling in love with him again? Though his spirits were lifted by the thought, he did not wish to be. He looked into her eyes and smiled the best he could.

"I must get my strength back quickly," he said.

"It will come in time, love," Eshe replied.

"I don't have time," Obaseki said. "My brother is coming and I must be prepared."

Eshe's face became grave. "You will stay here. You have an entire army to deal with your brother."

"I could have a million men, but only I can confront my brother," Obaseki said. The message from Fuluke was clear. What the ancestors had set in motion was almost complete. Any path he took would have led to this moment, this final confrontation.

"Moyo! Moyoseki!" Eshe's head jerked to the window as the roar of Obaseki's given name boomed through. She ran to the window and leaned out.

"Seki, I wish you could see this," she exclaimed.

"I can," he replied, his eyes closed. Through the vision of the spirits he saw crowds of people filling the streets, all chanting his name. He felt the love, respect and fear they held for him. It was the lesson the ancestors created him to learn.

El-Fatih entered the room with servants carrying Eshe's items. Glancing toward the window, he smirked.

"It seems the word of your awakening has spread throughout the city."

"So it has," Obaseki replied, managing a smile for his friend. "Tomorrow I will be on my feet. I wish you to teach me what makes the Tuareg such fearsome fighters."

El-Fatih's smirk grew into a smile. "It will be difficult. You may be a god, but you are still not a Tuareg. Despite this I will do my best."

"That is all I ask." Obaseki felt a wave of fatigue rising inside him and closed his eyes.

"I must rest now. Eshe, will you stay beside me?"

"Of course, my love." Eshe smiled and for the first time in many seasons Obaseki believed her love for him was true. He closed his eyes and fell into a dreamless sleep.

Eshe watched her husband drift asleep in fear. Was he only sleeping, or had his brother's wound finally claimed him? She leaned close, placing her cheek near his nose. The faint sound of his breathing calmed her; she sat straight, gently stroking his hand.

El-Fatih's hand touched her shoulder lightly. His touch was unsure, but his voice was steady.

"He has returned to us as I knew he would."

"How could you be so sure?" Eshe asked, turning her head so she could see him. "He was so close to the ancestors."

"He is not a man. I believe he was healing in his own way."

Eshe looked at her lover, knowing the words she was about to utter would hurt.

"All I thought about while he was gone was how I failed him as a wife. He was dealing with so many things and I paid him no attention. I was too busy with my own needs."

El-Fatih removed his hand from Eshe's shoulder. "It must be difficult bonded to a man such as him."

Eshe smiled; relieved that El-Fatih saw the path she was leading him down. She expected no less of him; it was the reason she was drawn to him. Whatever selfishness she indulged with him had to end. Obaseki was her husband and would need her help to recover. But it was more than that. Looking into Obaseki's eyes took her back to when they first met. She remembered the shallowness of youth in those eyes as he clumsily harnessed his powers to save her mother. To look into his eyes now was like gazing into a deep, calming river which every twist and turn spoke of paths well known and well-traveled. Obaseki's eyes showed her what she had longed to see. His wanderings were done; he had found his place. She only wished she knew what that really meant.

Obaseki awoke to a room illuminated by the soft light of early morning. The fatigue that weighed on him the day before was completely gone. He felt as if he'd only slept, not experiencing the turmoil of the past weeks. He opened his eyes wider and saw Eshe lying beside him, her sheer nightgown covering her body like morning mist. He was aroused and surprised by the feeling; it had been a long time since they'd touched each other in such a way. He ran his hand down the crest of her shoulder, following the slope of her arm and into the dip of her waist, then rising and lingering on her hip. She stirred, moaning pleasurably as she looked up into his eyes.

"Your sleep seems to have revived more than your spirit," she purred. She reached up and grasped his shoulder, pulling herself up to look at him eye to eye. They kissed, gently at first, then stronger as they both sensed his energy was real. They made love like new lovers, the passion spilling over into frantic motion and unbelievable need.

Obaseki held Eshe for a time, joyful to have his wife back completely. He kissed her cheek, then swung his legs over the edge of the bed and began to dress.

Eshe rose up on her elbows and watched him. “Aren’t you tired?”

Obaseki turned to her and grinned. “No, although I probably should be. I promised El-Fatih we would begin training today.”

“It must be true what he said then,” Eshe said. She made her way to him, slipping her arm around his waist. “You were not dying, you were resting.”

Her words raised the shadow in his mind, reviving his purpose. Obaseki removed Eshe’s arm from his waist.

“I was not resting, sweet flower. I was dead.”

Eshe’s eyes widened. “Dead?”

“Yes,” Obaseki replied. “I was among the ancestors. I walked among them with Fuluke. There—among the souls of my friends, relatives, and ancestors—I was told what I must do.”

Eshe’s eyes went from bewilderment to sadness. “You must confront your brother again.”

“Yes.”

Eshe looked away, a tear escaping her eye. Obaseki knew what she feared; that if he challenged his brother his death would be permanent. She was right, yet she was also wrong.

Distant footsteps told of El-Fatih’s arrival. “My teacher comes,” Obaseki said, trying his best to lighten the mood. El-Fatih strode into the room, looked at Eshe and quickly exited to a place where he could not see her near-nakedness.

“I deeply apologize, Moyoseki,” he said. “I was not aware. I assumed that the lateness of the day...”

“Don’t grovel,” Obaseki replied. “It doesn’t suit you. You have full right to expect me to be ready and my wife to be decent.”

He kissed Eshe’s cheek then left the room. El-Fatih stood midway down the corridor, clearly embarrassed.

“Come, my teacher,” Obaseki said. “It’s time to make me a warrior.”

He followed El-Fatih out of the palace into the courtyard. No matter how many times he’d seen these grounds, its beauty always amazed him. The lushness of it was in sharp contrast to the desert surrounding the plateau on which they existed. The courtyard was usually filled with servants, but today it was empty. A rack stood at the far end, filled with various weapons. El-Fatih marched to the rack.

"Knowing that you are of noble blood, I am sure you had some weapons training. I thought we would start by seeing what you remember."

He grabbed a wooden sword from the rack and handed it hilt first to Obaseki. Obaseki grasped it and felt a rush of energy overcome him. Memories flooded his mind, thoughts he knew were not his, but felt part of him just the same. The onslaught was almost overwhelming and he swayed, grabbing the weapons rack for support.

El-Fatih rushed to his side. "Are you sure you are ready?"

Obaseki steadied himself. "Yes, I'm fine. Let's continue."

El-Fatih hesitated, and then stepped away.

"We will begin with defense." El-Fatih extended his takouba, drawing a line in the air before Obaseki down from his forehead to his crotch.

"This is your center line. It is where all power revolves. Attack and defense originate here."

El-Fatih drew another line, this one horizontal and bisecting the center line.

"These are the four oases," he said. "Northern right, northern left, south right and south left. Each oasis is vital to the survival of the tribe. Each must be defended; each must attack."

Obaseki nodded in understanding. Though the terms were different, the concept was similar to what he was taught many years ago in Abo. The memories raced back to him and sadness accompanied them. Would he ever see his home again?

El-Fatih cleared his throat, drawing Obaseki back to his training.

"Today we will do a simple thrust and parry exercise. This will help you learn the oases and help you to become familiar with your center line."

El-Fatih took a fighting stance, slowly moving his takouba toward Obaseki.

"Attack north oases right," he said. Obaseki repeated the movement toward El-Fatih, who extended his takouba, thus deflecting Obaseki's slow attack.

"Defend north oasis right," El-Fatih said. They repeated the movement for each oasis.

"Now, let us begin the game," El-Fatih announced.

El-Fatih increased the pace. Obaseki, nervous at first, struggled to match El-Fatih's speed. But then a rush came over him, a sensation reminding him of Moyo's presence. El-Fatih seemed to slow, his movements easier to follow. Maybe he was tiring, Obaseki thought. The look on his face was clearly one of frustration as he thrust and parried in time with Obaseki. Obaseki raised his hand, signaling for El-Fatih to stop.

"Are you tired?" Obaseki asked.

El-Fatih threw down his sword. "I know who you are, Moyoseki, and I respect your power and what you have done for my people. Still, it is not right to deceive a person in order to shame him."

Obaseki was puzzled. "What do you mean?"

"This! Your skills are amazing! I begin slowly to spare you, and then I find myself struggling to keep pace with you!"

Obaseki smiled and place his hand on El-Fatih's shoulder.

"I did not deceive you, my friend. I possess no such skills. I think I am somehow tapping into the skills of my brother. He must be close."

"If that is so, your brother is a formidable warrior," El-Fatih replied. "It is good you tried to ambush him."

"I still have much to learn despite my new gift."

El-Fatih smiled. "Yes, this is true. Let us discuss more complex issues."

They continued to practice throughout the day, Obaseki's skills growing with every minute. His strength increased as the day moved on, much to the amazement and consternation of El-Fatih. As the desert winds carried the shadows of the evening over the eastern hills, the duo ended their session.

"Moyoseki, you are truly chosen by the gods," El-Fatih said. "Never have I seen such as you."

Obaseki looked at his friend and his chest tightened with sadness. The Ihaggaren leader's eyes spoke admiration and reverence, not the friendship that always eluded him. But unlike the years past, his remorse came with understanding. This was not his world, but his purpose.

"He placed his hand on Fatih's shoulder. "The ancestors have blessed me with a great teacher." They walked together toward the palace in silence as Obaseki contemplated his next move.

21

Ndoro knelt in the shifting sand, exhausted and angry. His body had failed him. He should still be running across the Mahgreb sands, arms and legs pumping in perfect rhythm until the walls of Yakubu came into view. Instead he was on his knees, staring into the darkness, the city of Yakubu still a distance away.

A hand touched his shoulder and he knocked it away, springing to his feet with his assegai ready to strike. Kumbala fell away, dropping his shield and spear.

"Inkosi forgive me!" he pleaded. "We are awaiting your signal to move."

"We will camp here and continue our march tomorrow night. It will give the Bedouins time to catch up with us."

"As you wish, inkosi." Kumbala trotted off.

Ndoro sat back down in the sand. Never before had he pushed himself to such a point. He felt the lie in his voice and knew Kumbala sensed it, too. It was a weakness he could not afford to show, especially now when the battle with his brother was so close. He had no idea what warriors his brother had gathered around him, but he was sure they would be formidable. His brother's magic was surely powerful and its effect on his followers would be immeasurable. The Diaka had fought many foes, but none strengthened with foul magic. Ndoro would have to be the example. He had to prove to his warriors that demons could be slain and the Diaka would prevail.

Camp was set up quickly in Diaka fashion. Ndoro was soon in the comfort of his marching tent, resting on his cot.

Kumbala sent servants with food and drink, much to Ndoro's surprise. He ate and drank heartily, confirming the toll his forced march had taken on him as well as his men.

His eyes heavy, Ndoro fought sleep. If he slept he would dream, and he feared where his dreams would take him. His brother was attacking his mind, but the fatigue was so great he was losing his struggle to stay awake. If he closed his eyes for only a moment, just enough for a short rest...

He fell into blackness, a fall that he realized would never end. Images raced by him, visions of his childhood, the desperation of his flight from Selike, the heady times of Songhai, the founding of his kingdom and the building of his empire. Now it all meant nothing, a moment in the stream of life that flowed around him. The face of his brother appeared as he knew it would. How could a man filled with such evil be so much like him? His brother's mouth moved in the chant Ndoro had come to despise. The litany that drove them both to the coming battle; two must become one.

He awoke to the sounds of shouts and steel. He rolled from his bed, grabbing his weapons as his tent collapsed around him. Ndoro hacked at the canvas enveloping him, rolling to avoid being trampled by his unseen attacker. He ripped a hole in the fabric and sprang to his feet in time to avoid the downward stroke of a scimitar wielded by a camel-riding Bedouin. He threw his assegai with deadly accuracy, the thick blade striking the Bedouin in the throat and toppling him to the sand. Ndoro ran to the fallen man, jerking the assegai from his throat, then spinning about to access the situation. Bedouins charged through the camp, striking down Diaka as they rose startled from sleep. His few remaining bodyguards surrounded him quickly.

"Sound the battle drums!" Ndoro shouted. He dropped to his knees, searching for and finding torch sticks. A few yards away, a lone fire still burned; Ndoro sprinted for it, the Diatanee close behind him. Battle drums sounded as they reached the flames, Diaka spilling out of their tents and into the midst of the attacking Bedouins. Ndoro lit his torch and passed it to the closest Diatanee. The others fell in line, grabbing torches and rushing to help bring light to the camp.

A group of camel-riders charged the fire. Ndoro and the remaining Diatanee fell into formation, locking shields and extending their pikes. The riders turned to avoid the lethal barrier, slowing just enough to give the rallying Diaka their chance. The riders and camels went down under a wave of Diaka, orinkas, and assegais flailing against the flickering torchlight.

The Bedouin ambush became a Diaka rout. The remaining Bedouins fled the camp amid a hail of assegais and arrows, disappearing into the darkness. Ndoro immediately sent runners out with torches, establishing a perimeter around the camp. The wounded were tended to while the dead were carefully wrapped and buried temporarily; they would later be exhumed and sent back to their homelands. Bedouin dead were dragged out of the camp and dumped over the dunes beyond the sentries. The camels were butchered and the meat prepared for smoking.

Ndoro gathered his indunas about him at the remains of his tent.

"I expected the Bedouins to react, but not so soon. We must assume there will be other attacks. We must also assume there will be no help from Zimfara."

The indunas shifted nervously as Ndoro continued.

"We must abandon our march on Yakubu, at least for now. We cannot advance unless we know our flank is secure."

"We will make camp here until Jawanza returns. Use anything available to create a perimeter and take stock of your supplies. You have your orders."

The indunas dispersed. As the Diatanee repaired his tent, Ndoro walked the camp, assessing the current conditions. He had underestimated the Bedouin response to his decree. Their attack was unexpected and from what he could see, devastating. He had no idea what was happening to his rear in Zimfara. Was Jawanza under siege, or was he marching to meet him? Ndoro cursed his brother. He was behind this, he concluded. Ndoro's miscalculation and the sudden, furious Bedouin response must be his doing; all the more reason for his destruction.

Ndoro reconvened with his officers at dusk. Sentries patrolled the makeshift perimeter, a collage of animal carcasses, wood, and sand. Tacuma archers were stationed behind the perimeter, their quivers filled with poison-tipped arrows. The wounded were moved to the center of camp with the few Bedouins that remained.

The mood among the Diaka was one Ndoro had only experienced once before at the hands of the Tacuma and Nakisisa.

He sensed the fear and it disgusted him, even though he understood its origin. They were in the center of the Mahgreb with no idea of their situation. Behind them the Bedouins were revolting; ahead of them was the unknown enemy.

Ndoro sat cross-legged by the fire, draped in his simba robe. He stood slowly, meeting the eyes of each man.

"We have traveled many miles together, my brothers. Beneath our feet are the bones of many armies that thought they knew the soul of the Diaka. The Bedouins, just like the others, have underestimated the strength of the Lion. They will come and meet our teeth. They will charge and feel our claws. Then they will truly know fear as they fall to the steel of the Diaka!

Shields and assegais rattled in the darkness, a gesture that swept the camp. Ndoro tilted his head back and chanted the familiar war chant of the Diaka, the song bursting strong and resonant from his throat. His army joined in and the chant rose from the camp like a mighty eagle, ascending the soft dunes and hard mountains. The Diaka sang loudly, warning all those within hearing that the lion was near and he was hungry.

The Bedouins emerged on the horizon with the desert sun. The undulating line of camel riders and men moved slowly, patient in their advance. There was no need to hurry; the Diaka had nowhere to go. This was the Mahgreb, their domain and their greatest weapon against those who thought these harsh lands were easy prey. The sand beneath the camels' hooves held the bones of many who had tried and failed to subdue these desert people, but still they came with dreams of conquest. The people, scattered among the sparse oases, were as harsh as the land they roamed. They convened as they always had during times like these, setting aside their tribal rivalries to push out the invaders. The Diaka had overstayed their welcome. It was time for the desert to claim it's due.

Ndoro stood on a small rise of sand built for observation. Below him the camp was mobilized. Archers were in position just inside the palisade wall, bows loaded and ready. Behind them stood the spearmen with their pikes, designed to thwart camel or horse charges. Inside the perimeter the Diaka waited, assegais at their sides, shields in position.

Ndoro and his indunas watched the slow approach of the Bedouins. There was no way to escape, not that the Diaka would entertain such a thought. They watched as the trot became a gallop, then transformed into a full speed charge.

A smile came to Ndoro's face as the Bedouins advanced. The archers loaded their bows, patiently waiting for the signal to fire. Their indunas raised their swords and watched as the charging line of horses disappeared into the hidden moat with the crashing sound like thunder and a maelstrom of dust and sand. The indunas dropped their hands and the archers responded, firing their poisoned tipped projectiles into the camel riders following the hapless horsemen. The riders, trying to avoid the deadly shower, moved forward and pushed those horsemen trying to avoid the pit into the cavern despite their protests. Some of the camel riders broke rank and circled the camp, waving their curved swords over their heads while they cursed the Tacuma archers. They kept their distance from the moat as they probed the boundary. After circling the camp twice, the camel riders rode away, leaving their dead behind.

"Clear the moat," Ndoro ordered. "Repair the palisades and replace the spikes."

Kumbala nodded. "It was a good plan."

Ndoro did not smile. "I doubt it will work again, but it may slow them down. Position the warriors around the moat with archers behind. The Bedouins will find a way over the pit. Have the men place torches outside the perimeter. Keep them burning all night."

Ndoro retired to his tent. The sun made its slow descent into the western hills, pulling the heat away with it. As darkness settled on the Diaka camp the sounds of Bedouins came to the ears of the sentries. It was a restless night; the torches constantly extinguished by brave desert riders dodging the poison missiles fired into the darkness. The warriors sent to relight them were equally endangered. No sooner did they cross the pit than they were set upon by hidden Bedouins waiting in the darkness. Skirmishes went on throughout most of the night until Kumbala ordered the men back. They were losing too many to the torches; he would have to concede the night to the Bedouins. By dawn, an uneasy quiet possessed the camp.

The sun peeked over the distant hills bringing the yells of attacking Bedouins. Ndoro sprang from his bed at the sound of the alarm drums, running out of his tent and into the emerging light. The Bedouins were charging from all sides. His archers and spearmen responded by spreading their line around the camp. Ndoro looked into the pit and smiled.

"Kumbala, light the pit!" he ordered. At Kumbala's signal torchbearers sprinted to the pit, throwing the fire into the heaps of grass and branches the Diaka had stacked into the pit during the night. The fires caught but spread slowly.

"More torches!" Ndoro shouted.

The Bedouins were too close for his order to be followed. They veered away from the parts of the pit on fire and rode for the gaps.

Ndoro's eyes narrowed. "Move the pike men into position. Make sure the Diaka are ready." He extracted his sword and braced his shield in anticipation of the Bedouin onslaught.

The Bedouin horsemen charged across the burning pit and were met by a fusillade of poison arrows. The bowmen fell back to reload, replaced by skirmishers flinging throwing-spears. The charge was stalled long enough for the pike men to form ranks before the archers. Their long thick-shafted spears forced the horse riders to divert.

By then the entire pit was ablaze, a thick black smoke rising about the camp. Fighters on both sides struggled to see through the swirling haze of dust and smoke. Bedouin riders charged through the infernal wall, bearing down on the disorganized pike men. The Tacuma archers threw down their bows and unleashed their swords, coming to the aid of the pike men.

"Diaka kimbia!" Ndoro shouted. The Diaka drums responded and the archers broke off their attack, running toward the man-made hill at the center of the camp. The Diaka swarmed down the hill into battle. The Bedouins dismounted and drew their scimitars, realizing their camels were a disadvantage against the seasoned Diaka.

Ndoro swung his sword with wild precision as Bedouins appeared before him like ghosts through the smoke. He had no idea who was around him, if they were losing the camp or gaining the advantage. He was alone, fighting for his life with the ferocity of his namesake. If this was his day to die, he would make sure the Bedouins remembered it well.

He was shoved from behind and spun about with a slash of his sword. The blade struck a Diaka shield blocking the terrified face of one his guard.

"Shumba!" the man yelled. He turned his head and shouted to his comrades. "Diatanee together!"

Other guardsmen emerged from the smoke, smiles of relief on their faces. They quickly formed a ring about Ndoro.

The attacks lessened, though the sound of battle could still be heard in the distance. Ndoro and the Diatanee moved through the camp, gathering the army about them and forming rank. War drums called for order and the warriors responded, each induna calling out for his unit and the warriors responding in kind. Ndoro gave his orders to the drummers and the army moved together in classic Diaka formation toward the sound of battle.

They emerged from the camp smoke into the midst of the mêlée. The men that fought the Bedouins were not Diaka, Sesu or Tacuma; they were other Bedouins. Unlike the ones that attacked the camp, these Bedouins wore blue-checkered keffiyahs. The Diaka surged toward the battle and the Bedouins fled. The Diaka continued to charge, heading for the blue-turbaned warriors. With a wave of his hand, Ndoro ordered the sounding of the drums. The advancing Diaka stopped instantly, though it was obvious they did not wish to. Ndoro and the Diatanee approached the Bedouins, Ndoro confident in his decision to call back his warriors. This Bedouin army was smaller than the one that attacked the camp, but their tenacity was obviously enough to draw the other Bedouins from his camp.

The leader of the Bedouins emerged from the horde mounted on a magnificent white camel and flanked by a contingent of heavily armed riders. He was draped in a white, blood-stained robe, his headscarf held on his head with a gilded agal. The two leaders faced each other, acknowledging each other with slight nods.

"Welcome to our desert, Great Shumba," the Bedouin chief announced. "I am Sheik Anwar Bashir, headman of the Madani."

"I'm impressed by your hospitality," Ndoro replied, "though your reception was not needed."

"Do not confuse our intentions," Anwar replied. "We attacked the Dulbe because they had no right on our land."

Ndoro was impressed by Anwar, despite his haughty manner. It was obvious any confrontation at the moment would result in the Bedouin's death, but he gave no indication of being in danger.

"We have no quarrel with the Madani. Our destination is Yakubu."

Anwar folded his arms across his broad chest. "A great man chooses great enemies. I have no feud with the Tuaregs and their leader. But if you seek surprise, you have already lost the advantage."

Anwar nodded toward the eastern horizon. Ndoro looked and saw two men draped in blue robes sitting on camels. They reined the beasts and turned away, descending into the hazy horizon. The Diatanee moved to follow, but Ndoro signaled them to a halt.

He turned his attention back to Anwar. "We must talk again when our business with Yakubu is finished."

"If you are still alive," Anwar replied. He mounted his camel. "May Moyo be merciful." The Madani rode off, disappearing into the distance.

Ndoro trudged back to camp in silence. The fires in the pit had burned themselves out, columns of smoke twisting into the night sky. Healers tended the wounded as the warriors worked together to gather the dead. Medicine priest hovered over the bodies, performing the proper rituals to appease the spirits of the dead on both sides. The doubts he felt before the march resurfaced, fueled by his anger with Anwar's words. To the people of the desert, his defeat at the hands of his brother was a forgone conclusion. Had he underestimated Obaseki's power? Maybe he needed more time to gather more intelligence and strengthen his forces before moving on Yakubu. As he reached his tent, he felt weighed down by doubt.

"There is no more time," the voice of Nakisisa said.

"I won't be rushed by a spirit," Ndoro replied aloud, not caring who heard him. "If you do not attack Yakubu now, your defeat is as certain as sunrise," Nakisisa insisted.

"Death has clouded your vision, Nakisisa," Ndoro snapped. "I am at half strength and wounded. I don't know whether Jawanza will return. I have lost the element of surprise. I will not suffer obvious defeat at the whim of dead spirits."

"The fate of this world does not depend on the battle of two armies. It depends on the confrontation between two brothers."

Ndoro stared into the distance as Nakisisa's words formed truth in his mind. Obaseki had understood this long ago; it was why he came alone to Abo instead of leading an army of thousands.

"Kumbala," Ndoro called. "Gather every man able to walk and as much provision we can spare. We march tonight for Yakubu."

"But Shumba, we are not ready," Kumbala replied. "We are less than half strength."

Ndoro place a hand on Kumbala's shoulder. "We must move with what we have. Jawanza will return soon to take care of the wounded. He will follow us as soon as he can."

Kumbala's expression told Ndoro he was not convinced.

"I trust the ancestors on this," Ndoro finally said with great difficulty.

Kumbala's eyes widened. "I have protected you many years, Shumba, and never have I heard those words come from your lips. If the ancestors tell you this, then it is a good decision." The captain of the Diatanee trotted off to fulfill his duties.

Ndoro turned to face the direction of Yakubu.

"I am coming, brother," he whispered.

22

The city of Yakubu pulsed with tension since the return of the scouts. The word of the desert battle spread throughout the city despite El-Fatih's best efforts to prevent it. The Bedouins had delayed Shumba's advance but not stopped it. It was only a matter of weeks before Ndoro's army would stand at the foot of the plateau, banging their assegais against their shields, calling for the blood of Moyoseki.

El-Fatih forced such thoughts from his mind as he reached the outer defenses. The ancient founders of the High City chose well when selecting the plateau as their home. Two sets of dunes surrounded the heights like necklaces, each mound approximately one half mile between them. Low Town crowded the area between the outer and inner dunes; a holding area for those newly arrived to Yakubu. A second city occupied the space between the second set of dune hills and the base of the plateau. It was known as Rig'at and was older than Yakubu. Its mudstone and marble buildings were the oldest of the city and once held the Ihaggaren. Legends said Moyo appeared one night a thousand years ago in a roar of fire and thunder, drawing the Ihaggaren to the top of the plateau and to glory. The oldest building on the plateau, the temple of Marina, was constructed around the landfall of Moyo.

El-Fatih's mind was occupied not only with the tremendous job at hand, but also with the growing doubt he now harbored inside toward Obaseki, doubts that surfaced the day he rescued the medicine-priest from death in Abo. Why would a man with such power have to resort to a stabbing to kill an enemy? During his training, El-Fatih's doubts subsided because of the alacrity with which Obaseki learned to fight. But those misgivings resurfaced during the meeting with the scouts reporting the Diaka battle with the Bedouins. Obaseki seemed uninterested, his eyes gazing at some invisible amusement. He barely acknowledged the scouts and did not notice when they completed their report. When El-Fatih asked him of his plans, his reply was just as disturbing.

"What will happen will happen. Two must become one."

El-Fatih ordered work crews to the summits of the dunes. Legend spoke of a stone wall built along the peaks, connecting the dunes to form a reasonable defense. He was determined to find them if they existed. The walls on the outer dunes would be used as observation only. He had to concentrate his forces behind the second dune where the maze of houses would allow them to slow down the Diaka. Those living between the walls and the old city would be evacuated to Yakubu. Boulders were set in place to block the streets that weaved up the side of the plateau in case the Diaka broke through the second wall. At best the Diaka would be driven back. At worst, the people of Yakubu would have to settle in for a long siege.

El-Fatih left the excavation work, heading back to the royal palace. The gate swung wide upon his approach and his personal guard immediately fell in time with his steps. As they made their way to the courtroom, El-Fatih prepared himself for his briefing with Moyoseki, hoping the medicine-priest would be more concerned about survival of the city he had revived.

He entered the courtroom. Obaseki looked up from his simple stool, flanked by Shani and Eshe. With a slight gesture he dismissed the women.

"My lord," El-Fatih said as he prostrated before his oba.

"How go the defenses?" Obaseki asked.

El-Fatih smiled, his hope renewed. "We are excavating the old ramparts to strengthen the defense of the outer city. If Shumba's army is as large as reported, we can defend ourselves behind those walls."

"Not the normal Ihaggaren response to a threat," Obaseki observed.

"I have more serious concerns than the honor of the nobles," El-Fatih replied.

"You speak of me."

El-Fatih gazed away from Obaseki. "You have changed, Moyoseki, and I am concerned. You show great power in your healing and I know the power of Moyo. It is strong enough to destroy the Diaka."

Obaseki eyes drifted to his feet. "That is true."

El-Fatih's hands began to warm, a sure sign he was losing his temper.

"Unlike you, my lord, I listened to the report of our scouts. Although they were wounded by the Bedouins, the Diaka army is still immense. It is the largest army ever to cross the Mahgreb and they have the provisions to make the journey to Yakubu in full readiness."

El-Fatih hesitated; fearful to say what he knew was true. But if it would make Obaseki act, it was worth the shame.

"I cannot stop them."

Obaseki looked into El-Fatih's eyes and the Ihaggaren leader cringed behind his face veil. He didn't want the sympathy in those eyes; he wanted action.

"Yakubu is safe," Obaseki replied. "The Diaka will never see the inside of this city. Ndoro and I will settle our business beyond the outer dunes."

Obaseki place a firm hand on El-Fatih's shoulder, and for the first time in days El-Fatih felt confidence in Moyo's caretaker.

"Go and finish your preparations. When the Diaka appear before the first wall, send for me. I will not fail you, my friend."

El-Fatih prostrated before Obaseki, sure in the knowledge of his oba's power.

Obaseki waited until El-Fatih was gone before slumping on his stool, cradling his worn face in his hands. Shani appeared, gliding to his side with a mother's concern.

"What did you tell him?" she asked.

"I told him what he wished to hear. I had no choice. If El-Fatih loses faith, he and his people will disappear into the desert. If the Ihaggaren leave, the others will, too. Ndoro and his Diaka will turn back and claim victory. That must not happen."

"Must it be this way?" Shani's face was distraught.

Obaseki smiled. "You will not lose us, momma. Your sons will always be with you."

Eshe entered the room and Obaseki's smile grew wider. He was not sure of what the confrontation with Ndoro might bring, but at least he could control his moments before answering his destiny.

"Come, sweet flower, sit with us," he said. Eshe smiled and came to sit beside him. Together son, mother, and wife conversed, keeping at bay the clouds of the future with the glow of their present pleasure.

Chadamunda was in panic. In his first duty since passing through his manhood rites he was failing. The night before, his father's herd of goats grazed peacefully under a clear moonless night. Now he was running about desperately, gathering the goats from all corners of their small oasis, the darkening skies threatening a heavy and violent rain.

Chadamunda took a quick head count of the goats and cried in dismay. Two were still missing. He fell to his knees, preparing to ask for spiritual guidance when he heard the frantic bleating emanating from the opposite side of the dune that protected the fragile oasis from the scorching desert winds.

Chadamunda scurried up the steep side of the dune. He reached the top and cried out. As far as he could see an army advanced, running and chanting toward him, his goats standing in their path. The boy turned about and stumbled down the other side of the dune.

Chadamunda dared to look back and saw the swarm of warriors crest the dune, rushing toward him like a dark sirocco. He fled, his eyes focused on the mud-brick house before him. Terror shadowed him as the warriors closed the gap and enveloped him like the night. Countless hands lifted him from his feet and carried him along. Chadamunda closed his eyes and prayed. After a terrifying eternity his feet hit the ground and he stumbled, sprawling into the sand. The soft thumping of running feet surrounded him, and then slowly subsided. Familiar arms wrapped around him tightly, the comforting smell of his mother dispersing his fear. Daring to open his eyes, his house stood before him untouched. His father stood beside them, watching the horde of warriors climb and disappear over the next dune. Chadamunda's father looked into his eyes and fell to his knees. The family embraced in relief at what passed, but in dread of what was to come.

Ndoro ran with an energy that amazed him. Three days ago he began his run with the Diatanee and two thousand Diaka fit enough to make the arduous march to the outskirts of Yakubu. They had not stopped running since that day. Some strange magic was at work, pushing him to this confrontation with his brother, driving away any fatigue, thirst, or hunger that would cripple normal men running such a distance at such a pace.

The plateau came into view, its pinnacle peering over the tops of the rolling dunes embracing it. A diligent sentry with good eyes would have spotted them by now, raising the alarm throughout the city. If that was so, he had no way of knowing.

They climbed the next dune before them and Ndoro called a halt to their martial marathon. The sun had long been hidden by thick clouds that were alien to the barren sand before them. They rumbled as if irritated, tendrils of lightening racing across them with each bellow. For two hundred yards, a flat land of hard packed rock and sand stretched, punctuated by another dune. Ndoro spotted ramparts undulating with the crests and troughs of the sandy ridge. Beyond the fortifications rose the plateau, a pillar of thriving life amidst the heat and sand. The city perched upon the heights glowed with unnatural light, its beauty a stark contrast against the furious sky. Ndoro was impressed; it was no doubt a wealthy city, one that under other circumstances would have provided much reward after its conquest. His prize, however, lie in the death of his brother and the release from this strange force that drew him to this moment. He turned to his warriors; some were weathered Diaka who had fought with him since his days in Songhai, others that were yet blooded who waited anxiously to gain their first honor in battle.

He could find no words to inspire them. This was a personal journey; there was no city to conquer and no empire to build. He turned and ran down the dune into the valley, followed by his warriors in determined silence.

* * *

Obaseki sat alone in the council room. No torches lit the chamber, only the faint glow of the city lights. Outside in the skies the ancestors gathered, their dark faces blocking the sun and casting a calming darkness over the dunes and valleys. Their voices rumbled across the land, words that chanted stories of the past and present with flashes of future visions. Obaseki acknowledged their presence and drew upon their confidence and wisdom.

Fuluke appeared beside him, announcing his arrival with a warm breeze.

"My brother is here," Obaseki said.

"The journey ends," Fuluke replied. "Two must become one."

Obaseki rose to his feet. He wore his blue robes, his face veil hanging to the side. His takouba slung over his shoulder, Obaseki adjusted his daggers. He was exiting the chamber when a messenger burst into view.

"Moyoseki! The Diaka are here!"

Obaseki nodded. "I know. Where is El-Fatih?"

"He is gathering the Ihaggaren to meet them."

Obaseki charged past the messenger, running through the palace to the stables. He mounted his camel and rushed through the gates into the street. Thousands swarmed him, their cries of praise and fear drowning out his urgent orders to clear the way.

"You cannot reach him in time," Fuluke's voice said in his head. "He has made his choice."

Obaseki ignored Fuluke and continued to shout. To his relief, a contingent of Ihaggaren warriors appeared on camel-back and began shouting and beating the crowd back.

"Follow us, Moyoseki," the leader of the group said. "We will lead you to the gates."

Obaseki followed his escort through the city streets, the crowd growing as the word of the enemy outside the gate spread. Obaseki became anxious, his anger spilling into his voice.

"Damn all of you! Get out of my way!"

The power of his voice struck everyone in sight. People fled, their faces cringing in pain. Countless eyes that only a moment ago looked on him in admiration now stared in fear as they stampeded out of the way of the riders.

They galloped down the spiraling road to the outer city. As they passed through the Yakubu gates, the signal drums boomed with the thunder from above, signaling their advance. The gates throughout Rig'at swung wide as people cleared streets before the riders as they rode through the second city to the outermost ramparts. Obaseki saw the Ihaggaren gathered about the final gate, horsemen and camels in tight formation. He spurred his camel, but the animal was exhausted and refused to increase its pace. He watched helplessly as the warriors rode out to meet the Diaka.

El-Fatih heard the drums signaling Obaseki's approach, but ignored the warning. The warriors gathered about him moved nervously, their eyes unsure. No matter what Moyoseki thought, El-Fatih had taken the outriders' report to heart. The army marching toward Yakubu was formidable, their vanguard before the gates a sure sign of their strength.

"This is not just a fight for Moyoseki," he shouted over the thunder. "This is for your homes and your families. We have lost this city once; we will not lose it again. No matter who he is, Moyoseki is not Ihaggaren. The Ihaggaren do not let others fight their battles."

El-Fatih turned away from the blue-clad warriors to face the gates. He glared at the gatekeepers and they swung open the barricade amid the increasing thunder and lightning. He charged forward and smiled as he heard the rumble of hooves and the war cries behind him. Before him the Diaka stood, making no move to change their formation. They remained single file, a tall warrior adorned in a lion-hooded cape standing in the center, shield and spear in hand. El-Fatih pulled his takouba from its scabbard, pointing it at the man and focusing on him. The sounds of his cohorts were drowned out by the increasing violent sky, the lightening constant. With only a few yards between him and his target, El-Fatih smiled. His life had been good; he had lived long enough to see Yakubu returned to his people and become the great city it had once been. He had helped Obaseki restore Moyo to its rightful place. If this was his day to die, he had no regrets. El-Fatih raised his takouba over his head.

"For Moyo! For Yakubu!" he shouted. He was turning to face his companions when his life ended in a torrent of lightening.

Obaseki reached the outer gate just as the ancestors struck down the charging Ihaggaren. The death of so many at one time hit like an orinka; he rocked on his saddle, his hand going to his head.

The ancestors answered him before the question could form in his mind; it was necessary. The proper ritual had to be observed. If El-Fatih and his outriders had reached Ndoro, they could have killed him. It was that possibility the ancestors saw and moved to prevent. Even the ancestors could not control everything, Obaseki thought with a smile. Though the path he and Ndoro walked was woven before they were born, there was no guarantee either of them would follow their destinies. Fate was influenced by choice, and fortunately for the ancestors, he and Ndoro had chosen the best path. Obaseki looked into the countless faces above him. They were silent for a moment, absorbing the new souls from the scene below. He waited until the ancestors began to chant again and then rode out to meet his brother.

Ndoro was stunned to silence. The warriors lay only yards away, the stench of their burned bodies overwhelming. He had not expected an attack so suddenly; they would have surely been wiped out. For a moment he wondered what force struck them down, but the answer was hard for him to comprehend. Had the ancestors done this? Was his brother so powerful and dangerous that those he never trusted had chosen him? If Obaseki was so powerful he had come on a fool's errand and would surely die. For the first time in his life, Ndoro experienced pure fear. He looked down the row of Diaka and saw the fear in their eyes as well. He could pull back and wait for Jawanza. With the full weight of the Diaka behind him, Obaseki's great power would crumble. Obaseki's strategy might not be to destroy the army, but just to kill him.

A lone rider emerged from the wall on the dunes, loping toward the Diaka as the clouds rumbled again. Ndoro stepped forward, his hands tightening on his assegai and shield. His brother was coming alone; such was his confidence in his power.

The sky heralded his approach, the thunder rolling in a rhythm Ndoro recognized. There was no doubt of the power his brother possessed, but he was also sure now that he was the only one that could stop him. Was he not his twin? Somewhere inside of him he must hold such power as well. Until it manifested itself, he would rely on his martial skills. It was all he had.

Ndoro trotted toward his brother. The Diaka moved to follow but he waved them still. This was a personal confrontation. He did not want the brave men that followed him to be struck down as dishonorably as the Tuaregs.

Time disappeared; the voices of the ancestors continued to rumble across the sky and the land, its strength shaking the buildings. Obaseki halted his camel only a few yards away from his brother and dismounted. They approached each other, and then stopped, only an arm's length of space between them. The ancestors fell silent.

Ndoro watched Obaseki as he removed his veil, his hand tight on his spear. To see his brother's face was like looking into a mirror. They were true twins, identical in every way. Obaseki smiled at Ndoro, an unexpected expression considering the circumstances.

"Ata," he said.

"Atsu," Ndoro replied instinctively.

"So it must come to this?" Obaseki asked. Ndoro began to answer but realized Obaseki was not talking to him. His eyes were cast upward, staring into the heavy black clouds overhead.

"Is there no other way?" he asked the ancestors.

The heavens roared and Obaseki closed his eyes, a sorrowful expression on his face. Ndoro realized he did not wish to kill his brother. There were so many questions to ask; so much he wanted to know. No matter how many people surrounded him throughout his life, a void existed which that had not been filled. He realized the answer stood before him, and he'd come to destroy it before he had a chance to know.

Ndoro was about to speak when Obaseki's expression changed from sorrow to serious.

"Two must become one," he said.

Ndoro caught the blow from Obaseki's sword with his shield, the force of the strike knocking him off balance. He stumbled back frantically as he beat back the flurry of blows, amazed at his brother's speed. He slowly matched his pace, finally managing to thrust at his brother, breaking his rhythm and taking away his advantage.

Ndoro and Obaseki fought at an inhuman pace. The sky rumbled constantly, the rainless storm an aural reflection of the battle taking place under its dark canopy. As the two fought, the people gathered around them. Ihaggaren warriors mixed with the Diaka vanguard. The warriors were surrounded by the people of Yakubu. In the distance, the bulk of the Diaka army crested the dunes, marching cautiously under the strange scene around them.

Ndoro managed to break away from his brother. He was exhausted. His chest heaving, he circled looking for an opening. Obaseki looked back, a grim smile on his face.

"Obaseki, you must fight the demon inside you! Drive him from your mind. Free yourself so I won't have to!"

Obaseki shook his head in despair. "There is no demon possessing me. After all your journeys, you still don't understand." Obaseki shrugged his shoulders. "It was not your calling to understand."

The ancestors raised their voices with a force that shook the sand.

"You are the earth," Obaseki continued. "You see with the eyes of the world. You understand only that which you can experience with your senses. I am the sky. I see beyond the physical. I understand the spirits and the shadows. We are each one half of the whole, the complete circle from which a new future will be born."

Another deafening rumble erupted from the clouds and Obaseki glanced upward.

"They are all here." Obaseki dropped his sword and reached into his robe, revealing Moyo. The mayembe glowed, the intense light making him squint. Ndoro drew back, shading his eyes with his shield. Despite his fear he felt drawn to the object, the light persuading him to look in its direction.

"Two must become one," Obaseki said with a voice that seemed to emanate from outside his body. He raised the mayembe over his head, his eyes fixed on the heavens.

Ndoro seized the advantage. He lunged forward, driving his spear into Obaseki's chest. Obaseki clinched his eyes as the assegai shattered bone and entered his heart. His hands dropped in reflex, the mayembe falling toward Ndoro, the point aimed at his chest. Ndoro raised his shield but the horn tore through the tempered leather like dry leaves. It plunged into Ndoro's chest, the same spot where Ndoro had pierced his brother. But instead of pain, Ndoro was filled with calm. The mayembe's light enveloped the world around him until there was nothing but brightness and his brother, standing before him with the assegai protruding from his chest. Obaseki grasped the spear in his free hand and pulled it out. There was no blood. He looked at his brother and smiled.

"Now do you understand?" he asked.

Ndoro nodded. "We were never two."

Obaseki smiled like a proud teacher. "We were always one person; one person, two lives. It was necessary."

Ndoro felt wetness growing in his eyes. "Our burden has been heavy."

"Birth is never easy," Obaseki replied as he looked away.

"And now?" Ndoro asked.

Obaseki looked back toward his brother, closing his eyes. "And now, two become one."

The ancestors sang with deafening voices, their joy rumbling the very foundation of the earth around them. The future became a bright, constant stream of light that ran across their dark faces and streaked downward, striking the brothers with a jubilant force. The people—Ihaggaren, Diaka, Tacuma, Sesu, Bedouin and Mawena—prostrated themselves before the furious joy, feeling no fear but anticipation of what was to become. A rhythm danced in the voices of the ancestors, a universal cadence known to all as the song of birth and celebration. The song was sung in different languages, but its meaning was still the same.

The ancestors fell silent. Their purpose complete, they drifted back to the Zamani, releasing the sun to touch the sands with the feeble strength of dawn. As the people came to their feet, they looked to the spot where two brothers met to see only one man standing. He was naked before them, his eyes closed as his body pulsed with his deep breathing. The people murmured; which brother had survived?

El-Fatih opened his eyes and was in the world again. He sat up quickly and studied the scene around him, the same vision he saw moments ago from above as his spirit mingled with the ancestors. Around him his men stirred, each one looking at him with knowing eyes, then looking past him to the lone figure surrounded by the glass-like residue of the strike. They had been given back their lives with an obligation they were expected to fulfill. El-Fatih and his resurrected warriors stepped forward, prostrating before him and covering their heads with sand.

"Rise and be recognized," the man said. El-Fatih came to his feet.

"What do I call you?" he asked.

"Obadoro."

Jawanza saw the Ihaggaren approach the man standing. He felt tired as he watched the man accept them, confirming his worst thoughts. He raised his assegai and turned away. Ndoro asked that no revenge be taken for his death and his request would be honored.

"Come, Jawanza." The voice that reverberated in his head was that of Ndoro, but he knew it was not just him. The man that stood with the Ihaggaren was more.

Jawanza looked across the distance into his eyes. The fire was there in all its intensity, the smile on his inkosi's face welcoming and familiar.

"Diaka Kimbia!" Jawanza shouted. The Diaka responded, running to him with a newfound spirit. Somewhere in the outer city, a woman ululated in joy and others responded. The Diaka war drums sprang to life, singing the song of the ancestors and telling a story of rebirth. Diaka danced, Ihaggaren shouted, and the celebration spread across the desert and into the streets of Yakubu. Eshe and Shani embraced, joy and loss bringing them together. The message of the ancestors spread across the desert to Zimfara, crossed the grasslands of Selike and Mawena, worked through the forest to the wooded hills and valleys of Tacuma. Two had become one and, by doing so, joined many people into one. Obadoro looked across the thousands of strides and saw his future in the millions of faces of his people. Two journeys had ended; one journey was just beginning. The path of Meji lay before him. It was a path the people soon to be known as the Obana would travel for a thousand years.

MEJI GLOSSARY

Name	Pronunciation	Meaning/Relationship
Abo	AH-boh	Mawena capital city
Alamako	ah-lah-mah-koh	A city near Ifana
assegai	A (as in at)-say-guy	spear
Ata	ah-tah	first born of twins
Atsu	AT-soo	second born of twins
Azikiwe	Ah-zee-kee-way	Obaseki's uncle
Celu	SAY-loo	Ndoki's mayembe spirit
Diaka	DEE-ah-kah	the slave people
Dingane	DEHN-gah-nee	Father of the twins
Fuluke	FOO-loo-kay	Mawena medicine-priest
Gamba	GAHM-bah	Sesu warrior
Husani	HOO-sah-nee	Shani's bodyguard
Ifana	EYE-fah-nah	City of ghosts
impi	EHM-pee	a group of Sesu warriors
Inkosi	N-koh-see	Sesu for king
Jelani	JEH-lah-nee	Husani's brother
kimbia	KEHM-bee-ah	Sesu for "march"
Kossi	KOH-see	Mawena traditional enemies
umuzi	oo-moo-zee	cattle enclosure
Mawena	MAH-weh-nah	Shani's people
mayembe	MAH-yehm-beh	A animal horn containing a spirit
Moyo	MOH-yoh	Obaseki's mayembe spirit
Mulugo	MOO-loo-goh	Sesu medicine-priest
Ndoki	N-doh-kee	The medicine priest of Ifana
Ndoro	N-doe-roe	Obaseki's brother
nganga	N-gahn-gah	Sesu for medicine priest
ngwena	N-gweh-nah	crocodile
Noncemba	NOHN-kehm-bah	Shani's father
Obaseki	OBAH-se-kee	Ndoro's brother
Olodumare	olo-doo-mah-ray	Mawena main god

orinka	OR-ring-kah	war club
Oya	O-yah	an orisha - minor god or spirit
Paki	PAH-kee	a boy
Selike	SEE-lee-keh	Sesuland capital city
Sesu	SAY-soo	Dingane's people
Shani	SHAH-nee	The twins mother
Shumba	SHOOM-bah	Diaka for lion
Simba	SIM-bah	Sesu for lion
Songhai	SAHN-high	people of the Sahel
Soninke	SAH-nin-kee	another name for the songhai
Tacuma	TAH-koo-mah	Enemies of the Diaka
Thembile	TEHM-bah	Shani's handmaiden
Tuareg	TOO-ar-rehg	people of the desert
Unkulunkulu	oo-koo-loon-koo-loo	Sesu main god
Zuwena	ZOO-weh-nah	nursemaid

ABOUT THE AUTHOR

Milton Davis is a Black Speculative fiction writer and owner of MVmedia, LLC, a small publishing company specializing in Science Fiction, Fantasy and Sword and Soul. MVmedia's mission is to provide speculative fiction books that represent people of color in a positive manner. Milton is the author of seventeen novels; his most recent is the Sword and Soul adventure *Son of Mfumu*. He is the editor and co-editor of seven anthologies; *The City, Dark Universe* with Gene Peterson; *Griots: A Sword and Soul Anthology and Griot: Sisters of the Spear*, with Charles R. Saunders; *The Ki Khanga Anthology,* the *Steamfunk! Anthology*, and the *Dieselfunk anthology* with Balogun Ojetade. MVmedia has also published *Once Upon A Time in Afrika* by Balogun Ojetade and *Abegoni: First Calling* and *Nyumbani Tales* by Sword and Soul creator and icon Charles R. Saunders. Milton's work had also been featured in *Black Power: The Superhero Anthology*; Skelos *2: The Journal of Weird Fiction and Dark Fantasy Volume 2*, *Steampunk Writes Around the World* published by Luna Press and *Bass Reeves Frontier Marshal Volume Two*. Milton's story 'The Swarm' was nominated for the 2018 British Science Fiction Association Award for Short Fiction.